Magician
of Light

MAGICIAN
OF LIGHT

A Novel

J. FREMONT

SHE WRITES PRESS

Published 2022
Printed in the United States of America
Print ISBN: 978-1-64742-355-1
E-ISBN: 978-1-64742-356-8
Library of Congress Control Number: 2021923638

For information, address:
She Writes Press
1569 Solano Ave #546
Berkeley, CA 94707

She Writes Press is a division of SparkPoint Studio, LLC.

Interior design by Tabitha Lahr

All company and/or product names may be trade names, logos, trademarks, and/or registered trademarks and are the property of their respective owners.

This is a work of fiction. Names, characters, places, and incidents either are the product of the author's imagination or are used fictitiously. Any resemblance to actual persons, living or dead, is entirely coincidental.

For René Lalique—
the man who inspired me to write this novel.

CONTENTS

⁓⁓⁓

I. CONVERGING

Chapter 1: The Goddess. 3

Chapter 2: The Tomb. 11

Chapter 3: Treasure Hunter 19

Chapter 4: In Black and White. 25

Chapter 5: Egyptian Magic 32

Chapter 6: Eye of Ra 40

Chapter 7: Scarabs. 46

Chapter 8: Shadow Worlds 53

Chapter 9: Messages 61

Chapter 10: Badger 68

Chapter 11: Hathor's Mirror. 79

Chapter 12: The Blue Curtain 88

Chapter 13: Flying into the Unknown 96

Chapter 14: Out of the Box. 103

Chapter 15: The Jackal. 111

Chapter 16: Warning Signs 121

II. CROSSING

Chapter 17: Monsieur Stoddard. 129

Chapter 18: The Egyptian Room 139

Chapter 19: Theater of the Mind 148

Chapter 20: Amongst the Bluebells 152

Chapter 21: Train of Thought 157

Chapter 22: The Magic Lantern Show......164

Chapter 23: Prophecy.................169

Chapter 24: Two Paths.................176

Chapter 25: House of Eternity...........180

Chapter 26: Insanity.................188

Chapter 27: The Casket of Nephthys.......195

Chapter 28: The Lotus Box.............203

Chapter 29: Turning the Corner..........213

Chapter 30: Book of Poetry.............218

III. DIVERGING

Chapter 31: Fire of Ambition............229

Chapter 32: Perfume.................242

Chapter 33: The Last of the Flowers.......249

Chapter 34: Family Portrait............257

Chapter 35: Faces de Verre.............263

Chapter 36: Muddy Shoes..............273

Chapter 37: Passed On................281

Chapter 38: The Sands of Time..........289

Chapter 39: Dreaming................296

Chapter 40: The World of Creation.......306

Chapter 41: The Temple of Glass.........314

Chapter 42: House of Light............324

I

CONVERGING

Chapter 1:

THE GODDESS

"Come, René!" Louis Aine called.

René stopped, set down his file, and took off his apron. Calling out, "Coming, M. Aucoc," he grabbed his coat and hat, put them on, and hurried towards the three gentlemen waiting for him at the door.

Aucoc's son, Louis, closed and locked the door. "René, you are learning quickly and are so productive. Don't you agree, Father?"

The older man nodded perfunctorily. "Shall we take a carriage?" René smiled to himself. He knew Louis Aine was not one to lavish praise.

"It's a beautiful May day," replied Louis. "It will take us some time, but I feel like walking." Louis grinned at his father. "Do you have the tickets?"

Frowning, Louis Aine nodded again. "Oui." René also knew the old man did not like exercise.

"Didn't the doctor say walking would be good for your knees?" Louis chided his father. "We'll get a cab back."

Without replying, the elder Aucoc just started down Rue de la Paix.

René exchanged a grin with André, Louis's younger brother, as they followed the two older men. They were headed to the 1876 Paris Salon Exhibition, housed in the Palais des Champs-Elysées. Louis Aine was a silversmith as well as a fabricator of expensive traveling cases for the wealthy. Eventually, his oldest son took over the business and focused more on goldsmithing. Louis had produced finely crafted jewels that soon drew French royalty including Empress Eugenie.

Louis had been looking to expand and take on a protégé. Then Rene's father, Auguste, had died suddenly the previous summer and Louis decided to adopt René. This unexpected change of fortune brought René to his current situation of being apprenticed at sixteen to a goldsmith who catered to the rich and famous. He and André, four years older, had become friends.

Louis was a leader in the art and jewelry community due to his elite connections. Popular, wealthy, and intelligent, he kept abreast of Parisian style and served on influential boards. Clever himself, René was aware that his foster father had wisdom to impart in the ways of the business world. When Louis talked, his young ward listened.

"Can you believe there were four thousand entries this year?" Louis asked his father.

"Most of it was garbage," Louis Aine responded in a surly tone.

"Are you talking about the Impressionists?"

"Who else?"

"The Academie des Beaux-Arts must consider all art, Father, not just the classical. Besides, the young artists bring a fresh viewpoint." Louis turned back and looked at René. "Isn't that right, René?" He winked.

"Oui," René answered enthusiastically.

Louis Aine just harrumphed and said nothing as they continued walking. His son resumed talking. "Did you read Émile Zola's scathing art review regarding Georges Clairin's portrait of Mlle. Bernhardt? He said Sarah's serpentine pose was physically impossible and she doesn't have a pretty face. He commented that Clairin only rendered her vulgar sensuality and eroticism." Louis turned again and grinned widely at the young men behind him. "Only a lover can portray such intimacy." René chuckled because he knew, as the rest of Paris did, that Clairin had briefly been Sarah Bernhardt's lover as well as an ardent admirer of the actress and in her private circle of friends.

André piped in. "I read that Clairin's portrait was one of the most prominent of the Salon. Its composition was original and had splendid color."

Louis nodded. "Mlle. Bernhardt has made quite an impression this year on stage and in art. There are two portraits of her in the Salon. One done by a woman and one by a man. Speculation is that both are her lovers."

At this remark, René elbowed André and they exchanged another grin.

Louis Aine snorted and shook his head. "She provides endless fodder for gossip with her flamboyant theater performances and all her lovers . . . And I hear that she wears pants. What is the world coming to?"

"I think Divine Sarah is sexy," said André, "a femme fatale on *and* off stage. A Parisian goddess. I can't wait to see the painting." René nodded in agreement.

"Well, we shall see, won't we?" Louis Aine said with finality.

A carriage rattled by in the street, drowning out most of whatever Louis was saying to his father about the Third Republic's corruption. Not interested in politics, René stopped listening. André slowed his pace a little and René fell back beside him.

"We should go out this weekend," André said. "I never did celebrate my birthday properly this year. There is a particular cabaret that I would like to go to in Montmartre."

"Will they let me in?" René asked.

"Your mustache makes you look older. And," André smirked, "your pretty friend Claudette likes it." He motioned towards the mustache as if he were going to pull on it. René drew back his head, but gave his companion a wry smile.

André laughed. "Don't worry. I'll buy and you can pay me back. Besides, I have friends."

René nodded his head. "Oui."

They walked on in silence, which gave René the chance to contemplate all that had happened in the last year. After he had accepted the position with the Aucocs, he had been enrolled in Ecole des Arts Décoratifs, the School of Decorative Arts, to further his education in art and design. He enjoyed his classes, although some of the professors were boring. Much like the Aucocs, they preferred tradition over innovation. René had other ideas. He aspired to be inventive and experimental and to create jewelry with a variety of materials rather than rehashing old techniques and concepts. To him, it wasn't work, it was play. If he didn't enjoy what he was doing, he did not stay at it long. But he knew that the art schools had a huge impact and influence on young artists' métiers. Those who did not conform to expectations were not as likely to be selected by committees, win awards, or even be noticed by the public. To succeed with originality, he would have to produce something phenomenal. His work was cut out for him.

Soon the group came to the end of the street and turned onto Place Vendôme. As they walked through the large square, René imagined his future. He would be a well-known bijoutier like his benefactor. *But not just in France. The world. My jewelry will be works of art, worn by royals and others. Perhaps displayed for all to see in museums.* He smiled inwardly at his grandiose dreams. René glanced up at the imposing façade of a building and then at the window fronts of the expensive retail shops as they passed by. *Someday, I will be rich and famous. I will have a store here.*

The men finally arrived at the art show. There was a small queue to get in and the interior foyer was crowded. Once inside, the group split up and René and André headed to the sculpture garden. As they wended their way through the museum attendees, René wondered how many serious art dealers, collectors, and museum curators were present. The Salon could make or break a career.

The young men meandered through the statues stopping to look and comment on several pieces. Finally, they stood in front of *La Charité* by Paul Dubois, the show's recipient of the Salon's medal of honor. It was of a mother holding two sleeping babies. René admired the serenity on the woman's marble face, the drape of her skirt and the expressions of the dozing children. René had been drawing since he could hold a pencil, but he also appreciated carving and fashioning things from stone. One day, he knew, he would take classes in sculpting.

"Well done," André remarked, "very deserved of the prize."

"I agree," René replied.

"Let's look for Divine Sarah, shall we?"

"Oui."

The two walked around until they found Clairin's painting. René and André stood together silently studying the blonde actress. Sarah, dressed in a long, opalescent white dress, was reclining seductively on a pink divan and propped by a large golden pillow. Her portraitist had included her hound at her feet. Both subjects appeared carefree and languid yet alert.

"I like his use of light and color," André said after some time. "His composition is good. I disagree with Zola. Clairin has done well."

Examining the painting, René felt himself flush. It wasn't the light, the colors, or the composition that was captivating. It was her eyes. The canvas exuded the essence of Sarah, titillating and tantalizing. "Elle est une femme de mystére," he said softly.

André snickered. "You are so right, mon ami. I am positive that Clairin thinks she is a mystery, too." He stood a little longer and then began to wander off to view other paintings. René, however, remained behind. As he stood before the portrait of the woman in white, memories of a past incident flooded his mind. The painting reminded him of seeing another woman in white, eight years earlier. The sight of her was so odd that it was ingrained in his mind. Distinct memories as if it had happened but an hour ago.

His mother, Olympe, had come to retrieve him from his grandfather's house in the countryside. His grandmother long dead, eight-year-old René was left behind with his grandfather in Ay-sur-Marne while his parents got settled in Paris. This day, they had picked her up from the train station in Epernay. After hugging and kissing her son, Olympe was bear-hugged by her father, Antoine. A farrier as well as a winemaker, he wrapped her in his large, muscular arms before loading her luggage and them into his carriage. On the way home, the horse had thrown a shoe. When they arrived at the house, his mother stayed with his grandfather to chat while she watched as he reshod the beast.

On the ride home, his mother had told René that she had brought some things for him, so he offered to bring her bags in the house when they arrived. Inside, he opened them and found a leather binder with sheet paper and pencils. There was also a stack of bygone, illustrated literary magazines. He pulled one out from the stack and began to thumb through it, stopping when he came to a story that piqued his interest. "The Mummy's Foot" by Théophile Gautier.

The title of the story revived memories of the beginning of his fascination with Egypt, after his exciting visit to the 1867 Great Exposition in Paris the year before. The avenue of sphinxes, people in exotic costumes, and temples with Egyptian antiquities including the authentic jewels of Queen Aahhotep.

René recalled his grandfather liking the donkeys and camels housed at the stables behind the buildings.

Smiling at these memories, René took the magazine and the binder and, as the house was hot and stuffy, went in search of a shady tree under which to read the story of the mummy and, perhaps, draw some pictures.

It was a warm day with a light breeze. René continued to walk along the dirt track that led down to the river until he found what he was looking for. The canopy of a beech tree created a shady spot over a large rock that he could rest his back against. He sat down, opened the magazine to the short story, and began to read. The story was about a man who happens upon a mummy foot in a Parisian curiosity shop. The shopkeeper tells him that the foot is genuine and that it belonged to a real Egyptian princess, so the man buys it to use as a paperweight. René paused in his reading and whistled softly. *One hundred francs for a mummy foot. That's a lot of money.* The man has a vision that night of the princess and she leads him on a dreamtime adventure. When René finished the story, he took off his shoes and socks, then used the binder to sketch his own foot and drew bandages draped around it. *A mummy foot,* he thought proudly.

Satisfied with his efforts, René laid his head back on the smooth rock surface. The heat made him drowsy and he closed his eyes. How long he had been there he didn't know when a sudden sound aroused his attention. He sat up and looked around.

In the distance, in the break of the large bushes and trees that led to the river's edge, he saw a person dressed all in white. Thinking it was a mirage, as the heat shimmer caused his vision at first to be blurry, he could see that it was an old woman with only one foot. She was leaning on crutches and looking at him. Then the woman motioned him to come toward her. He hesitated and she motioned again, this time more insistently as if she wanted him to look at something. He was a little apprehensive, but René was bold by nature. As she began to limp away, he got up and followed her.

The woman passed between the bushes and he lost sight of her. When he moved beyond the barrier of undergrowth, he could see her waist-deep in the water. She was not old as he had initially thought but a beautiful young woman dressed in a simple, white linen dress. Golden bands encircled her slender tanned arms. Her eyes were lined in kohl and on her head, she wore a gilded headdress with a golden disc surrounded by horns. Motioning, she wanted him to join her in the river.

He was warm; the water would cool and refresh him. René paused and then, in the distance, he thought he heard his mother's voice calling him. Turning around, he saw that the bushes had disappeared and he could see his grandfather coming down the road. René turned back to the maiden, but she had disappeared along with the river. He felt his grandfather's hand on his shoulder, shaking it. "René! Wake up!"

René felt himself sitting on the ground again. Opening his eyes, he realized that he had been dreaming. His grandfather's brows were knitted, but he exhaled before chastising René. "Why do you always worry your poor mother?"

Chapter 2:

THE TOMB

A shriek was heard before, "Damn cat left another one!" Then a worried voice through the closet door. "Miss Haliburton? Are you, all right?" Lucinda looked over and saw the locked doorknob jiggle.

"Yes. I am," Lucinda replied.

"Don't worry, I'll fetch the key," the maid reassured her.

"Alright."

Lucinda heard the maid mutter to herself, "And pick up the dead mouse."

The first time Lucinda's mother, Sarah, had locked her in her closet, she had been frightened in the small, gloomy space. After the second time, Lucinda had hidden a candle, matches, and books behind her shoes, so she had been prepared for the third time her mother had violently pushed her in. The closet had since become her peaceful reading space when it was too rainy to ride the horses. Sarah left her alone and Lucinda was drawn into her stories, the most recent one a new novel about a horse called Black Beauty.

Lucinda wasn't bothered at all now by being imprisoned; rather, it was her mother's slaps she tried to avoid. As she sat in the darkened closet with her flickering candle, Lucinda remembered recently overhearing her uncle and grandfather talking about her mother's mental condition. Unbeknownst to them, Lucinda was under the enormous dining table with its heavy, fringed tapestry tablecloth of crimson and gold. She had gone underneath to fetch the big orange tabby, Sekhmet. Named so by her mother after the fierce Egyptian goddess even though he was male. He frequently left dead mice strewn at doorways, so was continually chased out of the house. Therefore, when inside, Sekhmet liked to remain concealed under furniture.

Once she had crawled under the table, Lucinda tarried momentarily. She remembered when, as a child, she would hide under it. Mostly to avoid the governess du jour but also her flawed family and the paintings of her English forebears. The antique portraits of her stately ancestors that were hung throughout the mansion. She hated the haughty occupants who silently watched her from their frames. Not that they, or anyone else living on Foxhill Estate, cared about how she felt. No one except Sekhmet and her grandfather, the baron. Lucinda placed the cat on her lap and petted it gently. Content, Sekhmet was settled when her uncle and grandfather passed through the dining room on their way to the conservatory.

"You know she inherited it from Mother," Roderick told his father.

"Yes, I know."

"Do you think it is time to consider another option?"

"What do you mean?"

Roderick stammered, "Well, um, Sarah's deterioration, I mean . . ." He paused. "Surely, this situation is not good for Lucinda. No one takes care of her; she runs about the estate as free as a wild dog. How many boarding schools has the girl been expelled from? I am sick and tired of interviewing governesses. They all say that she is immature, ill-mannered and unteachable. All she wants is to be outdoors. Walking, riding or grooming the horses."

"Nonsense!" said her grandfather. "I see her reading in the library all the time. She's certainly not illiterate or stupid."

"Well, that may be, but she's too old for that now. She needs to learn proper behavior on how to be a lady and become a wife. Not a scholar. Besides, I don't have the time to continually do this and attend to my business in London."

Lucinda rolled her eyes. *I wish you would stay in London forever.*

"Perhaps a boarding school in the north . . ." suggested Roderick.

"That's too far. You know I am opposed to that and so is she. She doesn't want to leave because of my health. At least *she* cares."

Roderick didn't reply to his father's barb. "I just think that she needs to be removed from this environment for a while. What about a visit to Egypt to see her father?"

Lord Haliburton stopped walking. As Lucinda looked at their shoes and the tip of her grandfather's cane, she thought of her father, who had left England for France and then to Egypt a long time ago. He was only a faded, misty memory now.

Her grandfather grunted. "Do you think it wise to send Lucie to that place? To that vulgar American? Don't forget that Alexander is the one who brought shame to our family in the first place."

"Well, it's not as if Sarah didn't play a part. Her erratic, licentious behavior is also to blame."

"I should have never agreed to visit America. It's my fault they followed her back here." Lucinda could imagine her grandfather shaking his head dolefully.

"What's done is done. You couldn't have predicted that she would find out about his mistress."

"I wish they had never met."

"I agree. His attempts at reconciliation by sending love letters telling her that she is a goddess are pathetic. Absolute nonsense about reuniting and floating down the Nile, stargazing, like Cleopatra and Mark Antony." Roderick snorted. "Do you know that Sarah only wants to be addressed as Cleopatra or Annabel these days?" When the baron didn't respond, Roderick continued. "Recently, she has taken to locking Lucinda in the closet, telling her that she needs to get used to her tomb."

"Why didn't anyone tell me?" Lord Haliburton asked angrily. "We must find the key and take it from her." Lucinda heard her grandfather sigh heavily. "Poor Lucie."

"No one seems to know where she is hiding it. The maids say that she flies into a fit if they try to search her room. She threw a vase at one of them the other day for addressing her as Lady Sarah. Screamed at her, 'My name is Lady Annabel!' Thank god she missed."

Lord Haliburton cleared his throat but said nothing.

Lucinda grimaced. *She's as mad as a hatter.*

Roderick seemed to be thinking the same thing. "Sarah's behavior is becoming unacceptable. One of the footmen said he saw her slap Lucinda."

Lucinda heard her grandfather sigh again as he quietly said her grandmother's name, "Annabel." Then he began to shuffle about. Lucinda noticed he shuffled when he was especially upset. "I thought we agreed that you were to intercept Alexander's letters."

"I was, until she coerced one of the maids to go through the post for her."

"Then you must be more diligent! Why didn't you tell me? I assume that you let the maid go as a warning to the other staff?" This last question brought on a coughing fit.

Roderick softened his tone. "Of course. I didn't want to upset or bother you, so I took care of the situation." He paused for a moment and then said, "But on another matter . . . As you know, the letter Merimee sent was not encouraging. His endeavors so far have been fruitless. You read what he wrote. That bastard countryman of his, Auguste Mariette, is creating problems for fellow excavators. He wants any treasure found to stay in Egypt or to go to the Louvre. We need to check up on what is happening with our funds. I can take Lucinda with a chaperone when I visit. Perhaps the presence of his daughter will take Alexander's mind off of his wife."

"I don't know, a girl her age in a foreign country?"

"Do we want Lucinda to fall prey to her mother and grandmother's problems or disease? She is nearly eighteen, the age that Sarah was when she first became involved with Alexander. And when Mother . . ." Roderick didn't finish the thought. "Perhaps if we send Lucinda away, she will escape their fate."

"I just don't think it is prudent."

I agree, Lucinda thought. *I don't want to see my father.*

"We can't just sit by and watch Sarah abuse her. Egypt is better than the asylum, is it not?"

Lord Haliburton tapped the floor hard with his cane. "We are not sending Sarah to that asylum in London. I made a huge mistake with your mother and I have regretted it my whole life. I thought Annabel would get better, but she just sank deeper." A tone of despair entered his voice. "Surrounded by incurables and imbeciles, she left into another world. I lost her there and I won't watch Sarah . . ." His voice trailed off and another coughing fit ensued.

Poor Grandfather, Lucinda thought. She was worried as her grandfather's coughing spells had become more frequent and prolonged.

When the fit was done, the baron continued. "Your sister just needs nurses and medication. I was talking to Dr. Perkins about it. He recommended talking sessions with him and water treatments. Hydrotherapy, he said. Did you know that Charles followed his father into psychiatry?"

Roderick replied evenly. "Yes, you mentioned it before. All I am saying is that maybe a change of scenery and seeing her father would do Lucinda some good."

You don't care one bit about my good, Lucinda fumed.

"Alexander has a profession at least," her uncle pointed out.

Lord Haliburton snorted. "He has that position only because I know Gaston Merimee. It's a good thing I sent Alexander with him and away from here. At least Gaston reports that he is pleased with Alexander's renditions of the temples and their hieroglyphs." The old man paused. "Perhaps you should go. We need to collect the drawings for my associate. The editor firmly believes there is a high interest for this type of book. He said that we should capitalize on Egyptomania."

Uncle Roderick remained silent, so her grandfather went on. Lucinda could hear the exasperation in his tone. "Certainly, they're much better than his previous drawings. I still can't believe he encouraged my daughter to *explore* her artistic inclinations. He just wanted her to pose nude for him in his art studio and then become his lover."

Lucinda curled her lip at this thought and watched as the baron limped forward using his cane, his son following him. "Did I ever tell you that the recorder for the parish register wrote 'misbegotten' by Lucie's name and would not remove it until I paid their exorbitant fee? I told them her parents were married first, but they didn't believe me. Pure extortion, I say!"

Lucinda took Sekhmet off her lap and crawled to the edge of the table. She lifted the tablecloth and peeked out at her uncle and grandfather as they reached the stairs. Lord Haliburton shook his head in frustration. "Drawing and painting? Why couldn't Sarah just have focused on embroidery like all other women? Simply scandalous!" Lucinda could hear the contempt and disgust in his voice before it became muffled as the men descended into the conservatory.

Rousing herself from these memories, Lucinda closed her book and blew out the candle. By the time someone came to rescue her from the locked closet, Lucinda had hidden her book and candlestick again behind her shoes. She was standing close to the door talking to Sekhmet, who was on the other side.

The cat had started mewing after the maid left to fetch the key and was now scratching the door. Lucinda could hear heavy footsteps approach and then a male voice. "Shoo!"

Lucinda stepped back as the key was placed in the keyhole and the door was opened. Her grandfather stood before her and beckoned her out. Lucinda left the dark closet, but the bedroom was not much better on this grey and rainy day. Even though the maid had lit the wall sconces, the room with its somber wallpaper was still dim and dreary.

"Lucie. How long have you been in there?"

"Just the morning, Grandfather."

The baron shook his head. "I want to talk to you." He indicated that they should sit on the tufted Egyptian Revival settee placed near the two tall windows facing the expansive grounds of the estate. Lucinda had spent many hours on this sofa covered in plush velvet the color of wine. The armrests were made of carved mahogany, the profiles of Egyptian goddesses. Her mother had seen it in a store in London and insisted that it be purchased. Then decided later that she didn't like it; it reminded her too much of Alexander. Sarah had the staff put it in Lucinda's room.

Her grandfather smiled and then looked at her earnestly. "How are you?"

Lucinda debated asking if he was referring to her mental or physical health. Was his real query, *Are you going insane like your mother?* Lucinda stifled the urge. She loved only two things about Foxhill Estate: her grandfather and her cat. Her grandfather loved her back even if she was "misbegotten". She knew that he loved his wife and daughter too. Even in their madness.

"I'm fine," she assured him, and placed her hand over his. "How are you feeling?"

The baron patted her hand. "I'm well. Don't you worry about me." However, his expression revealed uncertainty and he withdrew both hands before placing them on his knees. The sudden appearance of the sun from behind the clouds brightened the room. The sunlight streaming through the windows seemed to punctuate his next words. "I thought that you might want to visit your father in Egypt. Do you remember much of him?"

Lucinda shook her head. She fiddled with the lace at the end of her sleeve. "Wouldn't you miss me, Grandfather?"

"Of course I would, dear."

She returned his earnest look. "Do you suppose my mother would?"

"Yes," he answered emphatically. Seeing the doubt on her face, he added, "I mean, I think so. You know about her condition. I don't know for certain what she thinks or knows anymore."

Lucinda reflexively traced the wooden Egyptian face of the armrest. "Do you think my father wants to see me?"

The old man glanced out the window and watched as the sun was again obscured by the clouds, leaving the room darkened as before.

You don't believe Father will want to see me either.

Her grandfather looked back at her. "Uncle Roderick thinks that a change of scenery would be good for you. The sunshine would be beneficial. He wants you to be happy."

Doubtful. Lucinda noticed Sekhmet poke his head out from under the bed. Upon seeing Lord Haliburton, the cat quickly returned to hiding. "I would miss my orange kitty terribly. What if something happened to him while I am not here? What if he runs away?"

"Don't worry about him, I'll make sure that he gets taken care of. What if I let him come inside occasionally?"

"I don't know . . ."

The baron tried to cheer her up. "Don't you think it would be fun to see the pyramids? Perhaps the excavation of the Great Sphinx of Giza? It would be an adventure."

Lucinda sighed. "If you think so, Grandfather."

And so it was settled. Lucinda would travel with her uncle and a new governess to Egypt.

Chapter 3:

TREASURE HUNTER

"Here is the post, Dr. Merimee."

His Egyptian manservant, Eza, handed Gaston the mail. At Eza's feet, Badger sat and wagged his tail. The dog, a fine specimen of a dachshund, had been sent to Gaston by a German friend and archaeology enthusiast after telling Dr. Merimee that he needed a true friend in the desert. Badger quickly bonded to Eza and he adored the puppy, so Gaston gave the dog to him.

"Thank you, Eza," Gaston replied. While he drank his strong Persian coffee, he watched the servant and the dog start down the hallway, then put his cup down and called out to the pair. "Oh, Eza, will you lay out my excavating clothes and boots? I wish to visit the dig site this morning."

Eza turned back. "Yes, sir," he answered and then continued down the hallway.

Gaston smiled at the young man, who disappeared through a doorway. Unlike the boy's French father, who had been Gaston's assistant at one time, Eza had never been a disappointment to him. The professor turned his mind to the post and leafed through the letters. There were only three pieces: one from the local police chief, one from the Museum of Egyptian Antiquities at Bulaq and one from his benefactor, Lord Haliburton. Starting with the official letters, he saw that both were about the archaeological dig and his discoveries. The first one from the chief discussed charitable contributions to the police force. "Charitable?" Gaston muttered to himself. "No, extortion." The only way he could safeguard the dig site was to employ the police force to maintain security as well as secrecy. Tossing that letter aside, he read the other one. It was from a minion of Mariette's reminding him again of reporting any findings immediately. Auguste Mariette was the director of antiquities at the museum. Gaston knew that the only reason he had been allowed to stay was because of his nationality and his knack for diplomacy. *To keep the snakes from biting you, they must be fed,* he thought bitterly. To avoid prying eyes, he refolded the letters and replaced them in their envelopes. Then he turned his attention to the last one.

Reading the last letter, he softly cursed in French. This missive from England informed him that he was to have visitors in four to six weeks' time. The baron's son and his granddaughter, Lucinda. Roderick Haliburton was also bringing a chaperone for Lucinda and an old friend of Alexander's, an American linguist and photographer, Mitch Grant. Apparently, Roderick was going to be inspecting Merimee's endeavors for himself to determine whether the funds provided for the field expedition were to continue. "How am I to be expected to carry on with my work and entertain visitors? Especially them?" Gaston said out loud. He didn't voice his next thought. That of his doomed future if he didn't produce soon what Lord Haliburton wanted: ancient artifacts. Golden treasure.

Gaston poured himself another cup of coffee. As he sipped it, he thought about the first time he had visited the baron at his estate outside of London, several years before. The butler had shown him into the study, and Lord Haliburton got up, shook his hand and greeted him heartily. "Bienvenue, Professor

Merimee!" He introduced the two gentlemen with him. "This is my son, Roderick, and Alexander, my son-in-law. He is a draughtsman by trade."

"An artist," the slim, finely featured, dark-haired young man corrected as he extended his hand.

Gaston recognized him as an American by his accent. He shook Alexander's hand and then Roderick's. Lord Haliburton summoned the staff for drinks and bade them to sit. They began the discussion of Egypt with the baron explaining how his distant cousin James, now dead, had been to Egypt and had been the one to introduce him to Egyptology.

"So, Dr. Merimee," Lord Haliburton suggested enthusiastically, "tell us of your expertise and your proposed field expedition." He listened intently as Gaston began.

As the professor continued to speak, he tried to ignore Roderick. By his stony face, Gaston could tell that he was not interested in Egyptian antiquities and probably perceived this idea as a useless endeavor, seeing it as a drain on his eventual inheritance. Alexander spent most of the time examining his fingernails.

When Gaston had finished his proposition, Lord Haliburton offered a deal. "Dr. Merimee, I want to fund your studies and your archaeologic pursuits, but I am not wealthy enough to just throw my money away without some recompense. You do understand?"

"Of course. However, you may recall, as we discussed previously, the number of antiquities being allowed to leave the country is now being monitored closely by the Egyptian government."

"And, I assume, by Auguste Mariette as well?"

Gaston nodded. "Yes, as he is director of antiquities."

"Well," said Lord Haliburton, "because I am involved with several exhibitions at the Paris Exposition, I know that Mariette is organizing the Egyptian exhibit at the fair. I think that you should get acquainted with him. He will appreciate a fellow archaeologist who wants to preserve this ancient culture." The baron smiled conspiratorially.

"But he believes that the Egyptians or the Louvre should keep their treasures."

"Yes, yes, but this is why you are just the man to help both of us."

Gaston knew the baron was anxious to add to his small collection. "I am determined to find an undiscovered tomb that will satisfy all our needs, Lord Haliburton," Merimee assured him. *Treasure for you, eminence for me.*

"Certainly, I have no doubt in your capabilities, Dr. Merimee. But . . ." The baron paused slightly. "I also have a travel company and an editor who might be interested in publishing a picture book to stimulate interest in visitation to foreign lands. Having an *artist*"—he glanced at Alexander—"along to document these discoveries would be agreeable to me. Someone to render pictorial proof of actual tomb hieroglyphs so that they can be studied and translated. Imagine the implications."

"Well, I suppose . . ."

Lord Haliburton interrupted him. "Then it is settled. Alexander will accompany you back to France. His *artistic* flair will help you in designing an exhibition for the world fair."

Alexander began to object. "But I don't want to . . ."

The baron interrupted him as well. "He can help in the preparations for the expedition and then onto Egypt."

At dinner that night, Gaston understood Alexander's reluctance. The American was drawn by his fiery wife, Sarah, like a moth to a candle flame. A queer thought came to Gaston's mind. *He circles around her unaware of his impending doom.* The two couldn't take their eyes off one another, much to the annoyance of Lord Haliburton.

Gaston knew that the baron wanted drawings of Egypt, but it was obvious that he also wanted to get rid of Alexander. He speculated about this strange family dynamic before wondering about the baron's wife. *And where is she? Separated from him? Dead?* Gaston sensed an unnaturalness to the household as he observed the only child at the table, a young girl, watching her parents. *Perhaps it's the way they ignore her,* he thought. *She is invisible to them.* While Gaston was looking at her, Lucinda turned suddenly and stared into his eyes as if she had read his mind. This action startled him, and he averted his gaze. He was glad he wasn't staying long; dusty, hot tombs and mummies were more appealing.

The next day, Lord Haliburton had taken Gaston aside. "I want to show you something in private."

The old man led him into his study and closed the door. He went to his large desk and removed a leather-bound folder with dried and cracked edges. "This belonged to my cousin. I bought it from James when he returned from Egypt. Disowned by our family, he came to me for help in paying his debts." Lord Haliburton opened the folder. "He told me that he believed there were many undiscovered tombs in the valley west of the Theban necropolis. He knew Belzoni, the famous Italian archaeologist who explored Egypt."

Gaston had heard of him. *Glorified tomb robber, more like.*

Lord Haliburton picked out one of the papers, a hastily scribbled map titled *Valley of the Monkeys, 1833*. The baron waved it at Gaston. "I believe this is a treasure map to a lost tomb."

Tossing aside Haliburton's letter now, Gaston snorted at the thought of a treasure. *L'illusion,* he scoffed. For years, he had studied that map, that journal, and to what end? Nothing but frustration. He hadn't been able to locate that tomb. Any trace of it had disappeared under the blowing sands of over forty years. Standing up, he adjusted his robe and retied the sash. As he made his way to his dressing room, the professor thought of Alexander and how he had changed. Thinning hair, leathery skin, and a potbelly from drinking too much Egyptian beer. The desert milieu had not been good to him. That thought made Gaston wonder about Lucinda. *She must be a teenager now. It will be interesting to see what changes have occurred in her.* But he didn't have much time to muse as there was a knock at the front door. Around the corner, Eza and Badger, who was barking furiously, hurried past to answer it. Gaston heard an excited exchange as well as continued barking and growling, but before he could ascertain the cause, Eza bounded back around the corner, almost colliding with his employer.

"Look Dr. Merimee! A worker digging in the new area found these!" Eza held out his hand. In his palm laid several dusty, white beads. Gaston picked one up to examine it. Carved into the sides were tiny black hieroglyphics. The professor strained his eyes and squinted at one of the characters. It was a feather.

Chapter 4:

IN BLACK AND WHITE

René had just finished fashioning a mallet from an old chair leg. He examined his handiwork before setting the mallet on the workbench next to his favorite enameling tool, a large, white goose feather that applied the perfect amount of liquid glass to each cell. Louis had encouraged him to make his own implements for jewelry manufacturing; over the last year, René had spent most of his time learning filing, hammering, and piercing. Much to his disliking, René was also the errand boy and spent time maintaining the workshop. However, by applying the knowledge he learned from Ecole des Arts Décoratifs, he gradually had earned the respect of Louis.

Now that René was an advanced second-year apprentice, Louis was allowing him to spend more time making adornments and less time cleaning. Enameling had fast become René's favorite pastime, and Louis was instructing him in this ancient art. His first pieces were not a great success, but each new one was an improvement upon the last.

What his mentor and benefactor liked the most were René's drawings. Louis admired the jewelry designs, boxes, and vases that René had drawn for class, and had once shown his art portfolio to Louis Aine. There was no verbal acknowledgment, but René was pleased when the older man had paused and nodded in approval at one of his illustrations. His satisfaction quickly waned, however, when Louis Aine came upon René's composition of a coffin with an Egyptian death mask. The elderly Aucoc wrinkled his nose in displeasure and closed the sketchbook. "So morbid."

On the other hand, Louis had copied a couple of the drawings, made a few modifications and rendered them into beautiful pieces which the firm had sold. René frowned. *I should be making the profit from my work, not him. But I am just an apprentice.*

"René!" André called as he approached. "Nom de nom!" He shook his head disapprovingly. "Why are you still working? You are trying to make me look bad! Lèche-bottes."

René grinned and shot back, "Well, if you weren't so lazy . . ."

"I prefer to enjoy life. You should too," André said as he clapped the younger man on the shoulder. "Besides, I can't keep up with your ambition and talent."

"I can't keep up with your enjoyment," René replied. Lately, after work, he and André had been visiting the Montmartre cabarets more frequently, much to the chagrin of his mother. Olympe had been chiding him the day before about his late-night activities. When his father had first died and his mother had been in full mourning, her depression caused her to ignore René and his whereabouts. Olympe had been mostly listless and dispirited except when it came to fashion. The only things she seemed to enjoy were crocheting and buying new mourning clothes. How many black crepe dresses and lace handkerchiefs were necessary? Now that Papa had been gone over two years and Olympe was in the half-mourning stage of proper grieving, René supposed that those dresses would be put away and new ones purchased. Earlier that day, he had stopped at a close-by specialty mourning establishment to pick up the silk bonnet she had ordered. René presumed that his mother would be donning gray and purple soon, as well as slipping back into her well-intentioned but overbearing and domineering attitude regarding his lifestyle.

André was admiring René's new mallet. "Not bad, not bad," he said before setting it down and walking over to the small desk that René used as a design workspace. André had followed in his father's footsteps and become a silversmith and a woodworker; he crafted the fine travel boxes under Louis's tutelage. "What new masterpieces have you created?" he teased, before rifling through René's drawings laying on the desk and stopping at a rough sketch of the Madonna standing on a crescent moon. "What's this?"

"My instructor took us to the Louvre so we could study the masters and sketch their pictures. That is the *Immaculate Conception* by Murillo." André continued to flip through the pictures, then held one up of a praying nun. "We also went to Saint-Sulpice to practice figure drawing."

André nodded. "Did I ever tell you about seeing a nun walking down Rue des Capucines? Did you know there used to be a convent here before the neighborhood was renovated? I had returned from a friend's house late at night and thought the nun was a real person at first. It seemed odd that she should be walking by herself. She was going in my direction, so I followed her. The nun turned the corner onto our street and when I got there, she had disappeared. Une fantôme."

"A ghost?"

André chuckled. "Perhaps it was the absinthe."

"Yes, I think so."

André chuckled again. "I do have a habit of drinking too much absinthe," he admitted. "It can make one crazy." Then he chose another picture, a black rooster. As he examined it closer in the light, he offered a rare compliment. "Fine detail, especially the feathers." André turned the drawing to René and pointed to the bird. "This is you, mon ami, le coq noir." He winked at him. "Such a ladies' man. Tell me, what is your magic? Is it your mustache, your dimpled chin or your soulful eyes?" André coquettishly batted his eyelashes at René.

"You're just jealous."

André grinned. "Moi?" He returned the drawings to the stack and then straightened it. "Come on, don't be so coy. Come upstairs for a drink. Or two. Tell me the secrets of your charming ways."

"Not tonight. I promised my mother I would come home after work and bring her the bonnet I picked up."

"Fine. See you in the morning." André pulled some francs from his pants pocket and tossed them on the workbench. "Louis Aine wants croissants. Don't forget to stop by the boulangerie tomorrow morning. And say bonjour to Claudette for me." As he walked away, he called over his shoulder, "Does she know about all your *girlfriends* at the cabarets?" Snickering, he disappeared into the back stairwell that led to the upstairs apartments.

Grinning, René straightened up the workbench. He put his tools away and pocketed the money. After extinguishing the lamps, he grabbed his coat and hat, and walked out the side door into the narrow alley between the buildings. He locked the door, then headed to the street. Rue de la Paix was deserted. All the shops had closed for the night. René turned the corner and headed to the boulevard where he would pick up the omnibus. Thinking of André's story about seeing a phantom reminded René of his own apparition. *Why didn't I tell him about my ghostly nun?* Memories of her appearance five years earlier flooded back.

At the time, he had assumed it was his imagination. The incident had occurred after school when the schoolyard was empty of instructors and students. René's teacher had made him stay late, after reprimanding him about paying attention during class and destroying school property. In the last hour of class,

René had become bored and had begun doodling in his math book. The margin of the book's page was not large enough, so he began drawing a picture in his notebook. It portrayed the mistress of one of the older teachers, who visited him on a regular basis to bring his lunch. He had told everyone that she was his niece, but others knew better. René noticed that the men, especially his own teacher, ogled her slim yet voluptuous figure. Her dark, sleek hair upswept, its wanton stray curls drawing one's eyes to her slender neck. René closed his eyes and visualized her face before sketching it, focusing on her large, captivating eyes. Instead of the flamboyant hat that she normally wore, he embellished her head with a plethora of long curls ending in serpent heads. René grinned at his Medusa drawing before he noticed his teacher standing over his desk.

The instructor cleared his throat. "Ahem."

René looked up to see his teacher glaring down at him and the other students staring at him. Just at that moment, the bell rang. The other boys closed their books, got up noisily and began to gather their things to leave. René started to close his book, but his teacher placed his hand over it.

"Non. You will stay, M. Lalique."

Knowing he was in trouble, a few of the boys grinned stupidly at René before exiting the classroom. René returned his gaze to M. Girard. Noticing the drawing, the teacher picked up the Medusa sketch to look at it closer. Obviously, René's rendition was accurate as he clearly recognized her face. Looking at it longingly, his lips curved into a slight smile. Then he realized the boy was watching him and he furrowed his brows at René.

He pointed to the scribbles in the math book. "What made you think this was a good idea? Defacing schoolbooks is a serious offense, young man."

René looked contrite. "I'm sorry, M. Girard." He wondered what his punishment would be.

"Erase that right now!"

René complied and then looked up at M. Girard. His gaze had returned to the picture. Forcing his eyes away from it, he examined René's textbook. Satisfied that the vandalism had been taken care of properly, he closed it.

"One does not fare well in life if one does not pay attention to one's lessons," M. Girard began to lecture. "You are here to learn about finances and commerce. How do you think you can properly manage a ledger and a business without mathematics? You need to learn to be practical. Doodling and drawing nonsense will not take you too far, M. Lalique. Do you understand?"

"Oui, M. Girard."

"I have a good mind to report this offense to your parents and the director. What do you think about that?"

"I'd rather you didn't," René replied respectfully and honestly. He smiled disarmingly at his instructor.

It worked. The teacher's face softened and he said, "Well, if you promise to pay better attention in class . . ."

"Oui, M. Girard," René readily agreed.

"And no more scribbling in your math book . . ."

"Oui, Monsieur. I won't, Monsieur."

"I am going to keep this picture as evidence," Girard said, "just in case you forget your promises." He ripped out the drawing, walked back to his desk and placed it in his satchel but not before glancing at it once more. Then he leaned against his desk and folded his arms across his chest. "You have talent. You should enter the upcoming drawing competition."

"Oui, sir. Merci, sir."

"You may go now."

Pleased with the compliment and relieved that he did not receive any punishment, René gathered his things and left. Walking tall, he thought about M. Girard keeping his picture of the girl. His drawing teacher, M. Lequien, was much more critical of his work. Monsieur Girard had bolstered his confidence.

René opened the door and walked out into the school court-yard. He was crossing it when he became aware of the presence of another person. She was dressed like a nun and standing between the buildings. He had heard the rumors of other students saying that they had seen ghost nuns wandering on the campus; one boy had claimed that he had seen one walk through a wall. René had figured that his classmates were just embellishing on the history of the grounds. Originally, the institution had been a convent for the Order of Daughters of Mary Magdalene.

Detecting her from the corner of his eye, he turned to see the old woman staring at him. Her look was so magnetizing that he had stopped in his tracks. They held each other's gaze for a few moments; there was a feeling of familiarity between them. Then he watched her turn and walk through the distant wall of the building he had just left. Disappearing. *What did I just see?*

René ran away quickly.

Serendipitously, shortly after seeing the apparition, René had won his first design award. In addition to René's previous artwork, his mother had used this award as leverage to convince Louis to take him on as an apprentice.

Now, as he continued walking toward the omnibus, René mused, *Why did the nun appear to me that day? Was the illusion an omen about my future as an artist?* He wondered why André had never mentioned his ghostly encounter before now. Was it because of seeing his Saint-Sulpice drawing or could there be another reason? Was André's account foretelling something momentous? Perhaps another major life transformation?

Chapter 5:

EGYPTIAN MAGIC

His mother had her eyes on him as he walked down the hallway. Obviously waiting for him, Olympe stood by the front door. She was impeccably dressed in a slate-colored mourning dress with buttons made of jet. When he stood in front of her, she presented her cheek to him.

René kissed it and then the other. "You are up early."

"You have been working late so many nights at La Maison Aucoc, I wanted to know if you would be home early tonight."

"Non, Maman."

Frowning, she asked, "When is your class?"

"It is late afternoon," René replied as he removed his overcoat from the hall closet, "but Ambrose asked me if I would go out with him tonight."

"Who is this Ambrose?"

"Don't you remember? I told you about him. He is one of my schoolmates." René slid into his coat.

Olympe pursed her lips and was silent as she studied him for a few moments. "I was going to have Mme. Staffe prepare her duck confit and artichoke bottoms topped with sauce Béarnaise. Some of your favorites."

"I'm sorry, Maman." René placed his bowler on his head. "But I have already promised him."

Rather petulantly, she began, "I tire of being alone in this big house. Now that your father is gone . . ."

To sidetrack her, René kissed his mother's cheeks again. "Why don't you ask Mme. Bouchard over for dinner? I am certain that she will have something interesting to say."

Ignoring his suggestion, Olympe adjusted his coat collar and picked off some imaginary lint. "Where will you be going?"

"To his apartment for dinner and then to a bookstore event." He opened the door, went down the steps, deeply inhaled and then exhaled the crisp October air. Bidding au revoir to his mother, René began walking away.

Left standing in the doorway, Olympe dolefully called after him, "Don't stay out too late!" René waved goodbye without turning around.

René had met Ambrose in one of his fall classes. Ambrose was interested in wood-working and so René had introduced him to André. They instantly took a liking to each other. With genuine camaraderie, the three of them made a habit of frequenting the cabarets together. Ambrose was a good-looking young man with an elliptical face and long, aquiline nose. Some would say he had an effeminate countenance had he not worn a short, dense, neatly trimmed French fork beard giving him a roguish look. Lean and muscular, spending time at a boxing gym had kept him fit. With natural charm, Ambrose was a flirt and the women flocked to him. Both André and René appreciated this trait in a friend; they could seduce the ones that Ambrose overlooked.

After René and Ambrose left school that night, they made their way to Ambrose's cramped apartment on the south bank of the Seine. Ambrose lived above a bookstore; he had convinced the owner that he was an asset as a tenant. Abandoned early by his family, poverty and living on the streets had eventually led to him being a semi-professional Savate fighter, a French kickboxer. The bookstore owner had agreed to allow Ambrose to stay in one of the small, attached upper rooms in exchange for working in the bookstore for several hours a day and keeping an eye on it at night. Ambrose told René that he didn't mind sweeping, dusting, and arranging the books as he was also permitted to borrow the used ones to read and return.

Several years older than René, Ambrose delivered regular counsel on life; René didn't mind much as he missed his father's company. In addition to Ambrose being a self-proclaimed romantic to the ladies, he also considered himself a poet and philosopher. A self-taught intellectual, his starry-eyed nature was compatible to René's, since the younger man was also prone to imaginary flights of fancy and optimistic daydreaming.

Mythology and magic were frequently discussed, and Ambrose claimed he had a link with the spirit world. When his friend mentioned supernatural encounters, René shared his otherworldly stories with Ambrose. Recently, he had relayed André's tale of the phantom nun and that it had unearthed a forgotten incident, René's own strange experience with the apparition of a nun. Although Ambrose had listened intently without expressing doubt about the tale's veracity, René still wondered if it had been just a hallucination.

As they walked through the dusky streets, Ambrose bragged about being privileged to live in the student quarter of Paris. "This is such a grand place to be, such a source of inspiration. I can see Notre-Dame from my window." He turned to René. "Did I ever tell you that I saw Père Corot with his entourage of younger painters, all listening to his sage advice?" René shook his head. "His workshop is just down the street."

Later, as they ate their frugal meal of bread and cheese in Ambrose's apartment, René thought wistfully of the duck confit and artichokes which he had missed out on. He cheered himself by thinking of the evening event they would be attending soon.

The bookstore was open late for a soiree. Ambrose had been talking about this grand affair for a week. What interested René the most was a seer égyptien, an Egyptian fortune-teller, who worked there. Occasionally, she would pull out her deck of peculiar cards to perform a free reading for some lucky customer. The novelty of it and her supposed accuracy had increased her reputation as well as the bookshop's receipts. Madame Sphinx was "très belle et exotique" according to Ambrose.

"There is already a crowd," René said as he gazed out the window.

"Vins libre! La musique!" Ambrose sang out happily as he tidied up after dinner. "Of course!"

René didn't care about the free wine; he was anxious to see the beautiful and mysterious woman from Egypt. He saw a violinist and cellist carry in their instruments. "The musicians are here. Should we go down?"

"In a minute."

As René continued to watch more people meander into the bookshop underneath, he remembered his dream of that morning. He had been walking down stone steps with old men to a stone portico overlooking the sea. He noticed two books propped against the wall. Opening one, he found hieroglyphs written in gold on a black page. Unable to read the writing, he still knew it was about Egyptian magic.

Ambrose interrupted his thoughts. "I'm ready," he announced.

As they made their way out of the apartment, René wondered if his dream was somehow related to the woman at the bookstore. What did it mean?

By the time the two young men entered the bookstore, it was already crowded. They jostled their way to the back, Ambrose looking for the wine and René looking for the Egyptian. They passed an alcove that had been cloistered by a deep blue velvet curtain embellished with miniature stars of silver glitter. Ambrose elbowed René and told him that most likely the fortune-teller was in there. Speculating about when she would emerge, René followed Ambrose through the labyrinth of bookshelves. In a large room, they passed an upright piano; the trio of musicians played a piece by Mozart with attentive listeners gathered around. Finally, they made it through the door to the connected tearoom.

The smattering of tables and chairs had already been taken. Ambrose went to the counter at the back of the room and ordered two glasses of wine. Then he suggested that they browse through the books while they waited for Mme. Sphinx to appear. René agreed, and they returned to the bookshop. Ambrose immediately became engrossed in the books.

Looking around, René was amazed at how many volumes the owner had managed to fit in the space. Old wooden beams supported the bookshelves that raised up to the ceiling and books were even in the area over the pointed arch of the doorway. A chandelier filled with lit candles dangled in the middle of the enlarged open area, throwing flickering light across the darkened spines. Scintillating gold lettering on one of them located on a top shelf caught René's eye. It reminded him again of his dream. Wide-eyed, he thought, *What a coincidence.*

Placing his wine glass on the tiny end table in the corner, René moved the creaky ladder system over to where the book was located, climbed the ladder, and retrieved the volume after reading its golden title: *The Lotus.* Returning to the floor, he examined the front cover. Black with a single lotus flower embossed on it. René opened the thin book; the pages were yellowed vellum with irregular edges. Turning to the title page, he noted there was no publisher name or date before flipping past it to the next page. Elegantly handwritten was: *To understand this book of magic, you must first grasp the lotus and come before the Sphinx.* René turned the page and began to read the text.

CHAPTER 1: HISTORY OF EGYPTIAN HEKA
Heka is the word that ancient Egyptians used to rep-
resent magic. Magic was the foundation of Egyptian
religion. Heka was understood to be both a force and
a law . . .

René's reading was disturbed by noisy voices, jingling and a flash of color from the corner of his eye. He looked up to see a woman in a silver headdress walk by. Heading to the tearoom, like a goose and goslings, she was followed there by a small crowd of men. Still carrying the book, René quickly walked to the entryway to look at her. She was dressed in a full-length black linen caftan with shoulders of red and a bodice of red and black stripes that fell to an empire waist. Long earrings swung from her earlobes and colorful beaded necklaces were strung about her neck. René observed her glittery headwear made from silver metal discs sewn onto a black scarf before taking in the rest of her: sensual curves, full lips, light olive skin and large eyes. Older, but Ambrose was right, she was attractive. René continued to stare at her as did the rest of the men present.

Ambrose was now standing next to him. "Was I right, mon ami?"

"Oui."

The person tending the bar handed the woman a teacup and she raised it to her lips. A man standing close to her asked, "Madame Sphinx, will you be giving a free card reading tonight?"

The seer did not answer immediately. Instead, she looked around at all the patrons and guests as she sipped her tea. When her gaze fell on René and Ambrose in the doorway, she put down her cup and pointed in their direction. "I will pull a card for him."

Ambrose smiled as he stepped forward. "Moi?"

"Non. The one with the book."

With her startling blue eyes, upper eyelids lined in black, focused on him, René involuntarily took a small step back to meld into the shadowy room behind. A smile playing on her bright ruby lips, she moved towards him with a sinuous, graceful gait. A lioness ready to take down a gazelle.

Holding out her hand, Mme. Sphinx asked, "Oui?" René placed his hand in hers and she led him back to the indigo velvet door covered with stars. The other patrons had followed and stopped, their covetous eyes watching. She invited René to sit in the alcove, then entered after him and seductively drew the celestial curtain shut.

Trying to hide his nervousness, René smiled warmly at her. She beamed back. In a sultry tone she told him, "Vous avez une aura puissante," then gave him a titillating look with her icy blue eyes. Even if he did have a powerful aura as she claimed, René felt weak in her presence. The seer had a magnetic gaze; he didn't know if he could resist anything she requested.

Focusing on the deck of cards in front of her, she said, "Let's see what the future holds for you, Monsieur . . .?"

"Lalique. René Lalique."

The seer lit some incense, picked up her cards and began to shuffle them. Then she expertly fanned them out on the table in a semicircle formation. "Choose one card, René." His name dripped from her lips like honey.

René laid the black book on the table off to the side. Madame Sphinx glanced briefly at it before looking back at him. He began to reach with his right hand, but she stopped him. "The left hand receives," she instructed him.

With his left hand, René removed a card from the semicircle and placed it face up on the table.

Pictured on the card was an Egyptian goddess wearing a headdress with a disc surrounded by horns. In the same way the cards had been laid out on the table, seven stars were etched above the goddess in a semicircle. The name Hathor was printed underneath. Suddenly, René felt oddly nostalgic; he was unsure if it was the picture or the incense. Sensing an intimate connection with her image, René felt certain that he had seen the goddess before.

"Hathor, the Mistress of Life," the seer said, "is the embodiment of romance, perfume and dance." She traced her finger over the card. "The seven stars of Pleiades sit above her head. The Milky Way. Seven was a sacred and lucky number to the Egyptians. Her crown represents the marriage of spirit and matter." Looking up, she met René's gaze before circling the same finger above her head. "Finding and realizing the power, the magic, that lies within. The hidden pathway is found in our dreams. Do you remember your dreams, René?"

"Sometimes." A brief thought about his earlier dream flitted through René's mind before he focused on the seer's full, scarlet lips as they formed into a provocative smile.

"Luck and love are in your stars. If you learn to follow your dreams," she said trancelike, "your destiny is Hathor." Her captivating eyes were mesmerizing; René felt dazed. "Divine guidance is here. Your success or failure is determined by you." The seer blinked, her dark fringe of lashes momentarily touching her cheeks. The spell was broken. "You are very charming, M. Lalique. You will go far." She stood up and drew the curtain aside.

Understanding that the session was over, René got up. The crowd had dispersed except for Ambrose, who waited in the passageway patiently sipping his wine. As Mme. Sphinx closed the curtain behind him, René remembered his own wine. He and Ambrose went to fetch it, Ambrose questioning him excitedly along the way. Afterward, René realized that he had left the book of Egyptian magic on the table in the alcove. When he returned there, it was empty. The sphinx and the lotus were gone.

Chapter 6:

EYE OF RA

"She blinked. Had she imagined it? Or had something flitted by her? The sound of thunder overlaid the running rivulets of rain; constant patter and dripping on the window. The meow of an anxious cat came from outside. It was then that she heard the footsteps. She followed the sound to her closet."

Lucinda reached down and petted Sekhmet. The young cat was sitting next to her on the red couch. She was listening apprehensively to the story that her mother, Sarah, was telling her. Outside, the raindrops continued to pelt the window.

"She placed her ear against the wallpaper with the printed floral pattern. Was there an invisible staircase? She could hear the creak of the stairs being treaded upon. Who was there?"

Sarah had been walking around Lucinda's room and stopped to place her ear against the wall near the closet. Then she turned and looked at Lucinda as she spoke.

"Her brother, Roderick, was the one who showed the way to the secret room of their mother's. It was dusty and dark with only one small window. When she stepped inside, he tried to close the door. 'No!' she cried and wedged herself into the doorway. Then he smiled and laughed as he tickled her. Giggling, she fell backward. He wasn't really going to lock her in the nasty old room. It was all a trick, a joke on his part."

Sarah smiled sweetly at Lucinda. "Would you like to see the secret room of my mother's?"

Lucinda grimaced and shook her head.

"Please? For me?" Sarah cajoled. Walking over, she offered her hand to Lucinda. At her approach, Sekhmet jumped up and scurried under Lucinda's bed. Lucinda got up reluctantly and followed her mother to the closet. "The entrance to the hidden staircase is here." Sarah opened the door. "After you," she said and waved Lucinda in. After she stepped inside, the door slammed shut and the lock clicked. Lucinda heard Sarah cackle with glee. "There's no secret staircase, you fool."

"Mother! Let me out!" Lucinda pounded the door. "This isn't funny!"

Sarah's voice was serious and distant. "No, it isn't. Perhaps Roderick will let you out."

Now, trying to forget that horrible day on which her abuse had begun, Lucinda looked out the window of the carriage. She absentmindedly fingered the turquoise pendant on a leather thong that her mother had given her earlier that day before she and her uncle departed Foxhill Estate. Everyone had been made to agree that Sarah was to think that Roderick and Lucinda were headed to London and her new boarding school. Lying was necessary as Sarah would be furious if she knew that they were visiting Alexander. Everyone wanted to avoid a violent rage.

As their steamer trunks were being loaded onto the top of the hackney coach, Sarah had pulled Lucinda aside. "Your father sent me this Egyptian amulet, the Eye of Ra, for protection. I want you to have it." Sarah was calmer and more rational than she had been in months. She hugged her daughter briefly.

Confused by her mother's affection and her words, Lucinda asked, "Protection? Why?"

"I had a dream . . ." Sarah started before looking away.

"What was it?"

"It was nothing."

"Please tell me, Mother."

Sarah began to pace. "I was in a boat on a river with you and your father. We all seemed happy. Then I thought I saw a snake in the water. Swimming towards us. But it wasn't a snake. It was a cobra headdress on a woman. She was all red and had the face of a lioness. The Egyptian goddess Sekhmet." Her mother stopped and faced her. "She swam to the boat and grasped the side with her fiery hands."

"What happened then?"

"I was scared. I woke up. It made me worry about you."

"Don't worry," Lucinda reassured her, "it was just a silly nightmare."

Sarah narrowed her eyes at her daughter but said nothing. Her warmth gone, she turned and walked away.

Watching her, Lucinda swallowed the lump in her throat. *I will never understand you,* she thought as she clenched her hands.

"It's time to go Lucinda," Uncle Roderick called.

Lucinda walked around the coach to where Lord Haliburton stood. She hugged him tight and said, "I'll miss you, Grandfather."

"I'll miss you, too, Lucie."

On their way to the port, jostled sharply by the movement of the coach over the dirt road, Roderick looked up from reading his papers and spotted Lucinda's new necklace. Knitting his brow, he asked, "What is that? Where did you get it?"

"My mother. It's a necklace from my father."

Roderick leaned closer and squinted at it. "Is that an eye?" Lucinda detected a note of derision. He frowned. "Take it off. Reminders of the past have no use in the here and now."

GASTON HAD SURVEYED THE AREA where the beads had been found, before directing the workmen where to dig. He could hear the low grumbles and whispered complaints of the men, but he was firm. His native foreman, Ali Suefi, had expressed his opinion that no one in their right mind would dig there. He pointed out that any water flowing through the canyon would accumulate dirt at that spot and would make it nearly impossible to reenter.

"Perhaps it was not meant to be reentered," Gaston replied. "Perhaps they wanted to fool any robbers and for this tomb to remain intact. Just waiting for us to discover it." He smiled at the foreman. Ali Suefi said nothing as he readjusted his dusty turban and shrugged at his boss. He turned and walked away and then began barking orders at the hired peasants. As the dust and noise became unpleasant, Gaston removed himself from the area. When he reached a position higher up on the slope, he turned and surveyed the activity. The archaeologist understood that Ali Suefi did not feel as positive as he did. *How could he? He does not know about the secret map.*

Gaston watched the great circle of men. Diggers in their raggedy, dark linen robes with rips and tears, the tattered edges of their bell-shaped sleeves blackened by excavation. Some with pants and sandals, others with bare legs and feet exposed, ceaselessly working. Bent over, digging with their turiehs— Egyptian hoes—dislodging the earth and filling their baskets with it. Scraping the material downward, before long they had created a fold in the earth. Ali Suefi watched attentively to ensure that the dirt was handled and inspected carefully before being discarded.

Carrying the baskets to the designated dump spot, the dust blowing about their faces, the workers picked their way down the sandy, rocky slopes. Throwing the dirt down the hillside, they returned to refill their empty baskets. This chain of men was kept moving by the sub-foremen. A giant loop of humanity, a colossal conveyor belt of earth movers. It reminded Gaston of an enormous ant colony. Searching for tombs and treasure was a long and tedious process that involved removing what nature had deposited over thousands of years. The professor crossed his fingers as he hoped for a worthwhile discovery this time.

It had been four weeks after he had received the letter from Lord Haliburton when they found part of a human skull deep in the ground. The back of it had been smashed. Excited that they had discovered something significant, Gaston took the pre-caution of reducing the number of workers and compensated them with a generous severance pay. The remaining workers were first-class and the most trusted but, even so, Gaston knew that he would have to reward them dearly for their discretion as well as preserving any finds. The fewer men he had to pay, the happier Roderick Haliburton would be and the more likely that Gaston could continue with his endeavors.

The digging proceeded at an even slower rate as they removed the dirt to enlarge the pit area, the team always thoroughly combing through it to search for more human remains and other items. When they discovered additional bones, everybody except Ali Suefi was sent home. Besides four small bones, Gaston and his foreman had managed to uncover a partial chunk of a rib cage and a black scarab ring. It was now late afternoon; Gaston had stood to stretch his back when Eza called from above.

"Dr. Merimee, the baron's son and his party have arrived!"

Gaston swore under his breath and was about to look up when something caught his eye. He watched as his foreman and most skilled excavator carefully scraped the hardened earth away from one of the more exposed ribs. Gaston's eyes widened. "What is that?"

Ali Suefi stopped what he was doing. "What?"

"That!" Gaston pointed to the jagged edge of something fibrous just barely visible next to the mere point of another rib. It was pressed to the concave surface.

Ali Suefi bent over and examined it more closely. "It may be a piece of papyrus." He began to delicately remove the dirt in the surrounding area. Focused intently on what was happening, Gaston forgot about Eza's announcement.

Eza had climbed down the wooden ladder. He too watched for several moments before speaking again. "Excuse me, Dr. Merimee, what should I tell your guests?"

Exasperated, Gaston snapped, "What do I care? Can't you see this discovery is more important?" But then he saw Eza's dismayed expression. "I'm sorry, Eza. Can you please tell M. Haliburton that I am engaged but will be back as soon as possible? Hopefully within an hour. Make them comfortable. Offer refreshments. You know what to do." He smiled. "Merci, mon ami."

Eza left, and Gaston turned back to the matter at hand. Before an hour was up, Ali Suefi had managed to dislodge the item from inside the rib. As he lifted it up, Gaston could see that it was indeed a piece of papyrus. It seemed to have been cut into a rectangular shape like a card originally but, judging by the irregular and ragged, brown-stained edges, appeared to have been torn in half. As Ali Suefi handed the piece to him, Gaston could see there was something drawn on it. Faded by time and the elements, the inked symbol of blue and black was barely visible. Bringing it closer, he recognized the hieroglyph: the Eye of Ra.

Chapter 7:

SCARABS

Sweat beaded on Gaston's forehead and trickled down his face. Using his handkerchief, he wiped away some of the perspiration that had gathered. The newly dug-out burial chamber was unbearably hot. *The fires of Hell surely could not be hotter.* He brought his pick down hard on the dried mud. The discovery of the bones, beads, black scarab ring, and, ultimately, the tomb, had given him newfound fervor.

Gaston had been working hard for several hours. The ground was stony and unyielding. Trying to be a good excavator, he had been scraping diligently with his turieh. However, he had not made much headway and was starting to tire. He rocked back on his heels and took a long draught from his canteen, watching Ali Suefi in the flickering light cast by the oil lamps. Undistracted, the foreman continued to carefully scrape away the dirt, always looking for buried artifacts as he did.

As he rested, Gaston recalled the faint hieroglyph carved on the rock overhang above the pit. Discovered the same day as the torn piece of papyrus, the hieroglyph was a crudely sketched owl. A protector of the ancient Egyptian dead. Gaston felt certain it meant there was a tomb there. Informing Roderick later that day, he got his approval to continue exploring.

Under orders from Gaston, Ali Suefi had instructed the workers to dig farther under the rock face. Eventually they discovered the tomb entrance hidden by large stones. After the stones were removed, a rough-hewn corridor was uncovered. It led to two chambers: a smaller shaft tomb and a larger, deeper one. Again, Gaston had released most of the local workmen but paid them handsomely and promised future employment to ensure their loyalty and silence. But also, to guard against the hornet's nest of corrupt dealers and foreign robbers that bribed the poor Egyptians to steal from his discoveries. Wealthy men from other countries who wanted what he and Lord Hāliburton had been searching to find for so long. Ancient Egyptian riches.

To their great disappointment, the tomb had been plundered. Gaston speculated that ancient robbers had left the site open. Over many centuries, desert flash floods had filled the chambers with dirt and covered the entrance with boulders. However, in the last room, they found three things. A coffin, an offering table, and a carved slab. The wooden sarcophagus with its worn, painted lid pushed off to one side was empty and the bottom had been encased in four inches of hard mud. They had managed to uncover the base but nothing valuable had been discovered.

Gaston and Ali Suefi had then moved to a depressed recess at the back of the chamber. They were there now, kneeling in front of the raised stone offering table, excavating around it. Gaston looked at the pink stone slab carved with hieroglyphs sitting on top of the platform. It was a false door, a portal that the ancient Egyptians believed led to the underworld. He took another swig of water before beginning to dig again. To satisfy his patron, he needed to produce gold and jewels, not just a few trinkets, a false door, and some paintings.

As he dug, Gaston's thoughts turned to his houseguests and their first meeting. Making the introductions, Lord Haliburton's son, Roderick, looked older but had the same contrived and aloof sociability as before. Miss Meadows, the attractive chaperone, flashed a phony smile that made him uneasy. Lucinda, standing rearmost, nodded her head politely.

The only one who was not ill at ease was the American, Mr. Grant. Tall, beefy, with blond hair and a cleanshaven face, he firmly shook Gaston's hand and said, "It's a pleasure to make your acquaintance, Dr. Merimee. Call me Mitch."

At that moment, Alexander walked into the sitting room. Mitch smiled and strode over to him. Grasping his hand and shoulder, he said, "Alex, it's been ages. Good to see you, my friend."

To Gaston's surprise, Alexander grinned back. "I can't believe you're here. Yes, it has been a long time. You haven't changed much."

Mitch turned and motioned Lucinda over. "No, but look who has. I remember when she was just a baby."

Gaston observed that the little girl had grown into a lovely, young woman, inheriting her mother's fine features and her father's dark hair. Hers was woven into a thick braid that nearly reached her waist.

Lucinda timidly approached her father. Standing in front of him, she glanced at his stony face before dropping her gaze. Eyes downcast, she greeted him. "Hello, Father."

"Hello, Lucinda." Then, ignoring the rest of the company, Alexander turned to Mitch. "C'mon, I want to show you the dig site before it gets dark." The two men quickly disappeared through the doorway.

Silent, Lucinda watched them leave. Looking at her pained expression, Gaston thought, *Sacre bleu, what is wrong with that man?* Then Eza, with Badger at his heels, entered the room, and her face brightened. She knelt, Badger ran over, and Lucinda petted him. Wagging his tail, when she stopped, Badger nosed her hand for more loving.

When she straightened up again, Gaston took the opportunity to approach her. "Do you remember me, Mlle. Haliburton?"

"Barely," she replied with a bashful smile. "But it has been a long time. My grandfather wanted me to say bonjour to you."

Smiling at this memory now in the heat, Gaston stopped what he was doing and took another swig of water. He surveyed the hieroglyphs on the wall above them and thought of Eza. Gaston wondered if anyone else, including Lucinda, noticed his manservant's frequent, surreptitious ogling of their new houseguest.

If she did, Gaston could not tell because Lucinda was as shy as she was pretty. Her reserve and silence were especially pronounced around her uncle and her father. Alexander acted weird with everyone except Mitch Grant; they had returned easily to their former friendship. Roderick and the governess, Miss Meadows, seemed to have the closest relationship. They had only stayed a few days, and then Roderick had taken his niece and her chaperone to see the sites of Luxor. Mitch had remained behind to help Alexander make copies of the painted walls. Working side by side, the tall linguist was a stunning contrast to his slight friend.

An excited sound from Ali Suefi brought Gaston back to the present. "Did you find something?" he asked.

"Oui, look!"

Gaston retrieved one of the oil lamps and shined light over the spot where Ali Suefi indicated. He could see a tip of metal in the mud. "Bien joué! Keep digging!"

The foreman continued to unearth the object. At last, he lifted it from the ground, a scarab with cloisonné wings. The carved green beetle held a large cabochon of carnelian between its front legs with a half-circle base of turquoise at the bottom. An amulet made to be placed over the heart. Ali Suefi handed it to Gaston, who turned it over and saw hieroglyphs.

To whom did this amulet belong and where is the mummy? Gaston wondered. He took a deep breath to quell his excitement and placed the scarab in a cloth bag. Thrilled as he was by their find, they still had almost a cubic yard of mud to dig through to reach the back of the recess. They returned to their tedious work of removing earth.

Soon, his mind began to wander again, and Gaston recalled a conversation he had with Mitch one night after dinner. They were alone drinking brandy and smoking in the sitting room. The other houseguests had not yet returned from their sightseeing and Alexander had gone to town by himself.

Gaston spoke first. "So, tell me, how do you know Alexander and the Haliburton family?"

"I've known Alex since college," Mitch replied. "We met the Haliburtons at a high-society function in Philadelphia. That's when Alex met and fell in love with Sarah, his wife. Estranged wife, that is. Did you meet her?"

"Oui, I met her a long time ago at their London estate. A beautiful woman."

"Yes, she was something." Mitch sounded nostalgic.

"Her daughter, Lucinda, reminds me of her but she's not as vivacious."

Mitch paused and a lustful look flitted across his face before he took another swig and set his glass down. "Yes. She doesn't always have to be the center of attention like her mother."

More silence ensued as they puffed on their Turkish cigarettes. Again, Gaston broke the silence. "What is the real reason you are here, M. Grant?"

Mitch peered at him and then gave him a toothy grin. "Well, Doc, the truth of the matter is, the baron has been toying with the idea of publishing a book about Egypt. Since I studied hieroglyphs, and am a writer and photographer, I guess he thought I could be of use in evaluating his project."

Gaston considered this response. "Is that so? I can't help feeling that there is another reason."

Mitch chuckled. "You caught me, Doc. As you may know, Alex is trying to win back Sarah. Roderick told me that Lord

Haliburton thinks that Alex is making Sarah crazy with his letters. I mean *insane*. Lord Haliburton thought, as Alex's friend,
that I could convince him to let her go."

"Do you think it's possible?"

Mitch shrugged before facing the window. Finally, he
admitted, "I don't know. He's different now, so cynical. Really
gone to pot. I feel bad for his daughter." He turned to Gaston.
"I told Roderick I would try. I mean, I could hardly turn down
a book deal . . ." Mitch flashed a charming smile at Gaston
before downing his drink.

Thinking about those drinks now, Gaston realized his arm
was tired and he was thirsty. He stopped digging and picked up
his canteen. It was empty, so he told Ali Suefi that he was going
to take a break and fill their water containers. As he walked by
the antechamber of the tomb, he overheard the two Americans
talking. He glanced in the doorway as he crossed by slowly.

"Did you know that scarab beetles orient to the Milky
Way to find their direction?" Mitch asked Alexander. Mitch
was holding the large piece of thin paper that Alex was using
to trace the ancient Egyptian figures and hieroglyphic script.
He was tracing over a scarab.

"No, I just copy them."

"Did you know that the ancient Egyptians considered the
scarab a symbol of rebirth? They represented life energy in
a continuous cycle. Metamorphosis. Life, death, life, death."

Alex snorted before moving to trace another hieroglyph on
the edge of the paper.

Gaston stopped on the other side of the entry. He wanted
to listen to their conversation without being seen.

"Their god, Khepri," Mitch was saying, "was the beetle-
headed god who rolled the new sun, Ra, across the sky to the
underworld and then renewed it each day to repeat the cycle."

"I understand that," Alex replied forlornly. "The same thing
day after day. Sometimes, I dream about returning to England,

but Sarah has never answered my letters. Not even one." He sighed. "I don't know what I'll do when this work is finished."

Mitch cleared his throat. "You know, maybe she hasn't forgiven you for having that affair. Sarah was possessive and jealous; she may never forget." He paused a moment. "Perhaps it's time to let her go? Move on with your life?"

"Easy for you to say. You didn't love or cherish her like I did." Mitch's tone was sharp. "I cared for her."

"But you finished college," Alex said bitterly. "Don't remind me of past mistakes." Gaston heard movement and then Alex announced, "This one is finished. You can let go."

From his vantage point, Gaston watched Alex walk to the stack of tracings in the corner placed away from the candles they used to illuminate the wall pictures. He heard Mitch say in a cheerful voice, "What you told me about using candles instead of oil lamps to light up the wall paintings and the tracing paper was so interesting. Not as much smoke and the yellow beam does make the thin parchment translucent. The drawings *are* easier to copy." Rifling through his pile of work, Alex didn't answer. Mitch persisted. "And the mirror system is genius. Positioning the mirror so that the sunlight is reflected in here to provide additional lighting is fantastic. The only flaw is that additional workmen aren't here to readjust its position."

Not bothering to look at Mitch, Alex grunted in response.

Now, Gaston heard resignation in Mitch's voice. "It's getting dark in here and it's time to move the mirror. I'm hungry. Should we take a break?"

"Sure, why not?" Alex picked up the papers. "I've done enough for today. A beer or two sounds good right now. Will you blow out the candles?"

Chapter 8:

SHADOW WORLDS

René placed the brass holder with its burning candle on the corner table. He had searched in vain. The lotus book with its gold-lettered spine was nowhere to be found. *Perhaps Mme. Sphinx took it away,* he thought. He and Ambrose were in the bookstore. They stood in the antiquarian section as before. Ambrose was unfolding an old city plan of Paris. He had found the dated map folded in a book about the Latin Quarter called *Trou et Coin de Paris.* The book was about the city's occult corners, inhabitants, and places. Eager to show the map to René, Ambrose spread out the fragile, yellowed parchment next to the candle plate. He pointed to a street. "Look here. Rue Zacharie was once called Rue des Maléfices, the street of Hex, where, I believe, there lives a secret society. Sorcerers and witches. Have you ever walked down it?"

Shaking his head, René didn't remember doing so.

Ambrose smiled. "I have. It has a certain presence." He refolded the map and placed it between the pages before returning the book to the shelves. Then he turned to René. "There is a shop of curiosities there. We will bring a gift to our hostess." Consulting his pocket watch, he advised, "If we go now, we will have time to tarry a few moments before the sitting." They put on their overcoats and top hats and, after Ambrose locked the store, began to walk.

The Egyptian fortune-teller had requested that René and Ambrose attend a séance at her home. According to Ambrose, she normally charged money but was so entranced with René that she had foregone payment. René readily agreed when Ambrose told him about the invitation.

In the twilight, they traveled silently the few blocks to their destination, passing a large church before turning down the narrow street. Halfway down it, they arrived at the store. "Here," Ambrose said as he faced the inky façade painted black with red trim. The door was flanked by four tall and narrow windows. Above the door was a bright gas lamp shining on red lettering: CABINET DES CURIOSITÉS. René noted a hodge-podge of strange items in the display window before hearing the doorbell tinkle as Ambrose stepped inside.

The odor of mustiness hit René as he followed Ambrose into the shop. They ambled their way through the dimly lit, dusty store, maneuvering between the large antiques and shelving packed with smaller items. In the middle, off to one side, was a glass case built in a wooden enclosure. Standing inside, with her cash register behind her, was a tall, skinny woman with a long neck in a blue dress. The saleswoman wore a wide-brimmed hat with two white ostrich feathers stuck into the hatband. Instead of the usual draping of the feathers around the crown, these feathers stood straight up. With her pinched face, big nose, and small eyes, she reminded René of a great blue heron. Her voice cemented the impression.

"I was just about to leave," she croaked. "Can I help you?"

"Perhaps," Ambrose answered as he approached the case. "We are looking for a small gift. Our friend is very exotic and Egyptian. What would you recommend for her?"

"What does she like?"

René remembered the clairvoyant's beads. "She likes perles."
Misunderstanding him, the woman answered, "Pearls?
Let's see . . ." She scanned the items in the glass case until she
found something. "Ah, this one." It was a glass perfume bottle
set in bronze; the front was covered with mother-of-pearl. She
slid back the door, reached in, and brought it out. Placing it
on top of the glass counter, she said, "This is beautiful. The
golden stopper is made of amber."

René admired the piece as Ambrose inquired about the
price. When they agreed to buy it, the woman told them, "Let
me make it presentable," and rummaged around under the
counter, procuring a small box, paper, and a ribbon. As she
wrapped their gift, René saw a man with a large basket strapped
to his back pass by the windowfront.

The saleswoman also glanced at the window and then at
the clock hanging on the wall above the cash register. "Will
that be all?" They nodded yes. "Très bon. It's closing time. The
pêcheurs de lune, the moon fishermen, have started to appear."

Ambrose pocketed their purchase and led the way out of
the store. Darkness had fallen quickly; shadows had grown
in the street of Hex. René could see the man ahead of them.
The old ragpicker had shed his basket; it sat in the street next
to the pile of refuse that he was probing with a long stick. As
they drew nearer, they could hear him muttering. A cold wind
suddenly buffeted their faces and René shuddered.

Ambrose must have sensed René's discomfort as he leaned
in and whispered, "Do not be concerned. He is harmless." He
called out to the man, "Salut, Le Chameau! C'est moi, it's me,
Ambrose! Have you found any bones?"

The Camel, as he was called, stopped what he was doing
and looked up. He held the lantern towards them, the swinging
light illuminating his body. The man's wrinkled visage, droopy
stance and dingy tattered coat reminded René of a mummy
arisen from his tomb. Le Chameau grunted in response and

returned to shifting the pile of junk with his pointed cane. René was unsure if the man was scavenging or checking for rodents before reaching into the mound of debris. He obviously discovered something to his liking as he stabbed forcibly into it and pulled out several filthy rags with his stick. He set down his lantern before plucking them off and tossing them into his basket, then straightened up as René and Ambrose came closer. The pungent stench of the old man was overwhelming, and the gloomy atmosphere made his stare even more disconcerting. René concentrated on keeping his face passive.

Ambrose spoke. "Le Chameau, this is my friend, René."

Not particularly pleased to be introduced, nevertheless René tipped his hat. Le Chameau looked from man to man and, then to René's surprise, he smirked and displayed missing teeth. "I know you." Uncertain of whom was being addressed, René forced a small smile and looked away. This reaction seemed to upset the old man. He pointed his stick at René. "The Hidden One has spoken. It is she who holds the magic mirror."

Perplexed, René asked, "What?"

But the ragpicker had lost interest. He hoisted his basket onto his back, picked up his lantern and proceeded to shuffle to the next pile, ignoring them. René gave Ambrose a questioning look, but Ambrose only shrugged in response. They watched Le Chameau move down the restricted lane for a few moments. Now René understood the nickname: the silhouette of the basket on his stooped figure made the old man look like a lame camel as he hobbled away. Seeing that he was headed the direction they wanted to go, René hesitated. "Should we turn around?" he asked Ambrose.

"Don't be foolish, we're safe."

Leading the way, Ambrose strode past the man, René following quickly behind. Breathing a sigh of relief when they got to the corner, René paused momentarily to watch the lamplighter ignite the streetlamp. A hand clamping on his arm startled him. He turned to see the ragpicker scrutinizing him with sunken eyes, dark circles beneath them. René involuntarily drew back from the man, but Le Chameau held on with a claw-like grip and said, "Beware of the screeching monkeys. They will tear away the veil." He lifted and turned René's arm. Into his palm, the moon fisherman laid a dead beetle and forced René's fingers to fold over it. "The black scarab is where the answer lies." He then let go of René's hand and melted into the darkness of the dirty passageway.

Fearing that the man would reappear if he threw the beetle away, René dropped it into the pocket of his overcoat. "Let's get out of here," he whispered urgently to Ambrose.

But, determined that the ragpicker and his strange utterings would not dampen his spirits, when they were on the bridge crossing over the Seine, René fished out the beetle and flicked it into the river. "Crazy old man," he said and then rolled his eyes at his friend.

"I wonder what Le Chameau was rambling about," Ambrose mused. "Most of the time he is coherent. He must have been bewitched tonight." Ambrose chuckled lightly. "What awaits us at the alchemist's street? I hope Mme. Sphinx and her other guests are more agreeable and charming." He consulted his pocket watch. "Let's hurry."

By the time they had entered Rue Nicolas Flamel across from Saint-Jacques Tower, René had forgotten the ragpicker's words. Ambrose led René to a set of dark wooden doors, one of which opened to a stairwell. René followed Ambrose upstairs to Mme. Sphinx's apartment on the fourth floor. When Ambrose knocked on her door, it was opened by a domestic servant. Behind her in the foyer stood the seer. René felt his stomach flutter as he looked into her crystal blue eyes twinkling above her translucent gold-beaded face veil.

The maid ushered them inside. Taking their coats and hats, she hung them on a hall tree before retreating. The subdued lighting and perfumed atmosphere of the apartment were intoxicating, and Mme. Sphinx looked stunning in her black turban. "Bonsoir," she said. "We have been waiting for you."

Ambrose handed her their present. "We brought a small gift for you."

Through her lacy veil, René could see the seer's ruby lips part slightly in a coquettish grin as she took the box. "Merci."

Madame Sphinx led them through the vestibule to her other visitors. Her flowing, floor-length dress of black velvet with long bell sleeves swayed elegantly and the tiny glittery star appliqués caught the light as she moved gracefully towards the salon. Upon entering the room, René noted the colorful Persian rug and silken wall hangings as well as the people seated around the large circular table. Three lit candles flickered on the table. Mme. Sphinx placed their gift on the ornate wall buffet and then introduced them to the other attendees. René observed each guest as she announced them. Two men and a young lady, the daughter of one of the men.

After directing René and Ambrose to sit in the empty chairs, Mme. Sphinx sat and addressed them all. "I will deal five cards. As I shuffle, think of a question that you want answered. Each card will have some meaning to everyone; one may be more significant than others. The ancient ones may choose to speak about them as well. I cannot promise what spirits will appear, if any." She reached for her well-worn deck placed next to the candles. Closing her eyes, she breathed deeply as she manipulated the cards.

How do I become famous? René wondered.

The fortune-teller stopped shuffling, opened her eyes and laid five cards face down on the table in front of her. She flipped the first one up. Pictured was a copper-colored mirror with a handle fashioned with the head of a woman. The artist had drawn her with cow ears. Madame Sphinx began to speak. "Hathor's Mirror. The Khaibit, the shadow of reflection, lives here. It's not an illusion but merely a different image of reality. This being dwells on the threshold of the spirit world, choosing the paths that one will take."

She turned over the next card. "The scarabs of green and black." Although the card reminded René of the dead beetle that he had tossed into the river, he appreciated the detailed drawing. Two stems, each end topped with a lotus blossom, encapsulated the two beetles; curving around they formed a lemniscate. "This card tells us that the living and dead coexist. They are together just on either side of the veil between life and death."

René thought of the ragpicker. *What did he say? Something about monkeys tearing the veil.*

The seer continued. "These scarabs represent us. Only the state of being changes. Material, light. Some-thing, no-thing, seen, unseen."

Moving to the next card, she revealed its image. A child sitting on top of a lotus flower in water holding a curved feather. A hieroglyph was depicted beneath the waves. "Heka, the Lord of Oracles," Mme. Sphinx began. "This card represents magic." Pointing to the waves, she said, "Heka is born from dreams and visions in the realm of the middle. The sea of consciousness. The feather he holds is the vehicle in the shadow world. Without feathers, there is no flight for the soul." Pointing next to the hieroglyph, her many metal bracelets clinking together, she explained, "This is the ancient Egyptian symbol for mouth or utterance. It is here that words of power emerge. Magic is born."

The seer turned over the fourth card. There was a jar with a monkey head for a lid. "The Jar of the Baboon." She glanced at the assembled group. "A canopic jar where the ancient Egyptians stored the dead's important organs. This one is where the lungs were kept. It is associated with Nephthys and the sense of hearing called Sedjem." Madame Sphinx focused again on everyone, ending with René. She held his gaze momentarily, then looked at the cards. "Perhaps, the ancestors are saying to watch what you say or to hear what others say to you. Magical words are being spoken."

She then turned over the last card. Two scrolls were depicted in an X, each tied with a turquoise ribbon. There was a lengthy pause before Mme. Sphinx said, "It seems as though I am channeling the energy of this card. It is blockage or indecision."

An enigmatic look came upon her face. "Let us join hands and close our eyes, and perhaps the spirits of old will tell us what they mean."

René held Ambrose's hand and gently clasped the young lady's gloved hand. The pretty girl smiled briefly at him and then closed her eyes. Hesitating, he looked at Mme. Sphinx. Meeting his gaze, she began to chant in an unintelligible language and then shut her eyes. A tremor of electricity seemed to flow through his hands and arms; René dismissed this sensation as his imagination. Just about to close his eyes, he saw the briefest shadow, like shimmering heat, move across the table. All the candle flames bent to the left as if they were responding to a passing current. Disbelieving the phenomenon, Rene blinked. *Is this really happening?*

Chapter 9:

MESSAGES

S uddenly, Mme. Sphinx straightened up and an intense
shudder convulsed her body. René's eyes widened when
she began to speak in a baritone voice:

> *"I am Heka, the Lord of the Oracles. You have come
> with a question to the One Who Answers. With the
> utterance of the Ur Hekau, magical words, the door
> bolts to the portal to the Shadow World will open to
> thee. Leap to enter the secret horizon which is neither
> here nor there, the Waters of Chaos. It is here that you
> will find what you seek."*

Mme. Sphinx stopped talking, slumped, and flattened
against her chair; René was reminded of a balloon when the air
was released. He felt the static electricity in the atmosphere, his
forearms were prickling with sensation. Before he could wonder
about what would happen next, she sat forward with a jolt and
opened her eyes wide, then turned and looked at all the séance
participants. Remarkably, they still had their eyes closed. Were
they hearing or feeling what he was? Again, her gaze ended on
him, yet she looked right through him.

She began to speak again but this time in an altogether different, higher tone.

"The flower of life is held within us, vessels of beauty and magic. Without us, there is nothing. We are that to which all is measured. We are here to carry you to your destination."

Again, the seer collapsed into her chair. René thought he felt a brief, light brush across his left cheek, like a feather duster touching his face. Mme. Sphinx's head lolled and her hands let go and fell noisily to her sides, rousing the others.

The young lady let go of René's hand and her father's. She clasped hers together at her breast. "What's wrong with her, Papa?"

The circle was broken, the magical moment gone.

"I don't know, ma chérie," her father answered.

Only the barest shift of the fortune-teller's veil with her breath assured them that she was alive. After a brief time, Ambrose gently grasped her shoulder and shook it. "Madame Sphinx, are you alright?"

His voice aroused the woman and she opened her kohl-lined eyes. Her head remained motionless as she blinked several times as if being woken from a dream. Finally, she righted her head, sat up and readjusted herself on her seat. "Forgive me, but I feel faint. I must ask you to leave. I promise I shall correspond with any additional messages from the spirits." Walking to the buffet, she picked up a bell and rang it. Her housemaid arrived and was instructed to assist with the guests' departure.

René noticed the daughter and father exchange a quizzical look. *Maybe they think she's strange, that her messages are gibberish.* They were, however, polite and did as they were asked. The seer briefly conversed privately with each visitor before bidding them adieu. René was the last to leave. Ambrose had stepped out into the hallway when Mme. Sphinx detained René with a hand on his arm. "Tonight, the spirits called me back to my homeland. I had a vision. The vulture goddess has spoken, Nephthys calls to thee. You will receive a letter from me in the mail, but I want you to have this." She placed the card of the two scarabs in his hand. "We will meet again."

HER LETTER ARRIVED TWO WEEKS later. René had just come down from his bedroom. "Who is this from?" Olympe asked. She handed René the envelope with no return address on it.

René saw the flourished script and knew it was from the seer. He placed the letter in the breast pocket of his frock coat. "A friend."

"What friend?"

Walking into the salon, René sat in one of the wingback chairs and picked up the newspaper. "You don't know them." He began reading.

Olympe persisted. "From school?"

"No. A mutual friend of Ambrose and mine."

Olympe sniffed in displeasure. "You have never introduced me to Ambrose, yet you boys go out with André all the time. Louis told me so."

Without looking at her, René said, "I promise to bring him by sometime." Hoping she'd get the message, he raised the newspaper to hide behind it.

She didn't. Olympe adjusted her lavender dress for comfort, then sat in the adjacent chair. "I don't think it is appropriate for you to be out at all hours of the night."

René gave up. He lowered the paper slightly and peered at her over the top of it. "Do you want me to become an artist, Mother? What do they say? The company you keep? If I want to succeed in art, then I must associate with artists." He stared at her for a moment and then slowly raised the paper again.

She sighed loudly. "I would much prefer that you *associate* with Louis or Louis Aine. Surely they have much better advice for a young man in *their* profession."

Looking around the newspaper, René gave her a look of disbelief mixed with displeasure. "Louis is married with children and Louis Aine is nearly fifty with bad knees. I highly doubt either of them can or wants to go dancing."

Olympe pursed her lips trying not to smile. "Do you think it is wise to be out drinking and dancing in *those* places, with *those* people?"

"Where else am I to dance?"

"Cousin Vuilleret has repeatedly invited us to his house for soirées. He tells me there are many young and beautiful debutantes that attend."

"I am eighteen! I don't want to court, I just want to dance!" René ducked back behind the newspaper, hoping once more that his mother would cease her nagging.

Olympe was silent for a few moments and then said softly, "You remind me of your father. So bullheaded."

Hearing the woeful tone in her voice made him put the paper down. "Désolé, Maman," René apologized before reaching over and gently squeezing her hand.

"I just worry about you. Being around women of ill-repute and crazy drunkards in dance halls. All the absinthe. You just don't know what could happen. After all, you and Grand-Père Antoine *are* the only family I have now."

Having heard this complaint too many times, René consulted his watch and stood up. "I must go. I need to stay late tonight; I am working on a project for school. Don't wait up for me." He bent down and gave Olympe a light kiss on both cheeks.

"Mon fils," she asked, "are you happy?"

"Oui, Maman. Je suis content."

When he got to the corner, René reached towards his coat pocket but saw the omnibus coming and decided to delay reading the letter. As he waited under the tree, he thought about his end-of-semester assignment. The students had to submit some illustrations for a project they would render the following spring. Ambrose had mentioned that he wanted to be hired by Louis and André, so René suggested that he make a traveling case for the assignment. Ambrose was delighted with the idea. Now René needed one for himself. He wanted to make a brooch, but he couldn't decide between a flower, an animal, a bird . . .

After boarding the crowded omnibus, René climbed the stairs to the top of it. He found a seat, took out the fortune-teller's letter and read its contents.

Dear Monsieur Lalique,

Thank you so much for the perfume bottle. I will cherish it always.

I want to explain what happened to me the night of the séance. During the time that my body was possessed of spirit, I was in another land, another time. The Shadow World. Egypt in the time of the Pharaohs. I was in a temple of glass. I saw two birds drawn on the wall. A voice said to me, "Tell him to be a Magician of Light."

When I came back into my body, I knew the message was for you. The hieroglyphs were pictures of small birds like swallows. Perhaps you will find the meaning in it.

After the séance, that night I had a dream that I was in front of an old table with a box and two scrolls tied together with a turquoise ribbon. I heard, "The Jackal surrounds her." Then the scrolls were gone. I knew that Anubis, the guide, had placed them on the scales in the Underworld. One for Nephthys and one for Hathor.

This dream referred to the oracle card drawn and its meaning of blockage. I don't know for certain its entire meaning. All I can say is that the shadow of Nephthys has been cast. Please take care. My heart tells me that we will meet again. Till then.

Yours faithfully,
Mme. Sphinx

René refolded the letter. Whatever he was expecting to hear from her, it was not this weird and vague nonsense. She had been so optimistic before. He recalled his question: how to become famous. The only answer he seemed to have gotten was magic. *How absurd was that? What did her vision mean? A magician of light? And her dream . . .*

He pictured her laying out the séance cards and thought of the one she had given him. The two scarabs, card of the living and the dead. He then remembered his previous dream of the two black books. Two scrolls, two books, two swallows. Were they related? And the bookstore card: *Hathor.* Now the fortune-teller was focused on the goddess with wings, Nephthys. René recalled the feeling, during the séance, of the sensation of feathers being drawn across his face and he shivered involuntarily.

Becoming conscious once again of the ambient city noise, clopping hooves of the plodding horse and scraping wheels of the omnibus, René placed the letter back in his pocket. As the omnibus crossed the intersection, the horse drawing their vehicle neighed loudly at another horse by the corner. Sudden movement and sound across the street drew René's eyes to the source. Disturbed by the whinny, a flock of birds had exploded from a nearby tree. The winged whirlwind circled above it before swooping away to another tree. A cloud of fluttering, they settled in the interior of its branches.

How strange, René thought. *Is this a sign?* Then inspiration hit him. He would make a brooch of two swallows for his project. As he began to envision it in his mind, he smiled to himself and quickly forgot about the foreboding letter.

Chapter 10:

BADGER

Lucinda was in the large sitting room with its view of the Western Desert. The house, sitting atop a small hill, faced the valley of tombs beyond. Unaccompanied except for Badger, who was sleeping on a cushion next to her chair, Lucinda had taken one of the pillows from the sofa and placed it on the floor for the dog. Her head buried in a book she had found on the bookshelves, suddenly Lucinda felt someone's gaze on her. She looked up and straight into Eza's eyes. They stared at each other momentarily before she smiled.

The manservant cleared his throat. "Would you like some tea, Miss Haliburton?"

Eza's looking at me again. I don't mind, though, as he is so polite, sweet, and rather good-looking with that mustache. "No, thank you. But please call me Lucinda. I think we have spent enough time together." Beckoning him over, she laid the book next to the summoning bell on the end table beside her. Badger awoke and sat up. His tail wagged at seeing his master. "I imagined that Egypt was going to be interesting, but it has turned out to be dreary, and hot. I never thought I would miss Foxhill Estate, but I do. Well, not all of it. Just my grandfather, the horses, and my kitty." She indicated that Eza should sit in the wicker chair opposite her, then looked down at Badger and patted him on the head. "If it wasn't for you, Badger, I would be terribly homesick by now." Badger gazed loyally at her and then turned his attention to the pillow. He pawed at it several times, then turned in circles until satisfied that he'd found the most suitable position. Plopping down, he laid his head on his front paws and closed his eyes again.

Lucinda glanced at Eza. His downcast face made her look away and pretend to take in the scenery of the picture window. "I mean, of course, I like being with you in the stable. Grooming Hana is fun; she's such a nice donkey. But I am not used to this heat." Returning her gaze to him she asked, "Does Professor Merimee ever give you a day off?"

Shifting in his seat, Eza faltered a little. "Didn't you like the pyramids, Miss . . . I mean, Lucinda?"

"Oh, the sightseeing was fine, but . . ." She leaned towards him and whispered, "I didn't like the company much. They ignore me when they are together. Especially her." Clasping her hands together, she placed them under her chin and tilted her head. "The *lady*-in-waiting." Lucinda batted her long eyelashes and giggled conspiratorially as she leaned back in her chair.

Eza grinned at Lucinda's mockery of her governess, Miss Meadows, but said nothing.

Lucinda grinned back. "You didn't answer my question."

"What?"

"Do you ever get a day off?"

"Well, um, not usually." Seeing the frown on her face, he added quickly, "but I could ask."

"It's just that, well, I mean, there is nothing to do around here. My uncle forbade me to go to the bazaar by myself, and she refuses to go." Leaning toward him again, Lucinda whispered, "Miss Meadows can't balance on a donkey without two Arabs on either side to hold her up." Sitting back in her chair, she scoffed at the shortcomings of her governess. "She told my uncle that she is afraid of heathens and camels." Rolling her eyes, Lucinda added, "The tombs are labeled too dangerous, but I think that is complete nonsense." Looking out the window again, she sighed deeply. "I don't just want to sit here all day by myself, or worse, with her as company. And my father, well . . . Staring at the dreadful portraits of my ancestors seems more worthwhile."

Eza nodded. "I understand. I get lonely too."

"Is your family around here?"

"My mother is nearby."

"What about your father?"

"He went back to his homeland. He was Professor Merimee's assistant but returned to France."

"Oh, I'm sorry, I didn't mean to . . ."

'No, don't worry about it. He's been gone a long time."

Wanting to change the subject, Lucinda asked, "How old are you?"

"Twenty."

"You look older. I mean . . ." She paused and touched her face above her upper lip. "With your mustache."

An awkward moment of silence passed. "How old are you?" he asked.

"Eighteen."

At that moment, Miss Meadows strode into the room. Eza jumped up and excused himself. "Just ring if you need my services."

The governess threw a hostile look at him before pointing to Badger and reprimanding Lucinda. "Why is that dirty *beast* laying on a good pillow? Remove him at once!" Lucinda ignored her. Picking up her book, she tried to read again.

From the doorway, Eza slapped his thigh and called, "Badger! C'mon boy!" until the dog ran after him and they both disappeared.

Miss Meadows picked up the pillow and placed it back on the couch. She then wandered around the room, pretended interest in the books, and stared out the window before finally leaving. *Thank goodness she's gone,* Lucinda thought. Now able to focus, she became absorbed in her book. By midmorning, she'd had enough. Picking up the bell, she rang for service.

Eza reappeared with Badger. "Yes?"

Lucinda smiled at him. "I think I would like that tea now."

"I shall have Mahmud bring it to you."

"Oh." She bit her lip. "I thought, well . . ."

Eza gently shook his head. "I need to bring food to Professor Merimee in the tomb. He won't stop digging until he is satisfied that there is nothing to be found."

Lucinda jumped up. "Could I go with you? Just give me a minute to change. I don't want to get this dress dirty." As she hurried past him without waiting for an answer, she added, "Besides, when working in the stables or climbing into holes, one should always wear boots." Badger followed her out the door.

"Come to the kitchen when you are ready," Eza called after her.

When Lucinda entered the kitchen, she was carrying Badger under her arm. "I am taking him with us. Miss Meadows doesn't like him." Unable to dissuade her from this idea, Eza fetched a rope for a leash and tied it to Badger's collar.

WHEN THEY ARRIVED AT THE DIG site, Gaston had already emerged from the tomb and climbed the ladder out of the shallow pit. "Eza! It's about time! We're famished."

"I'm sorry, Professor Merimee," Eza said as he untied the strap and took the food basket off Hana. He set the basket down. "Miss Haliburton wanted to come along and bring Badger."

Observing Gaston's knitted brow, Lucinda tried to mollify him. "Is this fine by you, Professor?"

Gaston's face softened and he nodded at his houseguest. "Yes, of course. Welcome to the tomb." He removed the cloth sack slung around his neck. "Your father is inside working with M. Grant's help. While we dine, you can visit them. Eza will take you in."

Eza had spread a blanket and was unloading the basket and setting out the meal and dinnerware. After the men began to eat, Eza and Lucinda climbed down the ladder into the pit. Eza set Badger down, and they picked up the lamps left at the tomb entrance before going in. Cooler and rockier than she expected, Lucinda was glad to have changed her attire as she picked her way carefully along the uneven, rough floor of the dim, narrow hallway with a low ceiling. She glanced at the barren, roughly hewn walls. *This is not a royal tomb.* Comparing them to the highly decorated temple walls she had seen, she thought, *I don't know what more treasure Professor Merimee believes he will find.*

The hallway began to dip slightly and, very shortly, they came upon an opening. Leading the way, Eza entered a doorway, maneuvering around the mirror that was placed there. Holding Badger's leash, Lucinda followed him and was amazed. Besides the light from the mirror, numerous candles illuminated the chamber. Colorful pictures and hieroglyphs filled the walls and ceiling. Her father was in a corner on his knees, busily tracing, with his back to her. He did not bother to look up when they entered.

Does he know we're here, Lucinda wondered, *or is he just ignoring us as usual?*

Mitch, however, who was standing and holding the tracing paper, certainly noticed their arrival. "Lucinda and Eza!" he greeted them. "And Badger, of course."

"What?" Alexander exclaimed when he heard the dog's name. He stopped what he was doing and turned around. "Why is that animal here?"

Lucinda responded meekly. "Miss Meadows doesn't like him."

"I don't care what that gold digger likes or doesn't! Get him out of here!" Alexander pointed to the doorway and then turned back around and started to work again. "In fact, all of you should leave. You're disturbing us."

Lucinda said nothing but sneered at his back.

Mitch caught her look. "I can show you the other chamber, Miss Haliburton." He looked down at her father. "Can you spare me for a few minutes?"

"Fine, I don't care," Alex grumbled under his breath. "This piece is done anyway." He stood up, took the paper from Mitch, and placed it on a pile before picking up another smaller piece of paper. "I can do it by myself."

"I'll be back," Mitch assured him, but Alex was already back at work. Mitch grinned at Lucinda and then tilted his head to one side as he shrugged resignedly. *He's so handsome and debonair,* she thought before giving him a bright smile.

Suddenly, Mitch's gaze became more intense and roamed over her before they locked eyes. In the moment before he looked away, she felt his desire. "Let me carry the lamp," he said. She handed it to him, and he started towards the doorway. "Come on, let's look at the other room."

Her heart fluttering, Lucinda hesitated briefly. She looked over at Eza. A scowl was on his face; he must have noticed the older man's look too. He met Lucinda's eyes before dropping his gaze to the ground. "If that is all, Miss," he said, "I should get back to Professor Merimee."

"Alright, I am going to stay here for a little while."

"Yes," Mitch said dismissively as he passed by, "we will return shortly to the house for lunch." He then disappeared into the hallway.

Without replying, Eza turned on his heel and walked out the other direction. Lucinda felt the color rise to her cheeks. *I've never had this much attention. But I like it.* Smiling inwardly, she and Badger trailed Mitch out of the chamber without another word to her father. Shortly, the hallway became noticeably darker and began to slope downward more dramatically.

"Careful, here, Miss," Mitch told her as he picked his way over a particularly rocky spot. Smiling, he held out his hand to her gloved one; her heart raced again at his touch. After she was on stable ground, he let go of her hand and she felt her fingers tingle.

At the end of the passage, she and Badger followed Mitch into the largest room. Flickering light from numerous oil lamps and candles lit the chamber. A glint from above made Lucinda look upward. Gleaming gold-leaf stars dotted the brilliant midnight blue ceiling. Lowering her eyes, she saw a wooden sarcophagus sitting in the middle of the room. Its lid was askew. The sight of it froze her. For the first time, she fully comprehended that she was indeed in someone's burial place. "Is that empty?" she asked Mitch.

"As Professor Merimee would say, 'Unfortunately, yes.'"

As they approached it, she thought, *A dead body used to be here.* Lucinda peeped inside and saw hundreds of eyes painted on the interior walls. A shiver ran through her. "Do we know whose tomb this was?"

"No, that's what we are trying to figure out," Mitch answered as he indicated the shadowy walls and then pointed to the back one.

Lucinda followed his finger and could see where Professor Merimee and his assistant had been digging. It was a raised area with steps at the back of the tomb. Murals covered the other walls completely, but the back wall had an addition: a large, narrow, rectangular stone panel. The pinkish stone was sitting atop the partially dug-out platform, and the center of the panel was recessed and framed by successive moldings that gave the illusion of depth.

"This is what they called a false door," Mitch explained. "The ancient Egyptians believed that a door like this one served as a passageway between the living and the dead." He pointed to the platform. "This offering table is where they would lay offerings of food and drink to the Ka of the deceased. The Ka could interact with the world through this door."

"The Ka?"

"Yes, what the Egyptians called the life force, a spirit double."

Lucinda's eyebrows raised. "A spirit double? You mean like a ghost?"

"Well, sort of, but not exactly." Mitch shrugged. "It's hard to explain."

Lucinda glanced around the dark and stuffy room and took a deep breath. Focusing on the false door, she asked, "Do you think the Ka is here? Still wandering around?"

Mitch laughed. "No, I don't believe that." He pointed to one of the painted hieroglyphs on the wall above the door. "See that picture of the woman with the headdress that looks like horns and a disc? That's Hathor. And the other woman with a bowl and a box on the top of her head, that's Nephthys. And that symbol is for the heart." Mitch moved closer to the door, then looked up and studied the hieroglyphs.

Badger was getting restless and tugging at his leash, so Lucinda dropped it. He ran over to the farthest corner of the back wall and started sniffing around the dark floor.

Lucinda listened carefully as Mitch raised his light and began to translate the paintings on the wall while pointing to the corresponding pictures. "These seven symbols are door bolts. The jackal-headed man is Anubis, the Guide to the Underworld. This is Nephthys again with her vulture wings." He indicated an oval below the goddess. Unlike the other symbols, this one was carved into the wall. "This is called a cartouche. It was used to surround the symbols of a name. See, this circle with a dot represents the sun. These three symbols represent the heart and windpipe meaning beauty or, as the ancient Egyptians would say, nefer, and that symbol, a seated woman, represents a queen." Mitch's voice dropped, and he seemed to be talking more to himself than to Lucinda. "The Beauty of Ra? A royal queen? Hmmm, this is interesting . . ." He stopped talking and continued to study the writing. Placing the lamp on the offering table, he dug into his pocket, brought out a scrap of paper and a pencil, and copied the images.

While Mitch was scribbling, Lucinda looked around the chamber. Badger was smelling the lower wall. Wondering why, she started moving toward the dog. As she walked by the wall, she peered at the pictures and tried to remember some of the hieroglyphs that she had studied in Professor Merimee's books on Egypt. There, near the edge of the wall above Badger, was a large vulture painted high above two symbols: an owl, representing the letter m, and a loaf of bread, the letter t. *Mt.* She recognized the word. *Death.*

Noticing Badger pawing at the wall, Lucinda crouched down. Scratching just below a five-pointed star in a circle carved into the wall, his nails were gouging out the soft stone. *What if he destroys the tomb? I don't want to get in trouble for bringing him.* She glanced at Mitch, but he was still copying the drawings. She scolded Badger quietly, but he was intent on what he was doing and did not stop. "Badger, no!" she said more forcefully and yanked on his leash, but he had already created a slight depression in the wall.

Mitch stopped drawing. "What's going on? What's Badger doing?"

Lucinda stood up and pulled Badger away from the wall. Blocking the damage, she shrugged her shoulders. "Just sniffing around. I think he needs to . . . you know . . ."

Mitch motioned for her to pick up the dog. "Well, let's get him out of here. Professor Merimee would have a fit if he found dog waste in here."

"Yes, of course. You should get back to my father anyway." When Lucinda bent down to retrieve Badger, she noticed something sticking out of the wall where he had made the dent.

Mitch had picked up the oil lamp and was heading towards the entrance. "Besides, lunch should be ready. Are you coming?"

"Yes." Lucinda and Badger followed Mitch back into the hallway. When he stopped at the doorway of the second room to rejoin Alex, she said, "I'm going to take Badger out now."

Mitch nodded. "We'll return to the house shortly."

Lucinda hastened towards the exit. She had to get rid of the dog and come back into the tomb before anyone else noticed Badger's discovery. When she emerged from the tomb, Gaston and his assistant were still eating. Eza was there too, gazing out over the desert landscape. Lucinda caught his eye and motioned for him to come over. She lifted the dog up. "Could you take Badger back to the house with you? I need to go back and help them." She motioned her head toward the tomb entrance.

Eza nodded his head apathetically and took Badger from her.

"Thanks," Lucinda said and headed into the tomb once more. Tiptoeing past the second room, she peeked in briefly, noting that the men had their backs to her. She darted by and returned to the burial chamber. Hurrying over to the wall where Badger had been clawing, she picked up a nearby candle and brought it close to the hollow made by the dog. Sure enough, there was an object there. Someone had placed it in the wall and covered it with soft mortar. Lucinda tried to scrape away the plaster with her fingernail, but it wasn't strong enough.

What could she use? She needed something sharp. Glancing around, she saw Gaston's turieh on the floor. Using the sharpened edge of the tool, she prodded and poked at the loose, sandy mix around the object. Finally, Lucinda extracted the object from the wall. As the treasure fell into her palm, she heard a whooshing sound, and a large shadow fell across the light.

Sucking in her breath, Lucinda jerked around, expecting to see someone, but the tomb was empty except for her. Holding her find to the light to examine it better, the ancient black artifact felt icy cold to her fingertips. Suddenly, a draft of stale, frigid air buffeted her face. Lucinda noticed the candle flame fluttering and trembling in an unseen air current. A terrifying thought occurred to her. Was the Ka of the dead owner here? She jumped up and ran from the chamber.

Chapter 11:

HATHOR'S MIRROR

B ack in her room at Professor Merimee's house, Lucinda smiled at her silly fear of an imaginary ghost. Sitting on her bed, she pulled the artifact out of her pocket to examine it better. Fitting nicely in her hand, the polished stone had been hewn into a little frog. The shiny black rock was filled with teeny, tiny specks of white that reminded her of the Egyptian night sky with its myriad stars. Turning the frog over, she noted tiny hieroglyphs carved on the bottom of it. She wondered who had stuck it into the wall. Why did they cover over it? Should she show it to anybody?

Lucinda laid down on the bed and rested the frog on her chest. *Maybe I'll show you to Eza.* Then she frowned. *What if he tells Professor Merimee about you?* She looked at the distinctive features of the frog's face. "I found you and so, rightfully, you are mine. Hmm, what shall I call you?" The first name that came to her mind was Mitch. Recalling his look of passion, she giggled nervously. Lucinda sat up and whispered to the frog, "Mitch, it is."

Noise from the hallway alerted her to someone's presence. Quickly hiding the frog under her pillow, Lucinda looked up to see Mitch standing in the doorway.

He smiled broadly at her. "Here you are. Lunch is ready." After escorting her to the dining room table, he pulled out her chair for her.

Miss Meadows finished pouring a cup of tea for everyone and then stared reproachfully at Lucinda. As Lucinda arranged herself in her chair, the governess complained to Uncle Roderick, who was sitting at the end of the table. "Mr. Haliburton, even though we are in a foreign and philistine land, don't you feel that English manners should be maintained and observed?" She glared at Lucinda again before turning her attention back to him. "Young ladies should dress appropriately for meals and not wear outfits suitable *only* for *dirty* stables."

Lucinda smirked inwardly. *If I had known you were going to carp about it, I would have changed my clothes. And if Mitch and Uncle Roderick weren't here, I'd put my feet, in my dirty boots, on the table just to spite you.*

Mitch interceded for her. "Well, Miss Meadows, it is a rather dirty business excavating treasures buried so far under the drifting sands." He then focused on Lucinda's uncle. "It's my fault, Roderick. I kept Miss Haliburton in the tomb far too long explaining the hieroglyphs to her."

Roderick narrowed his eyes at his niece briefly and then turned back to Mitch. "So, Lucinda was at the dig site?" Receiving a nod, he regarded Miss Meadows coolly. "I thought we agreed that visiting the tombs was unsafe."

The governess sniffed. "I was trying to keep her under control and away from the servants. Do you know that she spends all her time with that Arab boy and his dog in the stalls? Combing that donkey. In the dirt and muck with a cow and chickens."

"It's called grooming," Lucinda corrected, "and I'm not a child anymore. I'm bored. I wouldn't have to be in the muck and dirt if I had something to do. Other than looking at *drab* desert cliffs." She glared at Miss Meadows. "But I have no one to accompany me." Lucinda then turned to her uncle. "She won't walk anywhere, and she refuses to ride a donkey."

All eyes turned to Miss Meadows. "I . . . I don't like animals," she stammered and bit her lip.

Mitch intervened again. "Alex has enough tracings to begin making more permanent copies, and I need some time out of the dark. I would be willing to accompany Miss Haliburton to sightsee, to the bazaar or the ruins. We need more photos of the temples for the book."

"Without a chaperone?" Miss Meadows looked doubtful. She turned to Roderick. "Do you think that's wise?"

Roderick looked questioningly at Mitch.

Mitch smiled at him and then at her. "You are more than welcome to join us, Miss Meadows. I can arrange for three donkeys just as easily as two."

Caught in her own trap, the governess relented. "Since you are a family friend, I suppose it would be fine to visit the local town." She cast a disapproving eye at Lucinda. "But I must insist that she wear more fitting attire for a *lady* in the future."

Roderick chimed in this time. "Yes, I agree with Miss Meadows. From now on, Lucinda, no more riding habits. You are not eleven years old anymore. If you want my respect, then you must respect me and my wishes. You are not to be wandering around the dig site anymore. Or spending time with servants in the stables. If you want to be treated like a lady, then you must act like a lady. Not a tomboy."

Before Lucinda could respond, Eza entered with a tray of food and they all fell silent while he served them. Roderick took a sip of tea and replaced his cup in its saucer. "Eza, did the post come yet? I am expecting a letter from my father."

"No, milord. Mahmud should be returning with it soon."

"If a letter should arrive for me, have him bring it to me in the sitting room."

"Yes, milord. Will that be all?"

Roderick gave a silent nod and began to eat. Eza bowed slightly and retreated from the room without having once looked at Lucinda. Pursing her lips, she wondered, *Why is he ignoring me?* After lunch, she excused herself from the table and returned to her room. Changing back into her morning dress, she then proceeded to the kitchen. Eza and Mahmud were there, eating their lunch before cleaning up and preparing for the next meal. Badger sat nearby, hoping for a morsel of food to come his way. He wagged his tail when he saw Lucinda and then focused keenly on Eza.

Mahmud stood up and bowed silently to Lucinda, but Eza only nodded perfunctorily. "Please, Miss Haliburton, if you desire something, ring the bell and we will come."

He's mad at me, Lucinda thought as she felt her face flush. *I just wanted to be friends. Have someone to talk to. Couldn't he see that?* She shuffled her feet. "Of course. I'm sorry to have bothered you."

Feeling hot in the warm room, Lucinda needed fresh air. She left the kitchen in a hurry, going out the back door into the expansive, enclosed courtyard. Striding past the mudbrick stalls lined with straw for the animals, she ignored the cook, who was filling the domed oven with loaves of bread. Crossing over to the arched entrance, Lucinda opened the gate and kept walking. She finally halted after she had made her way partially up the dirt trail leading to the valley of tombs.

She looked longingly towards the hills that hid the dig site and recalled her time in the tomb with Mitch. *Did he discover a queen's name?* she wondered. She thought of the black frog, how she had removed the artifact from the wall and then felt the swirling, cold air that had given her goosebumps. *Nonsense. It was just my imagination. Still, what else could be hidden there? Is there more treasure? Did Professor Merimee really discover a royal tomb? Will Grandfather finally have the golden artifacts he wants?"* These questions surged through her mind until she saw Gaston and his assistant barreling down the beaten pathway towards her.

As they came closer, she could see they were happy and excited. Gaston ran up to her and stopped. He was breathing rapidly, with triumph painted on his face. "We have found another chamber! Where is your uncle?"

"In the house. Probably in the sitting room."

Gaston brushed past her with his assistant trailing behind him. Ali Suefi threw a suspicious glance at her as if he knew what she had discovered earlier. Lucinda followed them into the house.

Roderick was alone, smoking a Turkish cigarette and reading a letter, when the men burst into the sitting room. He looked up, knitting his brows at the disturbance. But his expression changed dramatically as Gaston spoke.

"Milord! We have discovered another chamber! It was quite by accident. I had lost my pick and began to look for it. When I found it, I came across a small depression with a tiny hole in the wall that I hadn't noticed before. There was a draft coming from it. The area appears to be an opening that was plastered over. I enlarged the hole enough to see in. There is a chamber behind the wall. You must come and see!"

Roderick stubbed out his cigarette and stood up quickly, the forgotten letter falling onto the chair seat. Ignoring Lucinda, the men rushed out of the room. Wanting to follow them but forbidden from returning to the tombs, she meandered over to the chair and looked down at the letter. Picking it up, she noticed that the letterhead consisted of the name "Dr. Charles Perkins" and a hospital address. Lucinda began to read.

Dear Mr. Haliburton,

I am writing on Lord Haliburton's behalf. He refused to communicate with you as he did not want you to cut short your travels. I don't want to alarm you, but your father has fallen ill, and I am afraid that the cause is your sister.

As you know, your sister has been in therapy with me and my father, Dr. Thomas Perkins, for some time. Sarah's mental health is deteriorating. She is steadily losing touch with reality and the knowledge of her own identity. She has been relaying hallucinations regarding her absent husband, which lead to episodes of anger culminating in violence. These events have become increasingly more common and serious. Recently, she flew into a hysterical rage and began to unmercifully beat one of her maids. A footman came to the rescue and attempted to restrain Sarah. They wrestled and, in the process, fell to the ground. Unfortunately, your sister hit her head and became unconscious.

The footman was alarmed and gathered her up. Under the orders of your father, the servant brought her to my office. Your sister had come around by that point but was still agitated. I gave her a mild sedative and she went home for bedrest. Sarah seemed to be recuperating well except for sporadic headaches until she had another incident. After starting a fire, she experienced an epileptic fit. She claims to have no memory of this event.

Sarah's unsound mind and vicious behavior was proving dangerous to herself and others. These circumstances led to a unilateral decision by me. Very concerned, I had no choice but to remove her from the house. In my estimation, it was far too risky to

*keep her at Foxhill Estate. She needs full-time care
and attendance. I am confident that you understand
my position. Your father, on the other hand, is not in
agreement. In this case, however, he cannot override
my medical authority.*

    *This situation has caused him undue distress. He is
very depressed with a lack of appetite, bedridden and
his cough is worsening. I am uneasy about his declining
health and feel it is necessary that a close family member
be in attendance.*

    *My recommendation is that you return from Egypt
as soon as possible.*

Sincerely, Dr. Charles Perkins

Replacing the letter where she found it, Lucinda wrung
her hands. *Oh no. I hope Grandfather is okay. I'm worried
about him.* Unsteady, she placed her hands on the chair back.
*Mother started a fire? Did Dr. Charles put her in a madhouse?
What will happen to her there? Living with crazy people. Will
she ever come out?*

    Her thoughts were interrupted by Mitch entering the room.

    "Where is everybody?" he asked.

    "Professor Merimee has discovered a hidden chamber in
the tomb. He took Uncle Roderick to explore it."

    "Really? Let's go."

    "But my uncle forbade me . . ."

    "Surely not with a momentous discovery such as this!"
Mitch grabbed her by the hand; giving in to his zeal, she let
herself be led. They quickly made their way to the tomb. Once
in the passageway, they heard loud banging, the noise getting louder as they approached the last room. When Lucinda
stepped into the stuffy, smelly chamber, she saw Ali Suefi, Professor Merimee, and Roderick swinging large mallets against

the wall where she had discovered the frog. There was already a significant hole in the weak plaster.

Overheated, Roderick stopped to mop his brow. He looked at Lucinda but said nothing.

Mitch asked, "Would you like me to take over?"

Roderick nodded and, before long, the hole had been enlarged enough for them to climb into the dark space beyond. They stopped hammering and put down their tools. Gaston picked up one of the oil lamps and leaned into the hole. He surveyed the area and then brought his head out.

"There is a clearing on the floor below. Just a small drop." He looked at Roderick. "Milord, would you like to go first?"

"After you. You discovered it; you should be the first one in."

Gaston smiled and handed the lamp to Ali Suefi. The foreman shined the light into the gaping hole, and Gaston lowered himself through it, dropping to the floor. He turned around to take the lamp. Ali Suefi motioned for Roderick to follow. After he entered, he was also given light and disappeared into the shadows. Mitch went next. He then faced Lucinda and motioned for her to come over. "But my dress . . ." Lucinda stammered.

"Come on. Your grandfather would have wanted it."

She relented. He helped her down and then asked Ali Suefi for two more lamps. Lucinda realized they were in a cramped vestibule. She and Mitch were alone; the other men had gone into another chamber. Lucinda could see the light from their lamps illuminating the outline of another doorway. Even standing next to Mitch, she shivered in the chilling blackness and musty atmosphere. After taking her oil lamp, she stayed close behind him as he led the way into the adjacent room.

When Lucinda entered, she saw that the undecorated chamber was crowded with stuff, including furniture, boxes, baskets and jars lined along the walls. Her uncle, Professor Merimee and Mitch were gathered around the most impressive item. Placed in the center of the room, the wooden statue, set on a stone base, faced the doorway. As Lucinda took a few steps toward it, Ali Suefi entered the chamber behind her. The professor called him over to look at the relic. The figure was a reclining dog painted black with gold accents and very large ears.

"It is the jackal-headed god, Anubis," Gaston breathed in wonderment.

"What detail," Mitch gushed. "The eyes are painted with gold-leaf."

Lucinda glanced at the shiny gold eyes then looked away. A creepy, claustrophobic feeling came over her; she momentarily felt the same icy sensation as before. While the men admired the statue, she turned her attention to the things situated against the wall. Noting several wooden chests of varying sizes as well as clay jars, she walked past chairs, stools, tools, and what appeared to be a bed frame with gilded, ornate carved legs.

This clutter doesn't seem like much, Lucinda thought, and then she saw it: A foot-high, black statue of a woman sitting on a throne; the figure had the head of a lioness. The statue was sitting next to a pile of things stowed inside the bed frame, so Lucinda brought her lamp nearer to inspect the items. One was a travertine jar with a carved head for a lid, a baboon glazed blue with black eyes. A sparkle of light caught Lucinda's eye. Curious, she knelt and saw a tarnished metal disc attached to a white handle. It sat atop a box covered in a knotted linen net.

Three millennia of dust covered all the objects, but Lucinda could see that part of the white handle was carved into a woman's face with cow ears. She reached over the bed frame and picked it up.

A hand gently grasped her shoulder. "What did you find?" asked Mitch.

"I'm not sure." Lucinda held up the item so that he could see it.

"You've found Hathor's mirror."

Chapter 12:

THE BLUE CURTAIN

René looked in the mirror as he tied his black tie and readjusted his suit coat. Then, brushing his naturally curly hair back and to the side, he flattened it with his hand into a suitable wave. He picked up his tortoiseshell mustache comb and used it to arrange the thick hair beneath his nose. Replacing the comb on the bathroom sink, he surveyed himself one last time. Satisfied with his appearance, he checked his pocket watch and realized it was time to go. He returned to his bedroom to fetch his hat on the desk by the bookshelf.

Long forgotten, the letter of Mme. Sphinx had been stashed away in a book there. Shortly after René received it, his grandfather Antoine had died and his mother had returned to wearing black. It seemed that she was just as distraught over her father's death as her husband's, and her sadness and worry permeated their home. Insistent on always knowing René's whereabouts, she was clingier than ever. René was spending more and more time at school and in the shop to avoid going home.

As René picked up the hat, he thought about the planned activities for the spring afternoon and evening. He, Ambrose and André were meeting at the railway station to go to Montmartre and their favorite open-air café, Moulin de la Galette. René smiled at the idea of the dancing hall next door and the comely seamstresses that were sure to be there. Donning his straw boater, he quickly left his bedroom. He was in the front hallway, hand on the doorknob, when Olympe called out to him.

"Where are you off to?" Before he could answer, she added despondently, "Am I to spend another Sunday evening alone?"

René turned around. "Maman, I have not been out for weeks. I have been working nonstop for school and the Aucocs. I need a break." Using her own tactic of guilt, he asked, "Don't you want me to be happy?"

She looked down at the floor. "Of course I do."

He walked over to her and lifted her chin. "You know I love you, Maman." He embraced her and then gave each of her cheeks a quick peck. "Don't wait up for me. I will be out late."

On the sidewalk outside the railway station, René and Ambrose waited for André, who had not yet arrived. Ambrose scanned the street. "André is always late. Do the Aucocs own a timepiece?" He shook his head. "Speaking of them, what did they say about my class project? Did André give it to them?"

"Yes," René replied. "Louis said it was certainly novel and he liked the different woods you chose."

"Hmmm. Well, what did the old man say about it?"

"What does it matter? Your traveling box demonstrated fine skill. You received a high grade for it."

"In other words, he hated it."

"Louis Aine doesn't like the new Egyptian style. He criticizes my pieces, too." René did not reveal that he had overheard the old man say that Ambrose's box was amateurish and mediocre. Nor did he add that they had praised his own project, a finely crafted silver and enamel brooch.

Ambrose snarled. "That old fool is boring and unimaginative. He wouldn't know style if it hit him in the face. The only reason Louis listens to his opinion is because he is his father."

"I agree. Your box is great." At Ambrose's tiny smile, René joked, "Especially the silver key I fabricated for its lock."

Ambrose laughed.

"Don't worry about that old sourpuss," René reassured him. "Hopefully, he'll retire soon. André likes your stuff. He has more pull with his brother than you think."

Ambrose's grin widened. "Do you think so? I really need this job. I'm broke and I don't want to fight anymore." He cupped his neck with one hand and then rolled his head around. "The last one was brutal."

René grimaced in sympathy and then consulted his pocket watch to avoid looking at his friend's bloodshot eyes. He didn't want to tell him that Louis Aine still held a large influence in production decisions. Snapping the metal cover shut, he glanced up and down the sidewalk. "Where is André?"

Ambrose reached into the breast pocket of his coat and pulled out a cut crystal flask mounted in sterling silver. A removable drinking cup was attached to the base. "It's brandy," he offered, but René shook his head.

"Well, I need one." Ambrose opened the flask and took a long swallow.

René noted the slight tremors in Ambrose's hands as he replaced the container in his pocket. *He's drinking too much these days.*

Just then, André arrived, carrying a picnic basket.

"Finally," Ambrose said. "The train will be here any minute. We should get out to the platform."

The train ride to Montmartre wasn't long and soon they were strolling up the street on their way to the top of the hill and Moulin de la Galette. They could hear the noisy revelers and the brass band before they could see them. When they arrived at the café, the proprietor recognized Ambrose and tipped his hat to him. "Monsieur De La Fontaine, it is good to see you on this delightful spring day." René took in the scene as the businessman took their money. The café was bustling with activity.

The working class of Paris was having a grand time; cheap wine, absinthe and the famous galettes filled the small wooden tables set under the canopy of trees. Twirling to a lively polka, couples crowded the dance area, filling the air with the sounds of their laughter and merriment. As the three friends settled into some empty chairs, the band started a new song. André quickly spotted a girl he knew and the two of them joined the dancers.

René scanned the crowd for an attractive dance partner. Not seeing any in the near vicinity, he looked over at Ambrose, who was taking a swig from his flask. "Shall we find some ladies to dance with?" Ambrose shrugged and took another swig. René knew he was in a gloomy mood because André had purposefully been evasive in talking about work on the train ride. Based on experience, René also knew that Ambrose had to be distracted or he would fall into a deeper melancholy and then become unnecessarily argumentative as his intoxication grew.

Determined to sober Ambrose up, René opened André's picnic basket and found a knife, sausage, cheese, bread, two bottles of wine, glasses and plates. "Are you hungry?"

Ambrose shook his head. "You know, I had a dream about Mme. Sphinx this morning. We were standing in the alcove of the bookstore. A wooden box was on the table. She told me, 'Don't be afraid to draw open the blue curtain.'" He took another sip of brandy. "Did I tell you that, before she left for Egypt last year, I met with her again? She gave me this card." He removed the tarot card from the side pocket of his coat and handed it to René. "I kept it in my bedside table."

René looked at the card; he remembered the picture of the copper mirror. Ambrose continued. "She told me to beware of the shadow being that lives in Hathor's mirror. Then she told me that she had a dream about us, you and me. Something about a box and two scrolls." He looked at René and smiled forlornly. "I never really placed any significance in it until you suggested making a traveling case for our class project. The Egyptian theme really hit home. It seemed too perfect. Unreal, in fact." Scanning the sea of dancers, Ambrose focused on André. "When I awoke today, I thought for sure that Louis would offer me an apprenticeship." He gulped more brandy. "I guess that's all it was, just a dream and nothing more."

"Cheer up, mon ami. Don't worry. I have every confidence that you will find suitable work. But for now, shall we focus on the ladies? Or will we let André have all the fun?" He grinned at Ambrose, who smirked in return. "Let's walk around."

Ambrose replaced his flask and they began to wander around the grounds. After numerous single women smiled at them as they sauntered past, Ambrose began to strut. René pointed out some of the prettier girls, and soon they had found suitable partners to lead to the dancing area.

The afternoon passed into evening; dancing, drinking, and laughter filled the time. The sunset was a brilliant orange and pink, the puffy clouds golden. When the light waned, the crowd thinned. The people remaining moved inside the dancing hall. Gaslight pendants hanging from the ceiling produced softened light, adding to the romantic atmosphere. The girl that Ambrose had been dancing with the most had left. René noticed that the flask was reappearing at regular intervals, so he searched the smoky room for another companion for him. Soon, he noticed a lovely girl in a dark dress and a red hat standing alone near a wall. René tilted his head in her direction and said to Ambrose, "You don't want her to be lonely, do you?" He prodded his tipsy friend with his elbow. "Go on, go talk to her."

Ambrose followed René's gaze reluctantly, but perked up when he took in the woman's exceptional beauty. "You are right, mon ami. Someone who looks like her should never be alone."

René watched Ambrose amble over, a little unsteady on his feet, to introduce himself. Feeling a tug on his sleeve, he turned to see the girl he had danced with several times. She nodded her head towards the dancers, and René obliged by linking his arm in hers and leading her to the dance floor. Soon, he became immersed in pleasure. After the second polka, they stopped to catch their breath. Leaning heavily on his arm, his partner gazed alluringly at him.

"Would you like some wine?" René asked.

She began to nod, then glanced over his shoulder. "Your friend is in trouble." René, hearing the commotion too, turned to look.

Ambrose was arguing with a surly man standing alongside the lady in the red hat. The thickset man wore a gentleman's clothing, but his perverse expression and rough, burly hands said otherwise. Speaking English, the man had a jarring voice. Ambrose held contempt for the English, especially the ill-bred ones, and his inebriation got the better of him. He insulted the Englishman, who responded with a violent shove.

For a moment, Ambrose seemed to come to his senses and backed off. But then he muttered something as he turned away, and the woman in the red hat grinned.

Seeing her expression, the man lunged after Ambrose and grabbed his shoulder. "Wha' you say?"

Ambrose spun around. "Get your hand off me!" The tension mounting, a crowd began to gather round to see what would happen. Ambrose took a couple of steps backwards, gave an arm signal and shouted at the man, "Va te faire foutre!"

René pushed his way through the throng to reach Ambrose but not soon enough. The Englishman lunged forward and threw a wild punch, which Ambrose ducked. This miss made the man angrier, so he continued to advance, swinging ferociously. Even inebriated, Ambrose danced and dodged the thug's fists. When the man lost his balance momentarily, Ambrose moved in and sucker punched him, the blow hitting the Englishman square in the face. He tumbled sideways and backward. As he fell, blood erupted from his nose. Dazed by the punch and hitting his head, the Englishman lay on the ground groaning with blood streaming out of one nostril. The girl in the red hat ran to his side. Using the man's pocket square, she dabbed at the blood dribbling onto his upper lip. Then she helped him sit up.

Teetering and breathing heavily, Ambrose looked down at his opponent. "Cochon Anglaise," he grunted, and spat on the ground in front of the man he had just called an English pig. Boorish laughter was heard and then the spectators began to disperse. The show was over.

René grabbed his wobbly companion by the arm. "It's time to go home," he said, and began to quickly lead him outside. *André can find his own way home. It will be expensive, but I must hail a cab.* Ambrose stumbling, they made it to the street. *Just down the hill to the boulevard.*

Suddenly, they were accosted from behind. Ambrose cried out and fell forward. René, unable to stop the momentum, fell with his friend. They tumbled onto the cobblestone and separated. René saw the Englishman dart away and vanish into a dark alley. As he got up painfully, he rubbed his stinging knee and elbow and looked over at Ambrose, who was still lying on the road.

René hurried to his side, knelt and turned his friend over. Ambrose's face was haggard and pale, his breathing forced. Gently pulling Ambrose's coat away, René felt a sticky substance coat his fingertips. He glanced at his hand and then at the red stain spreading over Ambrose's white shirt.

André had followed them. "René! What happened?!"

"He's been stabbed! Call the police!"

André hurried down to the main thoroughfare. "Help! Help!"

Ambrose's eyes flickered open. He gasped and tried to speak.

"Shh, don't talk."

"But I want to tell you something," he whispered.

René sat and cradled his friend's head in his lap. "Save your strength."

"I have to tell you about the rest of my dream." Ambrose's voice faltered but his face was determined. René leaned closer to hear what he was saying. "It was before I saw Mme. Sphinx. I was walking in the desert and came to a crossroads. A vulture was there. I knew the path that I would take. That the choice had been made long ago. But I hesitated . . . I was scared." He coughed and his body shuddered. A trickle of blood escaped his mouth. Searching René's eyes, he said, "I'm not afraid anymore."

"Stay with me, mon ami," René beseeched. "Help will be here soon."

Affection emanated from his friend's eyes. "Mon ami. Merci." Then Ambrose looked at the twinkling stars in the night sky. "The blue curtain . . ." His body went limp.

As René took in Ambrose's fixated gaze, memories of his father's untimely death sprang up unbidden and tears began to course down his cheeks. He turned away and focused on the fingernail moon. *Why has this happened again?*

Chapter 13:

FLYING INTO THE UNKNOWN

One early morning near the end of May, René was alone in the Rue de la Paix shop while the Aucoc family was still at Sunday service. He sat in front of the buffing machine polishing an enameled brooch, working the pedal with his foot and thinking about his mother. It was Mother's Day and he was going to give her the bad news tonight. Having applied to Sydenham College of Art in England, he would be leaving her and Paris to study draftsmanship. He had received his letter of acceptance but hadn't mustered the courage to announce his plans to anyone. Out of respect, he knew that he must tell his mother first. Admiring the silver brooch, he hoped this gift might soften the blow.

He stopped pumping the treadle lathe and examined the piece. The silver was developing a lustrous sheen. *Just a little more,* he thought as he applied a small amount of white rouge polishing compound on the fluffy felt buffing wheel. As he began to polish it again, he contemplated the intense labor of his school project. The many hours that he had spent sawing, carving, and filing the metal base and then preparing the enamel. First, grinding the glass to a fine powder with a mortar and pestle and then washing it again and again with water to remove the impurities. Afterwards, mixing the powder into the consistency of thick ink and applying it to the metal with his goose quill. At last, into the kiln to fire. Each successive thin layer of liquid glass fired and cooled before the next could be added. Layers upon layers of fired glass to fill the silver cells. All done with precision and concentration. Just like his myriad new illustrations. Anything to keep his mind off Ambrose and his untimely death.

Following his friend's funeral, René had thrown himself into improving and enlarging his art portfolio. Receiving his acceptance letter from the college had filled him with joy, but his enthusiasm had been short-lived as fear crept in. *Is this a mistake? Should I just stay here and work with Louis? Can I achieve everything I hope to do with La Maison Aucoc?* Answering his own question, he thought, *Not with Louis Aine around. The old man should have kept his mouth shut and let Louis hire Ambrose. Why did I send Ambrose over to that girl? No. It wasn't my fault. It was Louis Aine's. Ambrose might still be alive if Louis Aine had given him a chance. I hate him.*

René stopped polishing his piece and forced his thoughts away from his dead friend. He walked over to his workspace and placed the brooch on the desk. Then he sat down and pulled over his stack of sketches to look at them. *Will the old man ever allow me a chance to be original?* René shook his head. *Non.* He leafed mindlessly through his drawings until he came to a certain image, a tiara, which confirmed why he had come to the momentous decision to leave Paris for England and the art college.

Memories surfaced of when, not long after Ambrose's passing, he had overheard Louis and Louis Aine in the shop talking about him. After lunch, René had come in the back entrance unnoticed and then paused in the darkened stairwell when he heard Louis Aine mention his name.

"You give René too much freedom to do as he pleases," the old man said to his son.

René peeked into the room. Louis and Louis Aine were standing at his desk.

Louis shook his head. "The boy has talent and potential. We must nurture that creativity by allowing him some autonomy. You saw his brooch. You know it is of excellent quality. He is a hard worker."

"Yes, he is," Louis Aine conceded. "That is why you must channel his energies in the right direction."

Louis fanned out some of René's sketches. "Just look at these drawings, Père. Artistic originality. I've never seen anything like this."

Louis Aine snorted and pointed to one of René's renderings. "The tiara's crown is too large. Too bulky. Too complicated. Are those supposed to be curling vines or an overgrown hedge? Plus the spikes are ill-shaped." He picked up the paper and stared at it. "What are they? Dragonflies with the heads of women?" The old man rolled his eyes and put the picture down. "Too strange, too vulgar."

Then he glanced down at the next drawing and read René's notes about it in the margin of the page. "An enameled grasshopper brooch?" he asked incredulously. "What woman would wear that?" Louis Aine didn't wait for an answer. "It is absolutely hideous. And, not to state the obvious, too intricate and too detailed. Who has the expertise to make that? And what would be the cost? Do you suppose that Empress Eugenie would pin that to her breast?"

"You have to admit that his designs are certainly novel."

"Novelty will only go so far in our business. People want to wear what others wear. What royalty want to wear is expensive gems, jewels in beautiful settings. Not gruesome insects."

"I agree with you, Père," said Louis. "But look at this ring with scarabs." He picked up the drawing. "I love the center setting with the two beetles surrounded by an infinity symbol. Just look how he devised the shank of the ring to end in two lotuses on either shoulder." Louis nodded his head in appreciation. "It's brilliant work! Simple and elegant yet distinct. I'm going to fabricate it."

Louis Aine didn't even bother to glance at René's picture. He just shrugged. "If you want to waste your time, that's your business."

Louis studied the picture once more. "I could make the scarabs out of lapis, perhaps peridot . . . White enamel for the lotus heads? Add diamonds for sparkle? Hmm . . ." he mused, "maybe engrave the bottom of the infinity symbol with 'now and forever'?" Beaming, Louis folded René's design and placed it in his waistcoat pocket. "It will be stunning."

Sneering at them before he left, René slipped out the back door. He couldn't listen to any more of Louis Aine's disparaging remarks or watch his adoptive father pirate his creations. René had spent the rest of the afternoon sitting on a neighborhood park bench, watching the constant stream of Parisians pass by as maudlin thoughts of his tormented past ran through his mind: His father's death, his grandfather's death, his mother's mourning depression and his latest anguish, the death of his best friend.

Now, René picked up his tiara drawing and studied it. Louis Aine was right; he had drawn the crown too large. René tore the paper in half and then again. Crumpling the remnants, he threw them into the trash basket and then stood up. "I'll show them!" Before the Aucocs could return from the cathedral, René placed his mother's gift in his coat pocket and then spoke to his illustrations. "Louis will come to regret listening to his father's pedestrian notions. Someday, he is going to have to pay for you." He stashed his designs in the desk drawer and locked it. "Handsomely."

"RENÉ!" HIS MOTHER CALLED TO HIM from the bottom of the staircase. "Come down, the guests should be here soon!"

"Coming, Maman!" René was sitting on the edge of his bed, holding the seer's scarab card. Recollections of the séance filled his mind. The Sphinx had said that this card represented the coexistence of the living and the dead. *Why did the seer give it to me the night of the séance? Did she see the future, Ambrose's demise, but not tell us?* After the death of his friend, the card and its image had become an obsession. René studied it over and over. Inspired by the illustration, he had designed his scarab ring. The sketch had been his tribute to Ambrose, the process cathartic. Until Louis pilfered his design, reopening the wound just as it was beginning to heal.

Forlornly, René put the card in the drawer of his bedside table. *I won't let Louis steal my work again,* he vowed. *I won't let him take any more of my ideas.*

"René!" his mother called again.

He stood up. *I can't put this news off any longer. Better to tell her now as she will have to remain composed for her guests.* He put his mother's present in his dress coat pocket and headed downstairs.

He found her in the sitting room. "Maman, you look beautiful."

Smiling, Olympe stood up and twirled around gently so he could admire her dark bluish-grey silk reception gown. "You like my new dress, mon chér?"

René placed his hands on her shoulders and gave her two, quick busses on her cheeks. Mustering cheerfulness, he replied, "Wonderful," then stepped back and turned away. "Would you like something to drink?" he asked as he made his way to the rolling cart with its liquor.

"Non." She sounded suspicious.

René poured a moderate amount of cognac from the decanter into a glass and drank it in one gulp. Setting the glass back on the cart, he paused as the liquor burned down his throat.

"Is anything bothering you?" his mother asked.

He turned towards her. "Actually, I have some news."

Olympe looked at him warily. "What is it?"

"I'm leaving for England at the end of the summer."

"What?"

"I'm leaving for England at the end of the summer," he repeated.

"Is Louis taking you there?"

He shook his head. "Non."

Olympe's brow furrowed. "I don't understand, mon fils. Please tell me why."

"I applied to Sydenham College of Art outside of London. They have a good school for draughtsman. I want to improve my illustration techniques. I have received my letter of acceptance. For the fall semester."

Olympe was beginning to look more perturbed. "But what about your apprenticeship? What do the Aucocs think about this plan?"

"I haven't told them yet. I wanted to tell you first."

"Why England?"

"I told you. There is a very good school . . ."

Olympe interrupted him as she placed her hands on her hips. "Isn't your French education good enough?"

René tried to placate her. "My schooling has been excellent. I just think it is time for a change. I want more training in the industry and the techniques offered by modern engineering. And I would like to study under some different influences. I am fascinated by William Morris, Japonisme, the movement towards aesthetic values . . ."

"Stop!" Olympe threw her hands up. "I don't want to hear it." Obviously distressed, she turned away from him and began to pace. Her lower lip trembled. "I just can't believe that you want to leave me. First your father, now you?"

"That's not fair." René sighed deeply. His mother's flair for the dramatic equaled that of the Divine Sarah.

"What's not fair is that everybody leaves me. I am always left alone. Sad, bitter and alone." Olympe flopped down in one of the armchairs. "I am nothing to you."

René lost his temper momentarily. "You're wrong! Why do you always try to make me feel guilty?"

His mother looked up at him with melancholy eyes. He lowered his voice as he moved towards her. "Don't you see? There is nothing here but death and sadness. I cannot focus properly. I must get away. Don't you want me to be successful?"

"Of course, mon chér. But why do you have to go away?"

"I want to see the world. And I want to fill it with my art."

"You can fill France with your art."

"I'm sorry, but I have made up my mind." Sitting in the chair next to hers, he reached into his coat pocket and brought out the small box wrapped with silver paper and a golden ribbon. "Louis wanted to sell this, but I told him that I made it for you. For Mother's Day." He handed the present to her.

Olympe carefully unwrapped it. She lifted the brooch out of the box and held it in her fingers to look at it. Two champlevé silver swallows in flight, their interlaced wings comprising delicate feathers covered in brilliant blue enamel. The leading edges of the wings and the birds' heads were turquoise, their necks a bright white. For their eyes, René had used tiny, luminous seed pearls.

Olympe admired the beautiful pin and tears gathered at the corner of her eyes. "C'est très beau." She looked at him with loving adoration. "You're right. You must go and follow your dreams."

"This brooch is a reminder to you and a promise of faithfulness. Just as the swallows return every summer, I will return to you, Maman." He indicated her dress collar. "May I?"

As he pinned the jewel to her collar, they heard the sound of the front doorbell. The first dinner guests had arrived. While Mme. Staffe answered the door, René dabbed at his mother's cheeks with his handkerchief. "It will be fine, Maman, you'll see."

"Easy for you to say. You won't miss me like I will miss you."

"Oh, I doubt that very much." He offered her his arm and they went to greet their visitors.

Chapter 14:

OUT OF THE BOX

At the bidding of Professor Merimee, Ali Suefi and Eza had spent the moonless night in the pit outside the tomb to guard it. Early the next morning, items had begun to be removed to the compound. Lucinda had heard the professor and her uncle arguing about protocol, but finally Gaston relented. Now, he and Uncle Roderick were standing next to the dining table placed in the sitting room by the large window. From her chair positioned nearby, Lucinda studied the table laden with objects. The shrine of Anubis sat on the floor in a corner of the room near the entryway.

Gaston stopped Roderick from ripping the netting off the gilded wooden box. "Monsieur Haliburton, shouldn't we let M. Grant photograph everything intact? For documentation, for your father?"

Reluctantly, Roderick stepped back from the table and grumbled, "I suppose so."

Mitch and Eza walked into the room with camera equipment and photographic plates, Badger trotting behind his master's heels. When he saw the statue of the reclining black dog, he stopped and barked at it. When the wooden Anubis didn't move, the dog tentatively stalked it. He moved toward it warily, stopping before he got too close. Sticking his head out and wagging his nose, Badger sniffed the air for a prolonged period. Satisfied with his safeguarding, he trotted over to Lucinda. The dachshund got on his hind legs and pawed at her until Lucinda reached down and picked him up. Miss Meadows, sitting in a nearby chair, held her tongue but wrinkled her nose in disgust.

Mitch was setting up the camera and tripod when Gaston asked him, "Where's Alex?"

Mitch shrugged. "I don't know. Have you seen him, Eza?"

"No, sir," Eza replied. "Mahmud said that he left for town yesterday afternoon. Apparently, he did not sleep in his bed last night."

Roderick snorted in contempt. "Probably sleeping off a hangover in a brothel."

Miss Meadows cleared her throat. When Roderick looked over at her, she pursed her lips and indicated Lucinda with a tilt of her head. Rolling her eyes, Lucinda grinned when her uncle ignored her governess and turned his attention back to the table. "Well, shall we get on with it? I'm anxious to see what's inside these containers."

"Sure, let's go," said Mitch. "I'm ready. Tell me what you want, Doc."

As Gaston moved close to the table, Eza asked, "Will that be all, Professor?"

Gaston nodded. "Yes, thank you, Eza." The manservant turned to leave. "Don't you want to see what we have found?"

"Thank you, but I have other pressing duties, sir." Eza bowed and glanced briefly at Badger, who was already asleep on Lucinda's lap, before leaving the room.

Wistfully, Lucinda noted that Eza had avoided eye contact with her. But all was forgotten when she glanced at Mitch and he winked at her. She felt the color rise to her cheeks and had to cast her eyes downward. A tiny grin came upon her lips, but when she peeked at her father's friend, he had already returned his attention to his camera.

Lucinda shifted her focus to Gaston as he donned protective cloth gloves. Selecting the first item, a black statue, he described it to Miss Meadows, the designated recorder. "Number one, a statue of the goddess Sekhmet, polished black granite." As the governess wrote down the information, Gaston positioned the statue on one end of the table, isolating it for photographing. While Mitch took the picture, the professor began to arrange the other things in a specific order. He had placed Hathor's mirror next in the queue with the canopic jar after it. Roderick pointed to the netted box. "Then do that one." Gaston moved the box next to the jar.

"Okay, Doc, this one's done," Mitch said. He prepped his camera as Gaston shifted the statue back to the general pile.

The documentation protocol was repeated with Hathor's mirror. The professor then picked up the jar with the blue lid and moved it into place. "Egyptian alabaster canopic jar," he dictated to Miss Meadows, "with a faience head of Hapy, one of the Four Sons of Horus. Still sealed." Mitch took a photograph of it. Afterward, Gaston carefully tried to remove the lid from the jar. "These usually hold organs of the deceased," he explained as he attempted to turn it, but the lid was firmly cemented in place with a mud seal. "I need a knife to loosen the bond."

Roderick lost his patience. "Let's do that later." His eyes riveted on the gilded chest. "I want to know what's in there."

Gaston maintained his composure. "Certainly, Monsieur."

The canopic jar with the baboon head was returned to the pile. Gaston picked up the small chest and moved it forward. "Would you mind if we took a photo first?"

"Fine," Roderick relented.

While Mitch took the picture and Miss Meadows dutifully recorded Gaston's description, Roderick tapped his foot impatiently. Finally, Gaston unwrapped the box from its covering. As he folded the net and laid it to the side, everyone had a chance to study the artifact. A chest of ebony perched on stubby legs, with a curved hinged top covered in silver leaf. Every side was decorated with small inlaid tiles of blue faience.

Gaston lifted the lid open by using its ebony knob; everyone leaned forward in anticipation. As the professor reached into the container, he exhaled deeply and withdrew two ancient scrolls. The relics were rolled papyrus, both tied with a faded blue strip of deteriorated linen. Gaston reverently laid them on the table and began to pick gently at one of the knotted ribbons.

Roderick, however, was not impressed. "Is there anything else?"

Gaston sighed but held his tongue. Instead, he described the inside of the box to Miss Meadows. "There are numerous items wrapped in linen." He began to remove the other contents one at a time, using both hands to gingerly pick each item out, then depositing them in a row on the table. Then he checked the interior again. Feeling around, he pulled up a piece of linen and exhaled again. He reached in and brought out a dusty bronze sword. "An ancient khopesh." The curved blade was mottled and tarnished but still impressive.

Roderick was excited. "Finally, something worthwhile." Taking the sword from Gaston, he examined it before setting it down on the table. "Let's see what else is wrapped up."

Forgetting about proper procedure, Gaston picked up an item and carefully unwrapped it. "This one appears to be jewelry."

"How lovely," Miss Meadows chirped when she saw the golden tiara with precious stone inlays.

Just then, Alex burst into the room holding a piece of paper. Delirious, haggard, and disheveled, he careened about then stopped and, wild-eyed, looked at each of them before landing on Roderick. Shaking the paper at him, Alex hollered, "How long will you let your sister suffer?"

Sitting forward and gripping the arms of her chair, Lucinda stared at her father as his outburst continued. "I have not driven her crazy. You have. You and your father. Keeping her confined, locked away. Ashamed of her. Disgraced by her condition. And you are the two who made her sick!"

Roderick took a few steps toward Alex. "Stop this raving madness. How dare you berate me. Question my motives. Denounce me in public." He looked at the paper in Alex's hand. "The gall, the impudence, to read a private letter."

Lucinda recognized her uncle's letter. Twisting her lips, she thought, *What's going on here? Why is Father lying? Is he drunk?*

Alex resumed his tirade. "You finally have your wish. She's imprisoned in a madhouse. Where the life of her will be sucked out. Where her heart and soul will slowly wither and die like your mother's did. And your high-and-mighty father will die of remorse because of it. Then you will get what you always wanted. All the inheritance. Are you happy?"

His fists clenched, Roderick glowered at Alex but remained silent.

Mitch walked towards his friend and said in a soothing tone, "C'mon, pal, let's not argue. How about something to eat?"

Turning from Roderick to Mitch, Alex's voice was filled with regret and anguish. "I was her only hope of salvation, her true love." As Mitch continued walking toward him, Alex shook his fist at him. "Stay back, I'm warning you! I thought you were my friend. Now I see what you are doing. Taking their side. You're trying to kill her too."

Roderick scowled at Alex. "Whatever my sister saw in you, I will never fathom. Don't think I don't know why my father let you two marry. Your shameless behavior is despicable. Haunting opium dens, drunken debauchery. Good god, man, pull yourself together." He shook his head in disgust. "We have put up with your brazen nonsense more than anyone should bear. We are done here and have no need for further interaction with you. No reason at all. You have befouled our existence for long enough. Consider these words your notice of termination." Roderick turned to Gaston. "I demand that this *barbarian* be removed immediately from the household. Forcibly if necessary."

Alex took this opportunity to lunge at the unsuspecting Roderick. Lucinda's jaw dropped as she watched her father wrap his hands around her uncle's neck and begin to strangle him. Taken off-balance, Roderick stumbled backward as he tried to pry off Alex's hands. Mitch leapt forward, and the three men began to grapple. The brawl continued, the men locked together, bumping into furniture and knocking things over. Finally, after a lamp broke and Roderick's face had turned grayish, Mitch was able to dislodge Alex's hands. Holding onto his wrists, Mitch forced him away, but Alex wrenched out of Mitch's grip and, in the process, tripped over the shrine of Anubis before he rolled into the doorway. Gaston gasped and ran to the statue to examine it for any damage.

Quaking, Lucinda stood up, dislodging Badger from her lap. Lacy blackness invaded her vision.

Coughing and spluttering, Roderick tried to speak. "You crazy son of a . . ."

A voice shouted, "I command thee mortals to cease!" which caused Badger to begin barking.

Startled, everyone in the room turned towards the sounds. No one had noticed that Lucinda had moved behind the table. Entranced, she stood staring, wide-eyed and motionless. Badger glared at her, a low growl rumbling in his throat.

Her hands were on the statue of Sekhmet. Through Lucinda, the voice spoke again. "Only we can help her now." Then Lucinda's body went limp and she crumpled to the floor.

WHEN LUCINDA'S EYES FLICKERED open, Mitch's face swam into focus. He was sitting on the edge of her bed looking at her. He was also tenderly holding her hand.

"Hey, there," he said, "welcome back. How are you feeling?"

Lucinda smiled weakly. "A little dizzy. How did I get here? What happened?"

"You fainted. What do you remember?"

"The fight with Uncle Roderick."

"Anything else?"

"No."

Mitch let go of her hand and stood up. "Well, I have some things to do. You should get some rest. I'm going to go."

"No!" Lucinda sat up quickly. "I don't want to be alone." She gazed at him innocently. "Can I go with you?"

Mitch hesitated a moment, then gave in. "I suppose so. I was going to develop the pictures that I took."

Lucinda swung her legs over the side of the bed and stood up. "I can help you."

ON THE THIRD STRIKE, THE MATCH ignited. Mitch lit the candle and placed it behind the curtains of yellow and red material. The candle produced very low light, but Lucinda's sight gradually adjusted. They were in Mitch's cramped, makeshift darkroom. Trying to ignore the harsh smell of the chemicals in the close quarters, she savored the fragrance, notes of bergamot and cedarwood, that emanated from him. She noticed that he avoided her gaze and focused instead on the stack of light-tight plate holders on the table. Using gloves, he selected one and handed it to Lucinda after removing the light-sensitive, glass-plate negative inside. She set the empty box on the ground next to the table where he worked.

Mitch carefully laid the plate into the developer solution, explaining the process to her. "You only want to touch the very edges of the glass or otherwise you will rub off the emulsion of silver salts. The emulsion side goes face up." He put on the lid and agitated the tank. After waiting a bit, he removed the plate. They looked at the negative of Hathor's mirror.

"Amazing," Lucinda marveled. "Like magic."

Mitch smiled. "Are we not engaged in magic? By preserving their images, we preserve them. That's what the ancient Egyptians believed anyway. If they wanted to destroy their enemy, they destroyed their image or name. They would write the name of their oppressor on a jar and then break it." Focusing back on the photographic negative, Mitch pointed to a disk of black above the mirror. "That's weird. Must be a reflection." He placed the plate into the water stop bath and then into one of the fixer trays. After he developed and fixed the rest of the photos, he removed the fifth and last plate from the developer tank.

Goddess Sekhmet had materialized. Lucinda noticed the abnormality immediately. "Look, there's that halo again."

"Yes, I see it. How odd." Mitch gazed at the negative.

"It's their Ka."

Mitch was still focused on the picture. "Huh?"

"I lied earlier," Lucinda said. "About remembering. I do remember something else."

"What?" Mitch turned to her. In the faint light, her eyes were pools of black filled with innocent regret.

"I heard a voice."

"A voice?"

Hearing his concern, Lucinda backpedaled. "I mean, I *thought* I heard a voice. It must have been my imagination, Mr. Grant."

His reply was a throaty whisper, "My name is Mitch."

Lucinda tilted her head. "What?"

"Call me Mitch."

Looking deep into his eyes, she again felt his desire. She wanted him to touch her, taste her lips. Stepping closer, Lucinda raised onto her toes, kissed him quickly on the cheek, then backed away. Filled with passion, he moved to her, and they embraced. His mouth found hers, and they exchanged an ardent kiss.

Chapter 15:

THE JACKAL

Holding her diary, Lucinda stood under an acacia tree and looked through the archway into the walled courtyard. Only midmorning, the sun scorched the rust-colored sand, and a mild breeze created a hot, dusty atmosphere. She watched as Eza emerged from the makeshift shed that he and Ali Suefi had hastily constructed per her uncle's instructions. He closed the door and snapped the lock shut before leaning against the door and yawning. Everybody was tired except for her uncle. His energy was unflagging, exhibiting the most interest in the archaeologic endeavors since he and his party had arrived. Roderick and Dr. Merimee had argued again about the hasty transfer of the tomb's findings into the temporary structure without proper scientific procedure, but her uncle had had the final say. The secured shed now housed all the funerary items except those being photographed and catalogued daily.

As the manservant winced, put a hand to his head, and proceeded with drooping shoulders to enter the kitchen, Lucinda sat on the ground with her back to the tree. *Poor Eza. I suppose he's sick of all this arguing too. At least my belligerent father is out of the picture. I'm glad they forced him to go to town.*

Uncle Roderick accused him of such depravity. Frequenting opium dens and drunken debauchery? He must be wrong about that. I just don't know what to believe anymore.

Trying to get Alex out of her mind, Lucinda opened her diary and read some of her latest entries. All about Mitch and their time in the darkroom. She flushed. *He's the only reason I want to stay here.* Filled with desire, she longed to be with him all the time. *Am I falling in love with him? Does he feel the same way about me?* Twirling a long, curly lock of hair with her finger, Lucinda imagined herself, wearing a beautiful white dress adorned with pearls and lace, walking down a church aisle towards him. Then she thought of her grandfather and bit her lip. *What would he think? Would he condone my behavior? Certainly not. But still . . . Would he like Mitch? Probably not. He didn't like my father, so I doubt he would approve of his friend.* She then considered her black frog and its namesake. *Mitch. What is going to happen when I go back to London? Will he follow me home?*

Lucinda focused back on her diary and turned to earlier pages.

Eza is still avoiding me. I feel bad because I really like him. I wish that we could be friends. He is charming and handsome. Those eyes, that mustache. I know he will find someone who loves him.

More blackouts. I don't think anyone has noticed. At least, no one has said anything to me.

Two dream snippets last night. In the first, I saw a large frog. He was sitting on the edge of a copper water basin. I was afraid of him. Then something about blue swallows and their song.

Another confusing dream. I was hunting for lace netting (like the doilies that Grandmother Annabel used to make) buried in holes. Then I saw these symbols.

She studied the three flags and the other characters of twisted flax, upstretched arms, a scroll and three dots. Wondering what they meant, Lucinda had drawn these crude hieroglyphs for Professor Merimee. He knew the symbols. Two words, he said, and then explained the flag meant Neter, or force. Three flags together meant Neteru. The gods of ancient Egypt. The other word she had written was Heka: magic.

She flipped the page. More words with another hieroglyph, a seated man with a jackal head:

On your journey
The watcher is the watched
The Jackal sees and knows
Follow Anubis to the Land of Red
Hall of Judgment
To the Scales to be weighed
Forty-two flags
Flutter and decide
The fate of the dead.

She had asked Dr. Merimee about this poem, too. He thought it referred to the Egyptian Book of the Dead and a certain spell. In the spell, the jackal god Anubis weighed the heart of the newly deceased against the feather of truth. One's fate was determined by the scales while the other forty-two ancient gods and goddesses presided.

Did I really write that? And how? Lucinda didn't remember doing it. *What's happening to me?*

Her next entry was the one that worried her the most.

The statue of Anubis has infected my mind. It is always whispering to me. Nobody else seems to hear it. It must be my imagination.

Grimacing, Lucinda shut her journal and put it in her pocket. *Am I going insane? Or have I let something out of the tomb? Ancient gods? Egyptian magic? A Ka to haunt me the rest of my life?*

Refusing to dwell on this possibility, she got up and entered the courtyard. Looking at the quiet house, she wondered if Professor Merimee was feeling better. Mahmud had informed the guests earlier that the doctor was unwell with a stomachache and would not be joining them for breakfast. Not wanting to go back inside, Lucinda went to the stable. Greeting all the animals, she paid particular attention to the donkey. As she stroked Hana's muzzle and talked to her, Lucinda was interrupted by a familiar voice.

"There you are. I've been looking for you." Mitch signaled her over. "We're going to Luxor. Do you want to come?"

THE BAZAAR WAS TEEMING WITH people, natives and tourists. Regrettably, her uncle and governess had accompanied them to the ancient temples and then the city, but, fortunately, they had just parted ways. Uncle Roderick would tend to some business matters with Miss Meadows along, while Mitch and Lucinda continued to follow the dragoman. As the servant purchased food and supplies, Mitch scouted for photo opportunities for his book and Lucinda meandered through the crowd, stopping by the various tables of the street vendors to look at trinkets, curios, and other souvenirs for sale.

Besides the knickknack vendors, there were other sellers stationed along the dirt road. Ones with their wooden, wheeled carts laden with vegetables and fruits, others dispensing water from their goatskin bags for a fee. On the street were men with jars strapped to their backs and veiled women carrying baskets on their heads. All walked beside loaded wagons and pack donkeys that were driven along the noisy thoroughfare.

Old men with white beards and leathery skin, seated on chairs woven from date fronds, smoked their pipes and watched the masses stream by.

Lucinda scanned the throng for Mitch, spotting him at an intersection. He was giving money to a man balancing a platter of flat bread loaves on his head. She made her way over to him.

As Mitch readjusted his satchel of plates, camera and tripod slung over his shoulder, he told her, "This man said I might find some interesting subjects to photograph off the main street. I'm going to take his picture and then tell the dragoman to meet us at this corner in an hour."

Lucinda looked over at a shop off the main avenue, attracted to the colorful display of Egyptian glass and pottery. "Sure, I'll wait for you over there." Not daring to touch Mitch in public, she gave him a longing look that raised his eyebrows before she crossed the street.

Entering the pottery shop, she saw small, colorful glass bottles on a counter and walked over to it. Soon, the shopkeeper joined her. Dressed in a mushroom-colored galabia robe and a compact white turban, he ambled behind the wooden partition. He was a short man with bushy eyebrows and neatly trimmed facial hair.

"Hello. May I help you with anything?" As Lucinda didn't answer right away, he began to pitch his wares. "This one is beautiful," he said, picking up a clear glass bottle painted with gilt in a distinctly Arabic design. "Look at this jewel." He pointed to the faceted red glass finial set in the metal cap. Unscrewing the cap, he motioned with the bottle. "See how easy it is to pour your fragrance into your handkerchief? Yes?" Lucinda nodded, so he turned towards the assortment of larger colored bottles behind him on the shelves. "We have many delicate scents to choose from: attar of rose, jasmine, lavender." Looking back at her, he added, "For your husband, we have sandalwood, cedarwood, musk."

Lucinda turned around to see Mitch standing behind her. Mitch shook his head. "Just a friend of this young lady."

The shopkeeper glanced back and forth between Mitch and Lucinda and smiled. "Of course." As Lucinda's gaze drifted back to the glass bottles on the counter, he asked, "Which one do you like best?"

"They're all lovely." She fingered a couple, but her touch remained longest on the most unique one. Twisted like a corkscrew, it was violet blue with dots of white enamel and gold-leaf paint.

"Ah, yes, I see. You like blue." He gave Mitch a knowing look. "Friends like gifts too." He turned around again and picked up a blue flask from the shelves. Setting it on the counter, he removed the glass stopper and then reached under the counter to retrieve a small square of cotton trimmed with a delicate lace edge. After pouring some drops of oil from the flask onto the material, he handed it to Lucinda. "This fragrance is from the famous Khan el Khalili Bazaar in Cairo. They specialize in perfume there. It is called Lotus in the Nile."

Lucinda held the handkerchief to her nose and inhaled the heady fragrance. Closing her eyes, she savored the spicy floral bouquet. "It's heavenly."

Mitch smiled. "Would you like me to buy you some?"

Her face flushed red. "I didn't mean that."

"I know. I just thought you might like a souvenir. You know, a reminder of your time in Egypt."

"Well . . ."

Mitch pointed to the corkscrew container. "We'll take this one filled with that perfume."

Lucinda attempted to return the lacy handkerchief, but the shopkeeper declined. "No. My wife makes them. It is our gift to you, beautiful lady."

"Thank you." Lucinda watched as he carefully dispensed the oil and screwed the cap on tight, then wrapped her gift in layers of linen and tied the package with a piece of flax cord. Handing it to her, he smiled. She placed it, along with the handkerchief, in the pocket of her skirt. Then she wandered around the store looking at the other merchandise while Mitch paid for the perfume.

"Thank you so much," she said when Mitch drew near. As no one was around, and the shopkeeper was distracted by another customer, she grasped his hand and gave him a quick kiss on the cheek.

"I need to take some more photos. Would you like to accompany me?"

"Only if I can help you develop them."

Mitch gave her a forced smile. "About that . . ."

She pressed against him. "I won't take no for an answer." She led him to the doorway. "Let's go take your pictures."

As they walked down the crowded street together, Mitch scanned for scenes or potential portraits. Lucinda, walking alongside, waited patiently as he captured these images and agreed to pose for him in front of a filigreed gate. Gradually, they moved farther from the main street and, eventually, turned into a narrow alley. There they found a peasant sitting against the wall outside a dingy tavern. The sound of muted drunks and clinking glass, as well as noxious odors, drifted through the tavern's open arched threshold. The smells created a toxic mix with the sour stink of urine coating the warm walls.

As the peasant's head was resting in his hand and his eyes were closed, Lucinda was unsure if the man had partaken of the tavern delights or was just napping. Next to him were two mummies. One was standing and draped in a shroud. Propped against the wall, its sheet of death fluttered in the breeze. The other mummy was stretched out on the ground, smaller, a child. Lucinda gasped and drew back. She quickly pulled the scented handkerchief from her pocket and covered her mouth and nose.

As hideous as the mummies were, Lucinda was riveted to the decayed spectacle in front of her. The small mummy was covered in dirty bandages, partially torn, and yellowed with age. The frayed strips of linen revealed a skeleton with a petrified ribcage and blackened head. Tangled bits of knotted hair framed the face; the eye sockets were empty and the mouth open with teeth bared. Skinny upper arms crossed over the mummy's chest, but they did not cover the hole where precious heart amulets had been stolen. Because they would fetch a good price on the black market, these protective, funerary items were long gone.

Moving closer to Mitch, Lucinda grasped his arm. "It's horrid."

He patted her hand to reassure her. "I agree."

In an instant, the peasant awoke, sat forward, and flashed a mostly toothless grin at them. Anticipating a transaction, he spoke to Mitch in choppy English. "You like? You buy real mummy. From tomb."

Repulsed, Lucinda slid closer and slightly behind Mitch as he shook his head. "No."

His hopes for a sale dashed, the man saw Mitch's camera and made another offer. "Picture? You take picture for baksheesh." He stood up and waved over the corpses. "Me and my mummies."

"Can we leave?" Lucinda whispered through her handkerchief into Mitch's ear.

Mitch put his arm around her waist. "Of course, darling."

"Darling? You bastard!" Mitch was violently shoved forward, causing him and Lucinda to separate. They turned to see Alex, reeking of alcohol and stale smoke, glowering at them with red-rimmed eyes. Looking worse than ever, he tottered before them, sullen, dirty, and unkempt.

Mitch spoke quietly to his friend. "Alex, pal . . ."

"I'm not your pal."

Lucinda could now tell that her father was more than drunk. *Was my uncle right? Is he on opium?*

Alex glared at Mitch. "First my wife, now my daughter?" Swaying, he looked at Lucinda. "Don't you see? He'll corrupt you, too."

Lucinda took a step backwards. "What?" She looked at Mitch. "What's he talking about?"

Alex moved toward her. "Listen to me. He's just using you. He's a liar."

"You're wrong." She continued to back away. "Mitch . . ."

Alex moved closer. "I'm just trying to protect you. Get you to see the truth."

Mitch stepped between them. "She doesn't want your truth."

Alex shot Mitch a hateful look but stopped moving. He reached into his coat pocket and then dangled something at Lucinda. The Eye of Ra, the malachite pendant that her mother had given her. "Your mother knows the truth."

At first, Lucinda was confused. "But how . . ." Then, seeing Alex's smug look, she snapped, "How dare you go through my things! Give it back."

"It's mine now." Her father fumbled as he put it back in his pocket. Then, like a dog with fleas, he scratched mindlessly at his stubbled face and then his red, raked arms before sneering at Mitch with droopy eyes. "You think you have me fooled, but you're wrong. I know about the treachery."

"C'mon, Lucinda, let's go." Mitch started to steer her toward the street.

"But my necklace . . ."

"I'll get you another."

Alex stumbled after them. "You won't get away with it!"

Mitch spun around. "For once in your life, do yourself some good, Alex. Learn to keep your mouth shut."

Alex shook his fist at him awkwardly. "For once in your life, be honest. I'll tell her the truth about her family. About you. Your lies and deception about everything. Your betrayal. Everyone who trusts you. Tell her about . . ."

Before Alex could say anything more, Mitch punched him in the stomach. Alex groaned and clutched his gut as he staggered backward. Losing his balance, Alex tumbled over and fell face first next to the mummy child. As he raised himself onto his elbows, coming face to face with its grisly head and gaping maw, Alex began to retch. Screeching in Arabic, the peasant scrambled to keep his mummies free from vomit.

Guiding her firmly, Mitch swiftly escorted Lucinda away from the mayhem.

Chapter 16:

WARNING SIGNS

His stomach was on fire. So thirsty, but the thought of drinking made him nauseous. Memories of the last few weeks ran through Gaston's mind. Finally, having found the ancient treasure he was looking for, he should've been overjoyed, but his houseguests had made him sick. *Thank God I saved the tomb drawings from that maniac.* Gaston shuddered as he recalled Alex's threat of setting them aflame. *I should have known that he couldn't handle seeing his odd relatives again. Good thing his crazy wife stayed at home.* The only action Roderick had taken that Gaston approved of was getting rid of Alex. *His friend Mitch is so different, so calm and helpful. Cataloging, taking pictures . . . And Lucinda. She's a bit strange but friendly and interested in the artifacts. Asking about the hieroglyphs. Why does her father treat her so poorly? No wonder the baron sent him away.*

Thinking of his benefactor, Gaston sat up and leaned against the pillows in his bed. *Surely, Lord Haliburton will continue to fund me.* Unless, of course, Roderick had his way. The only thing he was interested in was gold, jewels, and weapons. Each box that was opened, its contents examined, seemed to cause greater disappointment; Roderick didn't give a fig about any of the items.

Gaston recalled Mitch's assertion at dinner the previous night that they may have discovered the tomb of a royal queen.

"I saw her name in a cartouche. Neferure, the Beauty of Ra," Mitch told them.

"Not likely," Roderick argued. "Royalty would have more treasure than a statue and a gold crown."

"Yes," Gaston agreed, "but certainly she is a noblewoman."

Mitch shook his head. "But I saw the royal cartouche in two places on the wall in the burial chamber. Her name was above and hidden behind the false door." He looked at Gaston. "I have yet to translate all the writing on that wall, but I think it might be a spell, a warning perhaps, from the Book of the Dead."

"But what about the scenes in the smaller chamber?" Gaston pointed out. "They seem to be about a temple priest."

"Certainly . . ."

Roderick interrupted them. "There's little value in a bunch of scribbles on the wall. Besides, we have enough tracings to fill a book." Disdain filled his voice. Mitch frowned but kept silent. "Fortunately, the Anubis statue and Senet gameboard will hold some fascination for my father. And the sword is admirable. Better when it's restored."

Gaston tried to persuade Roderick. "We should cut the mud seal and open the canopic jar tomorrow morning. Maybe that will give us more clues as to the owner."

"I'm not interested in seeing ancient body parts or more bones. But if you find something valuable, then come and get me."

These memories of Roderick's distaste for the relics caused a sharp pang in Gaston's belly. Sitting forward, he burped up acid. *It's all about the bottom line with him. He wasn't even fascinated with the mysterious card with the Eye of Ra symbol. Was it an ancient oracle card?* Gaston recalled when he and Ali Suefi had found the torn card. *In a rib cage.* Another pang under his ribs caused him to groan and place a hand over the spot. He frowned. *Roderick doesn't comprehend their value. He sees them as ordinary, everyday things.* He doesn't realize the profound insight into Egyptian culture by learning their beliefs about the afterlife. Gaston shook his head sadly before pulling his bedcovers back.

Why do I have to deal with this philistine? I wish Lord Haliburton had come instead. He would have understood the magnitude of the find. Gaston swung his legs out of bed as he wondered about his benefactor's health. *Is something wrong with the baron? Is this the reason for all of Roderick's haste?*

Weak and dehydrated, Gaston got up slowly. He decided he would open the canopic jar tomorrow when he felt better. *I cannot let Roderick rush me through the process.* How many times had they had argued about the detailed and thorough documentation of the items? How many times had he stressed to Roderick the importance of cooperating with Mariette and the Museum of Egyptian Antiquities at Bulaq? Gaston's archaeologic permits would be withdrawn if he did not do as he was told by the Pasha and the Department of Antiquities. *I must alert Mariette about the tomb before he finds out on his own.* Gaston shuffled over to his desk, which had been moved temporarily to his bedroom. He knew what he must do. Write a letter in secret and have Eza deliver it.

MITCH HAD REFUSED TO TALK TO her about anything that had happened. Kneeling in front of her trunk, Lucinda stared at her rumpled belongings and thought about her father. How dare he go through her stuff and take things. She wondered if Alex had also read her diary. Picking it up, she went to the desk and recorded everything from that morning, including their encounter with him. Emotions flowed from her pen onto the page. When she had finished, Lucinda returned the diary to the trunk. She stashed all her precious items in the concealed compartment under one of the drawers, straightened the clothes on top, and closed the lid. Then she collapsed on her bed. The heat and the drama of the marketplace had been too much. She closed her eyes and swiftly fell asleep.

She is walking through the hallway of Foxhill Estate. At the end of it is Sekhmet with a dead bird in his mouth. A blue swallow. Then she is in front of the pink granite false door. Her trunk is there. She looks inside. There is the frightening mummy child with its empty eye sockets, gaping mouth and dark pit in its ribcage. Looking into the chest hole, she sees movement. Shadows, something. Alive.

Lucinda awoke with a gasp, her chest heaving with fear. She lay motionless for a few moments, assuring herself that nothing was there. She was alone; her room was dark, still, and quiet. Sitting up on the edge of the bed, she rubbed her eyes. How long had she been asleep? As her eyes adjusted to the dimness, she noticed an absence. Her trunk was gone. Lucinda ran out of her room, down the hall and into the kitchen to look for Eza. Finding it empty, she hurried on. Mitch and Miss Meadows were talking in the dining room, glasses of sherry in their hands. She burst through the doorway and confronted them. "My trunk is gone! Who took it?"

Miss Meadows put her glass down. "Eza put it with our luggage. Clean traveling clothes and a nightgown are on your bedroom bureau. We are returning to England. We leave tomorrow morning. Early."

Her eyes wide, Lucinda barked at her governess. "What? Who do you think you are? Taking such liberties?"

Miss Meadows snapped back. "How dare you take that tone with me!"

Lucinda stared at Mitch. "Did you know about this? Did you know we were leaving?" His expression betrayed him. "I, I don't understand . . ."

"I was going to tell you, but I never got a chance . . ."

"That's why you . . . Why my father said . . ." Lucinda's lower lip quivered as she glared at her governess. "So that's where you and my uncle went to take care of business. You were booking our passage home."

Miss Meadows crossed her arms over her chest. "That's right. We're leaving this land of savages before you become one of them."

Lucinda was furious. "Stop putting on airs. Nobody is buying your phony sanctimony. I hate you."

Roderick came into the room behind her. "What's going on here?"

Lucinda turned to her uncle. "This shrew"—she pointed to Miss Meadows—"was just telling me of *our* plans."

"Are you going to let this brat talk to me like that?"

"A brat? A brat?!"

"Quiet! Both of you!" Roderick boomed. He looked at Lucinda. "Go to your room. I'll have Eza bring you dinner. You can eat in there and calm down."

Lucinda glared at Miss Meadows and then at him. "I'm not hungry." She glanced dismally at Mitch before leaving the room.

THE SOUND OF BADGER BARKING woke Lucinda. The dog was jumping at her bed, but it was the caustic smell of fire that roused her from her deep sleep. Opening her eyes, she sat up. Thick, stinging fumes threatened to smother her. Coughing and disoriented at first, she finally realized that the house was ablaze. She could just make out Badger in the hazy, orange gloom. He scratched her legs as he pawed at her until she stood up and then he ran out the door. Weak, wobbly, and sluggish, she held her breath as she followed Badger into the darkened hallway.

Dense, black smoke obscured her vision as she groped her way along. Tears rolled down her cheeks, squeezed from her squinting, smarting eyes. Virtually blinded, she felt the oppressive heat and heard the cracking timbers. Unable to hold her breath any longer, she dropped to the floor and sucked in the corrupted air. Choking, she crawled along the floor, her nightgown tangling her legs and impeding her progress.

Where is everybody? Where's Badger? The fire behind her was growing, the flames hotter and higher with each passing second. Sounds of the collapsing building reached her ears. It seemed like an eternity as she crept along, the sooty smoke coursing into her lungs with each short gasp. She was running out of air. "Help," she wheezed.

Where is the door? Will I make it? Her heart pounding, Lucinda continued to blindly claw her way forward. Eventually, she had no more breath, her muddled mind unable to think. Her coordination gone, she collapsed into a heap. Faintly, she heard whining and then a tugging. Raising her leaden head, she squinted to see a blurry Badger pulling insistently at her sleeve. By sheer will, she began to drag her body along. Badger remained just ahead of her, continuing to look back to make sure she was following. Finally, they made it to the door, which was open just a crack. Badger nudged it wider and wriggled through the gap. Mustering her remaining strength, Lucinda pushed the door open and crawled outside. Unable to go farther she lay there, gulping the fresh air, clearing her lungs. Foggy, disconnected, vague voices, loud cracking, fiery chunks falling, landing around her. *Must move.* Then searing pain. Blackness.

II

CROSSING

Chapter 17:

MONSIEUR STODDARD

The pungent smell of sulfur hit René's nostrils. He lit the three candlewicks with the burning match before shaking out the flame and throwing the stick in the trash bin. Placing the cast-iron candelabra next to his box of art supplies on the table, he went over to the small window. It was Sunday morning and another grey day. As he looked out over the green English countryside drizzled by rain, René thought of its residents. They could be as cold and dreary as their weather. René would never understand them, nor they him. Not that his English hadn't improved greatly since he had been here; it was more a matter of rapport with the country folk. At least he had an affinity for a few of the livelier students at the art school. "Jolly fellows" they called themselves, made more so by the strong liquor they consumed when they visited the taverns, especially in London.

A comfy chair, covered in fabric of orange-colored flowers, was placed by the window. *One more weekend to be spent alone on Foxhill Estate,* René thought as he sat. His new lodgings were in the old laborer's cottage of the villa. Not that he particularly minded; it was better than the newly built, smaller home where he had spent most of the last year. Mrs. Sowerby, his former landlady, had prided herself on her cooking skills, but René soon discovered that his stomach much preferred French cuisine. This affection, plus his disturbed sleep from the loud, constant snoring through the paper-thin walls made him decide to look for other lodgings. When he overheard M. Stoddard talking to Mrs. Sowerby over her white picket fence, René found his current residence.

He glanced over at his art supplies on the table. He was working on a drawing, an entry for the latest draughtsman competition organized by the local newspaper. The submission date was soon, but the gloomy atmosphere had dampened René's mood. Lacking motivation, he reminisced about home and his mother. She had sold her inheritance, some vineyards in Champagne, to pay for his school. Her sacrifice would not be in vain. He would make her proud of all his accomplishments.

Maman's letters always roused flashbacks about Paris: the dance halls, strolling the boulevards, the theater productions. Cafés filled with multitudes of well-dressed Parisians relishing plates of delicious food. Poularde aux morilles, Gratin Dauphinoise, turbot grille sauce Hollandaise. Cognac and sorbet to finish. René had dolefully remembered these dishes of chicken, potatoes, and fish whenever Mrs. Sowerby brought out her specialties. Madame Staffe would have never dared to serve black pudding, jellied eels, or herring pie with the fish heads poking through the crusts.

To distract himself, René focused on the estate grounds again. From the window, he could see the grand mansion situated behind the newer, larger outbuildings that housed the manager, Samuel Stoddard, and his wife. Not your typical solemn and taciturn Englishman, Sam was fond of hearing his own voice. He gossiped incessantly and told René everything about Sydenham and its inhabitants whenever the chance arose. One recent Sunday, the groundskeeper had unexpectedly appeared at his door to collect the rent.

"Bonjour, Mr. Lalique," Sam said jovially. "I hope that I'm not disturbing you. I thought I would save you the trouble of walking over to pay the rent and get a bit of exercise after church. The missus is taking a nap. Sometimes, I get a little drowsy too. Nothing like a brisk walk to wake you up." He smiled broadly at René. "Is everything to your liking? No problems?"

"Non, M. Stoddard, everything is fine. Let me get the money." René turned back into the small, two-room dwelling. Uninvited, Sam followed him in and shut the door. "So how is school going? This is your second year, right?" He walked across the room to the table.

"Oui. It is fine."

While René retrieved his money from the bedroom, he could hear Sam fiddling with his art supplies.

When René came back into the main room, Sam said, "You probably miss Paris and city life. Some people find the countryside boring. I prefer it to noisy, dirty London. Anyway, we're close enough with the railway, eh?" Pocketing René's rent money, he wrote out a receipt but seemed reluctant to leave. Instead, he sauntered over to the window and gazed out. "I like this location. You're closer to the woods. You probably know the path that leads through it?"

"Oui, I walk it nearly every day."

"What did you say you're studying?"

"Drawing. I want to be a designer."

"Like an architect?"

"No, an artist; a jeweler."

"Oh." Sam scratched his head. He seemed to consider the idea for a moment but then quickly dismissed it. "I've always been a farmer myself." He glanced over at the teakettle before looking out the window again.

René felt as if he had no choice. "Would you like a cup of coffee or tea?"

"Why, a spot of tea sounds delightful." The tall, thickset man dressed in dungaree work trousers plopped into René's threadbare orange chair and began a monologue involving his life.

As René prepared their drinks, he listened to Sam spew out the details. He and the missus had recently worked at a horse farm in Cambridgeshire. Did he know where that was? Beautiful place up north. Before that, a gardener, a field hand, those damn Yanks with their cheap imports . . . Anyway, they'd both been hired here. The missus had been a lady's maid, but she was a parlor maid now. That's fine as she wasn't fond of the lady of the house anyway. "Household chatter holds that she was the former chaperone of the baron's granddaughter."

René raised his eyebrows at that statement, but Sam offered no further details. "I manage the gardens and the stables with a lad, Willie. A lot of duties but the wages are good. Nothing wrong with a good day's work, eh?"

Sam went on. "Rumor is that they used to own a lot more land. The baron just kept selling off parcels here and there. They must have made some bad investments. Could be money or his wife, but sometimes Lord Haliburton's son, Roderick, is snarly. Lady Haliburton does have a reputation for spending too much. She's haughty considering her previous station and has a temper too. A real porcupine says my wife. Oh, the missus does like to complain. She's a woman. That's just their natural inclination, isn't it?"

Watching René balance the tea tray, Sam paused for just a moment. "The missus doesn't really care for a certain room in the mansion. Cold, musty, and crowded with too many strange things. Silly missus is afraid to go in there. Of course, she listens to nonsense and rubbish from the other girls about it being haunted. Especially Mary. She's full of dark yarns, that one. Makes up tall tales as consistent as breathing."

René handed Sam his tea. "Thank you, young man. I myself don't indulge her prattle about the supernatural. You simply can't give rein to that sort of drivel."

After taking a few sips of his tea, Sam continued. "My missus gets her duties done as quickly as she can in that room. She does like the old man, I mean the baron, from what she's seen of him. It's a shame he can't enjoy his wealth. He's sick and bedridden most of the time. Quarantined because of the coughing. Nobody talks about it, but she's seen the blood on the linens. Thinks it's consumption. Not long for the world. Probably."

The groundskeeper then asked René if he had seen any members of the family. René shook his head while Sam took another sip of tea. "Well, I don't like to encourage idle talk, you know, but sometimes, scandal leaks through the grapevine. You hear the most peculiar tales."

Sam swallowed more tea, set his teacup in its saucer, and resumed his narrative as he focused on the mansion in the distance. Family problems. Mental illness. According to those in the know, it ran through several generations, striking only the women. Bad brains, you know. Hysterical and violent, they say. Like to start fires. Had to be institutionalized. Practically killed the old man to do it. He just couldn't come to terms with their insanity. The baron's son, he didn't care. They say he was glad they were committed. But the father pleaded with him and Dr. Perkins. Seems they all came to some agreement. The solicitor being called in and all. Old Dr. Perkins, that is. There's two of them, father and son. Both doctors for the mad. Alienists, psychiatrists, yeah? Finally, the young Dr. Perkins, Charles, buckled against his better judgment, and let the young one come home.

The granddaughter should have never been sent to the asylum but there was no one to care for her. Apparently, she was a little strange but not crazy before she left and then she had a harrowing experience. There was a terrible accident. She was hurt in a fire. Supposedly, she started it. In a trance, mind you. Then went back to bed. Sounds crazy to me. Seems hard to believe. But people were killed and so she had to be committed for her own good and others.

Sam shook his head before looking at René. "The story goes that after she woke up and escaped, she got hit in the head by a falling timber. At first, she seemed alright and then she saw the little dog next to her. Dead. Seems Miss Haliburton had taken a fancy to the poor thing.

"Anyhow, after that she had a horrific fit; nervous breakdown they say. Lost her memory and went blind for a while but she can see now. The missus says she regained her sight but not her mind. Hears her talking to nobody. She got scared when she walked by that room and Miss Haliburton was talking to that dog statue. Alone. Then she turns to the missus and gives her a queer look. Straightaway, the missus went to Mrs. Darrow, the housekeeper—talk about a porcupine, don't get on her bad side—and had to ask permission for the afternoon off. The missus stayed in bed all afternoon, it gave her such a fright."

Sam took another brief pause. "Women and their fragile constitutions. Where was I? Oh, yes. Miss Haliburton."

M. Stoddard grinned again at René, who was sitting at the table with his chin propped in one hand listening, before forging ahead with his story. "She's there. Alone. In the garden. Sometimes even when it is raining. Sitting by the fountain. You probably haven't seen it. Beautiful work by the firm of James Pulham no less; they did the glorious landscaping too. Spectacular terracing. You might have heard of them. Commissioned by the baron to surprise Miss Haliburton. Those cacklers said she didn't like it. Said she was a spoiled brat who didn't appreciate anything. Just cried when she saw it."

Sam swallowed hard as he averted his eyes and looked out the window again. "They've given up on her getting married; you know high society and all . . . They say she's tainted and as mad as a hatter. Melancholy is what I say. I've only talked to her once. She came down to visit the horses. Seemed rather normal to me. Lonely perhaps. On the quiet side. Shy, yes, but the horses like her, and she seems to like them. It's hard for me to find fault with an animal lover." He looked at René. "She was polite and well-mannered. Quite a beautiful young lady." Sam closed his eyes and sighed. "She's small and fragile. Reminds me of a fine porcelain doll." Opening his eyes again, he frowned. "What a shame. The baron should have never let her go to Egypt. That's where all the problems began."

Finally, something that interested René: Egypt and a pretty girl. He perked up. "They went to Egypt?"

"Oh, didn't I mention that? Yes. They brought back all that stuff from there and put it in what used to be the library. The Egyptian room now. The one that I was telling you about with the dog statue. The room that the missus doesn't like." Sam glanced out the window again and saw the small figure of his wife with her hands on her hips staring in his direction. "Crikey, there's the missus now!" He slurped the rest of his tea, stood up and put the cup and saucer on the table. "I'd best be off. Thanks for the tea, lad."

A sudden squall of rain roused René from his memories. He looked out the window and thought about the young heiress. *Is she insane? Monsieur Stoddard said she looked like a beautiful doll.* He imagined her based on Stoddard's portrayal. *Will she visit the stables again? Will I ever meet her?* René thought of the estate's garden, with its fountain. Did he dare trespass, just to get a glimpse of them and the girl?

René hoped the sun might make an appearance in the afternoon. Maybe Miss Haliburton would be in the barn with the horses. No harm in walking by to see and chat with M. Stoddard. He would be interested to know that René's grandfather had been a farrier. Or perhaps he would go to the school instead. His classroom was in the nearby Crystal Palace Park. For inspiration, he could walk through its magnificent halls, vestibules and many stylized courts: Medieval, Renaissance, Fine Arts, and others. He especially liked the Egyptian court. A facsimile of ancient Egypt, it reproduced temple rooms with their majestic facades, columns and statues. The court reminded him of his visit to the Paris Exhibition so long ago. *Has Miss*

Haliburton seen the avenue of sphinxes? he wondered. He was curious about her opinion of it. *Does it remind her of the real place?* Surely, she had been to see Crystal Palace, the monumental glass structure with its grand transept, fountains and greenery. He envisioned the two of them there together, walking beside the water lily pools, talking about ancient Egypt.

René laughed at his own foolishness. As if they would have a chance meeting at the stables. As if she would visit Crystal Palace Park with him. As if a lovely, rich English heiress would be interested in a poor French art student who was fascinated with Egypt. Now *that* was insane. René got up, went over to the table and flipped open his art tablet. Needing more light, he pushed the wingback chair out of the way and pulled the table closer to the window. He then brought the small wooden chair from his bedroom, sat down and began to draw.

THE FOLLOWING FRIDAY NIGHT, THE silence of the grove after the raucous drunks was unearthly, reminding René of his dream earlier that morning. Or rather, a fleeting piece of it. Ambrose standing by a fountain with an angel. Not focused on the damp, uneven footpath, René stumbled but regained his balance before tumbling into the wet undergrowth. Repositioning his top hat, he continued through the darkened woods. The small lantern that he carried swung with his gait, creating odd-shaped shadows on the surrounding trees. *I shouldn't have had that last beer with the jolly fellows.* Thoughts of the barmaid surfaced. Not a bad figure but her face. She had been giving him the eye all night, but he would have to be a lot more drunk than he was to consider being with her.

René emerged from the trees, paused, and glanced over at the mansion in the distance. The full moon illuminated the estate grounds in silver light. *Is Miss Haliburton as lonely as I am?* He pictured a lovely young woman in a long, flowing gown of sparkles and a jeweled crown, a scintillating diadem that he had designed. René wondered if she was a dancer and imagined a huge ballroom with a gleaming wood floor. The beautiful heiress was in his arms as they glided around it.

He looked toward his lowly cottage. There was no need to return to it just yet. He could sleep in; tomorrow was Saturday. René turned towards the garden area. If he was quiet and stealthy, nobody would mind if he admired the fabled fountain and the jardin célèbre. *Who would deny me enjoyment of the garden? Surely not M. Stoddard or M. Pulham.*

Even in the dark, it was not hard to find the fountain. René followed the sound of flowing water. Large and glowing in the moonlight, the grayish-white, artificial stone fountain sat at the bottom of the terraced garden in a secluded corner. The diameter of its basin was large and the height of the centerpiece was at least eight feet: a pedestal with a tazza from which the water cascaded over the edge into the basin below. Atop the saucer-shaped ornamental bowl stood a cherub holding a small dog in its arms. René remembered the story that M. Stoddard had told him; now he understood why Miss Haliburton had cried when she saw it. *How could the household staff be so ignorant?* René thought of the other dog statue in the so-called Egyptian room. Was it the same?

A cool wind rustled the curly hair at the back of his neck. Suddenly feeling a presence, he held up his lantern and looked around to see if anyone was there. He was alone. René looked back at the fountain angel and again thought of Ambrose and his death. For so long, he had suppressed his memories of that horrible day, but they came flooding back. *Why did Ambrose keep that tarot card? Why did he dream of the Egyptian seer that morning?*

Before leaving Paris for England, René had read the letter from Mme. Sphinx again with its mention of the Egyptian pantheon in their underworld. One name came back to him.

Anubis. Anubis the Jackal. Could that be the dog statue that Miss Haliburton talks to? The wind picked up again and René felt certain that eyes were on him. He looked around again. No one. An eerie feeling washed over him. As he turned to leave, he didn't notice the figure standing at the mansion window, watching him return to the walking path.

Chapter 18:

THE EGYPTIAN ROOM

A fresh breeze wafted through the window. René was bored, and the sun was out. Since both seemed to be a rare occurrence these days, on a whim he decided to wander down to the stables. It had been several weeks since the groundskeeper had visited. He wondered if Stoddard would be there and what gossip he would have to tell. Since his night visit to the estate's garden, René's curiosity about the Haliburton family had increased. Although today was warmer than usual, it was difficult to predict England's capricious weather; this time a year ago, it had snowed. René placed his bowler on his head and draped his coat over his arm. Collecting his drawing notebook and pencil, he thought he would practice sketching the horses.

After his grand-père had passed, René hadn't spent any time around barns. As he approached the stables, the mild wind carried familiar smells. The earthy odor of damp straw, horse manure and fresh hay evoked memories of his childhood. René thought longingly of the idle days spent fishing with his grandfather on the Marne when his father was occupied with business in Paris. Stepping into the barn now, he brightened when he saw Stoddard grooming a large black horse.

M. Stoddard looked up and smiled at him. "Bonjour, Mr. Lalique. Splendid day, is it not?"

"Oui."

He stopped grooming and glanced at the sketchbook in René's hand. "Doing some schoolwork?"

"I thought I might draw the horses. Do you mind?"

"Not at all, my boy." The groundskeeper pointed to a hook on one of the stable posts. "You can hang your things there. No need for a hat or coat." He bent, put his brush in the bucket of grooming tools and picked out a comb. "Perfect timing. You can sketch Albert here. He's a fine specimen named after the royal prince." Combing the gelding's tail, M. Stoddard explained, "This fellow was born five years after Queen Victoria's husband died. That would make him around my age if he was human. He's strong but docile, especially when I chat with him."

As he hung up his hat and coat, René smiled, understanding the calming effects of Stoddard's talking. Sitting on a bench near the stall, he rolled up his sleeves and began to sketch as the older man droned on about the late Prince Albert, British politics and the numerous royal scandals. Fixated on his work, René was only half listening until the groundskeeper said something about a goddess.

He stopped and looked up. "I'm sorry, what did you say?"

M. Stoddard guffawed. "I wasn't sure if you were paying attention." He pointed to a large orange cat that was sitting by the doorway. "The barn cat, Sekhmet. Even though he's male, he's named after an Egyptian goddess." Sekhmet blinked his eyes lazily at them and then began to groom one of his paws. "He belongs to Miss Haliburton. Did I mention that she's been coming down here? She's changed. Says she likes it down here and chatting. I can hardly get a word in edgewise." Another hearty laugh erupted. "She's been telling me stories. Mostly about Egypt and their magic. She calls it heka."

The word brought back a memory of René standing with Ambrose in the bookstore. He stared quizzically at Stoddard. "What did you just say?"

"Heka. Miss Haliburton said that's what they called magic in ancient times."

"Interesting that she should know that word . . ."

"Why? Have you heard it before?"

"I saw it in an old book. What else does she talk about?"

"Well, she talks a lot about some Egyptian soldier and a queen. The queen had a special cat too but that he got to live in the palace, not the barn. Another cat used to follow her around the temple. I wasn't sure what she meant by that." Stoddard smiled at René. "That young lady has quite the fanciful imagination. Even though she does seem rather sincere about it all. You begin to think she is telling the truth. I don't mind hearing her mystical tales as it seems to cheer her up and well . . . She is so lovely to look at and listen to anyhow." He blushed and turned around to work on the horse's mane.

René looked back at the cat. Sekhmet had laid down, closed his eyes and was sunning himself. Posed like a sphinx, René began to draw him instead. Meanwhile, the groundskeeper rambled on about Miss Haliburton as he combed Albert's glossy hair. "The missus says the girl spends most of her days in the Egyptian room. Sitting amongst the statues and reading those dusty old books. It is somewhat strange the way she talks about them. The ancient Egyptians, what they wore, what they ate, what they did, their gods and goddesses. As if she'd been there, lived it. Maybe, with her head injury . . ."

M. Stoddard was silent for a few moments before continuing. "The missus says Lady Haliburton doesn't like it. The lady of the house has a lot of opinions about how Miss Haliburton spends her time. She says a proper young woman should be at social functions, high teas, dinners and balls. You know, dancing and looking for a suitable husband. Certainly not with her sick grandfather or in the Egyptian room. Lady Haliburton confessed to the missus one day that she dislikes everything in that room. Doesn't want it in her house. Then the missus overheard her and her husband arguing in their bedroom. First, it was about Miss Haliburton and, you know, her mental problems. She told him that the Egyptian room wasn't helping. Said the ancient things were hideous and made by idol-worshiping, ungodly heathens. Calling it dirty junk, she said they should get rid of it all, sell it, once the old man was gone. I guess that made Lord Roderick mad. How dare she speak of his father like that? Then he told her to mind her own affairs and that he was going to keep a closer eye on her. Said she was getting uppity—not in so many words, I'm sure—and that he was monitoring her finances. No more visits to Paris. Practically shouting, the missus said."

The groundskeeper paused for a moment. "That's unusual. He's not one to yell. Keeps a cool head most of the time, that chap." He led Albert back into his stall, came out and closed the door. "The missus said she heard him remind the lady that this was his family home and that he was the lord of it. She'd better keep her mouth shut or he'd send her back to where she came from. Then, nearly bowling the missus over, he stomped out and slammed the door. Without another word to anyone, he left and spent three days in the city. No one is certain where."

René bent down to scratch Sekhmet's neck. The cat had sauntered over and was rubbing against his legs.

M. Stoddard smiled. "He seems to like you. He doesn't like most people, especially the help. Skittish, he is. Probably because they are always screaming and chasing him out of the mansion." He walked over and glanced down at René's quick sketch of Sekhmet. "That's quite good, young man. May I look at the others?"

René handed him the notebook. As Stoddard flipped through the pages, he nodded before handing it back. "She'd like it," he said, scrutinizing René's face. "Miss Haliburton knows you live in the old cottage. She asked me about you, said that you reminded her of someone. Something about your mustache." Flustered, René involuntarily touched it. "When did she see me?"

"I don't know, son. She must have seen you walking to school." Stoddard stared out the barn entrance. "Here she comes now. You can ask her yourself."

René followed his gaze and saw a petite young woman walking down the path from the garden. Jumping to his feet and feeling self-conscious, he thought about his rolled-up sleeves, no coat on . . . Dropping his sketchbook on the bench, he moved to get his coat, but it was too late. She had seen them and was waving. M. Stoddard waved back and started towards her, René trailing slightly behind.

Her slender curves were covered by a white cashmere cuirasse bodice with long sleeves and a deep V-neck that revealed her high-necked day dress of pleated yellow silk underneath. She walked gracefully toward them, the swing of her gait emphasized by the close-fitting garment. She wore a large brimmed hat with a curled ostrich feather. They met halfway.

"Good afternoon, Mr. Stoddard," she said. She glanced at René and then returned her gaze to the groundskeeper.

He nodded. "How delightful to see you, Miss Haliburton. Let me introduce our lodger, Mr. René Lalique."

"Monsieur Lalique," she greeted.

René nodded back. "Enchanté, Mlle. Haliburton."

She smiled briefly, her rosy pink lips barely parting. The heiress was everything René had imagined and more. "Mr. Stoddard told me that you are from Paris and that you are studying art here in Sydenham."

"Oui."

"How do you like it here?"

René smiled broadly at her and said truthfully, "It smells better than Paris or London, with less smoke. At least I can breathe here."

When she tittered lightly at his joke, he thought, *Elle est belle et charmant.*

Her blue eyes held his momentarily, then she demurely looked away, her gaze landing on Sekhmet. "There he is, my kitty. Is Sekhmet doing his job of keeping the mice at bay?"

Stoddard glanced over at the cat, who was lazily flicking his tail. "Certainly, he is." He gave her a smile. "Mr. Lalique was sketching him earlier while he was taking a break from his duties."

She turned to René. "Really? Could I see your drawing?"

"Oui." He ran off to fetch his sketches.

As Sekhmet scampered away, René barreled ahead, thinking of the pretty girl and how much he wanted to impress her. After handing her the book of drawings, she flipped through the pages, stopping to look at several thumbnails of Albert's head and then perusing the one of Sekhmet posed as a sphinx. "I really like this one. You are excelling in your studies." Closing the book, she handed it back to René. "I saw the excavation of the Great Sphinx in Egypt."

"Egypt must have been very interesting," René said. "I have always been fascinated by it."

She was silent for a moment, then tilted her head slightly towards the mansion. "Would you like to see some artifacts? They're in our Egyptian room."

René hesitated and looked at M. Stoddard for approval. A tiny nod gave René his blessing. "Are you sure, Mademoiselle? There is no trouble?"

"Why not?" She looked at him directly. "So, is that a yes?"

"Oui, of course. Let me get my hat and coat."

When he came back, Stoddard told him, "Miss Haliburton wants you to see the garden too. We think you will find it stupendous." He bowed slightly to her. "Well, Miss, I must get back to work. I do hope you will visit the stables again. Soon." Turning, he walked back to the barn.

Miss Haliburton led René towards the mansion on the hill. When they entered the garden, she was quiet and paused so René could survey the landscape. M. Stoddard was right: the manufactured garden was spectacular. There was a gravel pathway to the house winding its way through numerous formations of stone. Tiny blooms of bellflowers and rock rose spilled over and around the rocks. A river of color, the small white, pink, and purple blossoms cascaded down the green and grey hillside. Under one of the numerous trees, René spotted a wrought iron bench facing the angel fountain. He recalled the moonlit night when he had first seen it.

"I thought you might like to see it in the daylight. What do you think?"

René looked at her quickly.

She pointed to a second-story window in the closest wing of the house. "I saw you that night from my window. In the moonlight." Before René could explain his trespassing, she stopped him. "Don't worry, your secret is safe with me."

"Merci," he replied and followed her into the mansion. He had seen many such places in Paris, having been allowed to accompany Louis to patrons' homes. While he was impressed by this house's grandeur, he was not awed by it. Until he saw the Egyptian room.

Larger than René had imagined, the room was shadowy and musty with old books and curios that filled the floor-to-ceiling bookshelves on one side. On the other side was a wooden sarcophagus. The center of the room was congested with furniture. Closed, the heavy drapery kept out sunlight and warmth. Underneath the curtained windows sat display cases full of items. The darkest corner contained a statue of a reclining dog with large ears and golden eyes.

René paused in the threshold, his eyes adjusting to the darkness. A cool draft enveloped his body and a fusion of excitement and fear gripped his solar plexus. It was like teetering on a ledge overlooking an abyss.

"Welcome to my tomb," she said. Miss Haliburton removed her hat and the long raven tresses tucked into it fell over her shoulders to the top of her silk-covered bosom. In the shadows of the Egyptian room, she seemed very different, reminding him of someone. *Who? An enchantress. Une femme fatale.* He hesitated in the doorway. "Come in," she urged.

Removing his hat and gripping his sketchbook, René stepped forward. Once in the room, he noticed an aroma. Underlying the robust smell of antiquities and old wood was a subtle spicy, floral scent.

She smiled mischievously at him. "There's no need to be nervous. I won't bite." Walking toward the corner where the statue of Anubis was situated, she placed her hand on the jackal's shoulder. "I saw him first. In the tomb. What do you think?"

Formidable, René thought. "Wonderful, Mlle. Haliburton."

"Please, call me Lucinda. May I call you René?"

"Oui."

"Look at this." She went over to the display unit under the window. A long mahogany cabinet split into three units. The museum piece had sturdy turned legs and sloping, hinged, glass-paneled tops.

René examined it. The three separate cases contained numerous items. He studied the ones in the first case, focusing last on the small statues of clay people.

Lucinda followed his gaze and answered his question before he asked it. "The ones who answer. Also known as ushabtis, magical servants in the Afterlife. Spells from the Book of the Dead were written on them to compel them to answer when they were called upon." She pointed to the markings on the base of one. "Behold, me. I am here when thou callest."

They moved to the next case, where he marveled at the jewelry. Gold, lapis, turquoise, carnelian; armbands, a diadem, amulets, a carnelian scarab pendant set in golden lotus flowers. And a mirror with a white handle. But one thing really caught his eye, a blue glass bottle in a bronze stand with a carved turquoise stopper, the head of an ibis. *Incroyable.* René read the tag next to it: *Perfume Amphora.*

Transported back in time, he recalled Mme. Sphinx, the séance and their gift to her, the perfume bottle. *That's it.* This girl was like the seductive, mysterious seer. *Deux sphinx,* he thought as he stared at Lucinda.

She was looking at the white-handled mirror. Placing her gloved hand on the glass, she said, "I saw you coming. In the mirror. You were there with her. The lady of blue." She pointed to the ancient perfume bottle. "That was yours. Don't you remember it?"

Chapter 19:

THEATER OF THE MIND

S itting at her dressing table, Lucinda thoughtfully brushed her long curls. She was recalling her nightmare experience in the madhouse when a horrible nurse had chopped off most of her tresses. While imprisoned in the asylum, she had fallen into a deep depression and refused to wash and comb her hair. Not allowing anyone else to touch it, finally it had become so matted that no comb could pass through the tangles. The good nurse cajoled but to no avail. The bad nurse threatened and then made good on her promise of cutting it off. While those vile orderlies strapped her into a straitjacket and held her down. Horror-stricken with her appearance afterward, Lucinda had refused to look at her reflection until her beautiful locks had returned.

Finished with the brushing, she took a moment to survey herself in her mirror. *Pale and a little thin,* she thought. But much better than *those* months. The dark days following her accident when she was temporarily blinded and those people had come through the mist. Young Dr. Perkins—called Dr. Charles by the staff to distinguish between father and son—had told her that she suffered from hallucinations. That her visions were nothing more than phantasms. Even though they seemed so real. Even though she seemed to be transported back in time and place to a familiar distant past. Bits and pieces of an ancient Egyptian life that she remembered. Unlike her recent time in Egypt, most of which had dissolved away like the medicated sugar cubes that she watched the nurse or Dr. Charles put in her afternoon tea.

Before and after her sight returned, Dr. Charles was always there. Visiting. He told her she needed the medication because she had been violent. Very angry, which made her have fits of hysteria. Uncontrollable screaming that she was a lioness and that she would destroy them all. Drink their blood like beer. That's why she was imprisoned. She didn't remember any of it. Now there was no anger, just fatigue. The medication made her tired and all she wanted to do was sleep.

After drinking her tea, Dr. Charles would talk to her to keep her awake, holding her hand, sometimes patting it gently. The young doctor told her all sorts of things, including what might be causing her hallucinations. She could have temporal lobe epilepsy or Charles Bonnet Syndrome, le théâtre de l'esprit. Theater of the mind. A phrase, he said, coined by M. Bonnet in the 1700s. Sudden blindness, brought on by her recent head trauma, could be producing her illusions. If the eyes stop supplying information to the brain, he explained, the mind begins to generate its own images.

Checking herself again in the mirror, Lucinda pinched her cheeks to bring some color, then walked over to the window and looked down at the fountain. It always made her sad and she didn't know why except that something bad had happened in Egypt. Something about a fire. She had done terrible things. Or so they said. *This syndrome, did it also affect my memories?* There were misty images of the Great Sphinx and temple ruins, but the rest of that period remained as dark to her as the room in which she now stood.

It was dusk, and Mary would be here soon to light the lamps. Dr. Charles had said that darkness stimulated the hallucinations, but Lucinda knew different. Sun or shadow, day or night, they still came. Watching. In the Egyptian room by the pink granite slab. The portal where they entered and exited. The doctor told her that the visions would lessen in time, but he was wrong. Ghosts of the past were here to stay.

As Lucinda sat down on her crimson couch, fond thoughts of Dr. Charles surfaced. She liked him. He was so kind to her. Visiting her when she was held captive and bringing her the little canary in the cage to brighten her room. She had looked forward to their walks on the asylum grounds, elbows linked, meandering along the pathways chatting. The walks had begun when she was blind, and she had relied on his support and guidance. But even as she regained her vision, he continued to offer his arm as they strolled.

When she and her doctor passed through the common areas inside, the other incarcerated women, working, would give them suspicious glances. Lucinda knew they were envious as she had a private room, nor did she have to sew, cook or clean. Her grandfather had seen to that. Also, she suspected, the women's doctors did not give them as much attention.

The doctor had told her, on their walks, that he would like it if she just called him Charles. He was attentive to her, talking, questioning, and then listening so intently to her answers. About everything. The dreadful hydrotherapy, cold showers and freezing foot wraps, the mean nurse and bad orderlies, the good nurse. What about her canary? How was her little bird doing and were they both eating? He encouraged her to think happy thoughts and said that her hair was so pretty, wouldn't she like to comb it? Put on the new dress that her grandfather had sent to her? Wondering about her feelings, her dreams, and her hallucinations. She was honest with him. At first. Quickly discovering that she needed to pretend she was obedient and cheerful, she lied. If she kept her Egyptian specters a secret, he would think she was better. He would let her go home.

Lucinda smiled as she twirled a lock of hair around her finger. It was worth losing her hair to start anew. Dr. Charles was livid when he saw what the asylum staff had done to her while he was away in London. After he shouted at the bad nurse through closed doors, he had personally escorted Lucinda back to Foxhill Estate.

Lucinda continued to toy with her curl as she watched Sekhmet come out from under the bed. He was allowed inside now at night, but still preferred hunting outdoors. The cat settled himself on her lap and began purring as she scratched behind his ears. She was glad that he had gotten used to looking at the Egyptians standing in the corners. They adored him. But of course, the ancient culture worshipped cats.

Lucinda wondered if the new tenant liked cats. The one she saw walking every day. The one who stood in the moonlight admiring the fountain. *What's his name? He's so handsome. Just a boy compared to Charles. No,* she corrected herself, *he's a young man. With that dimpled chin and bushy mustache. That thick, dark, curly hair.* She thought she had met him previously. *I have been lost in his soulful eyes before. Eza? Was that his name? No.* The man was an artist. She had seen his drawings. *They were in the tomb in Egypt, yes? No.* They had been together in the garden and he had visited the Egyptian room. *Today. Yes, earlier today. This afternoon.* She had shown him the blue bottle from Egypt, hadn't she? *The jackal god was there with us. Or was it just another one of my visions? A dream? I wish my mind wasn't so mixed up. Why can't it be like it was before?* Perhaps she would go down to the stables tomorrow and visit with Mr. Stoddard. He would know the young man's name. He would remember.

Chapter 20:

AMONGST THE BLUEBELLS

The jolly fellows had gone to London earlier and had invited him along, but René declined. Greasy fried fish wrapped in old newspaper and a warm beer wasn't enough incentive. Plus, they usually got into predicaments—monkey tricks, M. Stoddard would say—and trouble would soon follow. Besides, he wouldn't find a prettier companion than Mlle. Haliburton. His late lunch done, René sat back in his orange chair. He gazed at the mansion in the distance and thought of the captivating heiress, and their time together in the Egyptian room, where she was different. Not the demure girl, but a distinct personality, provocative and seductive. *Two people in one,* he thought. *How is that possible? Is it her mental condition?* Perhaps the missus was right. Maybe the room was affecting the girl's mind.

Lucinda's assertion that the ancient blue perfume bottle had been his was certainly bewildering. *I must have misunderstood her.* He hadn't time to ask her, though, because their visit was cut short by Mary, her lady's maid, saying that Lucinda's grandfather was asking for her and she would escort René out.

He had wanted to see her again, but the last couple of weeks of schoolwork had kept him busy. She was mystifying, odd, but still beautiful and charming. René pondered a pretext for a social call, but the only thing he could think of was to visit M. Stoddard at the stables. *Even if he's not there, I can visit Albert the horse.* He downed the rest of his drink and got up.

The stables were empty except for the horses. When René entered the barn, Albert whinnied and stuck his head out of his stall. René greeted him and fed him a handful of oats and petted his muzzle. As René sat down on the bench and took out his pencil and pocket notebook, Albert retreated into his enclosure, so René looked around for something else to draw. He saw Sekhmet emerging from behind a pile of hay up in the loft.

"*Ici, minou, minou,*" he called. The cat sat at the edge of the loft and looked down at him. René tried again. "Here, kitty, kitty." Sekhmet's tail flicked idly but he didn't move. A quick sketch was done before the cat disappeared beyond the sheaves of dried grass. Searching for another subject, René spotted a patch of wildflowers just outside the barn. He walked to the rear entrance and made a rough drawing, then heard a female voice.

"Fancy meeting you here," she said. He turned to see Lucinda watching him, her attractive face framed by a straw hat.

A thrill ran through him. *Si adorable.* "Bonjour, Lucinda."

"Bonjour, René." She looked down modestly at her beige linen skirt and cotton polonaise jacket. "Forgive my dowdy attire. I was going out for an afternoon walk and came down to visit the horses first. I didn't know you would be here."

"Vous êtes belle," he replied without hesitation. In English he said, "I like the flowers on your blouse."

Lucinda thanked him and then, bashful, glanced over at Albert's stall, where his head had reappeared. She walked over to greet the horse and stroke his forehead. When the horse backed away again, she turned to René. "So, what are you drawing today?"

"Would you like to see?"

"Yes."

Taking his notebook, she looked at his recent drawings and then flipped through the older pictures. She stopped at a colored sketch of the swallow pin he had made for Maman. "This is lovely."

"It's a brooch I made for my mother. It's silver with enamel on the wings and necks." He pointed to the birds' faces. "And tiny pearls for their eyes."

"Really?"

"Oui. I was apprenticed to a famous goldsmith, a jeweler, in Paris before I came here to study."

"You have wonderful talent. I'm sure your mother loved it."

"Merci beaucoup. She did."

"You must miss her and your father."

"I do miss her." René hesitated slightly. "And him." He glanced away. "My father died when I was sixteen."

"I'm so sorry . . ."

René smiled at her. "Non, don't worry." Changing the subject, he asked, "What do you do for la créativité? Um, loisirs? How do you say . . . a hobby?"

Lucinda giggled. "Well, I guess my hobby is sewing, mostly embroidery. I do it because it makes my grandfather happy. It reminds him of my grandmother crocheting doilies."

"My mother crochets too; she works in fashion. She has hands of gold," René said proudly. "You know, my school teaches embroidery and cooking to the girls, in addition to art. Our classes are in the Crystal Palace. Have you been there?"

"Yes. Before I went to Egypt." Lucinda bent her head down and shuffled her feet, then looked up at him again. "As I said, I was going on a walk. Would you like to accompany me? I know a wonderful spot in the woods. Do you like bluebells?"

"Oui."

They began walking down the regular path that René used but, in the middle of the woods, Lucinda veered off onto a little-used trail, nearly hidden by the new spring grass. "I haven't been this way in ages," she said.

"It's very enjoyable." René fondly remembered his walks with his grandfather in the countryside. Now, strolling in the woods with a lovely woman, he couldn't imagine greater enjoyment. Except maybe a kiss from her. He looked at her face and smiled.

Lucinda glanced at him. "What? Why are you smiling?" She turned her head away before he could answer, but a tiny grin appeared on her lips. As they continued to walk, she looked straight ahead and not at him. They finally arrived at a dappled glade with an expansive flower patch. A carpet of green and many hues of blue, pale to intense, spread out before them. Lucinda gestured towards the flowers. "My favorites. This is my secret bluebell spot, realm of the fairies. Do you like it?"

"Very much."

She led him to a fallen log in the shade. They sat on the ground and leaned back on the moss-covered trunk. "I feel a little sleepy. Do you mind if I take a catnap while you draw? Perhaps a design I can embroider." Her eyes, mirroring the profusion of blue around them, were captivating. "Please?"

René could not refuse. "Oui."

Lucinda smiled, scooted down to lay her head on the log and closed her eyes. Before René drew the requested design for her, he sketched her profile. *Those lips . . .* Trying to quell his rising desire, he focused on his promise. After finishing several designs, he returned to using her as a model for a fairy. He was sketching the curve of her bust when she opened her eyes and sat up. René quickly flipped to another page.

"My goodness, I seem to have been dozing. How is your picture coming? Can I see?"

He showed her the pictures of the flowers. "I love this one," she said as she traced the curve of a stem with her finger. Discovering the snail he had partially hidden in the leaves, she laughed. "And your snail! The spiral of his shell is so elegant, so . . . poetic." Lucinda turned to her side and relaxed against the stump, her expression dreamy and quixotic. "Your work is brilliant."

René fought the impulse to throw down the pad and gather her in his arms. Instead, he said, "Merci, you are too generous." Flipping to a clean page, he began to sketch anew.

She watched him for a bit, then stood up and looked at the picturesque scenery. "I am going to London tomorrow. I have been wanting to have tea at the Green Dining Room in the South Kensington Museum. I hear it is lovely." She turned to René. "Would you like to join me?" Before he could answer, she added quickly, "I mean, us? Mary, my maid, will come, too. Of course."

"But of course." René closed his notebook and got to his feet. "I would be delighted to accompany you."

"We will take the train to Victoria Station. I have ordered some silk fabric from Liberty's. Have you heard of it?"

"Oui."

"Well, I thought that Mary and I could take a cab up there—I have an appointment with the dressmaker as well—while you go on to the museum. Being an artist and all, I thought you might like to visit it. They have many fine paintings and what-not. Then we can meet you in the dining room for lunch."

René grasped Lucinda's gloved hand and raised it to his lips. Looking deeply into her eyes, he said, "It will be my pleasure."

Chapter 21:

TRAIN OF THOUGHT

Mary finished buttoning Lucinda's dress and then picked up the garnet necklace and fastened it around her mistress's neck. When Lucinda looked in the mirror, she returned her maid's gaze. "What else will you be wanting, Miss Haliburton? I have laid out your hat, gloves and purse."

"This is fine, Mary. Why don't you gather your things and meet me at the carriage?"

"Yes, milady."

After Mary left, Lucinda admired her outfit in the mirror. *What will René think?* She straightened the black bow decorating the neckline of her black and white striped walking dress. Then, using her grandmother's garnet-encrusted hatpin, she secured her small black felt hat to her upswept hair. Remembering the events of the day before, she smiled before her mind drifted to the purpose of her errands today: She was having a dress made for the upcoming ball.

Visiting her grandfather's quarters earlier in the week, he had insisted Lucinda go to the dance so that he wouldn't have to listen to Roderick's wife's carping about it. As Lucinda embroidered, she listened to his own complaints. "*Lady*"—her grandfather emphasized the title sarcastically—"Haliburton was here earlier. She was haranguing me about you attending the next ball at Lord Home's mansion at Beulah Spa." The old man cleared his throat. When Lucinda looked at him, he said, "You can't hide here forever. And become a spinster." As he said that last word, a coughing spell erupted. "I won't allow it," he spluttered. Lucinda just smiled at him and continued to sew.

The baron sighed. "Roderick tells me that you spend an inordinate amount of time in the Egyptian room. I understand. I wish I could spend more time there. Lord knows, I spent enough money finding those things." He coughed again loudly. "I want to enjoy them more but with my health . . . and Dr. Charles says it's too cold in there."

Lucinda paused her sewing. "I will wheel you in your chair any time you want to visit. Dr. Charles is wrong about it being too cold. I would wrap you in a blanket and open the drapes. I'll speak to him about that."

Her grandfather looked over at the wheelchair in the corner and then back at her. "My dear Lucie, what would I do without you? You are the only one who cares about me. And I care about you. That's why I want you to get out of the house more. Socializing. The Egyptian room is no place to spend your youth." He patted his bed. "Come and sit beside me."

Lucinda put down her embroidery and went to sit at her grandfather's side. Grasping her left hand, he spoke to her earnestly. "We really must think about your future. You know, I won't be around much longer."

Lucinda frowned at him. *He's not looking well. I am worried about him, but I must not encourage this thinking.* She shook her head. "I don't want to speak of that, Grandfather."

"I'm afraid we must." He squeezed her hand gently. "What do you think of Dr. Charles?"

"He has been a good doctor to me."

"He speaks highly of you every time he visits me. I think he likes you tremendously."

"I like him, too, Grandfather."

His eyes searched hers. "Just like?"

"He has been a friend to me in my time of need."

"Lucie, he is an admirer. I think he is interested in more than just friendship."

Charles is only a friend to me, she thought. *I certainly don't love him.* She patted her grandfather's hand and then stood up. "Would you like to visit your Egyptian antiquities today?"

He sighed again. "Would you just consider the idea?"

Lucinda smiled sweetly at her grandfather, but did not answer him.

Checking her outfit once more, Lucinda donned her gloves. She recalled René kissing her hand the previous day and then how he had looked at her. *Those eyes. So magnetic,* she thought dreamily. Now that the charming Frenchman was here, she wanted to go to the ball, to reenter society to see if she would be accepted. All she had to do was muster the courage. Imagining dancing with René, held close in his embrace, her heartbeat fluttered. Lucinda gathered her purse. Today was another tiny step forward.

AS THE TRAIN SWAYED, RENÉ gazed at Lucinda leaning on the window using her small purse as a cushion while she napped. Her chest rose and fell with deep breaths. It had been a long day in London, but she seemed overly weary. He glanced at Mary's face. She returned his gaze with an intense look and then smiled fetchingly. He understood: Mary was his for the taking if he wanted. René smiled back and then looked out the window at the passing scenery. The maid had pleasing features and a fine figure, but she was not her mistress. Lucinda was appealing in so many other ways even if she was moody.

It's my fault for being late, he thought as he recalled Lucinda's judgmental stare when he walked into the dining room of the South Kensington Museum.

As he approached their table, he nodded to both women. "Bonjour, mesdames."

"We've been waiting for you, M. Lalique," Lucinda replied sternly.

"I'm sorry to be late," he apologized. "I lost track of the time viewing the exhibits. Perhaps, after lunch, we could look at some of them together. The collections of sculpture and glass are phenomenal and the jewels . . ." He looked at Lucinda. "They made me think of you. I could imagine them around your neck and dangling from your ears." He flashed her a disarming look. "Wouldn't you like to see them?"

Lucinda's expression brightened. "I would. Please sit."

From his train seat, René studied her face again. *So beautiful,* he thought, and then recalled the other reason he had been delayed: stopping at a shop before going to the museum.

He had gotten off the omnibus at Harrod's to buy Lucinda something, a little trinket, a surprise. Rejecting handkerchiefs and gloves, he continued to meander along the mahogany counter before seeing it: A small bottle of perfume with a white satin ribbon around the neck and a pretty label edged in turquoise and gold. The picture was his favorite flower, lily of the valley. Later, when they were walking around the museum and Mary was engrossed in an exhibit, he took Lucinda around a corner. Pulling the container from his breast pocket, he presented it to her. "For you, ma chérie."

René smiled now remembering her look of wonder, then joy, then the love in her gaze as she thanked him for the gift. Filling with desire again, he reached into his pocket and pulled out the small notebook he always carried. Finding a blank page, he began to draw Lucinda's comely features.

Mary spoke softly. "It's the bromide I put in her tea."

René looked up at her. "What?"

"It's the medicine she takes that makes her sleepy," Mary quietly divulged, "She has horrible fits if she doesn't take it. Dr. Charles told me so."

"I see."

René's brief response prompted the maid to continue. "He told me that, after her accident, her brain doesn't work right anymore and she will need this medication forever. Milady doesn't like being tired—she calls it weary of heart—but it's much better than having fits. I've seen only one, short but a terrible sight to endure." Mary leaned towards him and whispered even more softly. "Her mother was . . ." She didn't finish, just made a spiral sign around the side of her head. *Crazy*.

René wanted to return to his drawing, but Mary sat back and continued to gossip in a hushed tone. "They put the mother in an asylum in London, where the wealthy lunatics go. They say that old Lord Haliburton was against it, but young Dr. Perkins did it anyway. He visits her monthly and tells Lord Haliburton that she is making progress, that she's curable." Mary paused, leaned closer and spoke quietly. "I doubt it. Though I wasn't at Foxhill Estate at the time, I've heard stories. There were fits and she beat the servants. They finally put her away when she locked the door, started a fire in her room and nearly burned to death." The maid paused and motioned her eyes towards Lucinda. "Apparently, she did too and had to be put away in the loony bin. But Dr. Charles put her closer, south in Banstead. Rumor is, so he could visit her more often." Mary shook her head. "Like mother, like daughter."

René looked down at his notebook and muttered, "So, I've heard." Turning to another page, he started to sketch from memory one of the jewels he had seen in the museum case. His drawing, however, did not prevent Mary from talking.

Leaning back in her seat, she asked, "What are you drawing?"

"A necklace that I saw today."

"That day I saw you with Miss Haliburton looking at their Egyptian jewelry, did you like it?"

"Yes." He looked up at her. "I would like to visit again and draw some of the pieces."

"I myself don't like that room," she sniffed. "Neither does Lady Haliburton. It's haunted, you know."

René recalled what M. Stoddard had said about Mary and her occult stories. "C'est, oui?" Wanting to hear what she had to say, he flashed a charming smile at her.

A torrent of words erupted from her. "Oh, yes, very much so. That room is never warm. Even if the drapes are opened." She motioned her head towards Lucinda. "And she will immediately close them. It stays bone-chilling cold from the spirits that live there." Mary leaned closer to him. "Milady said they like it that way. When I asked who she was talking about, she pointed to the corner and said, 'Them.'" The maid looked at her mistress for a moment to confirm that she was still dozing. "Nobody was there, but I got a queer feeling." Mary sat back. "I took myself out of there right quick. I won't go in that room unless I have to. Usually it's to fetch her if necessary." She glanced briefly at Lucinda once again. "I heard Lady Haliburton say those things are cursed. She wants to rid the house of them, but his Lordship won't allow it. I don't understand the appeal of those creepy old things. They should have stayed underground where they found them." Mary crossed her arms over her chest. "In Egypt. Lady Haliburton says that country is full of heathens. England is just fine for me." The maid sniffed again. "Of course, they keep coming here. Foreigners flocking to our civilized nation. Most of them thieves and charlatans. Why, I heard from Willy, the stable boy, that another troupe of them has come to Gipsy Hill in Norwood. He said there is a magic lantern performance, an exotic picture show, going on at a hall in the village. There is a fortune-teller too. She has created quite a stir with her readings. Willy said his older cousin, the one from up north, called her a brown witch." Mary smirked at René. "Though he did add she's a bonny one at that."

Mary stopped talking when Lucinda made a small sound and then abruptly shifted in her seat. Her purse fell to her shoulder, causing her to awaken. She sat up. "My goodness, I must have drifted off." Looking at René and then Mary, she asked, "What did I miss?"

LUCINDA SAT ON THE EDGE OF HER bed lost in thought about the nightmare she had had on the train. *Back in the hidden tomb chamber, she was looking at the canopic jar with the faience baboon head. They were talking about her, whispering. There was a wall, with voices behind it. She was being imprisoned.* Then she woke up.

Lucinda got into bed and pulled the coverlet over her. *What did it mean? Why did I dream about the baboon jar?* As her head hit her pillow, a memory of the Egyptian trip surfaced. Her uncle was there, and they were taking pictures of the antiquities on the table. She remembered a man trying to take the blue baboon head off of the jar, but the lid was sealed. *Gaston. His name was Gaston.* And there was a dog on her lap. *Badger. That was his name.* Thinking of the dachshund, tears sprung to her eyes and rolled down her cheeks. *No.* Squeezing her eyes shut, Lucinda forced the sad thoughts out by thinking about René amongst the bluebells. He brought joy and light. Her grandfather was right, she should stay away from that room. She needed to forget about Egypt as it only brought darkness.

Chapter 22:

THE MAGIC LANTERN SHOW

Madame Sphinx is sitting at her table. In front of her, on the table, are two scrolls. She is unrolling one of them and he knows that it contains secrets from an ancient time. She looks at him. Then he is standing in front of a curtain. He reaches to open it.

René woke up and turned over in bed. His dream reminded him of what Mary had told him on the train a couple of weeks ago. Something about a magic lantern show and a fortune-teller in nearby Norwood. He had forgotten about it until now as his mind had been wholly focused on Lucinda. They had been meeting discreetly every day, weather permitting, in the bluebell grove. They conversed, but mostly he would draw and she would talk. He learned that, besides being beautiful, she was intelligent and well-read. Praising his work, drawings, doodles, and studies, she asked to keep them so she could treasure them and look at them often.

Gazing at the wooden beams above him, René wondered if Lucinda would go to the picture show with him. *I will ask M. Stoddard if it is a good idea to invite her.* As he sat up and swung his legs out of bed, he decided he would visit the stables later this morning before his afternoon rendezvous with her.

At the stable a few hours later, René hoped to find M. Stoddard but only Willy was there in the yard, carrying his bucket and brushes to the water pump.

"Hello, is M. Stoddard around?"

"He's on an errand. I'll tell him to come round to your place when he gets back."

René followed the young man to the water pump and watched as he filled his bucket. "Perhaps you could answer my question. Mary told me that you had mentioned something about a magic lantern show in Norwood."

"She did?" Willy picked up his bucket and tools, then walked over to a nearby carriage and set down his things. "She's a regular church bell, that one." He shook his head and began washing the carriage.

"Did you go see it?"

"Aye."

"Was it good?"

"Aye."

"I heard it's exotic. Is it decent?"

Willy stopped and looked at him. "You'll see no butter-bags, if that's what yer meaning." He went back to cleaning.

René smirked, having heard the jolly fellows use this term when commenting on a barmaid's breasts. "For a lady's eyes then."

"It's about foreign lands, with strange music and sound effects. The show starts off in total darkness. It didn't scare me, but some of the girls were frightened." He grinned. "Good for cuddling, though."

"Mary also said something about a fortune-teller. Do you know anything about her?"

Willy splashed water from the bucket to rinse off the carriage. "Mr. Stoddard is right. I need to watch what I say around the girls. Especially her." He walked back to the pump to refill the bucket. "Me cousin told me about the card reader. He's a regular chap, but he went to have his fortune told. There's been a bit of talk about her. They say that her predictions come true." Willy was silent as he pumped, and then spoke again as he headed to the other side of the carriage. "I don't believe in such trickery, but he was taken in by her. Not sure if it's what she told him or that she's a real beller-croaker."

René suppressed a laugh at the English slang of belle à croquer, a beautiful, desirous woman. He thought of Mme. Sphinx again. "So, she is very beautiful, yes?"

Willy nodded in confirmation.

"Merci," René told him. "Good day."

LUCINDA LOOKED AT THE CLOCK. It was time to leave to meet René. She closed the book she was reading and went to her dressing table. She dabbed the lily of the valley perfume that René had given her on her wrist and behind her ears, then arranged her straw hat on her head. She was anticipating a sunny day surrounded by bluebells. Smiling at her reflection in the mirror, she noted her complexion looked healthier. Her grandfather was right: getting outdoors had been good.

Lucinda decided to peek in on him on her way out and made her way to his wing of the house. When she turned into the hallway to her grandfather's suite, her former governess was there with Dr. Charles; they were talking in low voices. Lucinda halted as a foggy memory surfaced. Miss Meadows had been standing there with him. Mitch. Drinking sherry and whispering intimately. A brief feeling of hatred for them both arose from the depth of her being. She stared at Charles. *No, that's not Mitch. You're confused again.* Not wanting to confront them, Lucinda was about to retreat when the tall, blond doctor noticed her.

"Hello, Miss Haliburton, I was hoping to see you today. Lady Haliburton was just telling me that you have been getting outdoors and spending less time in the library." Dr. Charles never referred to it as the Egyptian room.

Lucinda nodded. "Yes. As a matter of fact, I was just on my way out." Then she looked at Miss Meadows. *I will never, ever address you as Lady Haliburton.* "Tell my grandfather that I will visit him later. Thank you." Without waiting for a reply, Lucinda turned to go.

"Wait," Dr. Charles said, "I was just leaving. I shall walk you out." He said goodbye to Lady Haliburton and added, "Tell Lord Roderick that I shall be in touch." Putting his hat on his head, he strode over to Lucinda. "Shall we?"

Lucinda couldn't refuse; it would be unseemly. Besides, the eagle eye of Miss Meadows was on her. "Certainly."

When they arrived outdoors, Charles escorted her down to the trail near the stable. He looked at the cabriolet waiting for him and then suggested that he first take a walk with her. She politely declined his offer, but at his rejected look, she tarried for a few minutes to assure him that she just needed time alone in nature. Wasn't that his recommendation?

RENÉ CHECKED HIS POCKET WATCH and frowned. She was late. He had already drawn many pictures for her. What could be keeping her? When he finally spotted Lucinda coming down the trail smiling and waving, his grumpy expression melted as he stood to greet her.

"I apologize for being tardy," she said. "Charles kept me. He wanted to walk with me, and I said no. He was sad, so I had to cheer him up."

René remembered Mary's gossip about Charles and Lucinda. A pang of jealousy stabbed his heart. "Who is this Charles?"

"Oh, didn't I tell you? He's my doctor." She glanced down at René's drawings. "May I see them?"

But René persisted. "Why does he want to walk with you?"

Lucinda turned and looked out over the flowers. "We used to walk together when I was sick. When I was blind. He's just a friend." She faced René, stepped closer and held up her wrist. "Can you smell it? I'm wearing the perfume you gave me."

Lifting her arm, René bent his head and inhaled. Smiling, he tenderly kissed the exposed skin above her glove, then gazed into her eyes. "C'est charmant. My favorite flower. Like you."

Lucinda smiled demurely, withdrew her hand, and looked down at his drawings again. "Shall we look at your sketches now?"

René suppressed his passion once more. "Oui."

As she browsed through the drawings, he watched her. Finally, he got up the courage to ask her his question. "There is a magic lantern show in Norwood. Would you like to go with me?" They looked at each other. "Mary can come too if you think you should have a chaperone."

Lucinda laughed, a golden sound to his ears. "Mary fears everything including shadows. I'm certain that we would have to drag her along."

"We? So, you will go?"

She placed her hand over his. "On two conditions."

Chapter 23:

PROPHECY

René had agreed to Lucinda's terms. She would go with him to the picture show, with Mr. Stoddard to chaperone, if he would attend the upcoming ball with her. Now here she was, in the carriage, ready to go to Norwood. Lucinda pulled the hem of her navy-blue dress close to the cabriolet seat so René could take his place opposite her and not tread on it. After climbing inside, he sat down and smiled at her. A thrill went through her.

Returning his smile, she asked, "So what is this show about?"

"I heard it was about exotic lands and there are sound effects. I hope it doesn't scare you."

"Not if you are with me."

The ride passed quickly as she alternately looked at him and out the window. When they arrived in Norwood, he exited the carriage first and then helped her disembark, tenderly enfolding her hand as she stepped out. Lucinda then reluctantly let go.

As they entered the lobby, she read the placard for the show: "Cleopatra's Phantasmagoria."

"Is this about Egypt?" she asked apprehensively.

"It seems, perhaps. Do you want to leave?"

No, I must face my fears. Lucinda jutted out her chin resolutely. "I'll be alright. Shall we find some seats?"

When all the patrons were seated, the lights were extinguished. The show started in complete darkness with a startling sound effect of thunder ending with a clash of cymbals. A booming voice began narrating about the wonders of Cleopatra's time. A hidden band began to play Arabic music as moving slides with pictures and photos of ancient Egypt appeared. Brightly colored and animated, the thrilling show was punctuated with more eerie sound effects and voices. The tempo and volume of the music increased as an animated snake crawled up Cleopatra's listless body. After her suicide, amid little shrieks from the women present, demons, skeletons and phantom caricatures were shown, making Lucinda's heart race. But when Cleopatra's gauzy soul was transported by the devils to her tomb, Lucinda squeezed her eyes shut to keep her panic at bay.

Over the horrible screeching and howling accompanying the animated fiends on the screen, she heard René's concerned voice in her ear. "Do you want to go?"

She looked at him and nodded. Luckily, they were in aisle seats and could exit quickly. René searched the street for the carriage with Mr. Stoddard and Willy and flagged them over as he supported Lucinda. Mr. Stoddard jumped down and rushed towards her. "Miss Haliburton, what's wrong?"

"The show was too much," René told him.

"Let's get you home, Miss."

But Lucinda didn't want to spoil the evening and she wasn't ready for it to end. "No. I'm fine."

Three worried faces looked back at her. "Are you sure?" asked René.

She nodded. "The sounds, they were too loud."

Willy made a suggestion. "The tea garden at the bottom of the hill has been staying open late for the post-show crowd."

Mr. Stoddard turned to Lucinda. "Does a cup of tea sound good to you, Miss Haliburton?"

"It's a splendid idea." She looked at René. "Do you mind?"

"Non, not at all."

While René and Lucinda went inside the tearoom, Mr. Stoddard and Willy remained with the coach. The couple found an empty table by the window and ordered some tea and biscuits. As Lucinda sipped her drink, René apologized to her. "Forgive me for inviting you to that show."

"Don't worry about it. I am feeling much improved. This place is better anyway." She smiled at him and then nibbled on a biscuit. After delicately patting her lips, she sipped some more tea.

Lucinda felt his eyes on her as she set the teacup in its saucer. Her bare hand lingered on the tabletop and he slid his over it. "Even pale, ma chérie, you are so beautiful."

Color rose to her cheeks, but she made no effort to pull her hand away. "I'm looking forward to the dance, aren't you?"

"Oui, I have been dreaming of dancing with you."

Lucinda smiled shyly and turned her head away. She gazed across the room for a few moments and then looked back at him. Leaning forward, she said softly, "There is a woman over there, she is staring at you." Lucinda glanced at the woman again, then said with surprise, "She's coming this way."

René looked over, and his jaw dropped. The lady, dressed in a belted caftan made of dark green velvet and gold trim, walked towards him. He jumped up and crossed over to her. "Bonsoir, M. Lalique." Extending her hand, he kissed the top of it. She spoke to him in rapid French and Lucinda understood snippets. "You are looking well. Returning to Paris, the bookstore, I heard about Ambrose, so sad, the loss of our friend." She patted his hand. "A coincidence to meet again." Looking over at Lucinda, she said in English, "Please introduce me to your friend."

"Oui." René guided her over to the table. "Madame Sphinx, this is Miss Haliburton. Miss Haliburton, this is Madame Sphinx."

Mme. Sphinx nodded to Lucinda. "Hello, Miss Haliburton. Nice to meet you."

"Nice to meet you."

"How do you know each other?" Mme. Sphinx asked her.

"Mr. Lalique is our lodger. Our estate is near the Crystal Palace where he studies art."

"Oh, yes," she said before turning to René, "when I asked about you, they said that you had gone to England. To study drawing and industry and become a great artist."

René put his hand on a chair. "Would you like to sit down?"

Mme. Sphinx checked the gold and enameled watch hanging from her chatelaine. "Merci, but I have to go to work. The show lets out soon and my customers will be here." She pointed to a nearby curtained doorway and explained to Lucinda, "I am an oracle. I read the cards." Mme. Sphinx turned to René. "Another day, perhaps? We could meet at the Crystal Palace. Contact me through the shop owner."

RENÉ WAS SITTING ON THE terraced steps of the Crystal Palace between the two giant, red masonry sphinxes that flanked the stairs. He had agreed to meet Lucinda here. When he had told her that he was meeting Mme. Sphinx for a card reading, Lucinda said that she wanted to do it, too. Nervously tapping his pencil on his drawing book, René hoped the cards would be favorable.

He readjusted himself on his stone seat and then continued to sketch one of the sphinxes. Then he drew Lucinda's sleeping form at the base of it. Adding stars in the sky, he titled the picture *Dreaming of the Stars*. He admired the drawing and then flipped the page to begin on another, a tiny illustration of her nude. Imagining Lucinda's naked curves evoked memories of her fragrance and the perfume bottle he had given her. This memory gave him the idea to surround her miniature body with the outline of a bottle. Then he drew a large stopper with a spray of lilies of the valley on it. Pleased with his effort, he smiled as he labeled it too: *Bouteille de Muguet*

"You are always drawing," he heard a voice say.

René looked up to see Lucinda standing before him. He stood up quickly. "Bonjour."

"And you are smiling. You must like what you did. Can I see?"

"Oui." He handed her the drawing book and watched as she perused it.

Lucinda nodded. "That is a lovely bottle. The stopper is so unique. It reminds me of my perfume." Bringing the drawing closer, she scrutinized the small figure and blushed. "Your picture is very . . . sensual," she said and handed back the book. "I would love to have a perfume bottle with that design."

He tore the page out and gave it to her. "Thank you," she said, placing it in her purse. "Shall we go find your friend?"

Remembering her fright from the other night, he searched her eyes. "Are you sure?"

"Of course. Don't be silly." She looked at the face of the nearby stone sphinx. "I can manage."

"Sûrement." René put his drawing supplies back in his satchel. "She is waiting for us at my lecture room. Since it is the weekend, no one will be there." He led the way, climbing the stone steps and following the wide gravel pathway to one of the outlying brick buildings. Mme. Sphinx was leaning against the handrail of the stairs leading to the entrance. She wore an attractive and modest gray silk walking dress. On her head was a teardrop hat of matching fabric decorated with feathers. They greeted her and went inside.

Once in the classroom, they sat at a table next to the windows, René and Lucinda on one side and Mme. Sphinx on the other. "Shall we start?" she asked.

She held a deck of cards. "I will read three cards for you. Your personal cards and a third, your dual card." Shuffling the deck, Mme. Sphinx then fanned the cards out face down on the table. "Choose one card each with your left hand, and place it in front of you, still face down." They did as she asked. Then she scooped up the cards and shuffled them again. Finally, she took the card from the top of the deck and placed it in the middle above their cards. Closing her eyes, she took a few deep breaths then opened her eyes again. "I call this layout the relationship triangle. Do you see the pyramid of power?" Pointing to their individual cards, she asked, "Do you see how your cards form the basis of your involvement?" Then she pointed to the dual card. "This one is the intersection. It represents the situation in its entirety, including outside influences." Mme. Sphinx looked at Lucinda. "I will read yours first," she said and turned over Lucinda's card.

"The Weighing of the Heart Ceremony card." Lucinda's eyes grew wide at the picture of Anubis kneeling between the scales that held a feather and a heart. "The jackal god is here to examine your heart." Noticing Lucinda's expression, Mme. Sphinx explained. "He weighs it against the feather of Maat, the goddess of truth and harmony. When this card comes up, it means your heart is unbalanced. I sense conflict in you. To find your truth, call on Anubis."

At the name "Anubis," René realized that Lucinda was trembling. He wondered if he should stop the reading. But Lucinda had said she could manage.

Mme. Sphinx reached over and turned René's card face up. "An auspicious card, the Black Scarab. It is the card of potential, prosperity, creation. The black color signals the unknown, the cosmos. A portal is being opened to you and all you must do is have the courage to step through it."

She smiled at him. "The black scarab will protect you from chaos." Then she turned over the last card. "The Three of Fire.

Hmmm, interesting . . . Traditionally, this card signifies business and commerce." The seer paused and then said, "Let me see if the story will reveal itself to me." Closing her eyes again, she leaned back in her chair.

René took this chance to study the card's picture and was surprised to see Anubis again. The jackal god was standing between two scepters. Holding a third, he looked at the water where, in the distance, a felucca boat was sailing away. René returned his gaze to Mme. Sphinx. A brief shudder went through her body and then she started talking, the tone of her voice different. "You are standing on a cliff looking out. Is there something better out there? Your eyes wander, searching the horizon for something new. Waiting for a response. There has been a separation. A long-distance relationship? Connected by dreams?"

Mme. Sphinx grew quiet for a few moments and began again. "There are plans to travel. Going to a different country perhaps? I see only the back of Anubis. Have you turned your back on someone? There are three staffs of power present, a love triangle." She took a deep breath. "The one you are holding is afire. A blaze of passion but there is a blanket of smoke. Someone is emerging from the cloud of gray. A woman. The one who answers. If you call to her, she will help you see beyond the gloom." The seer fell silent again for a few moments. "A name is being whispered. Sally . . . no. Ara . . . Clara? No. Sarah . . . Yes. Sarah."

Who is Sarah? René wondered. *I don't understand.*

Mme. Sphinx opened her eyes and glanced at him before turning her attention to Lucinda. Looking worried, she asked, "Miss Haliburton, are you okay?"

René followed her gaze. Lucinda's face was ashen.

Chapter 24:

TWO PATHS

Her grandfather surveyed the view of the estate from his wheelchair on the bedroom balcony. "You seem happier and have rosier cheeks. I've heard that you have been going out for a walk every day."

Sitting close by, Lucinda finished passing the dark green thread through her needle before answering. "Yes. I have." She considered telling him that she was falling in love, but she didn't dare reveal what she had been doing in secret. Even innocently, she was in the woods, unchaperoned, with a man. *Grandfather wouldn't approve. He wouldn't understand.*

"Where do you go?"

"Oh, through the woods, around the estate, down to see the horses."

"I see," he said. "I've thought about visiting Mr. Stoddard and the horses. Is he taking good care of them?"

"Oh, yes."

He craned his neck to look at her embroidery hoop. "So, what are you sewing? May I see?"

"Of course, Grandfather." She handed him the hoop with her handkerchief secured inside. Lucinda had copied one of René's bluebell designs onto it. She had finished with the blossoms of indigo and had started on the stems.

Her grandfather nodded with approval. "Your work is

beautiful. You inherited your grandmother's sewing capability." He handed the hoop back to her.

"Thank you." Lucinda felt a sly smile cross her face. *If he only knew who the artist was.* Picking up her needle, she continued stitching.

"You know, your mother never did learn how to do it properly." Her grandfather frowned but then closed his eyes and smiled. "Your Grandmother Annabel loved to sew and tat. She made lace collars for her dresses, doilies, and covers for everything. I loved watching her. It was so calming. For both of us." Opening his eyes, he pointed to the cover on Lucinda's footstool. "Even that."

Noticing that he was becoming downcast, Lucinda tried to steer the conversation in a different direction. "The sunshine and blue sky are lovely, don't you think?"

"Yes. It's a good day for a drive in the country."

"Would you like me to have Mr. Stoddard ready the carriage?"

"Perhaps." He gave her a small grin. "How is that temperamental barn cat of yours?"

"He's fine." Now was her chance. "You know Sekhmet likes people who don't chase him. He met the new tenant at the stables and sat next to him. Even let him pet him." She smiled at her grandfather.

The baron cleared his throat. "About that. Roderick mentioned that he had seen you with that boy. That you had gone with him to the Crystal Palace unchaperoned and had returned appearing disturbed. I don't think this type of activity is prudent, wise or proper for a young lady."

"Is Uncle Roderick spying on me now?" Lucinda retorted. "And what does he care? He hates me. I overheard him and Miss Meadows talking about me. She said I was defective and that they would be lucky to get me betrothed."

"Uncle Roderick does not hate you and *Lady* Haliburton doesn't know her place. She says inappropriate things. I don't know what possessed my children to marry who they did." He softened his tone. "But I would like to see *you* married. I would spare no expense; your wedding would be a grand affair. A reason for me to see everybody before I die."

Lucinda put down her hoop and touched his forearm. "Please don't talk like that, Grandfather. You know it upsets me." She tilted her head toward the teapot on the low table beside them. "Would you like some more tea?"

"Yes, please." Her grandfather watched as she filled his teacup and then set down the pot. "I know a man who would take care of my dear Lucie." Sipping his tea, he searched her eyes. "So I could go in peace."

She looked out over the balcony. "You mean Dr. Charles."

"Yes."

"But I don't love him, Grandfather. He's a friend."

"There are worse things than marrying a friend who cares for you. Besides, you might find that you fall in love with him over time."

"But his care . . . He gives me medication that makes me sleepy. He makes me feel like I am . . . dead." Lucinda sighed. It was no use keeping her feelings secret. She had to tell him about René and her plans. "I want to feel alive, Grandfather. You have noticed that I am looking healthier. It's not because of Dr. Charles. It's because of the tenant. His name is René Lalique and he is an artist. I'm in love with him."

Her grandfather's pallid face became paler. "An artist? Oh no." Visibly upset, he began to shakily place his teacup on the saucer.

Lucinda knew that he was thinking of Alexander. "He's not my father."

"I don't think so, Lucie . . ." The baron's unsteady hand nearly dropped the cup, causing a jarring clatter.

Lucinda shot out of her chair. Letting out an exasperated huff, she strode to the railing. *Everyone is always telling me what to do. Do they think I am an idiot? Crazy?* She turned to her grandfather. Unwilling to openly disobey, she tried reasoning with him. "I know that you think you know what is best for me, Grandfather, but . . ."

He put his hand up to stop her. "You are young and inexperienced, Lucie. I just don't want to see you hurt again. I don't think that you should continue down this pathway. Artists are fickle and unreliable. And he is French. We know how unstable *they* are."

"That's not fair!" Lucinda exclaimed. "You don't even know him." She began to pace, trying to control the rising fire within. "He's a gentleman. Polite, attentive and chivalrous. He adores me, and he truly cares. I am not an experiment to him." Her voice became more strident. "Something aberrant to study and analyze. Something to drug into oblivion. Something to condemn. A monstrosity to control. Like . . . a . . . a freak of nature!" She stood with her hands on her hips and stared at her grandfather. Defying him to contradict her.

He sat forward, but instead of being combative, his face was filled with anguish. "There's no need to get all worked up," he said, his voice soft and soothing. "Come here, my dear Lucie, please." At that moment, Lucinda truly gauged his frailty: translucent skin, tired expression, withering body. His looming death. Her anger abated, she complied. Placing her footstool next to his wheelchair, she laid her head on the blanket covering his lap. "You know that I love you more than anyone on earth," he said, "and I want to see you happy. But I must insist that the boy court you in the proper fashion. Would you deny an old man his happiness?"

She looked up at him. "Of course not, Grandfather." Then, taking a deep breath, she made her proposal. "I thought that we, René and I, could attend the ball hosted by Lord Home together. Aren't Uncle Roderick and Miss Meadows going? They could chaperone us."

The baron sighed with resignation. "That's one solution."

Chapter 25:

HOUSE OF ETERNITY

B oarding the train, René found a window seat. His visit to
London, with its hustle and bustle, made him miss Paris.
While the English countryside had been idyllic and inspi-
rational, two years was a long time to be away from home. As
the train pulled out of the station, he glanced at the packages
on his lap. He had gone to Harrod's to pick up a new white
cravat and shoe polish for the upcoming ball. *I want to look my
best,* he thought. *This is my first time with Lucinda in public
in her social circle.* René gazed out the window at the passing
landscape and pondered the beautiful heiress.

Part of her allure was that she was mysterious, but her
unpredictability was unnerving. One minute she seemed normal;
the next, he didn't know who she was. At the end of the session
with Mme. Sphinx, Lucinda had appeared pale and in a trance.
Then she departed abruptly without a word. René had had to
apologize to the seer for Lucinda's odd behavior. *Still, I cannot
get her out of my mind.*

His mind wandered back to the reading. *Who is this mysterious Sarah? How is she important to me and Lucinda?* Unable
to answer these questions, he considered the other card: the
Black Scarab. René had been excited to hear that his future contained traveling, prosperity, creation; everything he dreamed of

doing. Selling his jewelry to the world and becoming rich and famous. However, he did not like the idea of a love triangle. Obviously, his rival was Dr. Perkins. René's jealousy flared as he thought of Lucinda and her psychiatrist together. From what Mary had said, the doctor was in love with his patient. Defiantly, René thought, *Elle est mon coeur, ma petite amie.* His heart belonged to her. She was his sweetheart, not Dr. Charles's girl. *I will take her away from him.*

Still gazing out the train window, René reconsidered his destination. He would get off the train at the Norwood station, return to the tearoom and see Mme. Sphinx. Alone this time. He needed to ask her more questions about Lucinda. And Sarah, whoever she was.

"SHE'S NOT HERE?" RENÉ ASKED the proprietor of the tearoom. "When will she return?"

"She won't be back."

"What do you mean?"

"Exactly what I said. She won't be back." He wiped down the countertop. "Maybe she went back to the Continent."

"Why did she leave?"

The proprietor shook his head. "I guess she said something that somebody didn't like. They complained to the police. The constable and his officer came round. They spoke to her and her friends. Then they left." He returned to his cleaning. "I stayed out of it."

René speculated about what had happened. The police had most likely threatened her or even roughed up the foreigners to get them to leave. He quietly cursed in French.

The proprietor looked a little surprised, then studied René's face before pulling out an envelope from under the counter. After checking the writing on the front, he asked René, "Are you M. Lalique?"

"Yes."

"She left this for you."

René took the envelope from him. "Merci," he said and left.

RENÉ SITUATED HIMSELF IN THE orange chair by the window and opened Mme. Sphinx's letter.

Dear Monsieur Lalique,

Please forgive my hasty departure. I was given no choice. I regret being unable to contact you and that we would not see each other. I am confident that the owner of the tea shop will keep his promise and deliver this letter to you. I wanted to let you know that I enjoyed seeing you again and to tell you of something else.

After the reading with you and Lucinda, I had a dream that night. In it, I was holding the perfume bottle that you gave me, and we were together on the steps of the Crystal Palace. You were reluctant to walk inside, into the Egyptian court. Then we were in France sitting at my reading table with Lucinda looking at the Two of Scrolls. You said to me: I know that card. I have lived it before.

When I awoke, I remembered the séance. I had pulled that card before with you and Ambrose. I con-templated the meaning of it, my dreams and vision. The Crystal Palace and Lucinda are your destiny, but are there two stories here? Two paths that cross? Lucinda lives in between two worlds and the jackal-headed god surrounds her. Anubis is the Opener of the Way, toward the Heart but Death as well. You are clearly enamored of her; the flame of love burns brightly in your eyes. Don't get caught in the fire.

The Black Scarab calls to you to be loyal to your creativity. Do not be afraid to enter the Temple of Glass. It is your House of Eternity.

Yours faithfully,
Mme. Sphinx

René folded the letter and set it on the table. Shortly, there was a knock on his door. Answering it, he found Mary standing there.

"Good afternoon, sir," she said. "My mistress has sent me with a message. She would like to meet you at the garden fountain in half an hour. Shall I say that you will be there?"

He nodded. "Thank you."

Mary gave a little curtsy and excused herself. René watched the maid make her way back up the pathway to the mansion and then checked his pocket watch. He wondered why Lucinda had changed their daily routine.

When he arrived at the garden, Lucinda and Mary were already there. The maid was sitting on the nearby bench sewing, and Lucinda was standing close to the fountain. Watching the water cascade over the lip of the bowl and into the basin, she had a faraway look on her face.

René walked over and stood next to her. "Bonjour."

Lucinda looked at him with a vague expression. "Hello," she replied and then turned back to the water. After an awkward silence, she spoke again. "I used to be with him amongst the flowers in my garden, my courtyard. We, too, met in secret. He called me his lily of the valley. He said that no one was more beautiful than I."

Perplexed, René asked, "Who, Dr. Charles?"

Lucinda continued to look at and listen to the flowing water. "It was so long ago. So very long ago." She shook her head. "I just don't understand. Why? Why all the lies? The deception. But the very worst was he left me." Lucinda turned to René. "Why did he leave me to decay in the desert?"

"Decay? My English. I don't understand."

"No, you wouldn't." Suddenly, Lucinda seemed to be back to normal. "But it doesn't matter now." She grasped his hands. "You have found me and brought me back to life." She looked over at Mary, who was still focused on her sewing.

Lucinda leaned in and whispered, "Promise me that you won't ever lie to me, René. I must know what's in your heart."

He didn't know what she meant, but she was so earnest, he made a commitment he knew would be hard to keep. "I promise."

Smiling, she said, "I have told my grandfather about us. The baron is anxious to meet you."

"D'accord," he agreed.

"He did stipulate one thing. We can no longer meet alone in the woods. He said it was improper." She frowned a little, and then her face brightened. "But you can come now and we will meet him in the Egyptian room. He wants to visit his ancient relics."

René didn't like this idea, but kept silent as he followed her and Mary inside.

When they arrived at the Egyptian room, it looked different. The curtains and windows had been opened wide. A mild breeze and sunshine were streaming in. It wasn't warm but still pleasant. Mary went to fetch the baron, leaving René and Lucinda alone. They walked over to the glass case.

Lucinda pointed to a scarab with metal wings. "Isn't that beautiful? Such fine work. Look at the wings."

René studied the detailed cloisonné feathers. "Oui, it is beautiful."

"It's an amulet that was placed over the heart. The ancient Egyptians believed that the scarab was the protector of the heart. They thought by wearing scarab charms, they would have long lives."

"How do you know so much?"

"I remember . . . I mean, I read about it. Come here." Lucinda led him to the bookcase. "As you can see, my grandfather has an enormous collection of books." She picked one out and opened it to a page. "This book is about the gods and goddesses. Here is Hathor, the cow goddess. See her horned headdress?" She turned to another page. "And here is Nephthys. She was considered the friend of the dead." Closing the book, she asked, "Would you like to borrow it?"

"Oui, merci."

Lucinda handed the book to him. "I know you like jewelry, but would you like to look around at the other things?"

"Oui."

She led him over to a tall glass case. "There we are for all eternity."

René glanced at Lucinda. She was staring at the objects in the case. He recalled what M. Stoddard had said about Lucinda making up stories about ancient Egypt. As if she had been there. Did he mean existing in another time? Like a past life? *Non,* he thought, *impossible.* These notions were just fantasies, her imagination gone wild. He studied her until she turned to him.

As their eyes locked, he felt pulled in by her.

"I know you can't remember, but I do." Lucinda glanced at the doorway and the spell was broken. Placing her hands on his shoulders, she whispered, "I have a secret that you must keep. Can I trust you?"

"Oui."

"Dr. Charles is drugging me. He says it is necessary, but the medicine makes me drowsy. I feel like I am sleepwalking, in a dream all the time. When I met you, I wanted to feel alive again, so I stopped taking it. I pretend to drink the tea but throw it out when Mary isn't watching."

René just looked at her. *I know you're being drugged, but he's your doctor. Is it wise to go against his recommendations?* When Mary appeared in the doorway, Lucinda dropped her hands.

Without coming into the room, the maid spoke first to René. "The baron is ill. He regrets that he will be unable to join you. Perhaps another day." Then she gestured for Lucinda to come over to her. In a hushed tone, she said, "Milady, the baron's manservant told me that he had a horrible coughing spell and your uncle sent for Dr. Perkins. Your grandfather is asking for you. Perhaps you should go to him."

Lucinda looked at René. "Will you excuse me? But I would like you to stay. I won't be too long." She glanced at the maid and then back at him. "Mary told me that you wanted to draw some of the jewelry pieces. Do you have your sketchbook?"

He patted his coat pocket. "Oui."

"Good. You can design a piece of jewelry for me." She smiled broadly at him. "Look around while you wait. Maybe you will get some inspiration."

René watched Lucinda and Mary go and then walked over to the jewelry case. Placing the Egyptian book on one of the glass panels, he took out his drawing pad and quickly copied some of the jewels and amulets in the case. As he was drawing, he felt eyes on him and glanced around. Nobody. René continued sketching but, again, felt someone was there. Watching him. Turning, he saw the statue of Anubis in the corner. An involuntary shiver overcame René as he focused on its golden eyes glinting in the light. *It's just my imagination.* Too distracted to draw, he laid his sketchbook on top of the Egyptian book.

Scanning the room once more, he spotted the sarcophagus and made his way to it. It was different from the sarcophagi that he had seen in the Louvre. It was not stone or shaped wood with a painted face. Instead, it was a plain wooden rectangular box with only some hieroglyphs painted on the top. Fascinated, he wondered what the interior looked like. What if he just peeked inside for a moment? René glanced at the empty doorway, then shifted the lid. He carefully balanced it on the lip of the coffin before peering inside. There were hundreds of painted eyes.

"You must be the Frenchman whom Lord Haliburton has spoken of."

Startled, René lost his grip and the lid fell, making a racket as it thumped onto the Persian rug. A tall, older Englishman stood in the doorway. René noted his serious expression and clipped, neatly parted, straight blond hair.

Ignoring the coffin lid on the floor, the man said, "I am Dr. Charles Perkins and Miss Haliburton is my patient."

Chapter 26:

INSANITY

Dr. Charles joined René at the side of the sarcophagus. Sidestepping the fallen lid, he examined the inside of the open casket. "That's rather eerie with all those eyes looking at one. Good thing the person is deceased before going in it." He looked at René with a poker face.

René was unsure if the physician was joking, so he gave him a half-hearted smirk. Then he extended his hand and introduced himself. "Bonjour, I am René Lalique." As they shook hands, he added, "A friend of Miss Haliburton."

"So, I've heard." Dr. Charles released his hand and looked him over. "I have also heard that you are an artist and studying at the Crystal Palace."

"Oui."

"I heard that most classes there are for women." The doctor's smile looked more like a sneer. "So, what are your professional goals?"

What? Why does he want to know that? René thought irritably. "I am an illustrator. I want to design jewelry."

Dr. Charles stroked his clean-shaven chin. "Hmmm . . . A jewelry designer? Will that be a lucrative profession for you?"

His brows furrowing, René answered tentatively. "Yes. I

was an apprentice for La Maison Aucoc in Paris. Renowned goldsmiths."

"I see," the doctor replied dismissively with a wave of his hand. "Oh well, I haven't kept abreast of the latest fashions. Baubles, frippery and what-not." He walked towards the bookshelves. "You see, when I was your age, I was busy mastering the books in medical school and working beside my father in the infirmary for sick children. Lately, I have been employed in the burgeoning field of psychiatry. I work with those of unsound mind." Dr. Charles considered the books, then turned to face René. "Discipline is the key. I have a dignified profession and I take it seriously."

René tried to interrupt, but the doctor went on. "You do know that mental illness is a grave problem, don't you?"

"Oui, Doctor."

"Mary told me that you know about Miss Haliburton's plight. I have done a great deal of analysis regarding her condition. Due to a head injury, her brain is no longer healthy. She has seizures and memory loss triggered by emotional issues. Therefore, I must administer medications to her. To keep her calm. Do you understand?"

"Oui."

"Under no circumstance can she get overly excited. Is this clear?"

"Oui."

"Good." With a smug smile, the doctor walked to the tall glass cabinet and surveyed the items. "Her father was an artist. Did she tell you that?"

"Non."

Dr. Charles looked over in surprise. "She didn't? What has she told you about her trip to Egypt?"

"That she doesn't remember anything."

Nodding, the doctor continued his interrogation. "Mary also told me that you have been spending a lot of time with Miss Haliburton. What do you do?"

René purposely omitted details. "I draw while she talks about books. She is very well-read. Mythology, art, history. She likes to hear me read French poetry."

The doctor snorted. "Have you talked about her family history of mental illness? Her parent's estrangement? The photographer, Mitch Grant? Her health problems?"

Every question Dr. Charles posed was met with a silent shake of René's head.

He watched as the doctor began to pace. Glaring at René, he asked, "What personal information has she told you?"

"She cares a great deal for her grandfather and her orange cat."

A frown crossed Dr. Charles's face. "Oh, yes. That ill-tempered beast. He scratches; drew blood once. He belongs in the barn."

Amused, René suppressed a chuckle. Sekhmet was clever: he didn't like Lucinda's doctor either. To further goad him, René remained silent.

Dr. Charles strutted to the windows and surveyed the view. "Miss Haliburton was blind and incapacitated when she first returned to England and had to be admitted to an asylum. She alternated between catatonia and hysteria and was obsessed with Egypt. Particularly fixated on their ancient religion, she was having delusions about seeing spirits." He looked at René. "But with my treatments, including walking in nature, I was able to relieve some of her anxiety and mania. She has become docile and compliant. Miss Haliburton has responded nicely to her medications. No more fits, nor does she fall into trances and see those phantasms anymore." His chest puffed up, and looking out the window, Dr. Charles smiled broadly and ignored his companion.

You are a pompous ass and mistaken, René disparaged. *Your patient is not compliant, not taking her medicine, and still hallucinating. I should tell him that less than fifteen minutes ago, she was in a trance.* Instead, he kept quiet as he had promised her.

Dr. Charles finally turned back to him. "Because of my care, she has a better life. Therefore, she must adhere to my regimen. Her condition must be controlled and monitored. I am not sure of your influence on her, but I do know that she needs to avoid being in this ghastly room. As her friend, you should encourage her not to spend time here." The doctor paused to scan the space. "These primitive objects only remind her of her morbid past."

He fastened his eyes on René. "Her uncle, Roderick, told me about the incident in Egypt. Alexander, Lucinda's father, had been banished from the archaeologist's house. He returned uninvited and was arguing with Dr. Merimee. When Lucinda heard them, she was so upset that she stacked up a few combustible antiquities on top of the papyri artifacts and tomb drawings and set them afire. Then went back to bed as if nothing happened." Dr. Charles looked down. "I feel somewhat responsible as this all happened after they—she and her father—had read a letter I sent to Roderick regarding her mother's incarceration in the asylum at my behest."

He shook his head. "People were killed in the fire. Lucky for Lucinda, her uncle rescued her after she got hit in the head with a falling beam. The servant's dog was nearby and was killed by it. Apparently, she had bonded with the dog. When she came to and found out it was dead, she became hysterical, claiming she was Sekhmet, an Egyptian warrior goddess, and screaming about drinking people's blood like beer." He sighed. "Unfortunately, she had to be . . . restrained." Dr. Charles fell quiet for a moment. "Thank goodness the Egyptian officials were inclined towards getting her out of their country."

His gaze landed on René's open drawing pad. Without asking for permission, the doctor picked it up and skimmed through it. "Interesting doodling." Then he stopped on one page, his eyes widening. "Rather risqué." He closed the book, set it down and looked at René. "When will you return to France to pursue your career?"

"I will finish my classes, though I haven't really considered . . ."

"You know, Lucinda is a sensitive person. And as you said yourself, very devoted to her grandfather. I would hate to see her get attached or sentimental about you and then have you leave her. Returning to Paris and women's fashions." He glanced at the notebook and rolled his eyes. "It could potentially provoke another . . . event. You wouldn't want that, would you?" He didn't wait for an answer. "It is best that you not allow yourself to become too familiar with her. In fact, the best course of treatment would be to distance yourself from her altogether. Gradually, of course. Let her down easily. Let her get used to the idea that she is not in your future. That she is not important to you."

"But she *is* important to me."

"Perhaps you think so. Do you know how much effort goes into making a career? Especially one in art? Jewelry design? I don't think so." He let out a brief, derisive snort. "I know there are those who *believe* they have talent and can make a living at it. They are a dime a dozen. You are young and inexperienced, my boy, but you will learn. Do you think you can build your career from the ground up and take care of a helpless, crazy English girl? In a foreign land no less."

The doctor's condescending tone was too much and René responded angrily. "She is not crazy, she is . . . imaginative."

Dr. Charles chortled. "What a fanciful notion. Tsk, tsk, my boy. You can't even control your own anger. I highly doubt that you could control hers. Should you two disagree, that is."

René snapped. "You think you know everything about her, but you don't even know how she thinks, much less what she feels."

The doctor bristled. "I know more about her than you do. I have worked with the insane for years. Have you ever been to the madhouse?"

"Non."

"Case in point."

"Yes, that's right. A case. That's all she is to you. Another patient. A girl. Not a woman. You're not worthy of her."

Dr. Charles took a step forward and hissed at him. "How dare you . . ."

The sound of voices stopped him. The men looked over to see Lucinda in the doorway.

"Dr. Charles, I thought you were leaving." Lucinda looked from one to the other as she walked into the room with Mary, who was holding the doctor's hat.

"I am now," he replied. He took his bowler from Mary.

"I see you have met M. Lalique."

"Yes, my dear, I have." Dr. Charles nodded at her before placing his hat on his head. "I will return tomorrow to check on you and Lord Haliburton." Throwing a cursory glance at René, he said tersely, "Good day to you, sir." Without waiting for a reply, he turned on his heel and left the room. Mary trailed after him.

"Is something wrong?" Lucinda asked René.

"Non."

"Did you two have a disagreement?"

René resisted the impulse to tell her that Dr. Charles was possessive, controlling and trying to isolate her from others. Specifically, him. Instead, he said, "I don't like him. He is very arrogant."

While René was speaking, Lucinda had noticed the sarcophagus lid on the floor. "What happened here?"

"Oh, I'm sorry. It was an accident. I wanted to look inside. I lost my hold and it fell." He bent down to pick it up. "Let us put it back."

"No. Leave it."

René straightened and turned to her. Once again, the faraway look was in her eyes. *Maybe the doctor and Mary are right. The effect of this room is bizarre.* He glanced again into the sarcophagus; the eyes of the casket were staring back. Looking away quickly, he consulted his pocket watch. "It's time for me to go. I told the jolly fellows that I would meet them. We are working on our final projects."

Lucinda frowned. "Please don't listen to Dr. Charles. He is trying to keep me trapped." Taking René's hand, she led him to the partitioned glass case, opened one of the compartments, and picked up the blue perfume bottle with the ibis head. "The god of magic will help you." Pulling the stopper out, she told him, "Smell it and you will remember."

Before he could stop her, Lucinda dabbed the oil on his forehead between his eyes. The fragrance was intoxicating. Where had he smelled it before? Misty feelings of longing arose in him. He closed his eyes and listened as she spoke.

"I saw you in the bushes that day. I saw your look of adoration. I knew in my heart that you loved the divinity in me. I was not just a girl; I was a goddess. I knew you would return and free me one day."

A vision came to his mind's eye: A naked girl with a halo of golden light around her. René opened his eyes to gaze at the beauty before him, his heart aflame with desire.

Lucinda touched his face tenderly. "I love you. Don't you care for me?"

"Oui, I do, but . . ."

She traced his lips with her finger. "Shhh, no buts. We must believe in each other." As she leaned toward him, her touch and the smell of the perfume overwhelmed him. René could not resist. He drew her into his arms, and they exchanged an impassioned kiss. And then another and another.

Chapter 27:

THE CASKET OF NEPHTHYS

Looking in the oval mirror, she admired her face and smiled. Her weary look and pallid complexion had disappeared. Lucinda hadn't felt this way in a long time: pretty and brimming with delight. Everything was looking up. Her memory was better, she felt less sluggish, but most of all, René reciprocated her love. He had given her a renewed sense of purpose, a reason to live. She glanced down at his sketch on her dressing table. Labeled *Muguet et Jacinthes des Bois*, he had drawn lily of the valley and bluebells intertwined. Their favorite flowers embracing as they had in the Egyptian room. She felt her face flush with desire. To dampen her lust, Lucinda refocused on looking for her plain handkerchiefs to embroider René's design onto them.

She had already looked in the drawers of the furniture in her bedroom; the closet was next. After a few minutes, in the corner, she found something covered. Drawing back the blanket, she exhaled sharply. Her traveling trunk. It instantly reminded her of the trip to Egypt and Mitch. The time spent in the darkroom with him. Then more repressed memories surfaced. She had hidden things in it, her diary specifically. She laid the blanket to one side and kneeled in front of the trunk.

With some trepidation, Lucinda lifted the lid and discovered that everything was intact. With nothing out of place, in the drawer with the secret compartment, were her clothes neatly folded. She pushed them aside to expose the false panel. Removing it, she released the hidden latch and lifted open the concealed tray. There lay the stone frog, her diary, and the blue perfume bottle covered with the handkerchief. Lucinda removed the fragrant handkerchief and mindlessly stuffed it into her skirt pocket. Uncorking the bottle, she brought it to her nose and inhaled. A flashback flooded her mind: the Egyptian vendor, the shop, boldly kissing Mitch there, that night, the arguing, his deception . . .

No! Her hand shaking, Lucinda replaced the stopper. *I can't remember, I don't want to remember . . .* Starting to black out, she gripped the side of the trunk but lost her balance and fell to one side. She sat there for a few minutes and then stared again blankly at the secret items. Instinctively reaching for the frog, Lucinda took it in her hand. Turning it over, she read the tiny carved hieroglyphs: heka. Egyptian magic. "Mitch," she whispered softly and closed her fingers over the small statue as tears welled in her eyes. Her diary; the answers would be there. *But not today,* she decided, and replaced the frog. Weakly pushing the clothes over, she closed the lid of the trunk, threw the blanket over it, curled up on the floor, and closed her eyes.

But her mind would not be silenced. Recollections of the peasant peddler and his horrifying mummies and disgusting smells. Waking up to find her trunk gone, taken away. That horrible nightmare about finding the child corpse in it. Realizing it was herself in the trunk; she was the mummy with a hole in her chest. Lucinda began to tremble and could not stop. A voice was speaking to her. "Lily of the valley, lily of the valley, lily of the valley." The tremors increased.

"Miss Haliburton! What's wrong?" Mary's voice called. She felt the maid's hands on her, holding her, trying to stop the shaking. "Miss Haliburton, wake up, please," she pleaded. Mary kept her hands on her until the voice and quaking finally ceased. Lucinda opened her eyes. "Shall I call Dr. Charles, milady?"

"No," Lucinda replied firmly, then saw the look of dread on Mary's face. "There's no need for alarm. I felt a little faint. Perhaps I shall lie down for a bit. Can you help me to my bed?"

"Of course, milady." Once Lucinda was comfortable, Mary asked, "Shall I fetch you a small teacake and a cup of tea?"

"Just a biscuit. Leave the curtains open, thank you."

LUCINDA OPENED HER EYES, TURNED towards her window, and noted the long rays of sunlight streaming in. *It is nearly teatime. I wonder what René is doing. I want to be with him.* She decided that, instead of becoming melancholy, she would visit her grandfather. He always cheered her up.

As she neared the drawing-room, Lucinda heard loud voices from inside. She slowed her pace so that she could listen and recognized the familiar voice. "We must tell them. He will find out anyway when he has to sign the papers."

The other voice belonged to Uncle Roderick. "I can deal with the bureaucracy myself. We aren't going to hold them liable."

"I'm afraid it doesn't work that way. Your father's name is on the documents as well. His signature will be required."

Uncle Roderick sighed. "Fine. But Lucinda doesn't need to know."

What doesn't my uncle want me to know? Her recent flashback to Egypt replayed in her mind. *Something about Egypt? Something about Mitch?*

"I don't think withholding that information is wise, besides, your father will tell her. I think, as a professional with experience in this area, that I should be the one to deliver the news to Lucinda."

Her heart racing, Lucinda walked into the room. "What news?"

Both men spun their heads to look at her. Uncle Roderick cleared his throat. "He will tell you." Her uncle addressed the tall, blond man. "I will apprise the baron of our situation. I'm sure that he will have questions." Then her uncle strode out of the room without another word.

Why is Mitch here? When did he arrive? Lucinda approached him. "What news?"

Gazing at her tenderly, he replied, "I think you should sit down." He gently grasped her hand to lead her to the couch.

Lucinda balked and shook off his hand. "I don't know why you are here, but I think that you had better answer my question."

His eyebrows raised briefly. "As you wish." After clearing his throat, he told her what had happened. "Your mother, Sarah, committed suicide last night."

What? Suicide? Her mind was foggy; Lucinda was at a loss as she absorbed his words. Her mother was dead. *No, no, it's not possible. I'm never going to see her again?* Another memory surfaced. They were standing next to the carriage, together, before she left for Egypt. Placing the pendant in her hand. Then her father, outside the tavern, holding it in front of her face.

She bit her lip. "How?"

"I don't think . . ."

Lucinda was adamant. "How?"

"The gardener found her this morning in the orchard. Hanging in a tree. We don't know how she got out of her room or where she found the rope." His eyes searched hers. "I am so sorry for your loss."

Envisioning her mother dangling in the breeze with her head at an angle, the image of her father returned. His hateful smirk and the Eye of Ra. Swinging back and forth. Uncle Roderick said he died in the fire. A queer feeling of disconnection came over her. The world seemed to shift and fall away. *At least my parents are together now. Happy. Or are they?* She knew someone who would know. She would ask her.

As Lucinda hurried out of the drawing room, he was at her heels. "Where are you going?"

She didn't answer him. He commanded her to stop, but she kept going. Her eyes straight ahead, she became unaware of his presence.

REALIZING HIS PATIENT WAS IN a trance, Dr. Charles trailed behind her as she made her way into the Egyptian room. Going straight to the open sarcophagus, she stood before it and began to remove her skirt and petticoats. As he watched in amazement, Lucinda stripped down to her silk drawers and kicked off her slippers. She then threw her clothes into the casket, climbed into it and laid down on them.

"Lucinda." The doctor walked over to the box and looked down. Her eyes closed; she had crossed her arms over her chest. "Lucinda, please get out of this thing." She didn't move. "You must get out of there."

Still nothing except for her soft mumbling. "Magic, feather, vessel . . ."

"Miss Haliburton, get up!"

Lucinda opened her eyes and stared at him. "Please stop yelling. I can't hear what she's saying."

"Who?"

"Her."

"Lucinda . . ."

She gave him a look of severe irritation. "Nephthys. She is speaking to me, but I can't focus on what she is saying because of you. Go away."

"Lucinda," the doctor said sternly, "I realize you are upset about your mother, but this is not appropriate. Come now, get dressed and let us return to the drawing room. I can have Mary make you some tea and we can talk."

"No. No tea."

"As your doctor, I insist that you get out of there." He grabbed her wrists and started to haul her up.

She tried to pull away. When that failed, she began thrashing around and screaming. "Leave me alone, leave me alone!"

He let her go, and she scooted backward into one corner. Her eyes flashing, she glared at him, looking like a trapped animal. The doctor wagged his finger. "If you don't get out of there, I will be forced to fetch the servants and give you an injection." Lucinda remained there; flagrant hate transformed her features.

Dr. Charles left the room. When he returned, he found her dressed and sitting placidly on the sofa. The picture of sorrow, she was holding her head in her hands, her face buried in a handkerchief. He dismissed the servants who had come in with him and went over to her. Setting his medical bag on the floor, he sat down beside her. "Lucinda, my dear."

She looked up with a doleful expression. "All I wanted was to find out about my mother and father. Were they together and happy again? That's all. I was asking Nephthys. She's my friend. She's a friend to the dead." Lucinda's hands fell to her lap and nervously twisted the scented handkerchief. The seductive fragrance filled the air.

Dr. Charles inched nearer and placed his hands over hers, gently caressing them with his thumbs. "I am your friend too, Lucinda. I am here for you to lean on. Talk to me, I will listen." A teeny-tiny smile graced her lips. He scooted even closer. "Lucinda, we have known each other for a long time. Our families—my father, your grandfather—have history together. The baron and I, well, we talk about things. We are both concerned about your future. He likes me and he expressed that he approves of our courtship."

"But—"

"Let me finish. He thinks that we would make a great alliance. He even mentioned a big wedding."

"I don't know . . ."

The doctor placed his finger over her lips. "I love you, my dear." Looking deeply into her eyes, he promised, "You will never find anybody who will care for you like I do."

RENÉ SAT AT HIS TABLE IN THE laborer's cottage and flipped through the book that Lucinda had lent him. He turned to one of the pages she had pointed out, a depiction of Hathor looking magnificent in her headdress. The bygone memory of his childhood vision at his grandfather's house surfaced. Now he understood who she was, the woman in the river. He marveled at how many times this goddess had made herself known to him. René studied her picture and then began to turn the pages again. He stopped when he came to a picture of Nephthys with her wings outstretched; the book said she was the mother of Anubis. Again, he carefully noted the details. Inspired, René closed the book and began to sketch Lucinda dressed as the goddesses. When he was finished, he labeled the drawing *Vache et Vautour*. Cow and vulture. Satisfied with his work, he put down his pencil and moved to the orange chair, gazing out the window at the mansion in the distance.

Checking his pocket watch, it was the usual time for their rendezvous. René wondered what Lucinda was doing. He missed their afternoon tête-à-têtes sitting amongst the beautiful flowers. Thinking about his most recent drawing of the lily of the valley and bluebells reminded him of the ancient Egyptian perfume and Lucinda's kisses. Desiring more, he wanted to hold her in his arms and have kisses that lasted forever. But they were separated. Due, no doubt, to the meddlesome Dr. Charles.

He sneered as he remembered the Englishman with his straight blond hair and smug good looks. *How old is he? In his thirties, most likely.* The doctor had referred to him as a boy several times. *He has a real nerve, telling me to stay away from her. So audacious.* His jealousy flared as he continued to think of the doctor's covetous and controlling nature. Eventually, René worked himself into a frenzy over it and decided to confront Lucinda. He jumped up from his chair, ready to tell her everything that had been said. He would destroy Dr. Charles's reputation.

There was a knock at the door.

Chapter 28:

THE LOTUS BOX

René inhaled deeply to calm himself before opening the door. He hoped his visitor was Mary with a message from Lucinda. Instead, it was M. Stoddard with a parcel in his hand. "Bonjour, Mr. Lalique. I've brought the post." He paused as he looked René over. "Is everything alright, lad? You looked flustered."

René shook his head. "Non, I'm fine." He eyed the package. "For me?"

"Yes." M. Stoddard handed him the box. "All the way from Paris."

Glancing at his mother's return address, René smiled. "Merci, M. Stoddard." As usual, the older man continued to linger. "Would you like a cup of tea? The kettle is still hot."

M. Stoddard beamed. "Why, yes. Thank you for asking."

René put the box down and set about preparing the tea as the groundskeeper moved the orange chair next to the table and plopped down in it. He began to eagerly share his gossip. Had René heard about the incident with Miss Haliburton? Her mental breakdown? The entire household was talking. The missus just happened to overhear the young Dr. Charles, such a brilliant physician, talking to her uncle Roderick about it. It was the news about the tragic incident that caused it. They had found Lady Sarah that morning.

The name prompted René to put up his hand to stop M. Stoddard. "Who?"

"Lady Sarah. Lucinda's mother. The one in the mad-house. She committed suicide. Hung herself in the garden of the asylum."

That's why she became so upset when Mme. Sphinx said the name Sarah, René thought. He brought the tea service over to the table as he confirmed what Stoddard had just said. "Sarah? Lucinda never mentioned her mother's name."

"Yes, it caused quite a commotion in the manor." The groundskeeper poured tea into his cup, then resumed speaking. "The old man, His Lordship I mean, took the news badly. The missus reported that he had the worse coughing fit to date; she's never seen so much blood. Thinks that this incident may be the final blow to him. Says that he has been looking poorly anyway these last few weeks. But it was the granddaughter's reaction that everyone is chattering about. Poor thing. The doctor had told her the news and she went straight away to the haunted room—you know, where they keep the Egyptian things—and got into the coffin there."

While Stoddard paused again to sip his tea, René repeated this last detail. "She got into the sarcophagus?"

"Yes. And folded her arms across her chest like a mummy." He took another sip and continued. "The missus heard the doctor talking. Apparently, the girl removed her clothes down to her unmentionables, threw them into the box and got in. Then was babbling nonsense about conversing with an Egyptian spirit regarding her dead mother. When the doctor tried to get her out of the coffin, she became hysterical." The older man's eyes goggled at René. "He had to get help because, and these are the doctor's words, she was like a wild animal."

M. Stoddard paused, sighed deeply, and looked out the window. "Thankfully, she calmed down before he had to medicate or restrain her." He looked back at René. "I am afraid for her, young man. I don't want to see her get committed again. The story is that they chopped off her beautiful hair last time. I don't know if her fragile nature could take it. She might never recover."

"Non, that would be terrible."

Drinking some more tea and fiddling with René's pencils, M. Stoddard went on. "A conversation between the missus and Mary revealed another problem. Mary had found Miss Haliburton in her closet curled up like a kitten and shaking like a leaf before she had even heard about her mother's death. Said her ladyship was babbling. Lily of the valley, lily of the valley. Mary found a drawing of flowers on the dressing table. Lily of the valley." He searched René's eyes. "Mary claimed that you had drawn it. What's going on, young man?"

"Je ne sais pas," René replied honestly. "I don't know, M. Stoddard. I am worried, too."

"Perhaps you can talk to her. I noticed that you two aren't together as much anymore."

"Her grandfather forbade her to visit me."

"But you must visit her. I believe that you can help her." The groundskeeper finished his tea and stood up. "I have packages to deliver to her too. I will arrange it and let you know."

After Stoddard had left, René sat down in the orange chair to open his package. Inside was Ambrose's box and a letter from his mother. René felt a twinge of loneliness as he began reading.

Mon cher René,

I have missed you so much. I can hardly wait to see you again. In the meantime, I have been cleaning out your old things, boxing them and redecorating your room. Cousin Vuilleret has installed some new wallpaper. I

206 ✳ MAGICIAN OF LIGHT

*told him all about you and your studies. He wants you
to design for him when you return to Paris. He assured
me that there is always a need for new and innovative
designs in his wallcovering business.*

    *André brought this box by; he thought you would
want it. Apparently, Louis Aine wanted to throw it
away when they found it stashed under your old work-
station, but André rescued it. He said to tell you to
come back as soon as possible and that he misses his
cabaret friend. When I told him no more of that trouble, he just grinned. I do like him, but why can't that
boy be more responsible like his older brother?*

    *I worry about you as you are the only family I have
now. You sounded sad in your last letter. Cousin Vuilleret
has many connections to wealthy families with eligible
young ladies. We need to find a suitable partner for you.
In fact, he mentioned the daughter of a wealthy widow
that you should meet. After you get home and begin
working, you need to court gentlewomen of society, not
cavort with servant girls who frequent dance halls. We,
Cousin Vuilleret and I, will make the introductions.*

Please write me soon,
Love, Maman

With knitted brows, René refolded the letter and set it down.
*I miss you and love you dearly, Maman, but why must you
always interfere?* He certainly did not like the idea of designing
wallpaper nor did he want to get married. He needed to focus
on his jewelry-making career. René sighed and looked out the
window at the mansion. Besides, his heart had already been taken
by a beautiful lady. What would his mother think if he told her
that he was in madly in love with a crazy Englishwoman? *She
would go crazy.* Why was his mother insisting on an arranged

marriage anyway? What about love? And didn't she believe that
he was going to become a famous jeweler? That he would make
his own wealth through hard work and creativity?
This last thought reminded him again of the haughty Dr.
Charles with his sarcastic attitude. Then René recalled Mme.
Sphinx's letter. She believed in him. Determined, René reached
over and took out a piece of paper from his art satchel. He
began writing a letter to his mother to tell her that he was
going to be a jeweler not a wallpaper designer. But he didn't
finish it. Instead, he crumpled up the paper and threw it in the
trash. What was the use? Why tell them? He would show them
instead. He would accomplish his goals.

René studied Ambrose's school project. For a student,
it exhibited very good craftsmanship. *Ambrose would have
made beautiful necessaires. He could have created fine,
expensive vanity boxes for the wealthy under the tutelage
of Louis Aine and André.* The thought of Louis Aine made
René scowl, and then he wondered if the younger Louis had
ever fabricated his scarab ring design. René pulled Ambrose's
box closer and opened it. There it was, the silver key that he
had designed for it. *It could be made into a pendant.* An idea
occurred to René. He opened his drawing pad and began to
sketch another beetle ring to show Lucinda. It would cheer
her up and it was something to pass the time until he heard
from M. Stoddard.

*HE IS BACK IN MONTMARTRE. At the Moulin de la Galette.
He sees the small wooden tables set under the trees. On one
table is the box. The lady with the red hat is standing nearby.
Behind her is a blue curtain. Suddenly, Ambrose appears there
and smiles at him. Then he is in a boat, fishing next to an
island. He pulls the net out, but it is empty. There is a woman
swimming nearby. She has blonde hair.*

When René awoke from the dream, he remembered the first letter from Mme. Sphinx and her dream. It, too, had a box but with two scrolls. Was it also Ambrose's box? What did the scrolls mean? He then wondered about his own dream. Why is the net empty? Who was the woman? Retrieving his pocket watch, René saw it was time to get up. He wanted to paint gouache on his drawing of the goddesses for Lucinda before his midmorning meeting with her.

RENÉ STOOD BEFORE THE MIRROR AND combed his hair and mustache again. Satisfied with his appearance, he put on his coat, then picked up Ambrose's box and tucked it under his arm for his walk down to the stables. M. Stoddard and Lucinda were already in the barn, sitting on a bench. When he saw René, M. Stoddard excused himself and left. As Lucinda looked up at René, he noticed that her cheeks had lost their color. She reminded him of a wraith.

He smiled as he approached her. "I have brought you something." He handed the box to her.

"For me?" Lucinda took the container and admired it. She looked up and beamed at him. "It's exquisite. Did you make it?"

"Non, a very good friend of mine did." René sat down next to her. "When we were in school together in France. The French call them necessaires."

Lucinda traced the lotus inlays with her index finger. "I love the flowers." She faced him and smiled blissfully. "I love it. Thank you so much." She kissed him lightly on his cheek.

"Open it."

Lucinda chirped with merriment when she saw his drawing of her as the goddesses. "Vache et vautour. Hathor and Nephthys. And you painted it for me." She looked at him again. "It's wonderful."

René smiled tenderly at her. "There's more." He removed the drawing to reveal the silver key underneath it.

She picked it up. "The Eye of Ra."

"Yes. I made that. It is the key for the lock. Let me show you." He took the key, put his drawing back inside, closed the lid and placed the box on the bench between them. After locking it, he returned the key to her.

"The blue enamel is so pretty, and the design is unique. You're amazing." She leaned over and gave him a brief kiss on the lips.

"Merci." René placed his hand on the box. "Someday, this necessaire will be filled with jewelry that I have made for you."

Lucinda stared at the box. "You're going back to France, aren't you?"

"Oui, eventually. Would you like to come with me?"

"Really?" She seemed eager and then deflated. "I don't know . . ."

Sensing her distress, René changed the subject. "I heard about your packages. When M. Stoddard delivered mine, he said two had arrived for you."

Lucinda smiled with excitement. "Yes, it was my ball dress and the matching silk shoes. The dance is this weekend. You do remember, don't you?"

"Of course, mon amour. I have been dreaming about it since you invited me." She giggled happily. "Tell me about your outfit."

"No, I want it to be a surprise. I want to see your face when I appear before you wearing it." Her eyes sparkled.

"You're beautiful to me just as you are," René said sincerely, "but I am sure that you will be the belle of the ball."

Lucinda looked away. "I hope you think so. I know that you French are so fashionable." Then she returned her gaze to him, her eyes filled with love and adoration. Unable to resist, he moved closer and they exchanged an amorous kiss. A knicker and a snort from Albert made them look at the horse watching them from his stall.

René grinned. "Albert is a peeping Tom." Lucinda laughed, and René grinned even more.

Lucinda stood and picked up the box. "Let's go to the Egyptian room. I want to give you something."

When they arrived, she led him to the glass museum case. Putting Ambrose's box down on top of one of the compartments, she opened the adjacent one and retrieved a golden ring set with an obsidian beetle. As she placed it in René's hand and closed his fingers over it, he recalled Le Chameau, the dirty ragman, placing the dead insect in his hand the night of the séance.

Lucinda was speaking. "The black scarab. Wear it for me. At the dance."

"But your grandfather, your uncle, what will they think?"

"My uncle doesn't give a fig about these things anyway. He won't even notice." René still hesitated. "Put it on. Please." He reluctantly slid the ring onto his finger.

Lucinda smiled before surveying the jewelry once more. She tapped on the glass above a golden pendant of lotus flowers and a red scarab. "I will wear that." Then her face clouded over.

René noticed that her hand was trembling. Worried about her, he said, "You're shaking again. Lucinda, you must take the bromide. Dr. Charles says so."

But she didn't seem to hear him. A faraway look appeared on her face. "She took what was mine and now I am dead." Tears sprang to her eyes.

"What do you mean? Who are you talking about? Do you mean Lady Haliburton?"

Lucinda didn't answer as the tears rolled down her cheeks. René gently wiped one away. "Tell me what's wrong. I want to help you."

"Even though I loved him fiercely, he killed me. He destroyed our love. Please don't let him kill me again."

"Chérie, I don't know what you are talking about." René knew that Lucinda's mind had gone somewhere else. "Come, let's find Mary and your medicine." He put his arm around her shoulders and steered her towards the door.

But she resisted and pulled away from him. "They are here," she said. She turned and walked to the large piece of pink granite. "This relic was stolen by my uncle. It's called a false door by the uninitiated. It's the portal in the tomb through which spirits pass. Back and forth." Lucinda gazed at him and, for a few moments, they locked eyes Then she looked away. "It is how they enter."

"Who? Spirits?"

Lucinda pointed to the corner with the shrine of Anubis. "Them."

"There's nobody there."

"Can't you see them? Not even Anubis?"

"You mean the statue?"

"No. The jackal-headed man. He follows me, hunts me like a rabbit. Even if I wanted to, I can't get away from him."

René peered at the corner harder. Nothing. *Anubis surrounds Lucinda. That's what Mme. Sphinx had said. Is something really here?* Despite this thought, he said, "Don't worry. Anubis is not hunting you."

Lucinda looked at him in disbelief. "He told me that you are aware of him. You know that he is here." She closed her eyes. A current seemed to pass through the space separating them. "He is between us, René. He is part of me, us." A tremor ran through her.

Concerned, René put his hand on her shoulder. "Lucinda, tu vas bien?" But she didn't look alright. Her face was pale.

Lucinda opened her eyes again. "You don't believe your own instincts or me either. You think Mary and Dr. Charles are right to drug me. Everyone wants me to be quiet about them." She returned to stand at the glass case. "Deny their existence."

"No, that's not true."

Lucinda stared into the display box at the Senet game-board. "The Great Game, the Waters of Chaos," she mumbled and closed her eyes again, swaying on her feet.

"Lucinda." She didn't answer, so René shook her gently. "Lucinda."

Her expression was blank as she opened her eyes, and she spoke in a monotone. "I tried to cross the icy waters before the jackal tore me in two and the beetles ate my flesh."

"What?"

Lucinda remained silent as she looked over her shoulder at the corner. Then she turned back to René. "When the portal to utter darkness is open, cross the Waters of Chaos to gain foot-fall on the primordial mound. Don't get caught in the House of Netting."

She fainted and fell against him. René caught her limp body in his arms and carried her to the nearby settee, his heart racing. Trying to revive her, he clasped her shoulders and shook them. "Lucinda. Lucinda."

Suddenly, her body jerked and then stiffened before she started convulsing violently. René jumped up and ran out into the hallway, yelling for help. Mary and another maid came at once. After René told them of Lucinda's condition, the other maid went to fetch assistance. He and Mary ran back to Lucinda, who was now still but unconscious. Using her apron, Mary wiped the bloody spittle from around Lucinda's mouth. René looked up to see Lucinda's uncle standing in the doorway glaring at him. When a butler walked into the room, Roderick whispered to him. The servant approached René, still in shock, and grabbed his elbow to escort him away.

Chapter 29:

TURNING THE CORNER

They were sitting on her Egyptian divan. Avoiding Dr. Charles's face, Lucinda focused on the end of the armrest that she leaned on, tracing the mahogany head of the goddess with her finger. "I'm still having dreams of an ancient time. But I don't think I'm just dreaming. The scenes seem real, like another life that I lived."

When the doctor didn't respond, she looked at him. His face was passive and unreadable. "Are you talking about reincarnation?" he finally asked.

She looked at the wooden decoration again. "I know it sounds crazy. Ever since I visited Egypt, this old life has come back. The spirits followed me."

An exasperated huff made her shift her eyes back to Charles. His face was contorted with a sulky pout. "So you lied to me. You're still having the illusions. Did you also lie about having no memory of what happened in Egypt?"

"No. I really don't remember what happened." She searched his eyes. "I didn't want to stay in the asylum because I'm not mad. They're there. Just because you can't see them doesn't mean they don't exist. I can hear them, too. If you care for me as you say you do, then you would believe me."

"I do believe you are hearing voices, Lucinda, but I can't help you unless I know more about what they're saying to you."

"That's private."

"Well, do you want them to stop?"

Lucinda shifted in her seat. "Of course. Especially Anubis."

"Why?"

"He tells me things I don't want to hear." She smiled weakly.

"The medicine might help to make him, and the seizures, go away. You seemed to be doing better when you were taking it."

"No." She shook her head. "I won't drink it."

"Why aren't you following my advice these days? I *miss* our outdoor walks and our talks."

Lucinda detected a hint of jealousy and accusation in his tone. Did he know about her secret trysts with René in the woods? "Your tea makes me feel dead. I might as well be dead. Like my mother."

"No, Lucinda, don't talk like that." Dr. Charles placed his hand over hers and gently squeezed it.

She focused on their hands. *Could I learn to love him? What would he do if I reached out, tousled his hair, or ran my fingers through it? Would he recoil in horror or would he gather me in his arms and kiss me passionately?* She knew what René would do. She studied the doctor's face intently, looking for clues of his true nature. "What would you like me to say, Charles?"

He got up and began to pace. "What if there was another way? What if there was another treatment? Hmmm . . . Could that be the problem?" Dr. Charles seemed to be talking more to himself than to her. "I could address the underlying issues in the subconsciousness. Sweep them away, clean them out. Some say it is quackery, but it is only mental manipulation." He stopped and looked at her. "Hypnosis. I could try to detect any emotional strain encountered in Egypt that could be the trigger of your psychologic worries. Hopefully reducing your delirious states and resulting seizures."

"Would that work?"

"If it did, you wouldn't have to take the bromide."

"I don't know . . ."

"Don't you trust me?" His face was full of such tenderness, she couldn't say no even if she wanted to. She nodded.

"Good," he said, smiling. "You must trust me wholeheartedly." He pointed to the settee. "Why don't you lie down?" As she leaned back, he fetched her desk chair and sat in it next to the couch. "Are you comfortable? Would you like another pillow?" She answered by nodding and then shaking her head. "In order to rid yourself of these problems, I am going to take you back to an earlier period. We will proceed backward one step at a time, and we will talk about how you feel about what you are seeing. I will be right there beside you, keeping you safe. If you become uneasy, you must let me know by squeezing my hand." He clasped her hand and then tightened his grip slightly. "Like this. Do you understand?"

"Yes."

"We will travel back to your earliest memory of Egypt in this lifetime. I believe that if you can remember this moment, it may help the other life recede. What do you say? Do you want to try?"

It probably won't work, but I'll try, she thought and nodded. Dr. Charles let go of her hand and removed his pocket watch. Holding it up, he began to swing it. As it oscillated, shiny and gold, he told her to follow it with her eyes and listen to his voice. It was soothing and relaxing. The sight of his watch, coupled with his soft, easy intonation, left her eyelids feeling heavy. Back and forth the watch swung, catching the light and glinting every so often. They would travel and walk together holding hands. Hard to keep your eyes open, he said. Back and forth. Her eyes were tired. She felt sleepy. Down the steps. He would count them. When it was time to return, to walk back up the steps, she would hear him counting and then he would snap his fingers. And they would be back. "Do you see the steps? Down we go. One, two, three . . ."

Soon, she found herself sitting in the dining room of the mansion. She knew Charles was at her side. She couldn't see him, but she could feel him holding her hand under the table. When he asked, Lucinda told him where they were.

"Who is with us at the table?"

She looked at the faces of the people. "Grandfather, Mother, Father, Uncle Roderick and him."

"Him?"

"The Frenchman from Egypt. He's visiting Grandfather. I overheard them earlier in Grandfather's study. He was talking about digging things up."

"What's his name?"

Trying to remember, she watched the foreigner stare at her parents. She wondered what he was thinking, so she also looked at her parents. Then she felt his eyes on her, so she looked back at him, straight into his eyes. His surprised expression at being discovered watching her made her giggle.

"What's funny?"

"The professor doesn't like it here. I don't think he likes us."

"What's the professor's name?"

"Dr. Merimee."

"What else do you remember about this time?"

Like a dream, she found herself in another place: a darkened hallway outside her parents' bedroom. She could hear them arguing. "They're fighting," she told Charles.

"Who's fighting?"

"My parents. My father doesn't want to go to France or Egypt, but my mother says it's just for a little while." Lucinda didn't want to hear them argue, so she began to walk down the hallway holding the invisible hand of Charles. When she turned the corner, she realized it was a circle.

"When did you see Dr. Merimee again?" Charles asked.

In front of her was the sitting room window of the house in Egypt, looking out at the desert hills. Turning, she saw the professor rush in and show her uncle something in his hand. Walking over, she saw the half-torn card with its hieroglyph. "When he found a piece of papyrus in a rib cage with the Eye of Ra painted on it."

"Where are you?"

"In Egypt."

"What's happening?"

"Uncle Roderick doesn't care about the card until the professor says something about ancient writing on the rocks. He thinks it marks the entrance to a tomb." Lucinda gazed out the window again at the bleak landscape of rocks and sand.

"Tell me about the tomb."

Turning back, she spotted Uncle Roderick's empty chair. He was gone and there was only a paper sitting there. She looked at it. A letter signed by Dr. Charles Perkins. She didn't want to read it, she wanted to leave. She squeezed his hand.

"What's wrong, Lucinda? Tell me."

"It's your letter. He dropped it on the chair after Dr. Merimee ran in to tell him about finding the secret chamber. In the tomb." Looking up, she saw Mitch come in the door. He reached out his hand for her to grasp. Now she was holding two hands, each one pulling her in a different direction. They would pull her apart, rip her in half like the professor's ancient card. She must let go of one. She squeezed the doctor's hand. "Take me out of here, please."

He began to count. To her relief, they were walking up the steps. Back on her red divan, opening her eyes, she realized that her face was wet. Charles had let go of her hand and was dabbing her cheeks with his handkerchief. She saw concern on his face until he met her gaze and gave her an encouraging smile. "We shall see this through, my love."

Chapter 30:

BOOK OF POETRY

The devastating news had come that morning. René's professor had said that the school was closing for good but had given no reason. No more studies, art or otherwise. It was the last day of classes; their projects were due the following week. The teacher let them go early, so René and the jolly fellows went up to London on the train. The others were still drinking and merrymaking when he left them at the tavern and took the omnibus to the South Kensington Museum. He had hoped the quiet of the museum would give him inspiration. Instead, he wandered listlessly through the exhibitions while thinking hopelessly about his future. How was he going to break it to Lucinda that he would be returning to France? What would she do?

René's ambivalent feelings about her were driving him mad. He loved Lucinda, but did he want to marry her? Certain that she would not come with him to Paris unless she was his wife, he focused on her attributes: adoring, beautiful, intelligent, and potentially wealthy. However, what if her grandfather disowned her for following him to France? Could her uncle cut off her allowance at any time? *Would I love her the same if she was poor?* And then there were her medical problems. Recalling her convulsive fit, he never wanted to witness that again. Would she ever be cured? Could he take care of her *and* build his career? Or was her doctor, right? Was Dr. Charles the only one who could take care of her? René sneered as he thought of Charles. *I will find a French doctor who can help her,* he vowed. *Could Maman help? Could she learn to love Lucinda, too?*

René had come to the section of the museum that featured prints and drawings. He stopped in front of a piece by an Italian artist: Castiglione's drawing of Apollo and Daphne. The painter had drawn the figures with a brush, Apollo in pursuit of Daphne through the woods with the Greek god Eros hovering above. René admired the artist's skill and then read the adjacent label. Eros fired two arrows, one of love at the god and one of hate at the nymph. Under the spell of the arrows, Apollo would be forever rejected by Daphne. Rejection. His lips tightened. *Poor Lucinda. What will she think of my leaving?* René checked his pocket watch. If he hurried, he could catch the next train back. The situation had to be resolved. He had to tell her before someone else did.

RENÉ THANKED M. STODDARD AS THEY watched the servant girl disappear into the back entrance of Foxhill Estate. Returning soon, she said that Miss Haliburton welcomed a private visit and took René through the servant's quarters. When they were upstairs, the girl admitted him to Lucinda's bedroom. She stood near the window, the late afternoon sun creating a halo of light around her, causing him to relive their earlier time in the Egyptian room, the bouquet of the ancient perfume, their first kisses. Lucinda greeted him, then nodded at the servant. "Leave the door open." When the girl had departed, Lucinda motioned him over to look out at the garden and fountain below. "I miss our walks amongst the flowers. Did you know that you can't easily transplant bluebells? I have tried and they all died, even in the shade. They seem to prefer the woods."

"I prefer the woods and sitting beneath the trees with you. Mon cherie amour, my beloved Lucinda."

She looked at him wistfully. "So, you have something to tell me? I fear that it's bad news."

René nervously twisted the brim of his hat. "Surprising news. Would you like to sit down?"

"Of course." She led them to her Egyptian settee.

René placed his hat on the coffee table next to the book of French poetry he had given her. He admired the wooden armrests of the divan before sitting down.

"Well . . ." she prompted.

"The Crystal Palace school is closing. No more classes. Our last day was today. I was shocked when the professor told us."

Lucinda sighed heavily. "I suppose this means that you will be returning to France soon."

"Yes."

She looked away. "I completely understand. I wouldn't want to be around someone who has fits."

A pang of guilt overcame him. "Non. Mon amour, it is not that at all. I must return home. I have no money." René shook his head. "My mother sold her property to pay for my schooling. I cannot ask her to continue to support me."

"Couldn't you find work in London?"

"I have a position waiting for me in Paris."

"Well, that settles it." Lucinda hung her head low and her eyes welled. Quiet sounds of anguish escaped her lips as tears rolled down her cheeks.

René reached out and touched her arm. "Mon amour, don't cry. I love you. I want you to come with me to Paris."

Lucinda looked up. "Really?" She searched his adoring eyes before getting up and returning to the window. Drying her eyes and dabbing her nose with her handkerchief, she turned to him. "I love you too, but I can't leave here." She looked down at the floor. "I have started a new treatment. Dr. Charles is hypnotizing me. So that I won't have to take the medicine and I won't have seizures."

Hearing Charles's name, René's face twisted into a scowl. "We can find you a French doctor."

Lucinda kept staring at the floor. "Can you love a broken thing? It would be so selfish of me to ask you to do so."

René got up, embraced her and then lifted her chin. "You don't have to ask." He kissed her tenderly on the lips and looked deeply into her eyes. Lucinda smiled, kissed him back and then laid her head on his shoulder. They stood like that for a few moments before she pulled away and sat down. "But my grandfather, I couldn't leave him."

"He would understand . . ."

"No, it's not that. He's dying, René. I won't leave him to die alone. I could never do that to someone I loved."

Lucinda's words reminded René of cradling Ambrose's head. He kneeled in front of her and clasped both her hands. Kissing them, he said, "I wouldn't want you to. You must stay with your grandfather. I will return to Paris and make money. Then I will come and fetch you when you are ready." He smiled warmly at her.

"I love you so much." Lucinda fondled his cheek and then ran her fingers lightly through the hair over one ear. Wanting more caresses, he rested his head on her knee. She toyed with his curls briefly and then asked, "Would you read to me?"

René stood up and then sat down beside her. Scooting closer, she picked up the poetry book, opened it and drew out the small booklet of his poems that he had given her. "Yours first," she said as she handed it to him.

He opened the illustrated paper cover, decorated with bluebells, and began to read quietly. "Je reve aux baisers, qui

demeurent toujours, sur tes lèvres si douces, ma tres beau fleur
. . ." She stroked the back of his head and neck. Neither of
them noticed being watched from the doorway.

AS SHE CONTEMPLATED HER PLAN, Lucinda smiled
broadly. She would stay with her grandfather, continue her treatment, and get better. She would be the woman that René needed.
A wife to support him, one fluent in French. He would be a great
artist, rich and famous. They would get married and have children
to love and nurture. I'll miss Charles's friendship, but not this
place or anybody in it. Their malicious slander, horrible chatter.
She frowned. I must have not noticed it when I first came back.
Those early days of dullness, countless days of embroidery at her
grandfather's side, timeless days spent in the Egyptian room, endless cups of tea and hours and hours of sleeping. Some days so
tired she could barely stir from bed. And the dreams. Awake and
asleep, the specters filed past. Filling her head with exotic and
chimerical images until she didn't know what was real anymore.

Then he came. The artist. She watched him from her window.
Daily, he walked past the mansion and into the woods. Every
day at the same time, an alarm clock to stir her from her waking
slumber. His presence had coaxed her from the gloomy land of
the dead. Slowly, as she emerged from her tomb, she became
aware of the whispers. Then the talking. The gossip and the scandal surrounding her illness. The outright vicious comments of
her uncle and his wife. A family tradition, they said, and handed
down the sentence of guilty as charged: insanity by association.
Everyone except Grandfather, Mr. Stoddard, and René. They
accepted her plight. She wasn't a raving lunatic or a deranged
maniac. Somewhere along the way she had just lost her balance.

On the road to recovery and then came the news of her
mother. She had stumbled again, and now here she was, back
to hiding. Away from the world and its unkindness. But Dr.

Charles and the hypnosis would get her back on track. This was her chance to regain her footing and cast off the chains of her past. Then she would leave and begin life anew. In a glamorous city with a wonderful man.

Before René left her room, he had convinced her to meet him in the woods the next morning, prior to the ball. He wanted to sit amongst the trees and draw her face one last time before he left for Paris. Lucinda went to her dressing table and drew out the pendant of Neferure. Is it wise to wear it? It's so beautiful. Why not? She strung it on her gold chain and returned it to the drawer. Then she went to her closet and brought out the box that contained her dress for the ball. Lucinda held the gown to her body and swayed in front of the mirror, humming a long-forgotten tune as she admired herself. A knock on the door forced her to look away. It was Mary. "Forgive me for interrupting, milady, but Dr. Charles has arrived for your session. Shall I send him up?"

HE IS RECLINING ON HER RED COUCH, looking at the wooden armrest of the Egyptian goddess. There is a noise, a crackle then a snap. He turns to see a fire in the grate. The fuel is the other carved face. There is no screen to keep the fire contained, growing and growing, sparks flying as the embers pop loudly. The banging noise continues to intensify, and he feels the heat as the flames creep nearer, threatening to burn him alive.

René awoke with a start, the back of his head wet from perspiration. He had fallen asleep, fully dressed, after his supper. Sitting up, he rubbed his eyes. The sound of pounding on his door brought him fully alert. Glancing at his pocket watch on the bedside table, he wondered who could be knocking at this hour.

It was Mary bringing him a note. René opened it and read the line scrawled across the page: *Meet me in the Egyptian room.*

The maid waited silently outside his door while he gathered his coat. René was grateful for this opportunity to see Lucinda. When they arrived, however, she was not the one in the library. Her doctor stood with his back to them, looking out the window.

"We're here, Dr. Charles," Mary announced.

He turned around and nodded in satisfaction to the maid. René gave her a puzzled look, but she was smiling at the doctor. "Thank you, Mary. You may go." She curtseyed and left the room, closing the doors behind her.

As soon as she was gone, Dr. Charles immediately launched into a tirade. "I have been told everything."

"What do you mean?"

The doctor pointed to René's poetry book and a stack of his drawings on one of the tables. He snatched the drawing on top and held it up. René could see that it was the page he had torn from his sketchbook the day Mme. Sphinx had given them the tarot reading. He had barely glimpsed *Bouteille de Muguet* and the perfume bottle with Lucinda's naked figure before the doctor shook the picture at him. "What the hell were you thinking? What is this nonsense?"

"How dare you summon me here to be chastised at this time of night!"

The doctor snorted. "I'm surprised you were home." He took another disdainful look at René's picture before carelessly tossing it back onto the table. "And alone."

René started to object, but Dr. Charles cut him off. "Don't make up excuses, boy. I know about your kind, the *French*. I did my research." Opening the poetry book, he read René's poem to Lucinda in a mocking fashion. "I dream of kisses, which always remain, on your soft lips, my very beautiful flower." He sneered at René. "Reading smut leads to degeneracy." Snapping the book shut, he flung it on the table. "I know all about your philandering, and how you're getting on with the tipple. A useless drunk is never welcome in high society."

"I am not a drunk."

Dr. Charles placed his hands on his hips and, with a snide look, tilted his head. "Really? That's not what I heard. Why, just today, after you heard that the school was closing, you and your fellow delinquents went to London to visit sordid taverns." René was quiet. "That's right. I know all about your perversion. And the predicament you find yourself in." The doctor began to stroll around the room. "No more school, your lack of funds, a foreigner with no serviceable skills, no prospective work here. Really, my boy—and I don't put much stock in this type of thinking—don't you see that this is a sign from the Almighty?" He stopped. "Can't you read the hand-writing on the wall?" Noting the enraged look on René's face, Charles continued taunting. "Let me spell it out for you. This is your cue that you must leave. Go back to that godless city where you belong."

His fists clenched at his sides, René tried to control his fury. "You are a pompous ass. Everybody knows it, including Lucinda."

"What you obviously don't comprehend is that she has mental problems. Ones that can't be solved . . ."—his eyes darted towards René's gifts—"by mawkish rubbish."

"I cheer her up with my drawings. She cherishes my designs; she begs me for more. Just because you're boorish and can't appreciate the finer things in life doesn't mean others don't have culture or style. You will never fathom savoir-faire."

"*Savoir-faire* is not what Lucinda needs. You must over-come your naiveté and accept that your approach is detrimental. Don't you know that she could be overwhelmed by traumatic memories induced by your scribbles? Do you want her to have another attack of hysteria? Or an epileptic fit?"

René shook his head. "Non."

"Do you want her to commit suicide like her mother?"

"Of course not."

"Then you shouldn't pretend to be an alienist."

As René's shoulders sagged in defeat, Dr. Charles smiled. "Lord Haliburton and I agree that she is to avoid this horrid room, she is to follow my prescribed treatment and she is not allowed to be alone with you anymore. I am totally against it, but I conceded that she could attend the ball with you only if she agreed to all my medical recommendations." He nodded at the door. "It's time for you to leave here. Leave England. Do us all a favor and move on."

III
DIVERGING

$\mathcal{C}hapter$ *31:*

FIRE OF AMBITION

P en in hand, René was sitting at his workbench. When he was ready for a break, he walked to the entryway and glanced around the Parisian workshop. All his workers were busy and productive. To think it had been three years since he had combined his two workshops and moved his crew of thirty to here, 20 Rue Thérèse. A far cry from eight years previously when Jules Destape had sold him his jewelry business. René had been worried then that becoming the owner would interfere with his time spent drawing his creations. But, he reasoned, having twelve others to help him fabricate his designs would allow him to bring his art to life even faster. However, he had learned that having workers and their families depend on him was a lot of responsibility. *But is it more stressful than those early days when I designed wallpaper for Cousin Vuilleret? And my jewelry designs were rejected by Cartier and others? Non.*

René's mind turned to his latest source of tension: the purchase of a new kiln. He had been experimenting with his patented cire perdue casting technique using powdered glass and a binder packed into a metal mold. Working well for his small jewelry items, he wanted to create larger sculptural pieces with his wax. He had recently fabricated a four-inch-long perfume flacon, a tear-shaped bottle with carved fish on the sides, and a fancy stopper. Now that he had the fireclay molds made, he was eager to cast them with recycled glass. However, casting entailed using a larger oven that could heat the forms precisely. The newest kilns were expensive and needed correct installation. More room was needed, which meant remodeling the workspace. How was he going to afford to pay for both a kiln and the new construction? He looked at one of his expert goldsmiths, Victor, who had been with him since he took over Destape's workshop. *I could save some salary by letting go of his son.* But then he remembered that Victor and his wife had another baby on the way. How would their family manage without the eldest son's extra wages?

To rid his mind of this worry, René admired the plethora of flowers sitting on nearly every surface. Energized by their beauty, he returned to his small office and studied a sketch. He was trying to design a piece of jewelry that would catch the eye of his most important patron, Mme. Sarah Bernhardt. The world-famous actress had come into the Destape jewelry showroom when he worked as the manager for the firm. She was on the arm of the artist Georges Clairin, one of René's newly acquired society friends, who made the introductions. Meeting Sarah revived an ancient memory: He and André standing in front of Georges's portrait of the actress. The feeling the painting had evoked was reinforced by her presence. Femme de mystére. Older, thin, and fragile looking, the actress still had verve and mystique. His heart fluttering, René had taken her to all the cases, where she glanced at the precious stones and diamond-encrusted pieces seemingly unimpressed. Eventually, Sarah stopped at a counter where her attention had been riveted to one of his brooches. It was a droopy flower in profile, a peony cast in gold with champlevé enameling done in translucent white. Earlier, M. Destape had complained that the flower looked half-dead and too plain, but he placed it on a lower shelf in the case anyway.

Sarah pointed to the brooch. "Now that is interesting. Are there more like it?"

"Non," answered René.

Georges inspected the pin more closely. "That looks like something you would do, René. Is that your piece?"

"Oui."

Georges turned to Sarah. "Besides managing this store, René does freelance design for such houses as Cartier and fabricates them as well."

Sarah looked at René with new interest. "I like it."

"You should show Mme. Bernhardt some of your illustrations," Georges said. Sarah nodded.

René fetched his portfolio. The actress leafed through it and stopped at a picture of a bat brooch. René had drawn it with a natural grey pearl for the body and given it lacy wings of translucent enamel outlined in tiny diamonds. "When you create this piece," she said, "let me know and I will buy it."

He had eventually made that one and many other pieces for Mme. Bernhardt for on- and off-stage use. She had become one of his main patrons and introduced him to many more. His stardom had risen because of hers.

Now, several years later, René focused on his latest drawing. It was another brooch, a woman's head framed by butterfly wings. He wrote on the side of the paper: fret working and enamel for wings. Then he sighed discontentedly. It was a lovely piece but not one that would excite Sarah. Only the most outrageous and extravagant jewels satisfied her. He knew from visiting her with Georges that everything in her house was exotic, including her pets. He was surprised at the monkey who roamed freely, but it was her boudoir that had fascinated him. The furniture of black velvet and a skeleton of a man hanging before a mirror were certainly strange, but the full-sized coffin was most disturbing. Sarah was reputed to sleep in it. This thought reminded him of his first love, Lucinda, and her Egyptian sarcophagus. Thirteen years had passed since he had last seen her. He looked down at his black scarab ring, the one he wore daily without fail. Twisting it around his finger, he thought of the captivating young woman who had given it to him. *Such a beauty with her perfect pink mouth.* He had loved kissing those lips.

René's daydreaming was interrupted by Victor's son, Antoine, who had appeared in the doorway. "Pardon, M. Lalique, your wife and daughter are here."

Sacre bleu, I forgot about them. He had promised Marie that he would watch Georgette for a little bit while she went to an important meeting. "Show them in, please."

As soon as Georgette saw her father, she came running to him. He stood up and she bear-hugged his legs before looking up at him with her large eyes. "Bonjour, Papa."

"Bonjour, chérie." He kissed the top of her head covered in dark curls like his own. *She is getting so tall,* he thought as he studied his five-year-old daughter. With a pang of guilt, he wondered if he should not have moved out of their house nearly three years ago to live in the apartment upstairs. But he and Marie had been having stormy arguments about his affair with Alice, and René offered to leave. With bitter resignation, Marie had agreed to his relocation. For six years what had bonded their marriage were finances and Georgette.

"Bonjour, René," Marie said. She was holding Georgette's doll. "I won't be long, two hours, three at the most."

Three hours? What am I supposed to do with Georgette for all that time? He glanced at his worktable and then at Marie. "I have a lot of work to do."

"I've heard that before." She appraised the things on his workbench. "If it isn't work, *experimenting*, it is sculpture classes, or the theater or dinners with that actress and her dandy bohemians. Let's see, what did you call them? Oh, yes, artistic business engagements."

René ignored her. Marie was raised with old money. An aristocrat like her would never understand social and artistic progress.

She looked at him with disgust. "All the while spending my inheritance and not inviting me along. Leaving me and Georgette alone." Marie sniffed before suggesting, "Perhaps your mistress can watch her and your other daughter." Marie rarely used Alice's or Suzanne's name, barely acknowledging his child with Alice.

"Alice is out with Suzanne visiting her family."

"Well, then you will have to employ that creative brain of yours to figure out what to do." She handed Georgette the doll. "I need to leave, or I will be late." Hugging her daughter, Marie assured her that she would be back soon.

After René and Georgette had watched Marie depart, she asked, "Do you have a chair for me here, Papa?"

"Non, let's go upstairs. We can play with the toys there." His daughter smiled as he took her hand and led her out of the workroom.

When they arrived at the apartment, Georgette made a beeline for Suzanne's crib situated near René's after-hours worktable. She looked in at the rattles, blanket and stuffed toys. "These are baby toys, Papa. I'm a big girl." Georgette held up her doll clad in lavender silk. "Look, Maman made a new dress for Camille."

"Very nice."

"Baby Suzanne won't be allowed to touch her. She's not old enough yet." Georgette tucked her doll under one arm and began walking around the crib, her hand trailing on the rail. "You have to show babies what to do. They need more attention than big girls." She stopped walking. "I heard Maman tell

Mme. Dubois that you don't love us the way you love Alice and my little sister. That's why you don't want to live with us." She looked at him. "But I know it's because Suzanne is little. She needs you to watch out for her, right?"

"Yes, that's right." René controlled his anger and facial expression. *Damn her. Why is Marie discussing us with her friends in front of Georgette?*

Georgette nodded. "I can take care of myself, so you don't have to worry." She walked to the divan, propped Camille on it and arranged the doll's dress. "So, what should we do for fun? Go to the park?"

René hesitated. "It might rain today and, besides, it's too cold to go there." His gaze fell on his drafting table. "Would you like to make some pictures?"

"Oui, Papa, I would."

They got themselves situated and began to draw together. Soon, Georgette's paper was filled with scribbled images. She was working on a picture of a dog when she said, "I want a doggie, Papa, but Maman won't get me one. She said that I won't take care of it. She's wrong." The little girl stopped drawing to look at him. "Would you get me a puppy?" When he didn't respond, she persisted. "I will take care of it, Papa, just like you take care of Suzanne. Please, Papa, I want a puppy."

"A puppy is a lot of responsibility. I would have to talk to your mother first to see if she agrees."

"What do you care what she thinks? You don't even like her!"

"That's not true."

"It is true!" Georgette put down her pencil. "Fine. I don't care." With a sulky pout, she marched over and plopped on the couch.

"Don't you want to draw anymore?"

Crossing her arms over her chest, she said, "Non."

René tried a different tactic. "Would you like something to eat?"

She shook her head saucily.

"We could have a tea party with Camille."

Her expression softened; Georgette looked at her doll and then at her father. "One like Maman has with her lady friends? With cakes and bonbons?"

"Oui, chérie, let's see what we have." René beckoned her into the tiny kitchen. She watched as he prepared the tea and found some iced madeleine cakes. He brought everything into the salon, and he and Georgette, with Camille propped in a nearby chair, chatted and enjoyed their refreshments.

Georgette was droopy-eyed afterward. René suggested a nap, but she objected. "Camille and I want to go downstairs again."

They returned to his office, then walked into the glassmaking studio and over to the small muffle kiln. "What's this Papa?"

"That's an oven where I make my jewelry." As he looked at the kiln, an idea occurred to him. *What if I keep the kiln at the highest temperature just a little longer than normal? The glass should melt. They are small pieces.*

"Can I see some of it?"

René walked Georgette around the workshop, showing her all the stations while the workers stopped to talk to her. Soon, she began to yawn, so René suggested she take a nap on the couch in Papa's office. She curled up with Camille and a cushion against the armrest and was soon sound asleep.

Returning to the studio, René arranged the molds in the muffle oven then carefully loaded the cullet into the fireclay forms, making sure the glass filled them to the brim. Then he fired up the kiln and began to cast his first perfume bottle and stopper. As the heating cycle progressed, he checked it several times by quickly opening and closing the kiln door to make sure the forms were holding up. As long as no cracks were forming and the glass was melting and filling the cavity, he continued to turn up the heat. At the process temperature, he checked his pocket watch and held the heat there for the allotted time and then a little bit longer. He wanted to allow the glass to fuse and any bubbles in it to rise, pop and heal. To start the annealing process and not wanting devitrification or cracking because of cooling too slow or too fast, he carefully lowered the heat, holding the kiln at the proper temperatures and times. Excited by his efforts, he began regulating the final cooldown.

It was then that he noticed how hot the little studio had become. Sweating, he pulled out his handkerchief to mop his brow and heard Georgette screech. When he ran back into his office, she was standing at his worktable, with Camille in her hands, blubbering loudly. "What's wrong?"

Bawling, she held up her doll. There was a large, white stain on Camille's new dress. Georgette had opened two jars of his paint, purple and white. The white jar had spilled onto the drafting table and the paint was now covering his sketch and dripping onto the floor. Agitated by the destruction of his picture and her noise, he shooed Georgette away and retrieved a rag from a drawer to wipe up the mess she'd made. His scolding produced a fresh outburst of tears from her and more guilt for him. While cleaning up the paint, he tried to console her.

After Georgette's sobs had subsided, she tried to explain. "I was making you a p-p- picture of Camille and I wanted to p-paint it." She looked at her wrecked picture, the paint on her doll and the mess on the front of her dress. "I didn't mean to knock it over. Now everything is ruined. Maman will be mad." Sniveling, the little girl wiped her nose on her sleeve.

"Come on, let's try to wash off your dresses in the sink."

It was then that he noticed smoke curling around the door jamb. "Sacre bleu," he cried and flung the door open. Through the dense fumes he could see that his handkerchief, on the countertop near the kiln where he had dropped it, had ignited. The source of smoke was the oven. Coughing, he opened the window to clear the noxious vapors, but the fresh influx of air caused the kiln to burst into flames. René rushed into the sweltering space and tried to turn on the water faucet, burning his hand in the process. He knew he needed help. Running back to his office, he rousted the crew to help and scooped up his petrified daughter. Then he headed to the adjacent landlord's apartment. He beat on the door until the wife answered it. She took Georgette, distraught and wailing, from his arms.

Soon, René, his crew and landlord were carrying containers of water to douse the flames. They put the fire out shortly, but the room and its contents had suffered damage; the cupboards, shelves and the walls were charred and wet.

When René went to retrieve Georgette, the landlord's wife told him, "She's crying about her doll."

René returned to his office, but the doll wasn't there. He finally found Camille in a corner of the studio. Georgette must have dropped the doll when he picked her up. In addition to the white stain, its purple dress was damp, tattered, and dirty. Camille had been stepped on and one of her delicate boots was broken. Georgette would surely cry again when she saw the state of her toy.

Then he noticed the remains of the kiln. What about my bottle and stopper? There they were, the molds blackened but intact. Knowing that breakage could occur with the weakened clay, he should leave them alone for at least a day. But his eagerness to see his creations made him impatient. He was mulling over what to do when he heard a shrill voice from the doorway.

"I leave our daughter with you for little more than two hours and I return to this chaos!" Marie strode over to the kiln and peered inside. "To what do we owe this catastrophe?"

"A perfume bottle," René answered gingerly.

"A perfume bottle?" Marie huffed before lashing out at him. "Don't you know what's important in life? You are supposed to take care of us, not . . . your things! Your daughter is your creation too." Then she noticed René holding Camille. "Oh, no," she blurted and snatched the doll out of his hands.

Looking at it more closely, Marie's expression turned glum. "Georgette will be devastated. How could you be so thoughtless, René?" She backed away and shook her head in dismay. "I have been such a fool thinking that you loved me and Georgette. My friends were right. They knew I was just a purse to you. They warned me that you were marrying me for my money."

"Marie . . ."

She glared at him and shook her head again. "Don't. It will just make this part worse." After stuffing Camille into her satchel, she pulled out some documents. "I really tried for Georgette's sake, but I just can't do it anymore." Marie handed the papers to him. "You got your wish. I filed for legal separation today. I want all my initial capital plus interest. You will have to sell your business."

"You know I can't sell. Just give me some time."

"I don't trust you." Marie's lip curled as she motioned towards the kiln. "Do you blame me?"

"What about my employees? What will happen to them?"

She narrowed her eyes at him. "Fine. But the divorce won't be final until you pay me every cent you owe me."

"Don't worry, you'll get your money."

"Yes, I will," she said. "I've hired the best lawyer and accountant in town. Don't think we won't be keeping an eye on the finances. Your morbid friend Sarah with her lair of drug addicts and poets will have to foot your bills. No more decadent nights on the town. You can't make an honest woman of her, but you can stay home with your concubine. That should make her happy." With this final insult, Marie turned on her heel and left.

AFTER HIS CREW HAD BEEN SENT home for the day, the landlord had gone back to his apartment, and Marie had left dragging their miserable, tearful daughter away, René went back to his office and sank onto the couch. Strangely, he had no remorse about casting the bottle. What he regretted was telling Marie that he would watch their daughter in the first place. He should have told her no. René didn't care what Marie thought, but he wondered how Alice would feel about what had happened.

René was back in his studio when he heard the entrance door open and close. The voice of the landlord echoed in the stairwell, already filling in the details of the incident. When Alice entered the studio, with Suzanne on her hip, she gasped at the scene. In the twilight, everything looked worse. Neither spoke while she glanced around the room staring at the destruction.

Finally, she asked, "René, how could you?" Without waiting for an answer, she went on. "What if Suzanne had been here? What if we had been sleeping? You could have burned the building down. You might have killed all of us. But your work was more important."

Sighing heavily, he kept his eyes downcast.

Alice looked around the room again. "More money, more time working, to fix this mess." With a disgruntled look she walked away.

René followed her back to their apartment, sat on the divan and watched as she set one-year-old Suzanne down in her crib. Alice frowned at him. "I have grown tired of being nothing more than a distraction for you. A mistress who inconveniently got pregnant."

"That's not true and you know it."

"I let you do everything, have everything. All I have ever wanted is your attention."

"You know I love you and Suzanne." René debated whether he should tell her about Marie's decision. *But if not now, when? She will find out soon enough.* "Marie wants a divorce."

Alice brightened a little. "Now we can get married."

"Non."

"What do you mean, non?"

"She says she won't grant it until I pay her back all the capital she invested in my business."

"How long will that take?"

"I don't know. But we can't get married until then."

"A convenient excuse for you."

As Alice began ranting at him in much the same way Marie had, René stopped listening. All he could think of was the bottle and stopper inside their fireclay molds. Had the glass fused, had it filled the molds, how did the design look, were there any imperfections, had they annealed properly, would they survive, or would they crack? What did they look like?

Finally, Alice stopped talking. René glanced up at her.

With a flushed face and a hostile tone, she asked, "Were you even listening to me?" He remained silent. "I have pride, René. I know you love your daughters. You say you love me, but I'm not sure you do."

She was wrong. René loved them all, but he did not belong to any of them. He belonged to the world, to art. He had to create. "Mon amour, you don't understand."

"But I do. I do understand, René. The world loves you and you love the world. But I am weak. I need more than you are willing to give. I will not be the last in line for your love."

"Non, Alice. Listen to me . . ."

"Non, you listen." She walked over to Suzanne. The baby had been sitting quietly in her crib, clutching the bars of it, watching them. "Suzanne and I are sleeping in our bed tonight. You can sleep somewhere else. Here, on the couch, or in your office, or on the floor of your precious studio. That's where you want to be anyway." Tears of frustration sprang to her eyes. Quietly sobbing, she picked up the baby and held her tightly. As Alice carried her away, Suzanne watched him from around her mother's shoulder.

At that moment, René realized that the fire had changed something, had destroyed something more than his studio. He returned there to gaze at the forms. *Thank God, I saved them.* He could have lost so much more: the studio, the workshop, the showroom, Georgette. *How would I have felt if something terrible had happened to her?* He thought of her doll in her wrecked lavender dress. Suddenly, an image of Lucinda flooded his mind. *She wore a lavender dress that day,* the day after he had learned the Crystal Palace school was closing.

Chapter 32:

PERFUME

Lucinda emerged from the mist slowly, an ephemeral figure in an impressionist painting. At first an indistinct form, her tea dress appeared to be part of the silvery cloud that surrounded her. Billowy lavender silk decorated with flounces and lace floated through the pearly veil as she waved to him. He stood up and waved back.

She was out of breath. "Sorry I'm late. I dressed myself and hurried through the back stairwell hoping to remain unseen. I don't know if I was successful. And I didn't fix my hair as I didn't want Mary to know where I was going." Lucinda removed her bonnet and shook her hair loose, fluffing it with her fingers. "I hope you don't mind drawing my curls." Her eyes twinkling mischievously, she grinned at him.

"I only hope I can do them justice," he replied before taking her in his arms and kissing her passionately.

When they broke apart, she said teasingly, "You'd better start drawing. I don't want them to come looking for me." As they sat down, René grimaced at the thought of her odious doctor. "How would you like me to pose?"

"I would like to draw you in profile."

She leaned back on her arms and looked out over the dewy flowers. "Like this?"

"Chin up a little." He brushed back the hair from her face and arranged her curls over the sheer cotton chemisette revealed by the square décolleté of her dress. "Perfect," he murmured before picking up his sketchbook.

He drew in silence until she sighed. "So, tell me about your new job in Paris."

He looked up at her. "Are you sure?"

"Yes, I want to hear about it."

"Designing wallpaper patterns."

"Oh, really? I thought you wanted to be a jeweler."

He continued sketching while he talked. "I do. I will be. I can earn money with the patterns and create jewelry designs on the side. I will sell them to the major houses, Cartier, Boucheron, my old employer Louis Aucoc. And when I have made enough money and a name for myself, I will open my own shop, where I can make fantastic and exclusive creations for the rich." René paused. *Why was I so honest with her?* He had never revealed his dreams to anyone before; he hoped that she believed in him more than he did himself.

"Yes, you will be rich and famous," Lucinda agreed. "Your unique jewelry will be in museums, like the South Kensington."

She said it so freely, so sincerely, as if she could envision his dream, his future, better than he. Intense feelings bubbled up inside him, and he stopped drawing. "It means so much to me that you have confidence in my abilities." René grasped her hand and brought it to his lips.

Balancing to keep her position, Lucinda smiled. "Will you continue your art studies in Paris? Take more drawing classes?"

He let go of her hand and resumed sketching. "Perhaps. I want to improve my enameling techniques so I can learn to use it like paint. To enhance and color my creations. My drawings transformed into necklaces, bracelets, tiaras. Imagine a brooch that is a miniature painting. I want my jewels to reflect my artistry. Simple yet complex. The gemstones shouldn't detract from the design. They need to complement it. Like a pretty dress on a beautiful woman. One that enhances her beauty and curves." René studied her. "Such as that lavender dress on you."

Her face flushed at his compliment. "Thank you. I am trying to stay still, and you are making that hard."

René laughed. "I am almost finished." His hand moved over the paper with finesse. "I also want to learn how to sculpt and carve different materials. Stones like cameos, ivory, bone, horn. Perhaps glass." He thought for a moment. "Yes, definitely glass. I hope to create something that has never been seen before."

Forgetting her pose, she turned to him. "You will. I know you will. I believe in you."

"Maybe this one can be my first piece sold." He held up the picture so she could see it.

"Beautiful," she said dreamily. "May I have it?"

"After I color it."

Lucinda pretended to pout, then looked up at the sky. "Look, the sun is peeking through. The fog is lifting." She laid across the moss-covered stump in a languid pose. "Make another one with me looking at you."

THE DOCTOR WAS FURIOUS, BUT KEPT his face impassive as he interrogated Mary. "So, she went out this morning before you attended to her?" At her fearful look, Dr. Charles reassured her. "It's not your fault, dear, but, with her condition, Miss Haliburton must be guided. She is like a small child who doesn't know any better."

"Yes, Doctor, I understand. Whatever you think is best, sir." The maid curtseyed briefly and then hung her head.

"We certainly don't want her to return to the asylum and for you to lose your position, do we?"

Mary looked up quickly and shook her head. "No, sir."

As Dr. Charles scanned Lucinda's room, his eyes fell on Ambrose's box. "What's this?"

"The French boy gave it to her," Mary said meekly.

The doctor opened the box and saw René's drawing, *Vache et Vautour*. He removed it before letting the lid drop harshly. Charles studied the sketch with antipathy, then had a revelation. *Yes, that might work. But I need more ammunition.* He folded the paper and put it in his pocket. "You said that you found Miss Haliburton trembling in her closet the other day? Could you show me where?"

Mary led him into the closet and pointed to where she had found Lucinda. "She was right here, lying there and shaking terribly."

"What was she doing in here?"

"I don't know, sir. I just found her babbling to herself: Lily of the valley, lily of the valley. Over and over."

Dr. Charles looked around the darkened closet. "Can you fetch me a light?" When Mary returned with a candle, he used it to look for anything that might have caused Lucinda's fit. Nothing seemed unusual. "That's it? Do you remember anything else?"

"No, just her mumbling about the flowers." Then her face lit up. "Wait, I do remember something else. When I bent down to help her up, I could smell perfume. It was strong."

"Not her regular fragrance?"

Mary shook her head. "No, it was an exotic scent."

The doctor's scientific mind began to whir. *Smells can stimulate the primitive brain. Maybe the bouquet brought on some forgotten, traumatic memories. Now we're getting somewhere. Where would she keep the perfume in here?* He crouched down and noticed the trunk partially covered by the blanket. "What's this?"

"Milady's travel case, sir."

Dr. Charles hoisted open the top and began to dig through the items, shoving clothes aside to look for clues. When he discovered Lucinda's secret cache, he picked up the diary, opened it and read a few excerpts. He couldn't believe his luck. *This will be the undoing of that lowbrow Frenchman.* He closed the book and placed it in his coat pocket. Kneeling, he refolded the clothes neatly and was closing the lid when he noticed the blue bottle behind the trunk. He stood up, uncorked the flask and held it out to Mary. "Is that what you smelled?"

"Yes, sir, that's it."

Dr. Charles took a whiff. *Where have I smelled this scent before?* An image of the Egyptian sarcophagus flew into his mind, then one of Lucinda sitting on the couch nearby, wringing her handkerchief. *Yes, that's it. After her mother died.* He replaced the stopper and put the bottle in his breast pocket. "We need to keep this discovery confidential. Miss Haliburton would be very upset if she knew we went through her personal things. I don't want her to have another epileptic fit; it could cause permanent brain damage. We don't want that, do we?"

"No, sir," Mary said emphatically. "I understand, Doctor. You know what's best for milady."

"Thank you so much, Mary. You've been of great service to me."

The maid blushed and demurely bowed her head, but a tiny grin appeared.

Dr. Charles gently lifted her chin and smiled. "And to her."

RENÉ SAT IN THE ORANGE CHAIR and picked up one of his dress shoes, musing about the following night and the ball. Wanting to look his best for Lucinda, he dipped his cloth into the tin of polish and applied it to his shoes, working the mixture of soot, lard, bear grease and beeswax into the leather. While the polish dried, he looked out the window at the estate in the distance thinking about Lucinda and her doctor. Should he tell her what Dr. Charles had said? She was so happy, so excited, about the dance, their future together, that he was afraid to destroy her mood by revealing that her underhanded physician was trying to separate them.

René considered his idea of returning to France and then bringing her over later. *But after her grandfather dies, will it be too late? She will have been in the clutches of her evil uncle and the alienist, and they will have turned her mind against me. She must come with me now. But will she agree?* He had another thought. *Should I approach her grandfather? Will he believe me about the doctor? What would he do?* René picked up his horsehair brush and began vigorously shining his shoes in consternation. After removing all the excess polish from both shoes, he buffed them with a soft cloth. When they were done, René came to a decision. He would go to the stables to talk to M. Stoddard about it. The young man hoped the older man could give him good advice.

"MONSIEUR STODDARD? WILLY?" RENÉ walked through the barn and called out again. "Monsieur Stoddard? Willy?" But the stable was empty and one of the carriages was missing. *They must have gone to town.* Disappointed, he was about to leave when he heard whimpering. Locating the sound, he walked over to one of the horse stalls and opened the gate. Inside the empty stall was a young puppy. Sitting in the middle of the straw, its whining had turned into howling. However, when the pup spotted him, it jumped up and ran over with its tail wagging.

René bent down and petted the dog while it tried to lick his face. "Bon chien, good dog." While he played with the puppy, he saw a hand-painted sign on one of the walls: "Puppy for Free." As he got up to leave, he used his foot to keep the dog in the stall while he closed the door. Immediately, the animal renewed its plaintive yowling.

"Poor fellow, he's lonely." Willy had come into the barn. "He misses his mum and his littermates. Me cousin gave him to me before he left suddenly to go back north, but I can't take care of him and the horses. I'm afraid they'll step on him and he'll be crushed to death. Do you want him?"

René shook his head. "Non, I cannot take him. Is M. Stoddard here?"

"No, he's gone till tomorrow afternoon."

Damn! I wish he were here.

The puppy's cries had become high-pitched. Willy frowned and spoke louder. "The boss won't stand for this racket. I'm gonna have to give the pup away before he gets back." The two men walked out of the barn. "I thought about Miss Haliburton, but I don't know if they will allow her to have a pet." Willy shrugged. "I mean, with her condition and all."

René remembered M. Stoddard saying Lucinda had loved the dog in Egypt. Maybe a new pet to take care of would be just the thing to keep her from being melancholy. And if *he* gave it to her, the puppy would remind her of him. "I could show her the puppy tomorrow morning and see if she wants him, oui?"

"Sure, yeah, I mean I can't stand to listen to his crying all day. He needs a friend."

Chapter 33:

THE LAST OF THE FLOWERS

It was another cold, grey morning in England. A thick blanket of oyster-colored fluff covered the new sun. The woods, usually enticing, were dank and unappealing to René; he hoped that sunshine would appear soon and brighten his mood. A tug on the leash made him stop and glance down at his charge. The puppy had been walking alongside him, stopping frequently, and sniffing everything, had found a toadstool to explore. René consulted his pocket watch, then bent down and gathered up the pup with the thin rope tied around its neck. He wanted to arrive at their favorite spot before Lucinda got there.

He had met Willy earlier, asked him to find another servant girl to fetch Lucinda and handed him the note he'd written. When Willy asked why not Mary, René reminded him of her penchant for gossip. Willy nodded in agreement and had gone up to the mansion to carry out their plan. When René arrived at the fallen log, he set the animal down and tied the rope to a broken branch. While the puppy investigated the new territory with its nose, René wondered how Lucinda would react to his gift. Would she love it, or would it bring back bad memories of Egypt? Would the sight of it be too much, like the magic lantern picture show? Foreboding crept into his heart.

LUCINDA RECLINED AGAINST THE BACK of the tub while Mary placed another bucket of steaming water in it, then fetched a basin filled with warm water and rose oil. She brought it over and set it beside the stool placed near the tub. "I'm ready to do your hair, milady." Lucinda sat up enough to gather her hair together and drape it over the edge of the tub. Then she sank back into the warm water and closed her eyes. While Mary washed her hair, Lucinda remembered a snippet of the horrible dream she'd had earlier that morning: picking up a teacup and seeing maggots crawling beneath. As she wondered what it meant, Mary finished washing her hair and then wrapped it with a cloth. "Are you ready for a towel or would you like to stay a little longer, milady?" Lucinda opened her eyes.

"I'll linger a little while longer. Just leave my towel on the stool. Thank you, Mary."

"Yes, milady. I'll add another bucket to your tub."

Lucinda watched as Mary poured the hot water in and then left. She slid down into the water up to her chin and closed her eyes again. Thoughts of René ran through her mind and then, out of nowhere, a vision of the Egyptian perfume seller popped into her head. She was transported back to the shop, watching him pour the perfume onto the handkerchief. There, on the counter, was the unusual blue bottle with its dots of white enamel. The exquisite scent of Lotus in the Nile was in the air. Lucinda opened her eyes quickly and sat up. *Why can I smell it?* She inhaled again. Yes, she could detect the subtle scent of the perfume. *How is that possible? It must be my imagination.* The bottle was in the trunk, wasn't it? Lucinda got out of the tub quickly and dried off. Throwing on her chemise, she went into her bedroom, strode over to the closet door, flung it open and inhaled. Nothing, no smell. About to search her trunk, she was interrupted by a knock on the bedroom door.

"Yes?" she called.

"Pardon me, milady, but I have a note for you."

Lucinda cracked the door and saw the scullery maid. The young girl offered the folded paper to her.

RENÉ DIDN'T HAVE LONG TO contemplate his misgivings before Lucinda appeared in the distance. She was wrapped in a long, heavy coat with a hood and rushing toward him. "What's this urgent surprise? Is there anything wrong?"

"Non."

"I can't stay long. I must get back before my session with Dr. Charles this afternoon. Then I need to get ready for the ball."

Lucinda hadn't seen the puppy behind the fallen log. Hearing a new voice, it bounded out from its hiding place and ran to her. Eyes wide, she was silent as René explained. "Willy got him from his cousin but can't keep him in the barn." Tail wagging, the puppy jumped at her legs. When Lucinda bent down to pet it, the puppy wriggled in delight. "Willy and I thought you might want him."

"Could it be? But how?" She sounded bewildered. "I . . . don't know."

Her face hidden by the cloak, René was uncertain of her emotion. "Can you sit with us for a moment while you think about it?"

Lucinda didn't answer but kneeled and then sat against the log. The puppy immediately sprang into her lap and pawed at her chest, trying to get at her face. She held him up. "He looks like him." Putting him down again, she petted the puppy while it rolled in the creases of her coat. Then he clumsily crawled out of her lap and continued to explore the smells of the wet ground. Lucinda watched him for a few moments. "His name was Badger. He was a dachshund too."

"Badger?"

"Yes. The dog in Egypt. He died." She turned and looked at René with sad eyes. "The fire. I am beginning to remember because of my hypnosis sessions with Dr. Charles."

René looked away so she wouldn't see his contempt for the doctor. "You don't have to talk about it if you don't want to."

"I do want to tell you the truth of what happened and not what my uncle has told everyone. You have heard the gossip, right?"

"Yes."

"What did they say?"

"That you started the fire, that people were killed, and then you went crazy."

"Who told you these things?"

René didn't want to get M. Stoddard in trouble, so he incriminated her doctor instead. "Dr. Charles. He told me that your uncle said that after you heard your father arguing with Dr. Merimee, you burned an ancient scroll which started the fire." He looked at her, but she had withdrawn into her hood.

"That's not the way it happened." Lucinda paused. "Did he make up any other lies?"

René tried to recall what the doctor had told him. "He thought you were upset about a letter he sent there. About sending your mother to the asylum."

Lucinda shook her head, the large hood still obscuring her face. "I was upset about a lot of things the night before we left. I made a lot of mistakes, but starting a fire was not one of them." She fell quiet again. As René waited for her to continue, he watched the puppy rooting around in the long grass. "I fell for the wrong man." Lucinda removed her hood but stared at the field covered in dew as she told her story. "We met a photographer in Cairo, and he traveled with us to Professor Merimee's. His name was Mitch Grant and he was an old college friend of my father. He taught me about Egyptology and photography, and was nice to me. I developed feelings for him. The night before we were supposed to leave, I had an argument with him and my uncle's wife, Miss Meadows." Lucinda glanced at René, then focused on the flowers again. "She was only the nanny at that time. They had deceived me, and I was mad. I went to my room, they brought supper, but I didn't eat or drink, I just pouted. Finally, I decided that I wanted to talk to him. Find out why . . . Maybe apologize . . ."

Lucinda sat forward and pulled up a stem of bluebells. She began to pick the wilted blossoms off one by one. "I went to his room. The door was closed, but I could hear that he was not alone. She was there. That shrew. The future Lady Haliburton." Lucinda tossed the ruined stalk away and turned to him. "They weren't playing Whist."

"I'm sorry, mon amour."

"Thank you, but I know now that I was a complete fool." She sighed.

"What happened next?"

"I can't remember except that I saw Eza walking down the hallway."

"Eza?"

"Professor Merimee's Egyptian manservant. We were friends. He was Badger's master and part French. You remind me of him." She smiled dolefully. "The next thing I remember was waking up and the house was burning. Badger got me up. I followed him and crawled to safety." Lucinda pinched the bridge of her nose, but couldn't stop her eyes from welling up. Her voice cracking, she said, "And then he died. He saved me, but I couldn't save him." Tears streaming, she huddled in her coat and sank back onto the log.

Reminded of Ambrose, René scooted over and put his arm around her shoulders. "It's not your fault. I know what you are feeling I couldn't save mon ami either. The box I gave you, he made it. His name was Ambrose." He told her the story of the death of his friend. "I had told him to go talk to the girl. For a long time, I struggled with the thought that it was my fault that he was gone." Then René described the séance with Mme. Sphinx and her prediction. "So, is it fate? I don't know, but feeling guilty about it doesn't change what happened."

Lucinda smiled weakly at him before leaning her head on his shoulder. They sat quietly together for some time. The puppy, finally tired of exploring, nestled between them in the folds of Lucinda's coat.

René broke the silence. "But why would your uncle lie?"

"I don't know. He hates me?" Lucinda sighed mournfully. "I should have never removed the frog from the hole. Professor Merimee would have never found the secret room and none of it would have ever happened. Dr. Charles wouldn't have to get rid of the jackal that is hounding me."

René grimaced. "*He* is the jackal that's hounding you, Lucinda."

She sat up and pulled away from him. "How could you say that? He's trying to help me so I can get better. Resolve my problems." Disturbed by her movement, the puppy rolled off her coat and the leash jerked around his neck. Then the dachshund got up and pulled on the rope, trying to free itself. Lucinda loosened the tie from the branch. "Not give me more."

Hanging his head, René turned away from her, stood up, and walked a few steps away. "You're right. I'm sorry, I shouldn't have. I just thought giving you the puppy would make you think of me. I thought he could be our bond when we are apart. So you would remember us. Me." The puppy had trailed after him and was now cocking his head at René. He picked up the pup. "I understand if you don't want him."

"No, I'm so sorry. I was rude. He's a thoughtful gift. I do want him." Lucinda got to her knees and motioned René back. He gave her the dachshund and she kissed the puppy's head before setting him down. "But how could you think that

I would forget you?" Then she muttered something else as she tied the leash back on the branch.

"What did you say?"

"Dr. Charles proposed to me. I told him I was flattered . . ."

"You told him no, didn't you?"

"Well, I, uh, um," she stammered. "No."

Resentful and hurt, René stepped backwards. "What about me? Us? Paris?"

Lucinda stood up. "But I didn't say yes. I couldn't tell him no straight out. I mean, he has been so nice, so good to me." She frowned as René stepped farther away from her. "I didn't want to hurt his feelings. He hides it, but he is kind-hearted, a softie . . ."

René looked ahead at the forest and held his tongue. *Softie? Are we talking about the same man? That hardheaded smug clod that revels in telling others what to do?*

Lucinda came over and placed her hand on his shoulder. "You do understand, don't you?"

He glanced at her sideways. "Non. Mon amour, I don't understand. If you love me and respect him, you will be honest and tell him no."

Lucinda took her hand from his shoulder and bit her lip before turning away. Riveted on the drooping azure blossoms in front of them, finally she said, "You're right. I will tell him no." She looked back at him. "But I need to find a way to let him down easily. Please."

René crossed his arms over his chest and fixed his gaze on the petals of the dying bluebells.

Lucinda tilted her head. "You know you are the only one I truly love, right?" She leaned close and kissed him delicately on the cheek, but he didn't respond. "Don't be like that." She kissed him again. "Please."

René continued to pout as he walked away and plopped down on the log. Lucinda followed him and began to plant dainty kisses on his head. Her curls spilled around him, her coat fell open and he could see her chemise underneath. Kneeling in front of him, she put her arms around him and began to kiss his neck. Her affection, perfumed hair, and exquisite bust covered in lace was too much to resist. He buried his face in her velvety bosom. She lifted his head with both hands and kissed him on both cheeks. Then she hungrily sought his mouth and their lips melded together. When they separated, he got to his knees and embraced her waist with his arm. Then he gently lowered her into the last of the flowers and took his place beside her.

Chapter 34:

FAMILY PORTRAIT

René was searching through his bureau drawer for a suitable pair of cufflinks. Even though it was Sunday, his business associate, Francois, had arranged a meeting with him to discuss the design of perfume bottles. They were to meet for supper at La Fermette Marbeuf close enough that he could walk there. René had noticed that his clothes were tighter; he had gained weight since Alice's death the year before. Usually an early riser, he had taken to staying in bed longer, but had been trying to get out of the habit. This morning, he had failed. Awakening from a disturbing dream, he had lain there drifting in and out of consciousness. When he was finally alert, he couldn't remember any of it only that it had left him feeling out of sorts.

Mindlessly fingering his sets of cufflinks, a velvet-covered box caught his eye. Opening it, he gazed at his medal of honor and ran his thumb over the lettering: *Officier de la Légion d'Honneur.* Presented to him after the Universal Exhibition in 1900; the birth of his son, Marc, his second child with Alice, occurred two weeks later. Ten years ago. It seemed like an eternity. At the exhibition held in Paris, his ironworks stand of insect women, a display case of innovative works, had created a sensation. The press about it had rocketed him into an international superstar. His colleague, Henri Vever, had said, "You thought you were dreaming when you saw these beautiful things." Public opinion had finally swayed the critics. *A far cry indeed from when reviewers called my work "disturbing" and "utterly freakish."* He returned the box and medal to the drawer.

Finally, he chose a special pair of cufflinks: pressed glass in a silver framework. A single opalescent lily of the valley surrounded by two intertwined enameled bluebells, he had fabricated them at his smaller workshop devoted to glass in Clairefontaine. After adjusting his sleeves and the cufflinks, René looked at the photographs on the wall. Above his bureau were the ones he had taken of his property that bordered the Rambouillet forest. He had been inspired with the design for the cufflinks while walking in the forest and feeling joyful. His divorce from Marie had been finalized and his financial burden to her resolved. Discovering a patch of bluebells, the flowers had reminded him of his long-ago love, Lucinda.

René surveyed the portraits of his family also on the wall: Maman, Alice, Georgette, Suzanne, Marc. His eyes drifted to a picture of Alice with her brothers and her father. René smiled wistfully as he thought fondly of his father-in-law and remembered going to Auguste's house and studio to learn to sculpt. *Thank goodness he died before his daughter. How would he have taken her death?* René had been in London when he heard of Alice's hospitalization and surgery for her recurring female problems. Refusing to get out of bed after she returned home, Alice bled to death three days later.

Why? Why did Alice do that and why did Georgette tell me that? To make me feel bad? The divorce with Marie had put him through the wringer for five long years and he had resisted the idea of marrying again. Then Marc was born.

"Marie has remarried," Alice told him. "Now that Georgette is living with us, the least you could do is make me your wife. My father thinks so, too."

René had made an excuse. Something about his work being demanding. For the next two years, she hammered at him about making their relationship legitimate. Finally, he relented. Studying her portrait on the wall, he thought, *And yet, she remained dissatisfied.*

She never seemed to understand or care about his desires and ambitions. His career had been fruitful and his production profitable. His art, industry, and skill had made him a wealthy man. He had bought land on the banks of the Seine and built her and the children a magnificent home. All he wanted was to decorate it with beautiful things that he had created for them. For her. But nothing ever seemed to make her happy unless he sat with her in the salon, reading books or solving crossword puzzles. His work was his passion, but it seemed she wanted to keep him from it.

René looked at another small, framed photograph of Alice. *You were so beautiful when we met. My muse for my jewelry. How many pieces did I make using you as a model? What happened to us? Why did you become so needy? So clingy.* She once accused that fame had changed him, but he knew that his celebrity had affected both of them. With each passing year, as he expanded, she contracted. Her letters to him were depressing; she was always bored and sick. And jealous, definitely of his female clientele, maybe even his success.

I thought the trip to America and the World's Fair in St. Louis would cheer her up and brighten her mood. He frowned as he recalled that time and her letter to Suzanne saying she thought New York was ugly.

Perhaps I did travel too much without her. How many times had she accused him of staying away on purpose? He tried to reason with her; business meetings were necessary.

How was he to get more clientele? More sales? Little by little, their love for each other continued to erode. The more she complained, the more he escaped.

As he stared at Alice's young face in the photo, he fiddled with his mustache before casting his eyes downward. Focusing on one of his cuff links, he traced it with his index finger. Lonely, she was *so* lonely. *Didn't she know that I got lonely too?*

I never told her about Lucinda. She wouldn't have understood. She certainly hadn't understood about Claudine or René-Charles. René recalled his first return to London, the year before the St. Louis World Fair, to attend the exhibition of his drawings at the T. Agnew and Sons gallery where Claudine worked. He remembered Alice got suspicious after the second exhibit of his work at the same gallery in the spring of 1905. Eventually, Alice learned about his lover and new son. The discovery of his betrayal was the beginning of the end of Alice. She sank into a depression from which she never emerged. His wife was gone now, and nothing would bring her back. As René put on his jacket, he vowed to himself to never marry again.

When he walked into the dining room a few minutes later, Georgette was already at the table reading the newspaper. "Bonjour, Papa."

"Bonjour, Georgette." He sat down and took a sip of the coffee that had been poured for him. "Anything interesting in the paper?"

"I am reading about the neon lamp. There is an exhibition tonight with the inventor of it. Eight years in the making, it is an electric current in a sealed glass tube of neon gas." She smiled at her father. "Glass, your favorite subject these days." Georgette closed the paper, handed it to him and then focused on the food the servant girl had placed in front of her.

René began to read, but Georgette's noisy chewing made him glance at her, busy spreading jam on another piece of toast.

Her face has gotten fat. He also noted that the accordion pleats of the skirt of her green dress had spread. *Her thin waistline is gone as well. I tried my best to protect her. She's too young and immature to be pregnant with twins.* Single, galivanting about town, getting herself in trouble, with no man around. *Twenty-two years old and what has she accomplished?*

René had tried to encourage Georgette into getting an education, a job, hobbies, many things, but she never wanted to work at anything. Even marriage. When he had suggested she find a husband, she told him that marriage was a sham, a societal mechanism to keep women down. He wondered how she would be as a mother.

Georgette seemed to have read his last thought. "The doctor told me that both heartbeats are strong." She finished the last bite of her toast. "I am a little scared of giving birth, but he told me not to worry. He has delivered many twins with no problems. He said that he would put me to sleep with chloroform if necessary."

"He is one of the best."

"Suzanne and I are going shopping for the babies, but we were going to decorate the Christmas tree later. Would you like to help us, Papa?"

"I'm afraid I can't. I have a business meeting with M. Coty."

"How about after dinner tonight? We could wait till then."

"Non. It is a dinner meeting and will probably run long. You know Francois. Never stops talking."

Georgette frowned. "But surely not on Sunday, Papa. The restaurants close early."

"Doesn't matter. He will pay the boss to stay open for us."

"Please, Papa . . ."

"Non. I can't. The appointment is already made, and we are both busy this week."

"You are always working. You never have time for family. Especially me." Georgette looked and sounded just like Marie.

"When you run a business, you realize that money doesn't grow on trees. Somebody in this house must pay the bills. Perhaps one day you will understand. When you have a husband and a household to take care of, not just bastards."

Georgette's lower lip quivered, but she said nothing. She looked down at her rounded belly and then cupped it with her hands as if she wanted to cover the ears of her babies inside. René gritted his teeth. *I should never have said that to her.*

Before he could apologize, Georgette sassed, "You know all about bastards, don't you? And failed marriages."

"How dare you speak to me like that!"

"You're horrible at relationships because you don't care about people. Maman was right, you only care about things!"

René banged his fist on the table. "Then move back in with her and she can support you!"

Georgette's brash expression crumpled, and she began to sob. Just then, Suzanne and the server entered the room. While the girl timidly placed René's breakfast on the table, Suzanne pecked him on the cheek. "There's no need for temper, Papa. We don't want to upset the mother-to-be." She then put her arm around her half-sister's shoulders. "Come, Georgette, let's get ready to go shopping." Gently pulling on Georgette to get up, Suzanne then comforted her. She threw her father a disenchanted look as they walked out of the room.

Chapter 35:

FACES DE VERRE

René consulted his watch. *Still too early to leave.* Even walking, he would be at the restaurant too soon. His business tactic was to keep Francois waiting. Picking up his briefcase, he went into the showroom. Daylight was waning and the skies were overcast, but the display window was still attractive. René admired all his new glass creations spread out there. Georgette was right: his fascination with the medium had grown immensely over the last three years. But she was wrong about him not caring about his family. He loved them all. Well, certainly not Marie, but there was only so much time in the day. Besides, his work energized him while intimacy drained him. Loafing around or chatting about nonsense was a waste of time.

He walked over to the jewelry display case. The less expensive pieces were kept here; his masterpieces were kept in the safe at his prestigious store on Place Vendome or with their wealthy owners. Focusing on a small dragonfly made with moonstones and colorful champlevé enameling reminded him of his enormous Libellule brooch with its intricate composition. His friend and most important patron now, the financier Calouste Gulbenkian, introduced to him by Mme. Bernhardt, had commissioned it.

How many months had been spent making the dragonfly lady with those marvelous plique-à-jour wings? So huge that they had installed four hinges on each wing to hold the pieces together. Never meant to be worn, Calouste housed it in a glass case on a wall in his majestic Parisian home.

Calouste had told René that he had superlative talent and an exquisite imagination. An extraordinary compliment given all the valuable artwork and artifacts collected by his rich friend. Even though Calouste would buy more of his gems, René's interest had waned. Disillusioned with jewelry-making because of others imitating his style and producing facsimiles, he had turned to a new love: glass. For Cyclamen, Francois's newest perfume, René had designed the bottle. His six dragonfly women in green patina encircling the bottle had been a triumph. He was eager to show the other designs in his portfolio to the perfume maker.

René checked his watch again before going to the window front and peering upwards. The dark clouds threatened rain again; it always seemed to be raining since Alice's passing. René fetched an umbrella and his overcoat and started out for La Fermette Marbeuf.

As he made his way to the restaurant, René's mind turned again to the morning squabble. He regretted making Georgette cry but felt worse about losing his temper and disappointing Suzanne. After Alice passed, the two sisters had formed an even tighter bond. Suzanne had matured quickly, becoming protective and maternal. René understood how much even he had come to depend on his younger daughter's support and advice. She had an artistic flair of her own, so he focused on cultivating her talents by furnishing supplies and encouragement. Suzanne was so much like him—creative, ambitious, a designer's aesthetic—it was easy to relate to her. Beautiful like her mother but not so moody. *And dutiful.* He would call for her and she would come running.

Unlike his son, who had taken the death of his mother hard. Marc had acted out and railed against his father's authority and so had been packed off to a boarding school. René supposed it was his fault; he hadn't spent enough time at home because of building his business. *My children don't really know me.* A brief memory of his father flitted through his mind. *At least I am not dead. I provide for my family.* They didn't know that everything he did, all his work, was for them.

René arrived at the restaurant. The maître d'hôtel informed him that M. Coty was waiting and led him to the table. Francois had already ordered wine and appetizers. René sat down and opened his portfolio. They agreed on several of the designs, including a stamped metal label for a wooden display sampler box for retailers and the vessel for the oriental fragrance, Ambre Antique.

Then Francois brought up a sore subject. "The containers must stay affordable."

René frowned. "The bottle for L'Effleurt made by Baccarat is so plain, so ugly, and the stopper is banal."

"I disagree."

"Imagine how much more attention there will be with my flacon and stopper," René argued. "My design will be a girl rising through the smoke, par fumé, but I will stylize the vapor more. What's your slogan? 'Somewhere inside romance blossoms'?" René pointed to his drawing. "The lady will look as though she is being born from flower petals."

"Hmmm . . . That sounds intriguing." Francois took a drink of his wine and ate two appetizers while he contemplated René's suggestion.

René had a bit of an edge: Francois knew that René's services were constantly in demand. He had already designed an entire bottle for Piver perfume as well as made furnishings for the mansion of the owner of the perfumery, Jacques Rouché. Other established perfume houses had approached René for glass manufacturing, as well as many architects for interior décor. René knew, as did Francois, that it was his name that was in part selling the fragrances. The elite wanted luxury and Lalique provided it. But he also wanted to capitalize on the middle class, to enable them to own a piece of his artwork, and Francois's business was the way to do it. He showed Francois the picture again. "See how the stopper is two cicadas?"

Francois shook his head. "Non, who wants an insect? Maybe I could design the stopper."

René tapped his fingertips on the tabletop. *Why are you always meddling in my area of expertise? I am the visual designer. You are the fragrance designer. You're just upset because your product is inferior.* He shot a forced smile at Francois. "The House of Piver seemed to like my scarabs. I heard that L'Effleurt is not selling so well." He paused. "Perhaps it isn't the bottle."

Francois frowned but nodded. "I am making some modifications to the formula." He took another swig of wine. "Do you think you can handle the output?"

"The factory at Combs-la-Ville can handle the production," René promised. "I have expanded the workforce and secured the patent for my new process. I can make them cost-effective."

"I'll think about it." Francois patted his stomach. "I'm hungry, let's order."

While they ate dinner, Francois began to ramble on about politics and René's mind drifted. He recalled how Alice had thought the perfumer was uncouth and gauche. René didn't care about Francois's vulgar nature; it was his industry acumen that drew René to him.

Francois had told René a tale of phenomenal packaging and marketing to women, the modern consumers, the likes of which the world had never seen. Put the product in an elegant bottle and then let them sample the bouquet. A dab of L'Effleurt, a dash of Styx, a touch of Ambre Antique . . . Perfume will rule the world, he said, convincing René that they would get rich beyond their dreams. Together as a team. Francois had ordered fifteen new bottle designs. René welcomed the money, but it was the fact that Francois would help spread his creations amongst the masses that he appreciated. René firmly believed that when an artist had found something beautiful, he must try to allow the greatest number of people possible to enjoy it.

René's attention shifted back to Francois when he suggested ordering a bottle of expensive brandy. Then, when Francois heard his name called out, René looked over at two pretty girls heading towards the table. Their bell-shaped dresses of vibrant silk rustled around them.

"Henriette, chérie," Francois exclaimed and stood up.

"René, you know Henriette."

Of course, René knew Francois's mistress. He stood as well, grasped her hand and kissed it. "Mais oui. Bonsoir, Henriette." He extended his hand to the other woman. "And this lovely lady is?"

As the girl offered her hand bashfully, Henriette said, "This is Camille, my cousin. She is visiting from Provence."

René brushed his lips softly over the back of her hand before letting go of it. "Je m'appelle René. How do you like Paris?"

"It's wonderful."

"Come, sit down and join us," Francois offered. While he regaled them with stories, René became distracted. Instead of listening, he studied the faces of the young women. Camille resembled Lucinda, but her name reminded him of his daughter and her old doll. *Why am I so upset about Georgette being with child? Perhaps I am not ready to be a grandfather.* The situation brought his age, his mortality, to the forefront of his mind. He had so many things he wanted to accomplish in this life.

The first thing he needed to do was make up for his rudeness to Georgette. *She is irritable due to her condition. And jealous that I am spending more time with Suzanne. What can I do to make her happy with me again?* A new dress? Non. Something more personal. A jewel? *Oui, I will make her a pendant.* He would have it fabricated for her birthday in February. But what? *A flower? Non. An insect? Non.* He wanted to use glass. *A face? Perhaps.* Looking at the pretty women in front of him, inspiration hit. Two babies, two faces. A motherhood pendant. René wondered if the twins would be fraternal or identical. He hoped they were girls. *I will use amethyst, her birthstone, and yes, that gorgeous opal.* A recent purchase, his favorite gemstone would be a drop on the bottom of the pendant.

Smiling to himself, he took out his fountain pen, his pocket notepad and began to sketch. He drew the contours of Camille's face.

Francois finished a story with, "As you know, Mme. Sarah Bernhardt wears that fragrance. Right, René? Monsieur Lalique is a good friend of hers," Francois informed Camille.

Camille was starry-eyed. "Mme. Bernhardt? *The* René Lalique?"

Before René could reply, the restaurant manager arrived at the table. Francois excused himself and followed the man to the bar. The restaurant had closed, and everyone had gone home except for their party. As René had predicted earlier to Georgette, he knew Francois was paying the manager extra, including tips for the servers.

Camille turned to René, who was still drawing. "What are you doing, M. Lalique?"

"Designing a pendant." He stayed focused on his picture, thinking about how he would frame the faces. Vines, leaves, flowers?

"May I see?" René reluctantly gave the sketch to her. "Is that my face?" He nodded. Smiling, she handed the picture back to him. "Are you always this serious, M. Lalique?"

"Oui, he is," Francois said, returning to the table. "Come on, René, put down your pen and have some fun." He poured more brandy in everyone's glass.

René joined in the conversation for a while, but quickly returned to mulling over his project. Once an idea took hold, he could rarely shake it loose from his mind. His eyes fell to his cufflinks. *That's it,* he thought. *I will surround one face with bluebells and one face with lily of the valley. I must begin now.* With that, he excused himself and got up from the table.

With pouty lips, Camille tilted her head at him. "Why so soon, M. Lalique?" She reached over and touched his hand. "I can make you smile," she said with a knowing look.

So young, so lovely, so tempting. Non, too soon. He kissed her hand and told her that she was enchanting, but he must go. He signed his doddles, ripped out the notebook page, gave it to her and told Francois that he would be in touch.

WHEN HE ARRIVED HOME, THE household was dark. René went into his studio and drew some more, fleshing out his design. He contemplated sculpting it but instead fell asleep on his divan.

He is there, in the field of bluebells. He sees, in the middle of the patch, a cloud of smoke arising. Lucinda emerges from it.

A distant voice calling. "Monsieur, Monsieur."

René opened his eyes after being gently nudged. His chauffeur stood over him. "I'm sorry to wake you, Monsieur, but it is your daughter."

Groggy, René sat up and blinked. "What? My daughter? Suzanne?"

"Non. Mlle. Georgette."

"What's wrong with her?"

The driver shifted nervously. "I didn't know where you were. We have been looking for you. Mlle. Suzanne requests that you come as soon as possible.

When he arrived at the address, Suzanne met him in the foyer. Behind her was Marie, staring at him with empty eyes. "Never around, can never be found."

René snapped at her. "Marie, I don't need your chastising right now."

With that, Suzanne lost her composure. She broke into tears as she fell into his arms. "Please forgive me, Papa. I told her to get down, but she didn't listen." Leaning against his chest, she wept harder.

He hugged her tight and petted her head. "There, there, chérie, tell me what happened."

"It was an accident. She was decorating the Christmas tree and standing on a footstool. I told her to get down. She slipped and fell." A new flood of tears erupted. Finally, Suzanne backed out of his embrace as she choked out the words, "There . . . was . . . blood. I brought her here."

René looked at Marie. "Where's Georgette? I want to see her."

Marie glared at him. "You are too late. As usual."

"What?"

She remained silent.

"Stop wasting my time. Where is she? Upstairs?' He tried to move past her.

"She died, René. Our beloved daughter is dead." Her anger gone, replaced with sorrow, Marie looked at him forlornly. Then, her head sagged. "Dead." Her voice was feeble and lifeless.

What? I don't understand. He stared at the top of Marie's head. *That's not possible. It can't be.* He looked at Suzanne. "Non."

Dabbing her eyes with her handkerchief, Suzanne nodded. "Oui, Papa, it's true. Georgette's last words were, 'Tell Papa that I never wanted to be a burden to him. I just wanted happiness.'"

He shook his head. "Non. She was never a burden."

Suzanne sniffled. "She said, 'Tell him I'm sorry I couldn't hold on.' Then she closed her eyes and was gone." The memory brought fresh tears.

"The babies?"

"Identical twins," Suzanne replied miserably between sobs. "Girls. Both dead. Stillborn."

Gray, leaden pain filled René's chest. "Two girls. Dead." He felt sick.

Marie broke down and René hugged her close. Whimpering, she buried her face in his shoulder until she had regained her composure and then gently pushed him away. Without a word, she turned and shuffled off into the salon.

René headed towards the stairwell to see Georgette. Suzanne tried to follow him, but he stopped her. "I wish to be alone with her." He kissed Suzanne's grief-stricken face before dragging himself up the steps, each footfall an effort. After entering the bedroom, he removed his coat and hat and laid them on the chair in the corner. Georgette was in the bed with fresh bedcovers drawn just past her waist. She had been clothed in a clean nightdress with lace at the throat. Her colorless face was serene. For the second time that night, he was reminded of her doll, Camille, from so long ago. René sat on the edge of the bed and tenderly caressed his daughter's porcelain white cheek. Her long dark hair had been arranged by someone to frame her face and drape over her bosom. He glided his fingers from her cheek to a nearby ringlet and smiled wistfully; she had always complained that she had inherited his unruly curls. He toyed with the curl briefly and then gazed at her lifeless face before turning away. It was then that he saw them shrouded in shadows atop the dresser. Two small, neatly wrapped, white bundles. *Oh, Lord, that's them. Her babies.* His chin slumped, and he could no longer look. Instead, he grasped Georgette's hand, cool to the touch, and wept until his anguish was spent. When the constable and mortician's assistant arrived to take her away, he leaned over and kissed her pale forehead.

Returning downstairs, René discovered that Suzanne had gone home. He put on his hat and coat before stepping into the street, then watched as they loaded his daughter and the bundles into the undertaker's wagon. His shoulders sagging, he got into his coach. The chauffeur drove him home but instead of going inside, René walked to the river. He crossed over the Pont de l'Alma halfway and stopped.

Electric lights illuminating the structure, he stared out over the river and at the Eiffel Tower across the way. Thinking about Georgette's earlier accusation, he realized that, again, he had sacrificed the evening with his girls for business. *Would she still be alive if I had been there with them?* As he stood there, he felt a drop of rain on his face. Glancing down at the black river, he watched the engorged Seine hurtle by in a hurry to meet the sea. He knew he should go home, go inside so he wouldn't catch a cold. But René was riveted there, remembering another night of rain and sorrow. From the distant past, like the current below the memories rushed in.

Chapter 36:

MUDDY SHOES

The oppressive clouds of the morning had remained in the sky but had turned inky as the day progressed. At the appointed time, dusk now falling, René stood on the portico of the mansion, thankful that the ornate structure was keeping the rain off of him. He looked down at the bouquet in his hand. Lily of the valley wrapped with a blue silk ribbon. Readjusting his top hat, he heard the butler opening the door. The servant admitted him to the entrance hall, where he waited until Lucinda arrived followed by her uncle and his wife. René offered Lucinda the bouquet.

"Lily of the valley. How beautiful. Thank you." After handing the bouquet to the housekeeper to put in a vase, she asked René, "How do you like my gown?" Twirling in place, her perfume radiated from the eddy.

Not quite scarlet yet not burgundy, her gown was a rich red. Bright threads were woven throughout the dark ones; with the candlelight, the gown was luminescent. Lucinda had painted her lips to match, a sensational contrast against her pale skin. Monsieur Stoddard was correct: she looked like a living porcelain doll. "Si belle, Mademoiselle."

Color rose to her cheeks and she cast her eyes downward. "Merci, Monsieur." As the housekeeper helped her don her fur capelet, Lucinda's eyes twinkled at him.

René offered her his arm. "Shall we?"

During the coach ride to the party, Lucinda was quiet and looked out the window. Unable to read her mood, René remained silent as well and watched the passing scenery in the fading light. They were traveling an ancient highway through the wooded acreage to arrive at Lord Home's mansion, located on a ridge. When René extended his hand to help Lucinda out of the carriage, his eyes fell on her red silk shoe with its sparkling vamp and small bow. He recalled his dream of that morning. In it, he is looking down at his polished shoes and then at a dirt hill he must climb. Worried about his shoes getting dirty, he sees three people at the top of the hill, two men and a woman. They see him and start to descend. He knows that they are going to help him get to the top.

Linking her arm in his, René escorted Lucinda as they followed her aunt and uncle into the main hallway. After their coats were taken, they entered the salon. Hundreds of people had already arrived and congregated in small groups, waiting for the announcement of dinner. René noted heads turning as he and Lucinda walked by. *Mon amour is so beautiful, they cannot keep their eyes off her.* He wanted to slip his arm around her waist and hold her close, but refrained.

Trying to ignore the attention, René kept his eyes forward but caught snippets of the conversation in passing. A pompous, portly gentleman said loudly, "You know I have been appointed to a Parliamentary committee on rules and regulations regarding the lights on fishing boats. Yesterday, we examined Captain Walker. He had much to say concerning the safety of the trawlers with side lights . . ."

Lucinda tugged on René's sleeve and whispered to him after they had passed the man. "How utterly boring these people can be."

They exchanged smiles and he squeezed her hand. He continued to smile until he spotted Dr. Charles conversing with two elderly gentlemen. Lord and Lady Roderick were headed straight to him. René's buoyant attitude disappeared. Thankfully, they were saved by the dinner bell but not by the seating arrangements. Across the table from each other, René threw amorous looks at Lucinda, who batted her eyelashes and suppressed tiny grins. All while chatting with the guest sitting next to her, the overbearing Dr. Charles.

After dinner, when the doctor was detained by another socialite, René moved quickly to Lucinda's side. He escorted her to the ballroom as the music began and extended his hand. "Would you care to dance?"

She placed her hand in his. "I have been waiting an eternity for you to ask."

They began to waltz. Lucinda's closeness and her fragrance reminded him of their tryst that morning. "You are wearing a new perfume."

"Yes, I got it in Egypt. It's called Lotus in the Nile. Mary placed some in my bath water this morning and then put the bottle on my dressing table. When I asked her about it, she said she found it on the floor of my closet. It was her suggestion that I wear it tonight. Do you like it?"

"Non," he replied, "I *love* it, chérie. Just like the most beautiful woman here. In my arms."

She blushed. "I love you too."

Twirling around and around the floor, they danced until weary. Then rested briefly before dancing anew. Finally, René led Lucinda to a seat. "Let me get us something to drink." As René approached the refreshment table, he overheard two women gossiping. Their backs turned; they didn't notice him there.

"With such a sullied reputation, I'm surprised that she is out in public and with painted lips. And can you believe that red dress?" said one.

"No, such a garish color," the other answered. "But she is mad like her grandmother and mother. Did you know that Lady Sarah committed suicide?"

"I had heard that. The Haliburton legacy tarnished again."

"Do you know who she is dancing with? Their tenant. And he's French. Ugh."

"She does look like a French whore." They both tittered.

"What more shame can she bring upon that family?"

René cleared his throat loudly and the women turned. Flushing red, they moved off. René picked up two glasses and returned to their table, but Lucinda wasn't there. She was on the dance floor, swirling around, a shimmering top, her skirt floating from side to side. René frowned when he saw her partner. Dr. Charles.

A gruff voice spoke at his side. "They make a handsome couple. Lord Haliburton thinks so anyway."

René turned to see one of the elderly gentlemen the doctor had been talking to earlier. The man introduced himself. "I am Dr. Thomas Perkins. What's your name again?"

"René Lalique."

Dr. Perkins nodded perfunctorily. "So, Mr. Lalique, my son tells me that you will be returning to Paris soon."

René tried to maintain a neutral face. "Oui."

"He told me that you want to be a jeweler."

The old man reminded him of Louis Aine. "Oui."

"Not much of a talker, are you?" René detected the same snide tone used by the younger Dr. Perkins.

Now more than ever, René wanted to take Lucinda away from here. As he pondered how he could accomplish that, Lady Haliburton appeared.

"Dr. Thomas, Lord Haliburton wants to introduce you to one of his London colleagues." After the doctor had left, she glanced over at Lucinda and Charles, then down at the glasses of wine René was holding. She looked deeply into his eyes. "I've never had the chance to talk to you. Looks like she won't be drinking that anytime soon. Do you mind?"

René reluctantly handed her one of the glasses.

Lady Haliburton raised her glass. "To Paris. My favorite city." As they sipped their drinks, she began to talk about her numerous trips there. Recalling landmarks, fashion, stores, museums, and her wealthy Parisian friends. She rattled off a list of names: had he heard of them, did he know so-and-so . . .

René tried to remain attentive, but he couldn't help occasionally searching for Lucinda and the doctor on the dance floor. He finally spotted them when the music ended. Following his gaze, Lady Haliburton stopped him before he could go reclaim Lucinda. "I saw your book of French poetry. I know some French but would welcome a translation or a lesson from you."

She flashed him a wanton expression. "Would you like to teach me while we dance?" Lady Haliburton had already set down her drink and was brazenly touching the arm holding his wine glass. He watched as she ran her hand down to his wrist, her fingers lingering there. As she took his glass and put it on the table, the orchestra began playing anew.

"I . . . I . . . I . . ." She took his hand and led him onto the perimeter of the crowded dance floor. Not knowing what else to do, René began to waltz her around. It was a lively tune and they glided and turned quickly with the tempo. Lady Haliburton leaned close to him as she clasped his shoulder tightly. Then, when the orchestra stopped, she reached behind and held his hand at her waist until the music started again. Unwilling but not wanting to cause a scene, he succumbed, and they danced for another two pieces. Finally, noticing Lucinda was gone, René politely but firmly excused himself.

He scoured the assembled mass as he wandered through it, avoiding the chattering circles of high society and searching in vain until he saw Lucinda hurrying out through the front entrance, clutching her fur capelet around her. Chasing after her, she was climbing into the carriage when he called out. "Lucinda, wait!"

She didn't answer. René ran into the wet night and reached the coach as Lucinda leaned back against the seat. Peering into the darkened interior, he saw her sorrowful face.

"What's wrong? What happened?"

She didn't speak, just tapped the side of the carriage to signal the driver.

"Non, wait, Lucinda, stop. We must talk."

M. Stoddard, once his friend, issued an order. "Step back, young man."

René backed up but gave him an imploring look before pleading again with Lucinda. "Mon coeur . . ."

Her head bent forward, Lucinda whispered, "Je t'aime. Pour toujours." I love you. Forever. She tapped again, this time more insistently.

The drizzle was turning into a shower. With a flick of the whip, the horses started forward quickly. Another flick and a command from M. Stoddard spurred them into a gallop. Muddy water sprayed from the wheels, soaking René's shoes and pants. Rain pelted his face as he dismally watched the carriage speed away, his fantasies and dreams disappearing with it. Rather than going back inside and enduring the English gawking, René remained there, staring at the empty stretch of road, until he was thoroughly sodden. After signaling a nearby coach to drive him back to town, René decided that, perhaps, it was time to return to Paris. He had had enough of this rainy island and its coldhearted people.

LUCINDA RAN IN THE DOORWAY BUT hesitated as her eyes adjusted to the darkness of the room. What had she done? She had fallen in love again. *How could I be such a fool?* She shook her head. *But he adores me. He doesn't like Miss*

Meadows, he told me. So why was he dancing with her? Flirting with her? Oh, Eza, why? Wasn't Mitch enough for her? That harlot had to seduce all of them. Take them away from me. She felt lightheaded, her memory misty. She tried to focus. *No, that wasn't Mitch. It was Charles at the ball. We were dancing.* Glass faces, hard and transparent, staring, judging, like the portraits when she was a child. Too many eyes on her, boring holes in her head. Feeling so hot. A little air, he suggested. Outside, he said. The rain had let up temporarily. *Yes, the cool air.* They had stopped by the old well fed by the mineral springs and looked into it. Very deep. Then they had sat on the bench by the old octagonal pavilion covered with ivy. Talking, they were talking. Then Charles had consulted his pocket watch. She remembered it swinging from its chain, the gold case catching the light from the gas lamp nearby. Glinting. Back and forth. Back and forth. Then nothing. And, now, here she was in the Egyptian room. What happened to Eza? Was that his name? No. Not him. The artist. Where was he? *How did I get here?*

Lucinda pulled her fur capelet closer to protect herself against the draft. Were the windows open? She looked towards them, but the drapes were closed. So cold. Needing to check, she drew the curtains back. The windows were shut. *I should light a candle.* Turning around, she saw him. The light from the hallway cast a glow on his silhouette. By the false door.

"Why don't you leave me alone?"

The shadow man was quiet, but she could see his gleaming eyes.

"They want me to go back in there. But I won't. I'll die first." She touched the pendant around her neck. "They want me to think that I am crazy. That you don't exist. But you do." She walked towards him. "So, tell me what to do." Still he remained mute, but his eyes followed her. Watching.

Lucinda looked at the sarcophagus and then back at him. "Should I ask her? Shall I get in and ask the goddess what to do?" Starting towards it, she saw the book and drawings on the table. The book of French poetry, his poetry, that he had read to her. Tracing the cover lightly with her finger, she thought of the times he had read it to her. So many times. She tasted the salty tears as they coursed past her lips. *No. Must be strong.* Lucinda huddled in her capelet, freezing. Considering the papers strewn on the table, she contemplated those glowing eyes again. A fire would warm her, wouldn't it?

Chapter 37:

PASSED ON

Lucinda laid down the newspaper after reading the article on the front page. The world's greatest actress, Sarah Bernhardt, was dead and Paris had turned out in droves to mourn her passing. Lucinda wondered how René had taken her death. She knew he had made jewelry for Bernhardt; surely they were friends. Lucinda tried to picture his young face. So long ago, eons it seemed. Glancing at the date on the paper—March 1923—what had it been, forty-three years? Closing her eyes, she conjured an image of them dancing together and looking into René's soulful eyes.

Her daydreaming was interrupted by the clinking of porcelain. She looked over to see Charles setting down a tea service on the sitting room table. He stepped over to her and kissed the top of her head. "Taking a little catnap, my dear?" he asked before settling himself in his chair.

"No, just closed my eyes for a minute. I was reading the paper."

Charles ran a hand through his white hair, glanced at the paper and rolled his eyes. "Another Parisienne dead. How unfortunate."

"She wasn't exactly just another Parisienne. She was a world-famous actress."

Charles scoffed as he poured their tea. "I read somewhere that she was anemic and thin but certainly a ham on stage."

"Critics are often unkind, but they can't deny that she gave memorable performances." Lucinda picked up her teacup.

"It's too bad the French army couldn't imitate her." Charles guffawed at the insult, which brought on a fit of coughing.

Not wanting to hear his crowing about the Great War again, Lucinda prompted, "Have you made the appointment for your chest X-rays, dearest? Your cough sounds worse."

"Yes, yes. I'm going in today." He didn't look happy about it.

She reached over, patted his hand and smiled at him. "Thank you, sweetheart. I know you don't want to cause me any worry."

After Charles had left for his appointment, Lucinda went into her bedroom closet and uncovered her traveling trunk. She hadn't looked at it for years. *So beautiful.* She ran her fingers over the pressed tin design before opening it. There it was, the lovely handmade lotus box that René had given her. Removing it from the trunk, Lucinda returned to her desk by the window and placed the box on it, then rummaged through the desk until she found the small manila envelope. Shaking out the key, the Eye of Ra, she opened the box. Lucinda took out a package of letters. It was quite the bundle, but she knew which ones she wanted to read. Untying the string that bound the stack, she selected the two letters stuck between the pages of a notebook and began reading the first one.

August 1903
Dear Mrs. Perkins,

To answer your inquiry, yes, life is treating us well. The missus is pleased with her new mistress. This Lady Haliburton is much more agreeable than the adulteress.

Yes, with the divorce, your uncle was forced to sell off more of the land (the old laborer's cottage included) and reduce the staff to pay for her place in France, but he refuses to sell the London flat or the manor house. Her new Ladyship's father has infused more resources, but the funds seem to be contingent on the amount of time your uncle keeps himself preoccupied. I must say, though, that he has become devoted to his young wife as much as she is to him. She travels with him a great deal of the time.

Like you, she is also fond of horses, and purchased a new thoroughbred after we had a conversation at the stable. We decided to name him Albert the Second after my dear departed companion. I can't believe the old fellow has been gone ten years now. Albert the Second is much feistier, but he enjoys a good combing and chat.

Last month, we had a surprise visitor. Your friend, Mr. Lalique, from Paris. He had gone to the manor house first, but the master and mistress were away in London, so the servants sent him down to the stables after he asked for me. We had a good talk. Still a nice fellow, although he has become much more reserved with age. Apparently, he has done quite well for himself. He mentioned that some of his work, his drawings, were being exhibited in London. He said that he decided to come by and visit since he was in the area for an extended stay.

He was very disappointed when he heard that you had married Dr. Charles and moved to America, and surprised that you had been there for twenty-three years. He mentioned that he was also married and showed me a picture of his daughter, Suzanne. Beautiful girl, simply angelic in a straw hat. He said that it reminded him of you. That he remembered you wearing a similar hat.

He asked whether you had taken the puppy or Sekhmet to America. I told him that Dr. Charles wasn't fond of animals and that they had been entrusted to my care. Again, he seemed dismayed but brightened up when I told him that we had named the puppy Deux and that the little dachshund had lived up to his breed's standard, that he was an expert rat catcher almost till the day he died. I told him that the dog and cat had become fast friends over the years and that Deux was devastated, as was I, when Sekhmet passed away.

When I asked him about Paris life, he said that he traveled a lot in his business and mentioned that he was traveling to America next year to the world's fair in St. Louis. He wondered how you were, and I told him that there was occasional correspondence from Dr. Perkins to Lord Haliburton and nothing seemed amiss. I failed to mention that we were pen pals. I wanted to inform you first that he had visited and inquired about you. Let me know, if he ever visits again, whether you wish for me to give him your address.

Your friend always,
Samuel Stoddard

Lucinda refolded the letter as she thought about her uncle's second wife. The new Lady Haliburton certainly had proven herself to be less self-absorbed than Miss Meadows. Having died just before the Great War with no other heirs, Uncle Roderick had kept his promise to her grandfather that Lucinda receives the estate upon his passing. Not wanting to return there, she had sold it to the new Lady Haliburton's father. In his infrequent letters during the war, Mr. Stoddard had passed on tidbits and kept Lucinda up to date regarding the affairs of her old home. He informed her that Lady Haliburton had generously provided the estate as a convalescent hospital for wounded soldiers.

Lucinda picked up the next letter.

May 1905
Dear Mrs. Perkins,
Your last letter made me happy to know that you are doing well and enjoying life. I was impressed to hear about your work with the Women's Auxiliary with the American Park and Outdoor Art Association. It sounds like you are kept very busy with committees, society meetings, social functions and what-not. Being a champion for nature and beauty is important.

As you have discovered, I included your friend Mr. Lalique's notebook. I received it from him at one of his art exhibitions in London. He had sent me an invitation to a private party after the gallery opening. I was surprised to get it, but then he mentioned that I reminded him of his childhood days and his grandfather. The opening was quite the fancy affair, I must say. Mr. Lalique was glad to see me but rather preoccupied with other guests and one of the organizers, a lovely young Frenchwoman named Claudine. I wish that you could have been there with me and seen his work. So many marvelous items. I didn't realize how talented he was until then.

I was sipping wine and looking at a large display case when a man came up to me. He asked me how I knew the designer. I explained our relationship to him; he was very interested in hearing about Mr. Lalique's life as a youngster. A foreigner, but a polite young man, Calouste said he was a collector. He asked me what

I thought about the exhibit, I said it was magnificent. He agreed. In his opinion, Mr. Lalique ranked among the greatest figures in the history of art.

Then he told me that all the pieces belonged to him, that he had loaned his jewelry collection for the show. Before he became engaged with another dignitary at the event, Calouste told me that someday he would have his own museum and Mr. Lalique's creations would be displayed for all to appreciate.

When I was leaving, Mr. Lalique stopped me for a moment and said he had something for me to give to you. He said the sketchbook wasn't much but that he wanted you to have it and to know how much your confidence and belief in him kept him going when he was starting out and the critics were harsh. I don't mean to be meddlesome, but I believe that you made a lasting impression on him. In fact, I think he was in love with you.

As you requested, I gave him your address. He directed me to Claudine to have her write it down. I don't know if he ever received it or if he will ever contact you. I hope that he does.

Your friend always,
Samuel Stoddard

Lucinda put the letter down and then dabbed at her eyes with a handkerchief. She wanted to believe Mr. Stoddard's words—she wanted to think that René had been in love with her—but he had never contacted her. For years and years, she had waited and wondered if the lovely Frenchwoman had given him her address. *Who was Claudine to him?* Lucinda had sent a letter to his store in Paris the year before the Great War. *He never bothered to answer it. But why would he have—to reply to small talk?* He was too busy to respond to trivial nonsense from someone as banal as she. And then there was the turmoil of that horrible war. *Silly me,* she chided herself.

Picking up René's sketchbook, Lucinda opened it and flipped through the pages, stopping here and there to admire the drawings. Turning to the picture of a swallow brooch, she smiled as she remembered that he said he had made it for his mother. She continued to turn the pages until she came upon a drawing of a sphinx with a nude woman below it. Reading the title, *Dreaming of the Stars,* she wondered wistfully, *Was that me? Or is it me now, dreaming of a star?*

Lucinda sighed and closed the book, clutching it tightly to her chest as she envisioned them kissing. *Maybe he never forgave me for whatever happened that last night.* The weeks after were gone. Drugged and sick, the only memory she had was of the windy arrival in America, disembarking from the ship, clutching her straw hat over her cropped hair. She never knew why René had left without saying goodbye. *Perhaps it was for the best.* Dr. Charles's patient had given her life to her doctor.

Lucinda glanced at herself in the mirror and touched her face, noticing the lines around her eyes. Still short, her hair was salt and pepper now, her youth gone. What did she have to offer René? *Besides, he's rich, famous, and married with children. Leave the past alone. Let it remain buried. That's how it should be. I can't change history.* She gathered the letters and retied them to the notebook. She put them back in the wooden box, returned the box to her traveling trunk, and threw the blanket over it once more.

She is in bed and the door opens. It is Charles and he is carrying a tea service. She watches as he pours it into a teacup decorated with dragonflies. The tea is overflowing, spilling out into the saucer. She looks up at Charles to see why he keeps pouring, but it is not him. It is René. She can feel him place his hand over hers.

Lucinda opened her eyes and gazed at the hand over hers before looking up at Charles sitting on the side of the bed. "Another nap, my dear? So sleepy these days. Must be our age getting to us." He smiled at her.

"Yes. I felt a little tired and lay down to rest. How was your appointment? What did the X-rays show?"

Chapter 38:

THE SANDS OF TIME

A s his chauffeur drove him to the cemetery, René recalled the dream he'd had that morning: In the bookstore where Ambrose worked, the gold lotus book is on the bookshelf in front of him. He opens it and the sketch of his mother's swallow brooch falls out.

René couldn't figure out what the dream meant. He hadn't thought of Ambrose or the bookstore in years, and he had given the notebook with the sketch in it to M. Stoddard with assurances that it would be sent to Lucinda. *When was that? Fifteen years ago? Or more.* René shook his head. *I should have written to her. Why didn't I reply to her letter? You know why. Him.* Now gray-haired, René wondered if Lucinda ever looked at his drawings and reminisced about their time together. He thought about his mother's gift, his first fine piece of jewelry. How Maman had treasured it. Now it was buried with her, the swallow brooch pinned to her lapel at her request. This morning's dream had inspired him to visit her grave and bring flowers. René glanced down at the bouquet in his lap and regretted, once again, that he had not made more time for her.

His mother had been dead nearly seventeen years, so why this dream today? *Perhaps it was Suzanne's watercolor.* She hadn't shown the new glassware design to him; he had come across it on her desk. It was a vase, spherical with a small base and the lip covered with silver, its surface covered with large beetles, their legs interlocking. He read her annotations: Gros Scarabees, acid-etched, brown glass? *It will be a beautiful piece.* As he thought of his daughter, his chest swelled and he smiled broadly. Suzanne had secured her own place in the world of decorative arts.

A revelation about the dream came to him. The vase reminded him of his own Egyptian-style works, especially the stage jewelry that Sarah Bernhardt had commissioned. She had encouraged his Egyptian motifs and had made them fashionable. The actress had died recently; crowds had filled the streets waiting for a glimpse of Divine Sarah's flower-decorated, horse-drawn hearse. Because she had been a sort of a mother figure to him, he had dreamt about his own mother.

After arriving at Père-Lachaise cemetery, René walked to the gravesite alone. He continued to reminisce about his old patroness, newly laid to rest. As he strolled up the large boulevard, past the ancient tombs, one of them caught his eye. The bronze stele, corroded green, was a bas-relief of bat wings on a flying hourglass. Stopping to view the monument, he recollected the bat brooch he had made for the actress as a young craftsman. *So simplistic*, but Sarah had liked it. She told him it matched her stuffed bat hat. René smiled thinking of it, of her. He realized that the two of them had turned to their dark sides for inspiration. That's how they had brought substance to their art, she to her characters and he to his creations.

Staring at the bronze hourglass, he recalled something that Sarah had said after her leg was amputated due to a chronic injury. "Change is inevitable, René. It's gone but I don't mourn its loss. I celebrate what is left. Eventually, all of me will slip away. Like an hourglass, we are the grains that pass back and forth between these two worlds. Nothing can stop the flow."

She's right—everything transforms with time, René thought, and glanced around his surroundings. Greenery was everywhere;

framing and clinging to the worn and crumbling stones, nature was trying to reclaim the space. The decayed yet alive space echoed Sarah's sentiments. The coexistence of life and death.

René continued on, turning down a winding walkway, until he arrived at his destination. At the tombstone, he read their names: Olympe and Georgette, his mother and daughter. Gone but not forgotten. Focusing on his daughter's name, memories of her committal service resurfaced. There had been a small gathering of people present but he could not bear to look at any of them, especially Marie, who blamed him for everything that had gone wrong with their family. Following the final prayer, he watched as Georgette's coffin was lowered on top of his mother's. Suzanne had held his arm during the entire service, but she let go to step forward and throw flowers onto the casket. His heart aching, René had picked up a handful of dirt and scattered the soil into the hole. Thankfully, there had been no handshaking or greeting after the funeral. When the crowd had dispersed, René wandered alone through the cemetery lost in his grief.

René laid his bouquet of lily of the valley on the grave. He silently paid tribute to his mother and daughter and then uttered a prayer. Chirping sparrows in the trees said it was time to go. It was such a pleasant spring day; it would be a shame to waste it being sad. *I need to cheer up and get to work.* Then he had second thoughts. He didn't need to work at all, so why did he? Coty had been right about perfume. After the war, American soldiers stationed in France flocked to the shops to buy fancy French perfume, elegant gifts for their ladies back home. The doughboys had lined his and Coty's pockets with millions of francs. *Coty the thief*, he thought ruefully. The public speculation regarding their separation was nonsense, that Coty had pushed him too hard, too much work, too little appreciation. But that hadn't caused the rift. It was because Coty had stolen René's design and taken it to another glassmaker to produce. Coty had complained that René's factory could not churn the bottles out quickly enough. *Because I value craftmanship. My products are works of art.* A businessman, Coty would never understand that; he was willing to sacrifice quality for quantity. He was too busy thinking about how big his company could get, how much more money he could make. After all, he was the Emperor of Perfume and he was, as he constantly reminded everyone, related to Napoleon Bonaparte.

Thank goodness I broke ranks with him. Now that René was no longer associated with Coty, he had more time on his hands. Marc was running the latest glass factory in Wingen-sur-Moder and Suzanne was busy creating new designs. He could withdraw from the business, stay out of Paris and, instead, spend all day in Chaville with his current lovely young companion, Marie-Jeanne. *Non, I'm not ready to retire. To die. There's still too much more that I want to create. I just need some inspiration.* Flowers. Women. Nature. Luxembourg Gardens would be a lovely spot to visit and see all three.

Back in the car, René focused on the people and streets of Paris. Perhaps a fluke, his driver had chosen a familiar, evocative route. As they passed by the corner of the Square of Saint-Jacques Tower, René thought of Mme. Sphinx's old place on Rue Nicholas Flamel and the night of the séance. Crossing the bridge with Ambrose and tossing the dead beetle into the river. An image of the old ragpicker pressing the dead insect into his hand swam into his mind. *Le Chameau.* René looked down at the scarab ring on his finger, thinking of Lucinda and the Crystal Palace and recalling their tarot reading with Mme. Sphinx. She had said the name Sarah. It had never dawned on him until now. René had always assumed the reference was to Lucinda's mother, but perhaps the message was also for him. Sarah Bernhardt had been the woman who had answered. She had been the important link to his success.

René directed his driver to the old bookstore. While the chauffeur waited, René returned to his past. The shop was mostly the same—the musty smell and the timeworn wooden bookshelves still crammed with books—but the customers were younger, more trendy, stylish. Mme. Sphinx's curtained alcove had disappeared, and he was sure that the golden lotus book was also gone but, perhaps, the shop had something that would bring understanding. René approached the girl behind the counter. "Do you have any books on dreams?"

ʜIS HEAD POUNDING, RENÉ SAT UP and rubbed his neck. Looking at the empty bottle of brandy on his bedside table, he thought, *Why did I drink so much?* Then answered his own question. *You know why. What you don't know is why she ran away.* He glanced at his damp garments thrown over the chair before recalling being stranded in the rain by Lucinda and M. Stoddard. Running his hands through his hair now, he sighed before being jolted by insistent banging on his front door. Dragging himself from bed, René threw on some clothes and slippers. When he answered the door, Dr. Charles stood there holding his medical bag. He curled his lip at René's rumpled appearance.

René grimaced. "What do you want?"

"The baron sent me to evict you."

"I paid my rent in full. I have until the end of the month."

Dr. Charles opened his bag and removed some bills from it. "Lord Roderick wishes to reimburse you. This money can pay for your passage back to France. Today."

René was puzzled. *Why is he doing this? And what about Lucinda?* He had to find out why she ran away. He needed to reconcile with her, to convince her to leave with him and go to Paris. "I don't want his money. I will talk to the real baron."

"He is the real baron. His father died last night."

René gasped and took a step back. "Oh, je suis désolé." But then, seeing the smug look on the doctor's face, René said scornfully, "Tell Lord Haliburton that I will be up shortly to discuss terms with him. Not his lackey." He began to shut the door on Dr. Charles.

Wedging his foot against the door, the doctor hissed through his teeth, "Look at this." From his bag, he produced the burned fragment of René's painted illustration. Even with the charred edges and singed holes, he could detect remnants of the goddesses. "And this," the doctor added as he brandished a blackened clump of stems. The residue of René's bouquet, only a few of the delicate flowers remained. Charles hurled the debris at René's feet. "All your drawings. She could have burned down the estate. Luckily, her maid saw her do it. Mary was able to put the fire out before there was damage."

"Mlle. Haliburton started a fire with my drawings?"

Dr. Charles nodded.

"Is she safe?"

"Yes. No thanks to you."

"What happened?"

"Lord and Lady Haliburton learned upon their return to the mansion that, after Lucinda started the fire, she had climbed into the sarcophagus and refused to get out. I was summoned, and when expelled from it, Lucinda had a fit of hysteria and started throwing things at us. From the museum cases. Then she tried to attack Lady Haliburton with one of the Egyptian artifacts. The sword. Lucinda told her that she was the queen, a goddess, not her, and she would die for her treachery."

René was silent.

"She had to be restrained and sedated."

René thought a moment. "Was the hysteria caused by her grandfather's passing?"

"She doesn't know yet and won't know until you are gone."

René's mind was racing. What had happened the night before? She had been dancing with the doctor, they had disappeared and then she had run out of the party crying. Why had she snapped? Why had she burned his drawings, the bouquet? Why had she gotten into the sarcophagus again? He needed to see her.

Dr. Charles read his mind. "Don't get any madcap ideas, boy. We've got our eyes on you."

"What happened last night?"

"I told you . . ."

"Non. The party. Why did she leave in such a hurry?"

The doctor hesitated. "She saw you flirting and dancing with Lady Haliburton. It brought up traumatic memories."

"I wasn't flirting! It was Lady Haliburton. I want to make that clear, tell Lucinda the truth."

"She's in a very fragile condition."

"At least, let me say goodbye to her."

"No. It would not be in her best interest."

René recalled Lucinda's last words to him: "I love you, forever." He couldn't leave without seeing her. "I demand that you let me see her. I will go to Lord Haliburton and, if he doesn't listen, then to the authorities and tell them that you are keeping her imprisoned against her will."

Dr. Charles laughed. "You'll do no such thing, my boy."

"Don't call me boy." René pushed his way past him.

"Before you go doing anything stupid, look at this."

René stopped and turned. He watched as the doctor removed something else from his bag and threw it at him. He looked down and realized the object was hair bound together with the blue silk ribbon from his bouquet.

"By her own hand," the doctor said somberly.

René picked up the hair and stared at the tangle of curls.

Dr. Charles spoke again. "She will return to the asylum for the rest of her life unless you do as I say."

"You wouldn't dare."

"Watch me. That's my offer. Leave today. Don't try to contact her, now or ever."

Chapter 39:

DREAMING

Lucinda looked out the picture window at the vista, past the tops of the leafy trees to the blue swells of the ocean. Her chin propped in one hand, she watched the rise and fall of the water and thought of her dream that morning.

She is walking down a dirt road and comes to a circus. She enters the tent to find a monkey running around in bluebells. Then she is outside in a field with horses. She sees a black one grazing. It is eating lily of the valley.

Lily of the valley. *Does my dream have something to do with René?* A wave of nostalgia enveloped her. Memories—of his bouquet, him, them, the field of bluebells—filled her mind. Hanging her head, she clasped her hands together over her chest to quell her heartache. Dealing with Charles's illness, as well as her other responsibilities over the last two years, she had managed to put René out of her mind. But the memories were resurfacing now that Charles had passed.

The day Charles came home from his appointment with the doctor after the X-rays, he had told her the results: tuberculosis, and it was spreading throughout one lung.

He had undergone subsequent treatments with gold salt and then surgery to collapse the lung, but nothing had worked. He continued to cough blood and deteriorate. Lucinda remembered their argument about the sanitarium. She wanted him at home, to take care of him as he had her. Charles, ever the doctor, had rattled off case study findings, statistics, and, finally, mortality data before she won the dispute. Until about six months ago, when they packed him off to the desert facility and dry air where he found it easier to breathe and—he hadn't voiced it, but she knew—easier to die. Not allowed visitors, all she could do was wait. When the day finally came, she was positive it was a relief to them both.

Lucinda turned at the sound of the new maid entering the salon with the day's mail. Mary had quit when she learned that Charles had died in the hospice. As Lucinda watched the maid leave, she thought about Mary and Charles together. Lucinda was confident that they had been carrying on an affair for decades. She was glad that he, as her friend and physician, had found passion. Whatever jealousy she felt was trivial, and besides, there was no time to worry about it. So many activities, committees, social affairs, she used their money and connections to do some good in the world. Furthermore, Mary was devoted to Charles. He had suggested that she come with them to America and continue to be Lucinda's caretaker. At least for a while. Mary eventually became the housekeeper with the keys. *Thank goodness those two never had children.* Their relationship was a small price to pay for all that Charles had given her.

Turning her attention to a specific piece of mail, Lucinda read the return address. It was from Mr. Stoddard. After his wife's unexpected death, the letters had stopped altogether. She had written him a sympathy card, but he had never responded. Although she continued to send Christmas cards, lately she had begun to wonder if he was still alive. Even so, she had sent him a quick note to say that Charles had died. Pleased that her friend had written back, she opened the letter.

July 1925
Dear Mrs. Perkins,

My sincerest condolences regarding your husband's passing. I hope that it was a peaceful one.

Please forgive me for not answering your cards all these years. Shortly after the missus passed, my other dear companion, Albert the Second, also died. I took their deaths hard, both too young to be taken, and I was just overcome with that and all the problems facing Foxhill Estate and our great nation after the war.

You may have noticed that I have a new address. I finally retired, as my health declined, and moved south for the warmer weather. I am now living with my niece and her family. She works at a nearby school run by nuns. It is a lovely coastal town.

I thought I would write and tell you some news that I recently heard from your uncle's widow, Lady Haliburton. She had been traveling over the Continent and stopped by to visit me before returning to Foxhill Estate. A delightful lady, she told me about her adventures but specifically her time in Paris. She was there for the International Exposition of the Decorative Arts and raved about it. She said what she was most impressed with was "The Springs of France," a fountain of glass, a phenomenal monument erected near one of the entrances.

She said it was so tall, over forty feet, and so beautiful with tiers and tiers of carved, crystal ladies. These figures were called "Source de la Fontaine," each one representing a river or stream in France. The fountain spouted crisscrossing water and was illuminated at night. Lady Haliburton gushed over the master glass-maker and his pavilion, especially his perfume bottles, commenting that his work was phenomenal. Guess who was responsible for this stupendous attraction? None other than our old friend, Mr. Lalique.

I told her that I knew him and that he had lived at Foxhill Estate as a tenant while he studied art at the Crystal Palace. She was flabbergasted but added that she understood where he had gotten his inspiration to build his pillar of glass. Then she said that, in her opinion, only a magician could have produced something so sublime. I must admit that I never suspected that nice chap would be so successful. I knew he had talent, but I didn't imagine he would achieve international fame in not just one, but two careers.

Thinking of him, of course, made me think of you. I felt truly sad when you told me that he had never answered your letter. I wondered if you ever regretted losing him. I feel, in part, responsible for the end of your relationship with him. You and I never really talked about the night of the ball or the day after. I wasn't sure if you didn't remember anything or just didn't say anything out of respect for your husband. However, now that Dr. Perkins is gone, I feel I must relieve myself of this burden of secrecy.

All these years, I remained silent about what I saw that night. I don't believe you or Mr. Lalique knew the actual version of what happened, and I never had the courage to tell either of you the truth. After I had stabled the horses that night, I went to check on you because you were so upset when I drove you home. I came upon you in your room, in bed, like a corpse, with a lily of the valley bouquet clasped to your chest.

Do you remember what you said to me? You asked me for a blanket and to let you die in peace. I saw scissors on your bedside table.

I was afraid. I thought you might kill yourself. So, when you closed your eyes, I took the scissors and fetched Mary. I told her to summon Dr. Charles. I returned later to check on you, and Mary was there. You were asleep on the bed, your beautiful hair shorn, and she was holding your curls tied together with a ribbon. When I asked her what happened, she told me that you had chopped off your hair and thrown it at Dr. Charles. I was confused because I had given her the scissors. Even with some doubts, I went along with her story. The next day, I saw Dr. Charles pay a visit to the old cottage. I don't know what he told Mr. Lalique. I only know that our young friend left shortly thereafter without a word to anyone.

I only learned later that one of the scullery maids was passing by your room earlier that night when she saw Dr. Charles burning something in the fireplace. When she went to get a closer look, she saw you collapsed on the bed and Mary was cutting your hair. The maid left in a hurry; she was afraid. She didn't know if you were dead or drugged or going back to the asylum. She confided all this to me much later, after you had already left for America.

Please forgive me if I did something wrong. I just believed Dr. Charles when he said that the boy was no good for you, that the French couldn't take care of you, that you would go mad in Paris. I see now that my mind was deceived. I should have listened to my heart. But I didn't want to believe that Mary was capable of such a foul act. Then I learned from Willy that, before she left with you to America, she had confided to him that she was in love with Dr. Charles. She said she would do anything for him. Follow him anywhere. I dread to think that the doctor ordered her to cut off your hair, but who knows?

I hope that this information doesn't upset you too much. I didn't want you to think ill of Mr. Lalique forever. Perhaps he was also deceived, and that would explain his behavior.

Well, I'll bring this missive to an end. Since the missus has been gone, I feel old and tire quickly. I must say that I've been blessed with a good long life and I shan't be sad to say goodbye to it. My only regret is that I can't look upon your beautiful face once more before I go.

Your friend always,
Samuel Stoddard

Lucinda refolded the letter with its shaky handwriting and set it down. Pressing her palm to her heart and sinking into her plush armchair, she thought, *Thank goodness I never cut off my own hair.* Lucinda's eyes flitted back and forth as she contemplated Mr. Stoddard's revelations. All those decades spent assuming she had had another mental breakdown, a psychotic episode from which her doctor had rescued her. But had Charles planned it instead? Had he told Mary to cut off her hair or did she do it of her own accord? And what had Charles told René that morning?

Lucinda sighed. *It doesn't matter. They are all out of my life.* Looking at the letter again, she realized something: *Mr. Stoddard is sick. I should visit him before he dies.*

At her desk, Lucinda got out some stationery and penned a letter to him. She wrote that she had business in London regarding Charles's English property and that she would love to see him. She would include plans to visit him in his new town and would telephone when she arrived in London to arrange a time. Lucinda addressed an envelope and placed her note in it. *So many things to take care of before I go,* she thought, as she began another correspondence, this one to the London solicitors.

LUCINDA WATCHED THE PASSING landscape from the moving train. On her way to New York to board the steamship for London, she had just finished lunch. Thoughts of her upcoming reunion with Mr. Stoddard ran through her head. What did he look like? What was his new home like? What would he think of her? What would they talk about? Would he bring up the past? She thought of René, too. What was he doing? What did he look like now? She closed her eyes and recalled sitting on her red Egyptian couch with him by her side. Running her fingers through his thick, dark curls. Then lying in the bluebells, tasting his lips. And then at the ball, twirling around the floor with their bodies pressed together. The rocking motion of the train soon had her dozing.

> *She is wandering through a hallway looking for something. As she passes through the intersection of two corridors, she stops in the middle. The other hallway is an arched colonnade; she realizes she is in a convent. She walks down the cloister. Stopping, she looks out one of the openings at a boy in the courtyard. She recognizes him but doesn't know who he is. He sees her and they hold each other's gaze.*

Something jostled her awake. Lucinda sat up and glanced down the train aisle at a young boy running from, and being chased by, his mother. She wondered about this coincidence with her dream. Who was the dream boy? How did she know him?

LUCINDA SMOOTHED THE WRINKLES out of her dress while she waited outside. The door was answered by a middle-aged woman, who invited her to enter. "Come in, my uncle has been looking forward to your visit."

Lucinda thanked her and followed the woman into her sitting room. An ancient man was asleep in a comfy armchair. His niece went to him and gently roused him. "Uncle Sam, your friend Mrs. Perkins is here."

When he was fully awake, his eyes twinkled and Mr. Stoddard smiled at her. A distant memory of him standing in the barn grooming Albert flashed through Lucinda's mind. As his niece left to fetch some tea, Lucinda approached him. "Hello, Mr. Stoddard. It's been a long time."

He nodded. "Yes. It has. Please sit, my dear."

After sitting down on the sofa, Lucinda expressed her condolences about Mrs. Stoddard and then the two made small talk about his new village, the house and where she had been living until his niece returned to pour their tea. When they were alone again, Lucinda brought up his letter.

"Thank you for your honesty," she said.

"I debated telling you. I didn't know if you would forgive me."

"There was never a question of forgiveness. You did nothing wrong."

"I wasn't sure how you would take it."

"Well, I wasn't happy about it." She gave a quick laugh. "But I am glad that I finally know. Thank you for your concern, but I never thought of committing suicide by scissors." Lucinda winked and smiled at him.

Mr. Stoddard returned her smile. "That's a relief." He rubbed his neck and changed the subject to Albert I's death and then the acquisition of Albert II. They spent the next few hours, over tea and then lunch, reminiscing, talking about René, and catching up. Then, as Mr. Stoddard was tiring, Lucinda proposed another visit to him the next day. His niece suggested that, since Mrs. Perkins was here for the week, they give her some tours of the local area; the outings and fresh air would do her uncle good. Lucinda thought it was a splendid idea.

SHE IS DANCING WITH RENÉ IN A CHAPEL. Angels are watching them. Then she is on the steps of the Crystal Palace. There are large glass lilies growing there.

Lucinda awoke and wondered about her dream. *It must be because of the trip.* She and Mr. Stoddard had visited his niece's place of work, the new school building on the campus of Les Filles de la Croix, a long-established order of nuns. A school for girls, it was founded by five French sisters in the early part of the century. The visit to the new building was interesting, the nuns were friendly and pleasant, and the children seemed very happy.

Lucinda got out of bed and went to the closet. She carefully chose an outfit for her visit with Mr. Stoddard, the last one before returning to the States. Then she opened her traveling trunk and rifled through it, looking for her jewelry box. *I can't believe my trip is over.* Seeing the English countryside, visiting with Mr. Stoddard and retelling stories about Foxhill Estate, especially regarding her grandfather and her orange tabby, Sekhmet, had filled her with nostalgia.

As she searched through her clothes for the box, the false panel of the trunk caught her eye. She opened the concealed tray and looked at the items kept there: Her little black frog and the perfume bottle wrapped in an embroidered handkerchief. She set the bottle aside while she admired the handkerchief with René's design and her fine stitches of colorful silk depicting bluebells and lily of the valley interlaced. She picked up the bottle again. A faded label of flowers, a yellowed ribbon and the liquid long gone, but still she cherished her little treasure from René. After a few more moments, she set it down and gently picked up the frog. Kissing its face, she then turned it over and read the bottom. Heka. *If only,* she sighed, *if only I had the magic to bring René back to me.*

THEY HAD BEEN TALKING FOR WELL over an hour and Mr. Stoddard's eyelids had begun to flutter. *It's time to go,* Lucinda thought. *I have to gather my things before leaving for the train to London this afternoon anyway.* She sat forward in her chair. "That was a delightful snack of scones and tea. Thank you. I hate to leave, but I must. You and your niece have given me a wonderful week of hospitality. I hope you enjoyed our time together as much as I did."

"I did. It was good to remember all those times," he agreed. "Again, I'm glad that my last letter didn't upset you too much. I was afraid of the effect it might have on you."

"No. But I'm glad you told me after Charles had passed." She smiled at him. "I don't know how I would have taken it if he was still alive."

"That's why I waited. I didn't want to cause any problems as you seemed happy."

Lucinda nodded. "Well, I really should go."

Mr. Stoddard held out his frail hand. "Can you stay just a little longer? There's something else you should know."

Chapter 40:

THE WORLD OF CREATION

René was meandering alone through his exhibit at the Museum of Decorative Arts. He had asked the director if he could stay after the museum closed to the public. Smiling broadly, a feeling of gratification swelled in him as he wandered through the retrospective show of his achievements in various media. A stupendous honor bestowed by the museum. Certainly, a high point in his long career.

Placing his hand on the top of a glass case, he bent over and peered at his creation below. A stunning Medusa piece, it was a jewelry pendant. One of his favorite subjects for his art, René admired her glass face and enameled, gold serpents surrounding it. The ornament evoked a long-ago memory of doodling in his schoolbook, the Medusa drawing, and his teacher's reprimand. René thought of the nun in the schoolyard. Was it his imagination, or did he see an apparition that day? The phantom nun reminded him of Lucinda. He contemplated her mental condition. *Could she really see spirits or was it just her imagination? Or was she truly mad?* René recollected the Egyptian room in the Foxhill mansion. *I did feel something there. Something unearthly.*

Pushing this idea away, he straightened and moved on through the rest of the exhibit before stopping in front of one of his vases. *How many vases did I design?* He couldn't remember because he had spent so many years sculpting. Molds and models of paper, clay, plaster, wood, cast iron, and steel. From jewelry and medals to perfume bottles, paperweights, lamps, tableware, car mascots, and statues.

René continued to stroll amongst his treasures and reflect on the time he had devoted to his work, to his passion. He knew he was blessed. The world provided for him to fulfill his desires, so many commissions he barely had time to breathe. Everything had grown; the business, the number of employees, even the glass pieces. He'd moved, almost exclusively, on to architectural components. Designing fountains, chandeliers, door panels and windows for ocean liners, yachts, trains, mansions, commercial buildings and chapels. His clients hailed from all over the world and included his wealthy English neighbor, Lady Trent. Florence had seen the doors of his French Riviera winter villa and had asked him to design some for her mansion nearby. She was so pleased with his efforts that, after her husband, Sir Jesse Boot, had passed, she had come to René with another proposal: design something for her church in Jersey. Something magnificent to honor her late husband.

René recalled walking, at night, around the grounds of his property at Cannes. Standing beneath the majestic trees, immersed in the moonlight. Magical, glowing, ethereal. *Something not of this world.* That was the feeling he wanted to create with this project at St. Matthews. Currently designing four huge angels, he needed a revised glass mixture to make them. His work was cut out for him.

René paused at one of the glass cases filled with his perfume bottles and thought of Francois. Coty had seen the museum exhibit and had contacted him recently. His request was simple: Would the renowned master of glass create another bottle and ad for his new perfume, La Fougeraíe au Crépuscule—fern garden at twilight—as a favor for an old friend? At first, René was hesitant but had acquiesced and then reconciled with his former business partner. René was shocked by the condition of Coty. His divorce and financial crisis had taken their toll; the perfumer's essence drained along with his money and dignity.

René surveyed the exhibit of perfume flacons. His eyes fell on one of his favorite designs: The Clairefontaine perfume bottle with its lily-of-the-valley stopper. Capturing the essence of the bell-shaped flowers on their delicate stems, he had designed it based on the drawing he'd done on the steps to the monumental glass edifice, the Crystal Palace, waiting for her. Lucinda. *I wonder what she looks like now. Is she still alive?* René shook his head. *What difference does it make? She has forgotten me because I never bothered to write back.* He swallowed hard before glancing around the pavilion and his works of art. *When did I have the time? I had so much to do.* René resumed walking through the collection. Possessed by the world of creation, there was nothing he could do but accept this reality. He would be forever searching for that new form, new technique, new material, new love.

NEARLY A YEAR LATER, SITTING AT his desk in his Parisian home, René read the memo his son Marc had sent from the factory. At last, the angels had been cast and were in the final stages of production. Which was good, because René had promised Mme. Trent that he would have all the decoration done for the church by the fall; Florence wanted to dedicate it to Sir Jesse in September. René trusted his son, but he knew that he needed to get down to Wingen-sur-Moder to oversee the production as well. He was consulting his calendar when he heard a knock. Looking up, he saw his manservant with an envelope in his hand.

"Pardon the interruption, Monsieur, but this letter just came for you."

"Merci."

René opened the envelope. It was a note from Francois.

Pavillon de Louveciennes
Mon cher ami,

It is too bad that we have not seen each other since last year. I know that you have been busy and, lately, I have not been myself. As you know, with the divorce, Yvonne took my company, my name, and my money. She finally purchased the yacht that we had been trying to buy together all these years. I never imagined that my life would come full circle.

So much toil in the early years with little recompence, and then I found you. My living was never the same. We found the way to tap a new market: Sell to the hearts of women. Pamper them, make them feel like a beautiful flower. I knew that perfume in a beautiful bottle was the key. We expanded the world of fragrance, the art of perfume, created bliss for the masses and made a lot of money for ourselves.

I learned that we are the architects of our own lives. Whether workers, drones or the queen, we are all busy bees in the hive. We make honey or die trying. So, was it a sin to enjoy the honey of life?

You and I, we did our part for our country. We helped during the Great War. You, making medical glass in your factory and medals for charity, and me, making my chateau into a military hospital and transporting the wounded French soldiers there. And what about post-war efforts? How much money did I, we, bring into France with our product? After the war, I helped restore France and so many of her beautiful chateaux to honor. Do you remember installing the glass dome in my office at Château de Longchamp? A tremendous effort but what a difference. Blue sky, nature. Do you recall what you told me? To seek beauty is a more worthy aim than to display luxury. I should have listened to you more, mon ami.

I miss the old days when we worked together. When I was the Emperor of Perfume. Do you remember the late dinners with Henriette and her friends? You wanted to work even then.

Ha, ha, here I am reminiscing, rambling like an old man and you probably wonder why. I guess I just wanted to say thank you for being my friend and business partner.

Votre,
F. Coty

René placed the note on his desk. *He's so sentimental but perhaps he's lonely.* He thought about his friend's heartfelt message. *You transformed my life as well. From a jeweler to a glassmaker. We were lucky to have come into each other's life at just the right time. Like magic.* Magic. What word did Mme. Sphinx use? Heka. He thought of Lucinda and their tarot reading in the Crystal Palace and then glanced down at his black scarab ring. *Are we the architects of our lives or just following a blueprint already made for us? Were we never meant to be together or was that our decision?* Filled with yearning, he stared down at his empty hands for a few moments, then refocused on the paperwork in front of him. *No use in missing what's gone. There's work to do.*

EAU DE COLOGNE, CORDON ROSE DE Coty. René studied the newspaper layout. It seemed impossible that Francois was dead. *He was so young, only sixty.* His friend had had a stroke and died of pneumonia not long after René had received his note. *I should have known something was wrong. He knew he was dying. He wanted to say goodbye to me.* He squeezed his eyes shut briefly before looking at the perfume ad again. *At least his name will live on.* René turned the newspaper page but didn't read the features as his mind was preoccupied with Coty. The businessman had supported many artists in his time with his wealth. Allowing them to create beauty and, for this gift, René forgave Francois his excesses.

His friend's death prompted René to ponder his own life. Seventy-four years. Had it been a good one? *I certainly had a prolific career.* He thought of the cire perdue vase with the two Gorgon faces that he had recently produced. *That was the last one.* His painful rheumatism was creating difficulties for working with wax. Remembering a special cire perdue piece that he had created, his perfume bottle in 1893 and the subsequent fire, he could have never imagined back then where perfume would take him. Into a whole other career; glassmaking. Rubbing his sore hands together, René touched his scarab ring, which made him think of Lucinda and the Egyptian artifacts. Suddenly, a memory materialized: He was looking at a blue, ancient Egyptian perfume bottle and she was telling him that it was his. *How bizarre. Why would she say that? Did she really believe that we had lived before? That we knew each other in another lifetime? How could that be? Non, pas possible.* He shook his head. That was just too crazy.

His manservant appeared in the doorway. "Monsieur, the car is ready."

THE CAR WAS IDLING, WAITING for traffic, when René glanced out the window. His gaze happened to fall upon a movie marquee: *Cleopatra* starring Claudette Colbert. It reminded him of the night he and Lucinda had gone to the magic lantern show. How much the film industry had changed since then. He thought about his own photographic efforts over the years. Where was that camera? *Maybe it's in the closet.* He was on his way to his chateau in Alsace and his Wingen-sur-Moder factory to inspect the angels and other church decorations before they were packed for transportation to Jersey. Crossing his arms over his chest, René settled back in the car seat. *I'm glad to be getting out of Paris. I'm looking forward to walking alone under the trees.* Smiling, he closed his eyes and imagined his six-acre haven in the countryside.

RUMMAGING THROUGH THE CLOSET looking for his camera, René had no luck. *Maybe it's in here,* he thought as he pulled a dusty box off the shelf and placed it on the desk. There was no camera, only folders. *What is this stuff and why did I keep it?* He sat down, picked up one of the folders and opened it. It was some correspondence and old invoices. He picked out two more; same thing. René removed the final folder. Inside were several items: a portrait photograph of Georgette along with her drawings and a packet. René unfolded the paper wrapper and found a lock of her hair. He refolded it and set it aside before picking up the pictures she had drawn as a child. Smiling wistfully, he leafed through them. At the bottom of the stack, an envelope sat on top of the last drawing, his illustration of the maternity pendant that he had never manufactured. His eyes watering, he traced his finger around the sketch. René set the stack of drawings on the desk but kept the envelope. Addressed to him, he opened it and removed the letter.

It was from Lucinda. Her greeting from twenty years ago. Why had he put it in this box? He glanced at the sketch again. Lily of the valley and bluebells intertwined. Why all these reminders lately? Coincidence? So many gone: Maman, Alice, Georgette, Sarah, Clairin, and now Coty. It seemed to be a sign. He must reach out and reconnect before it was too late.

René read Lucinda's words before touching her signature lightly. How would he approach her? What to say after all these years? How to explain why he hadn't written back? Was she even alive? What about the doctor? *Dead, I hope.* Then René had an epiphany. What about asking Lucinda to meet him in Jersey, at the chapel? He was supervising the final installation of glass there, just three weeks away. He glanced at the address in America. Would Lucinda receive his letter in time? Would she reply? Would she come?

Chapter 41:

TEMPLE OF GLASS

Rubbing his hands down his pant legs, René approached the church's entrance. He didn't know if Lucinda would be there as he hadn't heard back from her. The last installation of his glass pieces had been completed that afternoon; he was returning to Paris the next day. The large full moon had just appeared over the horizon when he grasped the glass handle to open one of the double front doors with its glass angel panel. René stepped into the vestibule and entered St. Matthew's. He stopped in the nave, next to his autographed glass font, removed his fedora, and looked towards the sanctuary of glass. Alone, a nun was kneeling and praying in front of it. He checked his watch and his heart sank. Either she hadn't received his letter or had decided not to come. Overwhelmed by sadness, he turned to leave. As he opened the front door, he heard his name called. Turning back, he saw the nun approaching him. A slim figure, her hair was hidden by her veil. As she came closer, he recognized the contours of her face and her blue eyes. Those same adoring eyes gazed at him.

"René, is it you? Is it really you?" Her face was beaming, her cheeks aglow.

It was as if they had never been apart. Love surged through him. He reached for her hands and, bringing them to his lips, kissed them.

She spread her arms and they embraced each other tightly before he finally stepped back. "I didn't know if you would come."

"Your letter arrived late because I have a different address." Lucinda smiled at him and then indicated the interior. "You did all this?"

"Oui."

"Can you give me a tour?" She offered him her hand. He took it and they ambled around, looking at everything while he told her about his glass production. They stood silent for a long time in front of his massive glass cross adorned with carved lilies and then entered the transept. As they stepped into the lady chapel with its giant glass angels, Lucinda gasped. "Oh, my goodness, they're so beautiful." She smiled at him. "Your work is extraordinary."

"Thank you." René searched her eyes. "Have you had a good life?"

There was a pause and then, "Yes. It had its ups and downs. A normal life, I suppose. Not like yours, of course. Rich and famous." She gave him a grin.

René returned her smile. "My life has had its ups and downs too. My first wife divorced me, and my second died." Lucinda laid her hand over her heart and winced. "Do you have children?"

Lucinda turned away. "I had one infant but lost it." She stared briefly at the glass angels before looking back at him. "And you?"

"Five but I had six. My first daughter died giving birth."

"Oh, I'm sorry. Suzanne?"

"You know her name?"

"Mr. Stoddard and I kept in touch over the years. He mentioned her. So, Suzanne died in childbirth?"

"Non. Suzanne is alive and has given me two grandchildren." Staring down at his feet, his voice cracking slightly, he told her, "Georgette was her name. Her babies died, too."

Lucinda touched his face. "Let's sit and talk, shall we?" She led him to the vestibule and a comfortable couch. He placed his hat on one of the end tables and, in front of it, set his bag on the floor. They sat and looked at each other for several moments.

Lucinda's face had aged but had a sereneness to it. An indefinable brightness. "So, you are a nun now?" René asked. "Monsieur Stoddard told me that you married *him* and went to America."

"I did. Charles died nine years ago, and I decided to move back to England." Then she explained, "I'm not a nun, I'm a sister. I took a simple vow. I work with the nuns at a girls' school, on the coast. I'd always been an advocate for the conservation of nature and promotion of the arts, but after Charles passed, I decided to become a champion for young women. Encourage them to see their potential, to be their best. I wanted to be an inspiration to them."

"You've been my inspiration as well." René reached into his valise, took out his gift and handed it to her. "I designed this piece with you in mind. I want you to have the first one produced."

"Thank you." Her eyes sparkling, Lucinda unwrapped the box and admired the perfume bottle. She focused on the delicate stopper, frosted glass fashioned into lily of the valley. "It's exquisite."

"I called it Clairfontaine, after the property where I designed it. But the idea came to me on the steps of the Crystal Palace before we met with Mme. Sphinx. Do you remember her?"

"How could I forget?"

René smiled. "When I first met her in Paris, before I met you, I had attended a séance at her place with Ambrose. She wrote me afterward and told me that she had a vision that she was in a temple of glass and there were two birds there. I only figured it out much later. She must have meant the Crystal Palace and us."

Lucinda set the gift on the end table next to her. "Ambrose?"

"My friend. He's the one who made the lotus box I gave you. Do you still have it?"

"Yes, and the key you made. I keep my personal things locked in it." She paused. "Did you ever get the letter I wrote you?"

René answered her honestly. "Yes." Reaching into his bag, he removed the folder he had found. "I kept it. Before I wrote to invite you to Jersey, I found it in here with some of Georgette's things." He handed her the folder.

She didn't open it but held it in her lap. "Why didn't you write back? Were you too busy?"

He hesitated. How could he tell her that he had tried to forget her but hadn't been successful? "Yes, I was busy. I had just bought another factory, my glassworks at Combs-la-Ville. During the Great War, it was converted for the manufacture of medical glass for hospitals and pharmacies." René stared ahead so as not to look in her eyes. "But the real reason was that I didn't know what to say to you. You were in America and I was in France. You were married, and I was a widower. I didn't know to what purpose rekindling our friendship would be." *Or where it would lead. I was afraid that I would fall in love with you all over again and get my heart broken once more.* "I visited Foxhill when I had an exhibit in London, but you were gone. I'm sure that M. Stoddard told you."

"Yes, he did."

"When I asked about you, he told me everything. You named our puppy Deux, but left him with M. Stoddard." René turned and looked at her. "It made me very sad."

Lucinda was quiet. René stared at her, waiting. Finally, she looked down at the folder. "Deux lived a long and happy life. Mr. Stoddard and Sekhmet would have been very lonely without him." She touched the black scarab ring on René's finger and placed her hand over his. "You still have it."

"I rarely take it off." René reached over and gently lifted Lucinda's chin and searched her eyes. "Chérie, why did you leave? Go to America with him?"

"Mr. Stoddard didn't tell you everything." She pulled back and withdrew her hand from his. "Before he passed away, he told me many things that I never knew." Lucinda stared ahead. "About my uncle. About the fire in Egypt. Mr. Stoddard kept them from me because he didn't want me to relapse. But when I saw him again, Charles was already dead, and Mr. Stoddard was dying. He wanted to get it off his chest. My uncle's second wife told him that Uncle Roderick had confessed to it on his deathbed. He was the one who started the fire." Lucinda looked at René. "And then blamed it on me."

René was appalled. "Why?"

"He didn't want my grandfather to know the truth. It was an accident, but they died . . ." As Lucinda's face contorted into a mask of sorrow, René held her hand.

Lucinda smiled weakly at him and then closed her eyes. "Professor Merimee was terribly sick in bed, unable to do anything. Eza tried to rescue him." She shed a few silent tears before wiping them from her cheeks. "Apparently my uncle was up late, smoking in the sitting room, and he fell asleep. When he awoke, the room was ablaze. My father's drawings of the tombs, the curtains, the bookcase all going up in flames. Worried about the remaining antiquities, he focused on getting *them* out of the house instead of the people." She looked at René. "Terrible, isn't it?"

He slowly exhaled and shook his head.

Lucinda gave a half-hearted shrug. "Because I was hit in the head, I was unconscious. My uncle said that when I woke up, I started babbling in an unknown language. So, he told the police chief that I had mental problems and had started the fire by accident. Of course, the chief believed him. The police said that the tomb was cursed, that a demon had been released and I was doomed. Uncle Roderick paid them, but it was easy to leave. They practically begged us to go. I guess they didn't want me or the unholy things in their country. Afterward, I became uncontrollable and that, I believe, is when I had my first seizure. Eventually, I went blind. And in my mind, I began to see a man with the head of a jackal. He would visit me and talk about the past."

"So your uncle put you in the asylum?"

Lucinda nodded. "Charles told me that the shadow man was a hallucination, but I didn't believe him. He seemed so real; I thought he was Anubis. After I regained my sight and returned to Foxhill Estate, I wanted to find out about this ancient god. So I started to read the books in my grandfather's library. Then other visions started to enter, and I wasn't sure why I was having all these visitors. I was in the Land of the Dead and confused. Who were these people? Where were they coming from? Who was real? What was true?" Lucinda smiled at René, gratitude in her eyes. "Then you came. Walking on the path through the forest each day. Like a ringing bell, you woke me up. I came out of my tomb."

A memory flashed into René's head. He recalled standing in the doorway of the Egyptian room and hearing her say, *Welcome to my tomb.*

Lucinda stood and began to slowly pace. "Finally, with hypnosis, Charles made me understand that it was all my imagination. He said that my mental illness was making me abnormally fixate on Egypt because of the stressful events that occurred there. In order to cure me of my madness, he took me away from all of it. Eventually, Anubis faded away. Back into the shadows." Lucinda stopped and looked through the doorway of the nave. "The moonlight . . . Your crucifix is glowing. It's so celestial." She gazed at him with reverence. "Your art, this church. It's utterly awe-inspiring."

René could not speak at first, then he whispered, "Je ne t'ai jamais oublié, mon amour." But she didn't hear him say it, how he had never forgotten her, as she turned back to look at his work once again.

She was focusing on the glass altar. "I realized over time, with therapy, that you were just part of a story that I made up in my trauma. I had mixed up characters, people; you became melded to the past. I thought you were Eza at times. Uncle Roderick must have seen the resemblance, too. That's why he didn't like you. A reminder of what had happened."

René didn't want to hear any more about her uncle. "Speaking of reminders . . .A peculiar memory came to me not long ago. I remembered you telling me that one of the Egyptian antiquities was mine, a perfume bottle. I'm not sure if that really happened or if it was just my imagination."

A distant look came over Lucinda's face as she stared down the aisle. "No. I remember it. In my insanity, I thought we had lived a life before in ancient Egypt. And that you loved me with all your heart, but we couldn't be together. You had to desert me."

René felt a pang of anguish. No, it wasn't true—she had abandoned him. "Is that why you started the fire? Burned my drawings?"

These questions roused her from her trance. "What? No. I didn't do that. Over time, I realized that Charles had hypnotized me that night. The dance . . . The rain . . . It's all so hazy . . . I do remember being very cold. I went to look for a blanket and decided to check in on my grandfather. I thought he was sleeping, but he was dead. I was so very sad, but he was serene. No more coughing. I thought it was good to be like that, lying there so peaceful, so quiet. I went back to my room and laid down. That's where my recollections ended." Lucinda returned and sat next to him. "Mr. Stoddard finally filled in the blanks." She told René the whole story of what had really happened that night. "Mr. Stoddard felt very bad, but Charles had convinced him that if I ran away with you, eventually you would tire of me, and I would go mad and be imprisoned in a French asylum. Charles made Mr. Stoddard afraid for me."

"So, Mary cut off your hair while Charles burned your diary from Egypt, the flowers and my picture of the goddesses?" Lucinda nodded.

René shook his head in disbelief as he looked at his gnarled hands in his lap. "That's not what Charles told me. He said that you burned my bouquet and the drawings and then climbed into the sarcophagus. When he made you get out, you got hysterical and threatened to kill Lady Haliburton." René looked at Lucinda. "He said that you cut off all of your hair. He had it in his medical bag. He threw it at me." His lip curled in disgust at the memory. "I hated your husband and I never understood why you chose to marry him."

Lucinda was quiet for a few moments and then spoke softly. "I never understood why you left and never said goodbye. Why you didn't ever try to contact me. Was it something I did that night?"

He shook his head vigorously. "Non, chérie. It's because he threatened to put you in the asylum for the rest of your life if I ever tried."

At this revelation, Lucinda's chest caved and a pained expression clouded her eyes. Finally, she broke the silence. "That's why he kept me drugged with lithium bromide. I lived in a hypnotic dream for a long time. Charles convinced me that you and I would ruin each other's lives. That you would never attain the greatness you desired and that if I cared for you, I would let you go. Over the years, I have told myself that he was right. That I did it out of love for you. But as I have gotten older, I see that I did it because I was scared. Scared that you *would* tire of me, leave me, forget me in the pursuit of your career."

Lucinda turned to René. "With him, I was his career. I was the anomaly that he could study up close, analyze, categorize and put on a shelf. Like one of your works of art." She gestured toward the chapel with a sweep of her hand. "Transparent, but breakable and delicate. If only . . ." She sighed heavily. "I guess it just wasn't meant to be." She gave him a conciliatory smile. "I still have the perfume bottle and your poetry. Mr. Stoddard told me later that it was he who hid them in my traveling trunk."

"Did M. Stoddard ever send my notebook to you?"

"Yes, he did. And when, over the years, I would dream of you, I would get it out and look at it."

"You had dreams of me? I have dreamed of you, day and night, over the years. I thought maybe you forgot me or hated me for never writing back."

"Hate you?" Love emanated from Lucinda's eyes. "I could never hate you. You saw the beauty in me that I had buried. You were the only man to truly love me." Briefly, she touched his face with tenderness. "Now, tell me about your life. I want to know about you. You seem to have conquered the world."

"Yes, I have done well for myself. I am planning on opening a new shop in Paris, hopefully in the next year. The work never stops. I always have something to do, new commissions, and am grateful for the business. I enjoy working and I am as happy as I could be. Except for missing you." He kissed her hand then held it gently. "And for getting old."

She caressed his gnarled fingers. "One cannot stop the river of time. It continues to flow."

"Chérie, our whole lives, cut in two, separate but connected . . ."

Lucinda shrugged nonchalantly, but he could see sadness in her eyes before she started looking around again. "Those angels. They're simply sublime." She got up and he followed her to the front doors. Opening one, she examined the angel's face there and then traced its contours. "Just heavenly."

Nearby, a radio was playing. A recent hit song had begun; the strains of the orchestra reached their ears. "Would you like to dance?" he asked and held out his hand.

"I've waited a lifetime," she replied.

He led her a few steps away, and they began to dance under the glowing moon as the instruments carried the tune. Soon, Al Bowlly began to croon, "The very thought of you . . ." The lovers gazed at one another as they floated along with the music. By and by, Lucinda laid her head on his shoulder. As they gently swayed together, René heard the lyrics, "I see your face in every flower, your eyes in stars above, it's just the thought of you, the very thought of you, my love . . ." He pressed her closer and wished the song would never end.

Chapter 42:

HOUSE OF LIGHT

The Mother Superior studied the middle-aged man in front of her. "We never knew that our sister had a son. She told Sister Colette, but made her promise that she wouldn't tell anyone until after her death. Sister Lucinda wanted us to give you your inheritance. We were glad that the adoption agency had your current address"—she consulted the paperwork in front of her—"in California." The Mother Superior looked up at him again. "It's good we were able to find you. Are you married, Mr. Bell?"

"No," he joked, "I'm a tried-and-true bachelor."

The nun attempted a smile. "As you know, there is a considerable cash settlement. But your mother also asked that you take her remains and spread the ashes in California." She indicated the urn on her desk. "Sister Lucinda requested a certain area, near her old home, I believe. I'll give you the address." Then she stood up. "Come, I'll show you what else she left you." They walked through the convent until she stopped and opened the door to a storage room. Inside was antique furniture, numerous boxes and an old steamer trunk.

Mr. Bell gave her a dismayed look. "What am I supposed to do with all of this?"

"Sister Lucinda was quite specific. If you want the cash settlement, then you must take her other things. She said she wanted you to have them."

"Fine. Can you pack and ship them to my address, please?"

"Certainly." The Mother Superior looked up at another woman coming down the hallway towards them. "Sister Colette, this is Mr. Bell, Sister Lucinda's son." The nun nodded. "This is Sister Colette. She and your mother were roommates."

Sister Colette stuck out her hand to welcome him. "I can see your mother in you."

The Mother Superior shook Mr. Bell's hand as well. "Sister Collette can show you around the grounds while I assemble the paperwork." Then she left to return to her office.

Mr. Bell and Sister Colette strolled between the stone buildings in the school complex, which was situated on a cliff. "When she wasn't teaching, your mother liked to come out and walk amongst the trees," Sister Colette said. She led him out onto the grassy area to the wooded area beyond as she talked about his mother and their lives as sisters. When they arrived underneath the trees, she took him to a spot where the trees opened to a view of the ocean. A cool sea breeze buffeted their faces.

They stood for a few moments in silence. "Why does she want her ashes in California?"

"I suppose because that is where she spent most of her life."

Mr. Bell shook his head. "I still don't understand. Why did she come here? Why didn't she stay in America?"

"Your mother was born in England. After her husband died, she returned to take care of some legal work and visit a friend. When she saw the school, she knew that's what she wanted to do for the rest of her life. Help young girls, children."

"Wanted to help children? What about her own child?" He grimaced as his head sagged a little.

Sister Colette placed her hand briefly on his shoulder. "Sometimes, we don't know all the circumstances of why certain decisions are made."

Lucinda's son frowned as he regarded the vista of water before them. "It's sad, really, that I meet her in death. I knew I was adopted and, when I got older, I tried to find my birth mother. But she had wanted to remain anonymous. Apparently, they told me, there was a history of mental illness. That's why she gave me up." He snorted. "That's amusing. Didn't she realize that not allowing me to know her would cause psychological problems?" He gave Sister Colette a questioning look.

"Well, I don't want to make excuses for my friend, but her husband may have forced the decision. She was heartbroken that she had to give you up. Sister Lucinda never talked about him much, but what she said . . . Well, I inferred that he was the one responsible for your situation." Sister Colette paused for a moment. "I think he believed he had everyone's best interests in mind." Then, looking at his hands, she said, "You have really long fingers. Are you a musician?"

Mr. Bell laughed. "No. You're not the first to mention it, though. I'm an artist, an illustrator."

Sister Colette smiled. "Well now, that's interesting. You followed in your dad's footsteps. Sister Lucinda mentioned to me once that your father was an artist. She showed me his sketchbook. He was quite talented."

A GLASS OF WATER HAD BEEN set on his bedside table. René wanted to get out of bed but was too tired and sore to move. He finally managed to sit up feebly and reach into the drawer of the table. As he removed the aspirin bottle, his eyes fell on the black scarab ring sitting on top of the handkerchief embroidered with bluebells. He hadn't worn the ring in several years, as his fingers and hands had become more deformed.

Rheumatism had swollen his knuckles so much that he couldn't even balance a pencil; he had stopped drawing years ago.

René took some aspirin then picked up the ring and studied it. He thought about Lucinda and how they had danced under the moon in front of St. Matthews and then afterwards. They had managed to exchange occasional pleasant letters over time, but as usual work kept him busy, especially when his new store on Rue Royale opened. Then he had been commissioned to make table services for the official Parisian visit of the king and queen of England. *1938. The year that Marie-Jeanne left me. I thought I would visit Lucinda in England then, but I was too late.* He remembered the day his letter to her had been returned unopened. It was accompanied by a letter from her roommate, Sister Colette, who was sad to report that Lucinda had joined the angels in heaven. René sighed heavily and scrubbed his hand over his face. After replacing the ring in the drawer, he laid back down. *At least she didn't have to endure another war.*

For the past three years, René had been disabled and cooped up in his grand house on the boulevard, doing nothing but watching the river, the people, the tanks, the war, flow by. The German vermin had infested everywhere. The insane shadow of occupation had wrung out the life of the city and squeezed out her light. Reading the newspaper with the politicians and the Nazis spraying their cotton candy propaganda around, while their tanks and soldiers were contaminating the streets. René glumly remembered eating a box of the sickeningly sweet pink fluff at the St. Louis Fair with Alice. Called Fairy Floss, it cost twenty-five cents. God, it was awful.

Awful. That had been their lives during the occupation. It had all been too much for him to live through again, and it wore him out as he witnessed his city come to ruin once more. Paris was mostly silent, punctuated only by notes of destruction. René thought about the eight months since the city had been liberated. What had he accomplished? Barely reading, just sleeping it seemed. What had happened to his energy, his vitality? The war had sucked it all away. The stinking war.

René knew he should be grateful that his factory, his livelihood, and he and his family had survived. It was only because of who he was that his household hadn't been invaded. But he had been separated from everything he loved. The war had cut him off from his younger children, his friends, his work, his social circle and his life. He thought about his old friend Calouste in Lisbon. *He was smart to leave here in 1942, but I miss him. He connected with my soul and recognized it in my art. He loved women and their shapes as much as I did.* A tiny smile played on René's wrinkled lips as he recalled Calouste urging, "Make me another goddess, my friend."

Another goddess. René recalled his burnt drawing of Lucinda as Hathor and Nephthys. The madhouse, like war, a terrible place to be. The artist hoped in some small measure that he had kept his lover from that experience.

His mind continued to drift through the memories of his life's path. Reminiscing about everything he had created, invented, patented. Except for his work and business relationships, his career had always separated him from others. But he had made a name for himself. Lucinda had once told him about the ancient Egyptian practice of surrounding the name of a person with a cartouche for protection. If the name lived on, the soul lived in eternity, becoming part of the fabric of the Universe. Had she meant the soul somehow stayed intact? Was that what was meant by immortality? Would he continue to live or just his name? What was his destiny now? Was he ready?

As the early afternoon sun streamed through the tall windows, René's eyes fell on the vase Suzanne had placed on his bedside table that morning. It was filled with lily of the valley, reminding him that it was May first. Every year on this day, his employees received a box of chocolates and a bouquet of his favorite flower. He admired the pure white blossoms nodding on their slender stalks between the deep green leaves, then closed his eyes again. He remembered telling a reporter once that as a child he had liked walking in those flowers in the forest above his hometown, that there were so many that one could imagine walking on pearls.

René felt the peaceful buoyance he had felt then. The evil cloud that had polluted the world for so long had finally been lifted. It made him feel hopeful, something he hadn't felt for ages. In the Alsace region, the German bastards had occupied Wingen-sur-Moder, his factory and beloved property, for six tedious years. Thankfully, while damaged, the factory was saved, and his precious molds had been recovered by the Allied forces. René had tried, just after war had been declared, to save them. On the nerve-wracking train trip from Paris to Alsace, he had nearly wrung his hat brim to pieces. And then what disappointment when he arrived: The factory was closed, the oven fires extinguished, and the gates shut. Not allowed inside, he had been turned away empty-handed by the guards stationed there. "It's wartime, old man, go home." Then, when he had gone to his house in Viroflay to get his youngest children, he was met again with emptiness. Marie-Jeanne had spirited them away at the beginning of the war.

The recovered molds reminded René of his glass angels at St. Matthew's. He wondered if the church on Jersey had survived the German occupation. He sincerely hoped so; the church was irreplaceable. René envisioned the tall glass panels of carved lilies, the heavenly symmetry of crystalline light, and sighed deeply. To make the angels, he had used a unique glass mixture. *What happened to that piece of paper with my formulation? Did I put it with Georgette's pictures?* He had handed the folder to Lucinda and then forgotten it. When he returned for the dedication of the church, no one had seen it or knew where it was. It was gone, she was gone, but it didn't matter. He had destroyed those molds long ago. *If they want to fashion glass, carve a sculpture of luminosity, they will have to figure it out on their own.* René sighed again. Very soon, he would no longer be around.

Like the others who were already gone: his grandfather, his mother, his oldest daughter, and his first best friend, Ambrose. Would he see Ambrose in Heaven? Did it even exist? Madame Sphinx was surely dead. Had she predicted Ambrose's death? Her vision of being in a temple of glass and hearing the words, *Tell him to be a Magician of Light.* What about her claim that Lucinda and the Crystal Palace were his destiny? To fall in love together but be ripped apart by life? *Maybe Mme. Sphinx saw in those cards that my work would be my everlasting love.* And then her final prediction: *The Temple of Glass is your House of Eternity.* He contemplated this idea. Yes, his jewelry had affected individuals, but his glass had touched many. It was his gift to the world, his legacy. How had she known?

His breaths were becoming shallow. René glanced at the windows. The light there was brighter, fiery like the holes in his glass furnaces but without the heat. The window frames were blurry and indistinct as well as the fabric hanging there. Blue curtains. René remembered holding Ambrose's head in the street. The glassmaker was being pulled into the light, being absorbed by it. He was becoming as transparent as one of his creations. Disappearing.

René closed his eyes. When he opened them again, they were there. By the dissolved window. All the women who had left him. Maman, Alice, Georgette, Lucinda. They were not lost; they were not gone; they still loved him. Their shimmery arms opened wide, stretched out like dragonfly wings. Waiting. Welcoming.

Viens, René, nous sommes ici. Come, René, we are here.

THE END

ACKNOWLEDGMENTS

Many thanks to my editors, Annie Tucker and Jill Angel, for their beneficial advice. They helped to bring my characters to life. Thanks to all the staff at She Writes Press for aiding me in this process.

My infinite gratitude goes to my husband, Ron, and my late mother, Barbara, for their support to make this book possible. And last but not least, my appreciation goes my son, Trent, for taking the time to read my story and giving me new perspectives.

AUTHOR BIO

J FREMONT is an author and veterinarian. For more than twenty-five years she practiced small animal veterinary medicine while also serving as an adjunct professor at a local university and community college. The mother of two adult sons, she lives in Southern California with her husband of thirty years.

In addition to writing, J is a passionate practitioner of the decorative arts, including gardening, jewelry making, glass fusing, photography, sewing, and other arts and crafts, and is the author of multiple short stories (via her website, drjfremont. com). Magician of Light is her debut novel with She Writes Press.

Author Photo © California State University, San Bernardino

SELECTED TITLES FROM SHE WRITES PRESS

She Writes Press is an independent publishing
company founded to serve women writers everywhere.
Visit us at www.shewritespress.com.

Hysterical: Anna Freud's Story by Rebecca Coffey. $18.95,
978-1-938314-42-1. An irreverent, fictionalized exploration
of the seemingly contradictory life of Anna Freud—told from
her point of view.

Little Woman in Blue: A Novel of May Alcott by Jeannine
Atkins. $16.95, 978-1-63152-987-0. Based May Alcott's letters
and diaries, as well as memoirs written by her neighbors, *Little
Woman in Blue* puts May at the center of the story *she* might have
told about sisterhood and rivalry in her extraordinary family.

South of Everything by Audrey Taylor Gonzalez. $16.95, 978-
1-63152-949-8. A powerful parable about the changing South
after World War II, told through the eyes of young white woman
whose friendship with her parents' black servant, Old Thomas,
initiates her into a world of magic and spiritual richness.

Eliza Waite by Ashley Sweeney. $16.95, 978-1-63152-058-
7. When Eliza Waite chooses to leave a stagnant life in rural
Washington State and join the masses traveling north to Alaska
in 1898 during the tumultuous Klondike Gold Rush, she
encounters challenges and successes in both business and love.

Portrait of a Woman in White by Susan Winkler. $16.95,
978-1-938314-83-4. When the Nazis steal a Matisse portrait
from the eccentric, art-loving Rosenswigs, the Parisian family
is thrust into the tumult of war and separation, their fates
intertwined with that of their beloved portrait.